The Ghosts of Summerleigh Collection

By M.L. Bullock

Text copyright © 2018 Monica L. Bullock

All Rights Reserved

ISBN 9781717817846

The Belles of Desire, Mississippi

Book One

Ghosts of Summerleigh Series

By M.L. Bullock

Text copyright © 2018 Monica L. Bullock

All rights reserved

Dedication

To all the little liars.

Haunted Houses

All houses wherein men have lived and died
Are haunted houses. Through the open doors
The harmless phantoms on their errands glide,
With feet that make no sound upon the floors.

We meet them at the doorway, on the stair,
Along the passages they come and go,
Impalpable impressions on the air,
A sense of something moving to and fro.

There are more guests at table, than the hosts
Invited; the illuminated hall
Is thronged with quiet, inoffensive ghosts,
As silent as the pictures on the wall.

The stranger at my fireside cannot see
The forms I see, nor hear the sounds I hear;
He but perceives what is; while unto me
All that has been is visible and clear.

We have no title-deeds to house or lands;
Owners and occupants of earlier dates
From graves forgotten stretch their dusty hands,
And hold in mortmain still their old estates.

The spirit-world around this world of sense
Floats like an atmosphere, and everywhere
Wafts through these earthly mists and vapors dense
A vital breath of more ethereal air.

Our little lives are kept in equipoise
By opposite attractions and desires;
The struggle of the instinct that enjoys,
And the more noble instinct that aspires.

These perturbations, this perpetual jar
Of earthly wants and aspirations high,
Come from the influence of an unseen star,
An undiscovered planet in our sky.

And as the moon from some dark gate of cloud
Throws o'er the sea a floating bridge of light,
Across whose trembling planks our fancies crowd
Into the realm of mystery and night,—

So from the world of spirits there descends
A bridge of light, connecting it with this,
O'er whose unsteady floor, that sways and bends,
Wander our thoughts above the dark abyss.

Henry Wadsworth Longfellow, 1807-1882

Prologue—Harper Belle

Desire, Mississippi
September 1942

Dressed in nothing but a cotton slip and a head full of rag rollers, I tiptoed to the rusty screen door. Poised impatiently with my hands on my skinny hips, I frowned at my sister's shadow as she crossed the front porch.

"Momma is going to kill you D-E-A-D, Jeopardy Belle! You better get in here before she finds out you've been out all night," I whispered disapprovingly at her silhouette as I reached up to unhook the screen door latch. My eyes felt like someone had thrown a handful of sand in them, but I could very clearly see my sister's petite frame and the outline of her long, wild hair.

Didn't she know I had gotten in late myself? Aunt Dot was sleeping in my room with me tonight. She'd been my chauffeur for the Harvest Dance. It had been the happiest night of my life, except for Jeopardy's absence.

I had to protect my sister from Momma's wrath. I had lain awake almost all night listening for the sound of her footsteps on the porch or her fingers tapping at my bedroom window. I'd just about given up hope that she would ever come home until at last I heard the creaking porch boards, the evidence of her late arrival. Maybe instead of covering for her, I should have told Momma or Aunt Dot everything—that Jeopardy went out smoking and drinking with whatever boy she took a fancy to just about every night of the week—but I couldn't do it. I could never bring myself to break her confidence. Doing so would mean I would abandon my role as the family peacemaker; I might have been a lot of things, but never disloyal, especially not to Jeopardy—she had so few friends. She needed me.

"Honestly, Jeopardy. I don't know why you have to be so stubborn," I whispered as I struggled with the latch. It didn't want to budge this morning for some strange reason. Daddy had installed it too high, so I had to stand on tiptoe to pop it open, but I finally got a good grip on it. Easing the door open slowly to avoid its obnoxious squeaking, I waited for Jeopardy to stumble inside. Once I smuggled her back into the house and up to her room, I was going to give her a real piece of my mind, and good too. Lightning popped across the dim morning sky; I expected it to illuminate Jeopardy's guilty face. How was it that she was the oldest? Not only was I the most mature of the Belle sisters, but I was also the tallest and the plainest. And this morning, I was certainly the most tired.

Was tiredest even a word? Thank goodness I didn't have school this morning, and thank goodness today wasn't the George County Spelling Bee. My brain was too sticky and exhausted to put two letters together, much less o-n-o-m-a-t-o-p-o-e-i-a. I couldn't abide it if Martha Havard won the spelling bee. I'd have to move to Mobile with some distant cousin just to escape the shame of it. Not that anyone in this house cared. Momma would show up for the Harvest Queen competition but never the spelling bee.

Suddenly the bottom fell out of the sky and rain trickled through the leaks in the tin roof porch, but to my surprise, my older sister was nowhere to be found. I closed my eyes and opened them again, but she did not appear. I flipped up the hook and opened the screen door, completely puzzled by this turn of events. I had seen her—I had certainly seen her! Suddenly, my tummy felt like a bowl of spoiled jelly, all wiggly and uncertain.

Something was wrong. Was I dreaming? Had I fallen asleep?

"Jeopardy? Don't play games with me." I stepped onto the wet concrete of the screened-in porch, and even though it was predicted to be a scorcher of a day after the rain, my feet were freezing. It was as if I were standing nude in the soda shop, the only place in town with air conditioning, and every hair on my body stood at attention. An unholy cold crept into my bones. *Where could she be?* We had no back porch furniture except Momma's rocking chair, and a full-grown girl of fifteen couldn't hide behind it. Even one as petite as Jeopardy Belle.

This had to be some sort of joke. "Jep?" She hated that nickname, but seeing as she wanted to play games with me, I had no alternative but to insult her. I searched the porch and even the narrow stairs leading up to it, but there was no sign of Jeopardy. I knew I had heard her footsteps; I had even seen her figure a minute ago. No way could she move on and off the porch that quickly, especially not in the clunky white high heels she wore last night unless she had managed to lose them somewhere. I prayed that was not the case because they were probably Momma's. Jeopardy was particularly fond of them, and she was one to take risks. Momma would be fit to be tied if her favorite pair of heels came up missing. She'd had to send away to Montgomery Ward to get those shoes.

A voice from behind me surprised me. "Harper? What are you doing out here? It's raining cats and dogs. You'll catch your death. Are you walking in your sleep again?"

I had no choice but to lie to Momma. She and Jeopardy carried on a lifelong feud, and I was one to strive for peace, even if that meant lying to one or the other if need be. I would do as much for Jeopardy to make her think more highly of our Momma. In some ways, it was as if I were the grown-up in our family.

Where are you, Jeopardy Belle? Maybe I *had* been dreaming or sleepwalking. I used to do it all the time before we moved to Summerleigh.

"Sorry, Momma. I didn't mean to frighten you." To my surprise, she hugged me. Hugs were distributed infrequently in our home and were rarer than a ribeye steak dinner. I breathed her in, enjoying her particular fragrance of peaches and cold cream.

"Come inside and help me make biscuits. You girls have choir practice this morning." She kissed my cheek and patted my back as we walked into the house. I swallowed the lump in my throat and resisted the urge to spill my guts to Momma. Maybe if I knew she wouldn't unleash her rage on Jeopardy, I would have been more forthcoming. In hindsight, I would regret not telling her everything right then and there, but hindsight is always twenty-twenty, as they say.

I heard my youngest sister crying loudly enough to wake up the rest of the household. As Momma lit a slender cigarette and took a puff, I said, "I'll get Loxley, Momma. She's probably soaked through her clothing." Caring for Loxley would provide me enough of a distraction to gather my wits and come up with some sensible explanation for Jeopardy's absence.

My mother looked tired this morning. I clearly saw the fine lines around her mouth and between her eyes despite the thick layer of powder she had applied to her face. She wasn't even thirty-five, but she didn't smile much anymore. When was the last time I'd seen Momma smile? It sure wouldn't be this morning. "I don't know why Loxley has to wet the bed every night. You girls aren't giving her water at night, are you?"

"No, ma'am."

She frowned again. "She's five now, too old to leave puddles behind."

"Yes, ma'am," I agreed. "I will clean her right up." Maybe if I softened the blow with some good deeds, my mother wouldn't get crazy angry when she found out that her oldest daughter was nowhere to be found.

"No, I'll go tend to Loxley, dear. You start sifting the flour." My stomach did a double clutch as I watched her walk away. I hoped she wouldn't go up to Jeopardy's room and discover one Belle missing. Momma walked down the threadbare carpet runner toward the bedroom where Loxley and Addison slept. Jeopardy and I used to share the smaller room just beyond, but she usually slept in the attic of our dilapidated mansion now.

I dumped flour into the sifter and added the salt and baking powder. *Darn you, Jeopardy!* I thought as I tapped the flour through the sifter, pausing only a few seconds to light the gas stove. The stove was the only luxury in this big old house; Daddy had really come through for us with the new Wedgewood stove. It was a beauty and cranked up with just one strike of the match. *I miss you, Daddy!*

Daddy had been something of a dreamer, but you couldn't help but love him anyway. He was so handsome and kindhearted that even Momma loved him, even if most of the time his head was in the clouds. I heard Momma once tell her closest friend, Augustine Hogue, that even when Daddy wasn't away at war, he was there in his mind. War does things to people's minds. Or at least that's what everyone says. *I wonder if Loxley is right. Does Daddy haunt this place?* When he was away on the battlefield, he rarely wrote; he always promised to write but never did. And now Jeopardy was missing.

Oh, Daddy. What do I do?

Reaching for the biscuit pan, I greased it with a faded checkered kitchen rag and set about finishing up the biscuits. Loxley must have made a real mess because it was ages before I heard Momma again. At least Loxley wasn't crying anymore, which meant she hadn't been spanked for her accident this morning. That meant Momma was in a good mood. *How long would that last now?* Once the biscuits were in the oven, I started the coffee percolator going and took the peach jelly and butter out of the refrigerator. The phone rang, and Momma answered it and put a pouting Loxley in the chair beside her. It was Augustine Hogue calling to share the news that there was a new opening at the church. From what I could hear of the conversation, Reverend Reed needed a new secretary now that Ola got married, and there was going to be quite a bit of interest in the position. Even Momma thought it might be nice to apply for the job.

I must have looked out the kitchen window a half dozen times, but there was no sign of Jeopardy. A bright September sun rose over the thick clump of peach trees in the backyard, and still nothing. It was late for the peach crop, but the trees continued to produce copious amounts of the succulent fruit. Any day now, Momma would send us girls up the trees again to collect peaches so we could sell them to our neighbors. Jeopardy had always been the best at climbing. *Where are you, sister?* I supposed in some homes it would've been strange to have a child missing for breakfast. But that's how things were around here.

Sometimes Momma and Jeopardy went days without speaking or even looking at one another. I didn't understand it at all, but I had to believe they loved each other. I kept my silence during breakfast, and thankfully Momma didn't ask about the missing Belle. Loxley chomped on her food, and Addison picked at hers but ate a few bites while Momma finished her phone call. She and Miss Augustine made quite a meal of Ola and Reverend Reed. I guess they'd closed their ears during the pastor's latest sermon about gossip and the dangers of "wagging tongues." Despite the evils of gossip, I was glad that Momma had something to distract her from Jeopardy's latest escapades.

"Girls, get dressed for practice. I'll tidy up here, and Harper can walk you down to the church. I guess your sister doesn't plan on participating?" Momma arched an eyebrow at me over her chipped coffee cup, and I stumbled over an answer. Nothing sprang to mind, and my stomach churned as if at any moment it would reject the few crumbs of biscuit I'd eaten and the glass of milk I'd swallowed. I was no good at lying, and knew I would fail miserably at any attempt. I knew I should have woken up Aunt Dot. She would know how to soften the blow.

I am going to fail you, Jeopardy. I can't do it, I thought as tears filled my eyes. Before I could open my mouth and confess my sister's sins, someone banged like a freight train on the screen door. Startled at such an early caller, we all trailed behind Momma as she went to answer it, and she didn't shoo us away. Unlike me, she didn't have a head full of rag rollers but looked pretty as a picture, complete with a neat dress and perfect makeup.

To our surprise, the caller was Deputy Andrew Hayes. I couldn't help but smile at him. He was almost as handsome as Daddy with his short brown hair, serious eyes and tidily pressed uniform. He spoke to Momma in low, serious tones, but I couldn't hear a word he said. He clutched Jeopardy's purse in his hands, along with Momma's stolen high heels. Momma's white hand clutched the doorframe as she listened to the deputy. Another vehicle pulled into the driveway at a high rate of speed. It kicked up dust and rocks, and Loxley began to cry. All I could hear was the beating of my own heart. Something bad had happened to Jeopardy. Something really bad.

This can't be right! I saw her this morning—she was just here! Momma turned around with Jeopardy's things in her hands. Her blue eyes searched mine and her lips moved, but I couldn't hear her either.

Suddenly I heard something heavy hit the ground beside me, and then the world went black.

Chapter One—Jerica Poole

A year ago, my alarm clock was much sweeter than the one that screamed at me this morning. *Marisol, I miss you, sweetheart.* I missed being awakened by butterfly kisses and warm arms around my neck, and to add to my agony it had been another dreamless night. After I beat the buzzing alarm clock half to death, I reached for my daughter's picture. Forever frozen in time, Marisol smiled back at me, showing her missing front tooth and a sprinkling of freckles across her nose. I kissed the dusty glass and whispered, "Another day, baby girl."

I took my time getting out of bed and knew without turning over that I was alone—again. Eddie showed up last night, and like a fool, I let him in. One moment of weakness. That was all it took to welcome chaos back into my life...but I'd been so alone lately, and Marisol's sixth birthday had come and gone. Eddie and I had shared a silent meal, avoiding talking about Marisol, and then made love, but it was an empty coupling without healing or emotions. It was not as it once was. I tried to remember that he was also a broken person, that he had also lost a child. He did not make it easy for me to have sympathy for him because as usual, sometime last night or early this morning, Eddie had left me. I had smartly hidden my purse in the cedar chest before our dinner together, but I had completely forgotten about hiding the contents of my medicine cabinet. The chances were good that my ex-husband had relieved me of my anxiety and depression prescriptions.

Please, God. Cut me a break.

Placing Marisol's picture back on the nightstand, I pulled on my robe. Rain slapped the side of the house—the weatherman had gotten it right for once. He'd warned the residents of Portsmouth, Virginia, that it was going to rain all day. *Yeah, that rain sounded ferocious, like BBs striking the windows.* I had first shift today, and I couldn't miss another day of work. I'd burned up my sick days with various personal appointments with therapists, wellness checkups—you name it. Nothing helped, nothing diminished my grief. I lost myself in an endless cycle of work, hence the ever-expanding collection of medications. It was better to pretend I did not feel than to actually experience the agony of my loss on a daily basis.

Might as well face reality.

I faced the mirror of the medicine cabinet and stuck my tongue out at myself. Why in the world had I let Eddie into my home, and how had he found me? Before this most recent hookup, I hadn't seen him for six months. I opened the cabinet, and sure enough, my meds were gone.

"Damn it, Ed!" I closed the cabinet and dug my purse out of the cedar chest. It didn't take long to figure out that he'd discovered my hiding spot. Everything was out of place, but at least he'd left my credit cards and checkbook alone. All my cash had disappeared. "Eddie! You bastard," I said under my breath. I couldn't have predicted that he would stoop that low, but his pill addiction apparently had a hold on him. *If you'll rob a grieving mother, your own ex-wife, of her cash and medication, you're pretty low-down.* "That's the last time, Eddie Poole. The last time!" I wiped a tear from my eye. I had a few groceries in the house, but I needed that cash for gas and my lunches all this week.

No sense in crying over spilled milk. That's something my grandmother used to say when she dealt with her son, my father. In other words, *It's too late to do anything about what's been done.* Yeah, that would have to be my motto too now. It was too late for Eddie and me. Our chances died along with Marisol.

I began my weekday morning ritual and prepared to face my day. I drank two cups of black coffee, got dressed in my pink uniform, smoothed back my hair in a bun and dabbed on a bit of makeup. Next, I put dinner in my mini crockpot: today's menu choice was a chicken breast, a can of chopped tomatoes and green chilies and half a can of black beans. I detested fast food but loved the salad bar at the restaurant near the nursing home. Unfortunately, I had no cash for lunch now. Unlike my ex, my crockpot never let me down. I turned the pot on low and grabbed my purse and umbrella. It was summer, so I didn't need a jacket, but a raincoat was obviously a necessity today. Luckily for me, I would be inside all day.

Count your blessings, as one of my therapists reminded me every week.

My car didn't want to start this morning, and I quickly forgot about counting my blessings when I finally coaxed the engine to turn over. Jetting down Twelfth Street, I pulled into the parking lot of the Sunrise Retirement Home. Since my shift began at 6 a.m., I had plenty of parking spots to choose from and I picked a close one. That was one of the advantages of coming in early. The night shift was basically a skeleton crew.

As administrative nurse and coordinator, I walked into any number of emergencies every Monday. What would it be this morning? I wondered if Mr. Munroe had made it through the weekend without a trip to the hospital. He really needed to go, but he refused to thus far. At least one of my favorites, Mrs. Nancy Grimes, had a visitor last Friday. The first in months. Sweet lady. She always had a joke to share.

But the one resident I hated leaving the most was Harper Hayes. Mrs. Hayes, who insisted I call her Harper, was a firecracker with a penchant for telling the honest truth—about everything. She and I became fast friends when I was pregnant with Marisol. In fact, my favorite resident of the Sunrise Retirement Home had given me an "All About Baby" book and showered my baby with gifts including a silver spoon, crocheted booties and a dedication gown. And when Marisol died, she'd cried alongside me. We were an odd family, the three of us. Yes, it was hard to leave her on the weekends, but she insisted on it. She reminded me that I needed to have a life outside this place. The truth was, I didn't have much of one. As last night had proved.

To my surprise, there had been absolutely no emergencies this weekend. None at all. I checked the boards twice for messages or notices, but there wasn't anything that required my attention. Nothing on my computer screen either. "Well, that's a change," I said to Anita, my right-hand nurse and work buddy. "No emergencies at all?"

She smiled, her dark skin glowing prettily. "Yeah, everyone was well behaved. Uh, you won't believe this, but Eddie's been calling this morning. He started calling a few minutes before you got here."

"He's got a lot of nerve. He's lucky I don't call the cops."

Anita tossed her pen on the desk in front of her and gave me an incredulous look. "Tell me you didn't. You went through all that to get moved, and then you let him in."

I buried my head in my hands and refused to meet her gaze. "I know. I'm a loser. This isn't an excuse, but I've been so lonely lately. I guess he just caught me at the right moment."

"More like the wrong moment. For someone with so much education, you sure do need your head examined." I accepted her gentle scolding, for I knew her heart.

"Believe me, it's been examined, and I don't think there's any hope for me."

One of the new nurses, Jenny, came to the desk and said, "There you are. Mrs. Hayes has been waiting for you, Jerica. She sent me to come find you and asked you to come see her at your earliest convenience."

It was my turn to raise my eyebrows in surprise. "And that's how she said it? That doesn't sound like Harper Hayes."

Jenny blushed and confessed, "She didn't say it exactly like that. I paraphrased for her."

"Oh, she's in one of those moods. I'm on the way. Thanks." I tucked my purse in the top drawer of my desk and headed down the hall to see my friend. I had barely stepped my foot in the door before she instructed me to come in.

"Thank goodness. I didn't think I would make it to Monday. Have a seat. I know you're busy, but I really need to speak with you." I joined Harper at the small table next to the window that overlooked the garden. I barely had the time to sit and visit with her during the day except during these early mornings.

"What are you talking about? Are you sick?" I frowned at her suspiciously. "You can't wait for me to be here to tell someone, Harper. What's the matter?"

"Hush now and listen. I have something to show you." She slipped a picture out from under a lace doily that topped her round table. "Look at us, Jeopardy."

"Jerica, I'm Jerica, Harper." My heart fell to hear her get my name wrong. Doing so once was forgetfulness, but she'd done it quite a bit recently and it worried me.

"Yes, I know that. Now take a look."

The black-and-white photo had crumpled, brittle edges, but the faces were clear. Four girls looked back at me, three with smiles and one with a faraway look as if she were seeing past the moment—as if she could see me. I shivered at the silliness of that thought.

"Can you guess which one is me?" She smiled like the Cheshire cat, and I stared at her and then at the photo. Picking out Harper was easy. You could tell the girls were related, but none of them looked exactly alike. Unwilling to wait for my answer, she said, "That's me, on the end."

I smiled at her. "You haven't changed a bit."

"Oh, you're such a liar, Jerica Poole, but thank you." Thank goodness she didn't call me Jeopardy again. But I wasn't lying. Of course, she looked much older than this photo, but it was Harper nonetheless. She had a wide forehead and neat eyebrows that had a natural arch to them. In the photo, she wore a Peter Pan blouse, and her soft blond hair was bobbed and curled.

"And which sister is which?"

"Now, this pouty thing with the bee-stung lips is my sister Addison. She's the only one of us who had brown eyes. She looked a lot like my father's family. Addison was a sickly girl but sweet." Addison had a cleft chin to go along with those full lips. She was certainly a pretty girl. "This ball of sunshine was my youngest sister, Loxley. Momma always braided her hair into two braids. She used to see ghosts all the time, right up until the day she moved away and married that boy from Mobile. Why can't I think of his name?"

"What?" I laughed at that. "Loxley must have had an imaginary friend or two, I gather?"

"No, they weren't imaginary friends; she saw ghosts just like you and I see cats or dogs. And this girl here, the one beside me, that's my sister Jeopardy. She disappeared in 1942." I was mesmerized by the girl with the wild blond hair. She looked so out of place, like a girl from another time had stepped into the frame. She wore a white sundress and had vulnerable-looking bare arms and that sad, faraway look in her eyes.

"She looks so tiny. She was the oldest, right?"

"Yeah, she was the oldest, but I was the tallest. I was the Ugly Duckling of the Belle family, taller than even Momma when I got older. Jeopardy was always a petite thing, with a wild streak a mile wide. Oh, how I wanted to be like Jeopardy." Harper clutched the photo in her hand and closed her eyes as if she were remembering some half-forgotten moment. I didn't want to interrupt her, but I was captivated by the photograph.

"Hardly an Ugly Duckling, Harper. And I'm taller than you. Tell me about your sisters. You said Jeopardy disappeared?"

"They are all gone now. I am the last Belle." She opened her eyes and tucked the crocheted blanket around her legs. "Chilly this morning. I wanted to see you, Jerica, because I am going to die soon, and I'm afraid I have failed to bring my sister home. I made a promise a long time ago. I promised Jeopardy I would bring her home, but I couldn't. I need your help. Please tell me you'll help me. I can't die knowing she'll never make it home."

Alarmed at her confession, I put my hand on her wrist to comfort her. "Hey, you aren't going to die on my watch. Let me call your doctor. If you feel off in any kind of way, we need to get him here."

"Don't do that. I need you to believe me. I can't explain how I know it, but I do—I am going to die soon, and I need your help. I can't find Jeopardy, and she's been gone so long. She can't rest until we find her. Please help me." For the first time in all the years I'd known her, Harper Hayes cried. I was so surprised that I couldn't imagine refusing her. I couldn't say no to her after she'd been so good to Marisol and me. She'd been there for me when I needed her most. I would have to return the favor.

"I'll help you, Harper, but we have to call Dr. Odom. I'll help you if you allow me to call him."

She wiped her tears away and nodded in agreement. "That sounds like a fair trade. Hand me my handkerchief, please."

I walked to her bedside table and retrieved one of the embroidered handkerchiefs from her neat stack. Handing it to her, I couldn't help but hug her even though I suspected she didn't enjoy hugs too much.

"I want you to have this picture, Jerica. I don't want you to forget Jeopardy Belle, not like everyone else has. Even me—I forgot her for a while. I tried to find her, but then I got so busy with my own life. Find her, Jerica. Find her and bring her home."

"I can't accept this picture, Harper. These are your sisters, not mine."

"No, I want you to have it. Just remember your promise. I'm going to hold you to it now, Jeopardy."

I didn't correct her but squeezed her hand and slipped the picture into my pocket before I walked out to call Dr. Odom. The whole thing was weird, but I couldn't refuse Harper. She'd been there for me, and how hard could it be to find her sister?

She disappeared in 1942...

Chapter Two—Harper Belle Hayes

Monday's child is full of grace...Nope. That's not how it goes.

"Mm-hmm," I answered the doctor absently as he poked and prodded me with his cold metal tools. I disliked doctors immensely, but I'd made Jerica a promise, and her promise would be harder to keep than mine. I had no doubt she could do it. Jerica had a quiet strength that would take her far if she could tap into it. So much like my Aunt Dot.

Tuesday's child will win the race. Uh-uh. That's not right either. How strange that Loxley had sung this in my dream last night and now I couldn't remember any of it. I used to know this song and about a dozen others by heart.

"Poke out your tongue, please," the young man said as he unceremoniously shoved a wooden tongue depressor in my mouth. *Good Lord! I don't have tonsillitis.* This silly doctor was messing up my concentration. It was easier to remember this poem when you sang it; we used to sing it, all us Belle girls together. Hard to sing with a Popsicle stick in your mouth. Jumping rope had been a happy pastime of ours; Jeopardy had always been the best at it, so much so that she got bored with it and went on to other things like boys and smoking, but the rest of us continued until we were all too big for the jump rope.

Dr. Odom mumbled something about potassium levels to Jerica, further proof that he was a fool. I didn't need a banana...I was dying. I knew this because Loxley told me; I saw my baby sister in a dream last night. And she had been as she always was, sweet-faced and wise beyond her years. Loxley had been Tuesday's child. *Full of grace...yes, I think that's right.* My eyes closed; I'd been so sleepy yesterday and today too. The next thing I knew, I was opening my eyes and back home. Back at Summerleigh, on the landing, in the full sunlight that shone through the big window. Loxley was there, her neat braids shiny and her blue checkered dress tidy for once. And in that moment, when I cleared the stairs at Summerleigh and ran to the end of the hallway to hug her, all the things that drove me crazy about her when we were young didn't matter anymore. I didn't care that she always lost her lunch money or that she peed the bed or had a habit of vomiting if she ate too much. I loved her beyond reckoning.

And Summerleigh...I had forgotten how magical the place had been when I was a child. I had loved it since the day I first clapped eyes on it. It had all seemed so rotten and broken, like a forsaken sand castle those first few days, but there was beauty there, beneath the rotten boards and peeling paint. Daddy never doubted the house's potential.

"Summerleigh is a prize worth having, and we'll work night and day if that's what it takes to restore her," he told us proudly. "I won this house fair and square—you should have seen my hand, Ann—and now we will keep it." Knowing Daddy, he totally believed this declaration. Momma didn't speak against the place after that, not in Daddy's hearing, anyway, but she sure didn't lift a finger to do any of the work required. Momma's hobbies were picking peaches, smoking her skinny cigarettes and talking on the phone. When Daddy was home, she did all the cooking. But if he was gone to take a load somewhere—he was an over-the-road truck driver after he left the military—I did it all. It was like she was Momma when Daddy was home, but when he was gone, I was the Momma. Funny how at the time it didn't seem strange to me. It was just life.

I remember her burning up the phone lines once the phone company managed to put one in the kitchen at Summerleigh. More than once I heard her whispering about Summerleigh and Daddy, but she didn't speak ill of either in front of me. Unfortunately, she wasn't the only one talking.

Everyone in town had talked when we left the West Desire Mobile Home Park for Summerleigh. People thought we were fools before, and they knew for sure we were now, Momma complained to Aunt Dot and me. But the thick-tongued gossips didn't deter Daddy. He didn't care when folks said that we were living above our means or that having Belles living at Summerleigh was like putting lipstick on a pig. We'd come from a long line of sharecroppers, and everyone in Desire knew it. But Daddy had brought us all up now, with his medals and many awards for bravery, so perhaps they would talk a bit less. That's what Aunt Dot told me even though her very own sister did not hold to that viewpoint.

I loved my Aunt Dot. People said I looked just like her, and when I was a child, I liked to fantasize that she—rather than the elegant but cold Ann Marie Belle—was my mother. If Momma had her choice, we'd all be back in the cramped trailer park where she could once again be the queen of her own social kingdom, of which Augustine Hogue was her chief ally.

Summerleigh had been a fine two-story mansion with five columns across the front porch and two smaller one-story wings on each side. Once upon a time, Summerleigh must have seemed a magical place, but by the time we carried our boxes and suitcases inside, it had stood empty for at least forty years. It felt less like a palace and more like a graveyard.

As with any small town, there was plenty of talk in Desire about the McIntyre family, the original owners of the house. Daddy quickly became obsessed with the McIntyre family history too. When he wasn't tinkering with something around the house, replacing wood here and there or scraping off old wallpaper, he was reading about them.

Yes, I remembered my first trip to Summerleigh. There had been a rickety gate and a broken walkway that led to the front door. The unkempt yard was full of untamed bushes and overgrown saw grass that hid things like field rats and a family of feral cats who dined on the rodents regularly. Oh, I hated finding those carcasses all over the place. One cat in particular liked to leave half-eaten rats on the front porch, as a kind of peace offering, I supposed.

Harper, are you coming?

Loxley's voice called to me now from somewhere beyond the noisy Dr. Odom's droning. Obviously, no one else heard her, and I was okay with that. I didn't want to share her. As he scribbled on his notepad, I announced, "I'm ready for a nap. Everyone out." Jerica frowned at me for my rudeness, but I was tired and Loxley was waiting.

They finally left me alone, and I breathed a sigh of relief. I had done what I needed to do; Jerica had promised to bring my sister home, to find Jeopardy Belle. I could rest now. Old age had finally caught up with the unstoppable Harper Belle Hayes, and I had done all I could do. I lay down on my bed and closed my eyes. Oh, I was so tired, much too tired to do one more thing.

But the peaches need washing and the quilts need beating, Harper. Momma needs you...

"Alright, Momma," I said to my memory. Now I remembered the poem. I recalled it perfectly!

Monday's child is fair of face
Tuesday's child is full of grace
Wednesday's child is full of woe,
Thursday's child has far to go
Friday's child is loving and giving
Saturday's child works hard for a living
But the child who is born on the Sabbath day
Is bonnie and blithe, and good and gay....

I could hear their voices, young girl voices all sing-song-y. Patent leather shoes tapped the floors as they jumped in time.

Harper...come on, slowpoke. Why do you have to be dead last at everything?

"Jeopardy?" I whispered. "Is that you?"

"Of course, dummy. Get your head out of the clouds and come on. How are we going to double-jump without you?"

I ran up the second set of stairs now. I could hear my sisters jumping rope in the big empty room on the top floor. That was the best place to jump rope when it rained. And it was raining now. I raced to the doorway, and my hands were on the doorframe. My eyes were closed, and I couldn't face it if I opened them and they were ghosts. I didn't want to see them like that.

Please don't be horrible, I thought. *Don't be ghosts!*

The rain stopped, and I felt comforting warmth, like the sun shining on my face. I opened my eyes and without a second thought walked into the room.

I was home at Summerleigh. Jeopardy smiled at me and handed me one of the ropes. I had found her after all! I kissed her cheek and took my place across from Addison. As always, Loxley and Jeopardy would jump first. I had questions for Jeopardy, so many questions, but strangely enough, I could remember none of them at the moment.

Monday's child...we began to sing together. Our shoes tapped, we sang, and I realized I was young again. My hands were young; I wore my pink dress, the one with the strawberries on the collar and hem.

I was home now, and I would never leave again.

Chapter Three—Jerica

I had been mistaken about Eddie's theft; he'd taken more than my fifty dollars. He stole my bank card too. How could I have missed that? Fortunately, my bank called my cell phone to notify me that there had been unusual activity on my card. I told them my wallet had been stolen, which was partly true. They were going to investigate, but as it stood now, my ex-husband had cleaned out both my checking and savings accounts. The bank encouraged me to file a police report, and luckily for me—or unluckily, however you wanted to look at it—I had a contact at the police department. I pulled Detective Michelle Easton's card out of my purse and called her the first chance I got.

During a long, embarrassing conversation, I explained what happened. She said, "I'll get the papers started, but you'll need to come by and sign them so I can start recouping your money. Over three grand, huh? Mr. Poole is looking at a felony or two with this one. And you still want to do this?"

"I don't have any choice this time, Detective. The bank insists on having a police report of the theft, and frankly, I don't know of any other way to get him the help he needs."

Easton went quiet as if she were thinking about my statement but didn't offer any advice. "I'll have it ready when you get here. Do you have somewhere to stay this evening?"

"Uh, no. Why?"

"Well, he may have a key to your apartment. You need to change the locks."

I glanced over my shoulder. Someone was coming into the break room, and I wouldn't be able to keep my shameful secret to myself with a dozen ears in here. It was bad enough that Anita knew. It was almost time to go anyway. "I don't have the money for that right now. He stole it! Besides, I don't have anything left for him to take. He's got my medication and my money."

"Wait, you didn't say he took your medication. That's another felony, possession of a controlled substance for starters. Whatever you do, come by here when you can. The sooner we get started, the better the chance we find him with at least some of your cash."

"Alright, I'm leaving now."

"Great, see you in my office."

I hung up, retrieved my purse and headed out with a wave to Marcheline, the evening supervisor. "See you later." Pausing in the doorway, I considered saying goodbye to Harper, but she'd been sleeping the last time I peeked in on her.

"Wait up, Jerica," Anita called to me.

"Yes?" I put a fake smile on my face.

"I'm not trying to be nosy, but you take this." She shoved a crumpled bill in my hand. "No argument. You do what you have to. If you need anything else, you let me know." She hugged me quickly and left me standing on the damp sidewalk. Opening my hand, I was surprised to find a hundred-dollar bill.

So that had been Anita in the break room. Well, I knew she would keep a confidence, and I was sure going to pay her back. I tucked the money into my pocket and climbed into my rust bucket. I leaned back in the seat pondering what I wanted to do. Two felonies? How long would that add up to? Obviously, Eddie would do prison time; he'd escaped that fate twice already, but this time...this time would be the real deal. And I would be the one to send him there. I believed what I had told the detective, that this would be the only way he would get any help, but now I was halting between two minds.

What should I do? Take the financial loss and let him slide or be the one to turn the key in the lock? Screw it. He didn't care about me or my pain. All he cared about was himself. I had to do this or else I would be letting him take me down with him.

I am sorry, Marisol. I am so sorry about your Daddy.

I heard nothing except my cell phone ringing. Unknown number...did I dare answer it? Of course, responsible me, I had to. What if it was a doctor or someone from my medical staff?

"Hello?"

"Hey, Jerica. Don't hang up."

"Don't hang up? Are you crazy calling me? I want my money back, Eddie, and my medication! You robbed me, you bastard. Me, of all people! You robbed me!" I didn't mean to start sobbing, but I did. It didn't last long.

"If you would let me explain...please, Jerica. Marisol..."

"Don't you dare mention her name! Don't you dare!"

"I lost a daughter too, Jerica."

Then I said the meanest thing I could think of, and saying it brought me no joy. "Well, at least she won't have to see what a complete failure you've become." Eddie went silent, but I knew he was still there. "The cops are looking for you, Eddie, and I am going to tell them every place I think you'll be. Every place! Don't you ever contact me again. Don't even say my name, or hers! You're dead to me!"

"You're an ice cold bitch, Jerica! Ice cold! You hear me? You turn me into the cops, and I'll make you regret it. Marisol is gone because of you! You killed my..."

I hung up on him and tossed the phone on the passenger side floorboard so I couldn't pick it up. I went straight to the police station and signed on every dotted line Detective Easton asked me to.

"What are your plans for tonight? Are you still staying at the apartment?" she asked me.

"No, I'm going to a hotel, but I have to get some clothes first."

Easton got up and slid on her jacket. "Alright, let's go. I'll drop this off at the Warrant Division, and then we'll go together. I don't trust him, Mrs. Poole. If he's got the cajones to rob you, of all people, there's no telling what else he'd do." I didn't tell her about his latest phone call. Why add years to the sentence? He was a low-down, dirty, backstabbing bastard, and I wanted her to find him. And I agreed with the detective. Eddie was perfectly capable of hurting me. I would have never believed it before all this, but now? Absolutely.

"Thank you."

An hour later, I was checking into a local hotel. I took the detective's advice and got a room that could only be accessed from the inside, and I parked my car away from the building. I missed my apartment and hoped that Easton would nab

Eddie quickly so I could return home without fear of repercussions.

After eating a bland meal from the hotel grill and showering, I felt kind of human and decided to try and get some sleep. I had forgotten to pack socks, and my feet were freezing. I shoved them under the covers and eventually fell asleep. I don't know how long I slept, but it couldn't have been too long. Or at least it didn't feel like it. I pretended that I didn't hear the phone ringing on the nightstand. It couldn't be good news. I didn't pick it up.

As I drifted off to sleep, I heard a young woman's voice calling me. At first it sounded like she was underwater, but then her voice became clearer. I could see her now. Her bobbed hair was pinned back on the left, and she wore a pink dress with strawberries embroidered on the collar and hem. She was tall and pretty and oh so familiar.

"Harper?" I whispered. She stretched her hand out to me, and I took it. I wondered if I was dead but didn't voice the question. Instead, I followed her, and then she disappeared.

I was somewhere I had never been before, but I knew where I was. Somehow, I knew.

I was at Summerleigh.

Chapter Four—Harper

July 1942

Momma's shiny black Chevy Master DeLuxe raced up the driveway toward Summerleigh, leaving a wide trail of dust in its wake. It was hot and sticky out; we needed rain to tamp down the powdery red dirt, but no luck so far. Momma and Augustine Hogue had gone shopping this morning in Momma's new car, a gift from her father, Mr. Daughdrill. Although he was our grandfather, we weren't allowed to call him Grandpa or anything like that; he preferred Mr. Daughdrill. I had no idea what Momma had done to earn such a vehicle. Our grandfather rarely appeared in our lives, only when my father wasn't around. There was no love lost between the two, that much was certain, but Momma had always stood by Daddy in her own selfish way.

Momma and Miss Augustine were laughing as they walked through the back door. Momma deposited her shopping bags on the kitchen table and walked through to the parlor without even a hello to me. The ladies removed their hats and took their seats by the radio. Amanda of Honeymoon Hill would come on in a few minutes, and they never missed their favorite program. Sometimes my sister Addison joined them, but not today. She remained in her bed with a toothache; it was less a toothache and more a heartache. I reminded her that Daddy would be gone for only a few weeks this time; this deployment was much shorter than the others. Daddy had a very special mission to accomplish, I told her, but it hadn't helped. Daddy was a larger-than-life figure, a handsome man with a beaming smile and a deep devotion to his Belles. He had been our hero before the war, and now he had become a hero to our entire community. Nobody could put him down now. He'd saved too many men, rescued too many soldiers for those naysayers to continue their mockery of John Jeffrey Belle.

Jeopardy was sulking somewhere upstairs. As soon as Daddy left the house, she began writing him a long letter, probably berating him for leaving or some such nonsense. Jeopardy wrote him daily while he was gone, although she wasn't always allowed to mail her letters. Momma would fuss about the cost of postage and remind Jeopardy that Daddy had better things to do than write letters to a girl. He had work to do, but that didn't discourage Jeopardy. She'd find a way to earn change enough to mail her letters.

I wrote Daddy too, but not nearly as much as Jeopardy did. I had other responsibilities like cooking supper, cleaning the house and caring for the garden. Besides, Daddy didn't write me back, not like he did with Jeopardy. And in the end, I didn't want to compete with my sister for Daddy's affections. Addison never wrote him because writing gave her headaches, she said, and little Loxley could barely write her name. Heaven knows if Momma ever wrote him, but he certainly sent her cards, letters and gifts all the way from Europe. Jeopardy always ended up with those trinkets; otherwise, they might find their way to a pawn shop or a yard sale. Momma didn't treasure Daddy's gifts like we did.

The ladies were laughing about something. I already had the tea brewed and cooling on the counter. And then the intro music came on and they grew quiet. I poured two glasses of tea, broke off a few pieces of ice from inside the freezer, dropped them in the glasses and carried them to the parlor. Out of the corner of my eye, I saw Jeopardy skulking on the stairs, but I didn't give her position away; I didn't have to. Momma spied her and called her down during the opening commercial. Amanda of Honeymoon Hill always had lots of advertisements at the beginning of the broadcast. I think I liked those better than the actual program. Someday I would get to try that fancy new Pepti Toothpaste.

"What are you wearing, Jeopardy? Is that the same dress you wore yesterday?" Momma frowned at her oldest daughter as she walked toward her. "And when was the last time you brushed your hair...or your teeth? Come here and stop slouching." Jeopardy didn't obey her. She stood with her hips shifted to the left, her right hand grasping the upper part of her left arm. Clearly, she didn't want to be anywhere near our mother. She always blamed her for Daddy's deployment, and even I didn't appreciate Momma's joyous attitude in his absence.

Miss Augustine huffed beside Momma as she cast a disapproving eye on the eldest Belle child. I wanted to intervene, but it would do me no good. No good at all. When Momma and Jeopardy tied up, it was best to stay out from between them. That had been Daddy's advice. You could just sense they were on a collision course for a fight, and I was getting nervous for Jeopardy. But then Momma smiled, her pretty face undeterred by her daughter's disobedience.

In a sweet, cheery voice, she said to Jeopardy, "There are two baskets of peaches on the kitchen counter. One goes to Mrs. Hendrickson and the other to Dr. Leland. Collect a quarter for each basket, or twenty cents if they want to return the baskets. You can take Loxley's red wagon if you think you can't carry them both."

"All the way to Leland's? That's over a mile away," Jeopardy whined.

"And the sooner you get started, the sooner you'll get back, but please tidy up before you leave. I can't have you leaving the house looking like you stepped out of a pigpen, Jeopardy Belle."

Jeopardy was ready to argue about it, I could tell. This was my chance to defuse the situation and save my sister from further humiliation. "I'll go with you, Jeopardy. I'd like to return Mrs. Hendrickson's paperbacks anyway."

"No!" Momma said sharply before the smile returned to her face. "Miss Hogue and I will need your help with canning that bushel of peaches in the sink, Harper. Why don't you start peeling them while Jeopardy runs this errand for me? And of course, you'll keep ten cents for yourself, Jeopardy, dear. I'm sure you'll want to buy paper and postage stamps for all those letters."

Jeopardy's face lit up, and she scampered back up the steps to brush her hair and her teeth and maybe change her dress. I was disappointed that I couldn't go, but at least I would be in the kitchen near the open window and not traipsing around in this heat. Five minutes later, as the ladies were deeply immersed in their radio program, Jeopardy loaded two baskets onto Loxley's Radio Flyer and headed down the lane. She didn't say much except goodbye, and I could see from the kitchen window that she was taking the shortcut through the woods. *Good for her.* The trip wouldn't be quite a mile long, and she'd have plenty of shade. I noticed she carried her favorite stick, just in case she needed to knock a snake in the head. We had plenty of black snakes around here. Summerleigh wasn't that far from Dog River, and the snakes got stirred up even more on hot days like this one.

After the radio program, Momma and Miss Augustine came into the kitchen. I assumed they were going to help me peel the peaches, but Momma had her hat on. "I'm taking Miss Augustine home. She has an appointment she forgot all about, but I will be back in a few minutes to help you." As soon as she opened the screen door, she paused. "It looks like it might storm soon. Have Loxley come inside, Harper. We don't want her to get sick, and you know she's prone to keep a runny nose in the summer."

"Alright, Momma. Could you check on Jeopardy? She might get caught in the rain, and I see lightning just up the road."

Her face tightened, and her eyes flashed at me. "I am sure she's on her way home now, Harper. Don't worry about Jeopardy; she's a resourceful young lady."

"I don't know how resourceful she'll be in a rainstorm," I whispered to her back as she stepped off the porch with Miss Augustine's bulky frame in tow. I washed my hands in the sink and went looking for Loxley. I hadn't seen her all morning, and finding her would be a chore. I didn't need another chore; I had a sneaking suspicion that I would be canning this bushel of peaches by myself.

"Loxley, come in the house. It's going to rain!" I yelled at the edge of the yard. I didn't have time to go wandering through the woods. "Loxley! You hear me? Come back to the house!" I waited around and didn't hear a thing. With a sigh of exasperation, I walked to the front of the house just in case. Loxley generally didn't venture into the unkempt front yard; she had a great fear of rodents, and there were usually plenty scrabbling around out here. But she did have a tendency to wander...especially when accompanied by one of her invisible friends.

"Loxley!" I didn't see hide nor hair of her, but after listening for a moment I heard her voice coming from the house. Sing-songy, like she was playing a hand-clapping or jump rope game with someone, but who? Jeopardy was gone, Addison was down in the bed, and here I was. You sure couldn't play a hand-clapping game with a ghost, could you? I would have to go fetch her and bring her downstairs before Momma got back home. Momma didn't like us to "lurk around up there," as she described it. Some of the floors were spongy and might give way if you trod on them, she warned us repeatedly.

I went around to the back door and through to the kitchen and peeked in on Addison. No, she was still there, sleeping in her bed. I walked back through the Great Room to the parlor and then up the first set of stairs. Suddenly, I heard footsteps running away from me.

"Loxley? Please don't make me chase you."

I waited, but she never came down the stairs. With an exasperated sigh, I climbed the steps. The footsteps returned, only this time they weren't running away from me but coming up behind me. "Jeopardy?" I turned, expecting to see her returned from her errand, but there was no one there. My skin suddenly felt icy cold as if I had stepped into an icehouse. My stomach did a double-clutch, but I didn't wait to ponder it. I scampered up the stairs away from the mysterious sounds in search of Loxley.

"Loxley Belle, you come out here right now."

"Up here…" she called from the floor above.

As quietly as I could, I raced to the end of the hall and ran up the stairs uncaring if they were spongy or not. The invisible footsteps had put the fear of God in me, and I didn't want to be up here. I couldn't shake the feeling that someone was behind me, following me, watching me.

"Loxley!"

"Here, silly. In the nursery." And there she was, sitting on the floor by the window, a sprinkling of jacks and a tiny red rubber ball in front of her. "Play with me, Harper."

I could see the dark clouds gathering through the dirty, curtainless window. I didn't care for this room. It had too many nooks and crannies, too many places for things to hide. "Loxley, who was in here? I heard footsteps on the stairs, and I heard you clapping hands with someone. Someone was up here. Who was it?"

"That boy. I think you scared him away. He doesn't like grown-ups."

"I'm no grown-up," I said with a nervous, uncertain smile. "What boy? Someone I know?" I sat down across from her. She picked up the ball and stared at me with her big blue eyes.

"No, I don't think so. He ran out of the room when he heard you coming. Will you play with me?"

A shadow passed by the door, but I pretended I didn't see it. Loxley glanced behind her and then turned back to me with curious eyes. I said, "I can play for just a minute or two. I have to finish peeling peaches before Momma gets back. I'm waiting on Jeopardy too. She went to deliver jars, and it's going to storm."

"Play with me first and I will help you, Harper," she promised with her sweetest expression.

"You mean you'll eat them all. Come on, then, you first."

We played a few rounds, and then I reminded her of my chore. Tucking the jacks and ball in her pinstriped apron pocket, she paused and stared at the doorway. I couldn't discern her expression. "What is it, Loxley?"

"I think we should go now."

The hair on my arms prickled up as I asked, "Why? Is someone coming?" I didn't hear any footsteps, but ghosts didn't always let you know they were there until they jumped out at you. At least that's what Loxley told me.

She nodded and took my hand. "We have to go, and Momma will be back soon." We were down two flights of stairs in no time flat. I didn't ask any more questions and gladly went back to paring peaches. Just as Loxley predicted, Momma returned without Miss Augustine and chattered away as she got the pot ready for the jars. The three of us worked together to get the peaches on to simmer, and Momma even allowed Loxley to add a dash or two extra of cinnamon. Loxley loved cinnamon.

Without my hearing her arrive, Jeopardy stormed in through the back door looking like she'd fallen down a hill. The sleeve of her dress was torn, her face was dirty, and there could be no doubt she'd been crying.

Momma didn't say a word, but I couldn't help but exclaim, "Jeopardy!" My sister didn't speak but stared at Momma with all the hatred she could muster. To my surprise, Momma smiled sweetly. What was happening? Suddenly, Jeopardy threw the quarters and a handful of twenty-dollar bills at Momma, but Momma didn't flinch. Jeopardy ran through the kitchen away from us all. Our mother continued to stir the pot and didn't go see about her. I went instead.

It was her footsteps I heard now. I knew the sound of her shoes well. She bounded up the stairs two by two all the way to her "castle" room in the attic. I heard her lock it, but I refused to go away.

"Jeopardy, it's me, Harper. Please let me in." The only sound I heard was her crying. "Please, Jeopardy."

She didn't answer me. After a few minutes, I walked down the hallway and waited at the top of the stairs. What could I do? I couldn't force her to open the door. A hundred horrible scenarios played in my head, but I couldn't figure out what just happened. Maybe Momma knew. I would certainly ask her. I looked back once more and to my surprise saw a woman in a white gown with long dark hair sliding through the locked door. And then Jeopardy's crying stopped.

I didn't stay at Summerleigh. I had never seen a ghost before, and the experience left me terrified. Ignoring Momma's call, I ran until I couldn't run anymore and found myself clear down the lane at Mrs. Hendrickson's yard. As always, the older woman was home, and I went inside and cried on her shoulder. I couldn't explain why I was so upset, but after a few hours, a half-dozen tea cakes and a phone call from Momma, I was prepared to go back to Summerleigh.

Or as prepared as I could be.

Chapter Five—Jerica

Taking an extra five minutes in the shower, I stood under the showerhead dumbfounded at the memory of my strange dream. In no way did I think I had imagined any of it. There was no doubt in my mind that Harper Belle Hayes had visited me and that I'd seen life through her eyes for a little while. As I scrubbed my body, I could smell traces of Harper's lavender perfume, taste the peaches on my lips and feel the heat of that long-ago summer day on my skin. Yes, I had been there. Loxley's curious eyes and Jeopardy's ripped sleeve came back to my mind; these were images I would never forget—not in a lifetime. I wasn't sure how Harper had done it, but she and I had connected in that dream, and I couldn't wait to talk to her about it. I knew for a fact my friend was a big believer in dreams, since she shared hers with me often, but this was certainly an unusual experience. I used to dream all the time, but I never did anymore since Marisol's death. Until now.

I rinsed the soap off my skin and stepped out of the hotel's shower surprised to hear my cell phone ringing. "Shoot," I complained to no one. I wrapped a towel around my body and another around my hair before padding off to the nightstand to retrieve my phone. Someone from the front desk of the care facility had called. Some emergency must have happened. I glanced at the bright red alarm clock display. I would be at work in thirty minutes, just as I was supposed to be, but I couldn't avoid returning the call. I was the administrator, and I couldn't shirk my responsibilities despite my current personal drama. There could only be a few reasons why anyone from work would call so close to check-in time. And none of them were good.

To my surprise, it wasn't Marcheline who answered the phone but Anita. "Good morning, this is Jerica."

Anita answered, "I am sorry to call you like this when I know you'll be here soon, but I have to give you this notice. Can't avoid procedure even though..."

"Notice? Who passed away, Anita?" I asked as I sat on the bed. I knew exactly who died, but my mind wasn't willing to process the heartbreaking truth.

"It's Miss Harper. She's gone, Jerica. Passed away in her sleep. I am so sorry."

My hands shook at the news. "Um, I'll be there soon, Anita. Thank you."

"Take your time. We're just getting her ready now, but the ambulance is here for her. Do you want them to wait for you?"

"No, that's not necessary. You sign the paperwork, okay?" This was one patient I couldn't say goodbye to. Not like that.

"You've got it. I'll see you soon."

Anita hung up, and I collapsed on the bed. This explained everything, how Harper came to me in my dream, how she could share a bit of her life with me.

She was dead.

Then I remembered the picture I had placed on my nightstand last night. I stared at those hopeful faces now. There they were: Jeopardy, Harper, Addison and Loxley. All of the Belle girls except for Jeopardy were smiling back at me.

I tucked the picture and my phone back in my leather purse, finished getting dressed and checked out of the hotel. *Screw Eddie. I'm not staying away from home another night.* I needed to go to my apartment anyway—I needed to brush my teeth and change into clean underwear. I had been so frazzled that I'd forgotten to pack underwear and my toothbrush as well as socks. I couldn't face the day with fuzzy teeth, and I wasn't one to go "commando" as my old roommate used to. That would put me getting to work even later. Well, it couldn't be avoided. With my hair still wet and with minimal makeup, I made the drive to my apartment and raced up the stairs to find that my door stood open.

Oh, God. Not this.

Without thinking, I stepped inside and immediately noticed that my television and satellite receiver were missing. The couch cushions were scattered as if someone had taken the time to dig for change—or knew exactly where I kept my "mad money" in a zippered plastic bag. I should have known it would be a bad idea to hide money in the couch.

"Hello?" I called, but nobody answered. As cold as it was in here, the door must have been open for hours. *Gee, I have great neighbors. Did nobody hear all this commotion?* The kitchen didn't have much missing except the microwave, but my bedroom looked a shambles. Someone had pulled out all the dresser drawers, and my clothes were all over the floor. My nightstands and closet stood open, and my computer and jewelry boxes were gone. I sat on the bare mattress and took in the sight.

Oh no! Eddie had taken Marisol's picture! The one from our last day at the beach. I checked around to see if it had fallen on the floor, but there wasn't a trace. He'd clearly stolen it as if in one last cruel act, he would steal her memory from me. Eddie wasn't joking. He clearly blamed me for the accident; he blamed me that Marisol was gone.

God, I had been such a fool to let him back in here. What the hell, Eddie?!

When I quit sobbing, I knew I had to call the police. Again. I'd left my cell phone in my purse, so I had to use the landline. Picking up the phone, I heard a voice on the line. A girl's voice. Nothing but whispers, desperate whispers. "Hello?" I said as I sprang to my feet. There was another phone in the living room. What if someone was hurt? I ran through the mess and raced to the phone. It was still on its receiver. There was no one in here. I hung up the phone and picked it up again and again, but nothing I did disconnected the sad voice. Whoever was there didn't hang up, and she was crying now. The whispers continued, and the voice sounded even more heartbreaking.

"Hello? Is someone there?"

"What happened in here?" Detective Easton stood in the doorway. I dropped the phone and nearly jumped a foot off the ground.

"You tell me. I thought you guys were watching this place! If I had to guess, I'd say that Eddie cleaned me out while I was hiding out in the hotel. What a great idea to leave my home unattended!" Angry words burst out of my mouth before I had a chance to think about reining myself in. Harper's death and now this? It was too much to handle.

"He's a likely candidate, but we can't know for sure he did this until we begin the investigation. Could you have left it unlocked?"

I ignored her stupid question, tossed a couch cushion on the couch and sat on it. "Well, he took my change stash, and nobody knew about that bag of change except Eddie. It was right here."

"Lots of people hide money in their couch, Jerica."

I shook my head and said, "You honestly think a stranger did this?"

"Could be a stranger, but Eddie Poole would be my first suspect. First things first, I'll need you to step out; this is a crime scene now. I have to get the crime team in here, and I'll need a list of what's missing."

"Marisol's picture, the one on my nightstand—he took it. It had to be him. Who else would do such a thing?"

"I am sorry, Jerica. We let you down on this one, but I'll get to the bottom of this."

I didn't believe her. I knew it wasn't going to be all right. I was never going to be rid of Eddie. He would always torment me, blame me for Marisol's death. Like I didn't blame myself enough. "I don't have time for this. I have to go to work—a patient has passed away. You do what you have to, Detective."

"Oh, sorry to hear that. Alright. Well, I'll call you when we're done."

"Fine," I said. "And don't bother locking the door. There's nothing left to steal."

I was too stunned to cry now. I drove to work feeling numb, just like the morning of the accident. One minute we'd been singing, and the next....

The ambulance was parked in front of the doors, and I watched as the paramedics respectfully wheeled the sheet-covered body of Harper Hayes out of the Sunrise Retirement Home. Some of the residents came to watch her leave; this would be hard on them. Harper had been everyone's favorite. Even the crotchety Ricky Jackson liked her, and that was saying a lot.

When the ambulance drove off, I wiped away tears and walked inside. This would be the second hardest day of my life.

Chapter Six—Jerica

Anita and I had barely finished Harper's paperwork when an older gentleman in a tidy blue suit appeared at my station. "May I help you, sir?"

"I'm here on business for Mrs. Harper Hayes."

Anita and I looked at one another. "I'm sorry to tell you that Mrs. Hayes passed away this morning. Were you a family member?" I asked politely.

"Yes, I know about her passing, but I am not a family member. I am a friend of hers from Mississippi."

Curious about who this unknown friend could be, I suggested that we speak privately in one of the empty consultation rooms. Closing the door behind us, I invited Harper's visitor to sit across from me at the small, round table. It was then that I noticed the man had a small leather bag with him. He put it on the table and unzipped it with trembling hands.

"I didn't catch your name, sir. I am Jerica Poole."

"Oh, good, just the lady I wanted to see." He removed two envelopes, one small and the other long and white. He placed the smaller one in front of me. "I am supposed to give you this, in the event of Harper's passing." He slid the sealed envelope closer to me. I didn't open it.

59

"What's this all about?" The hair pricked up on the back of my neck, but I kept an uneasy smile on my face.

"I know this all appears so mysterious, but I am here on behalf of Harper Belle. Excuse me, Harper Belle Hayes. My name is Ben, Ben Hartley. I am an old friend of the Belle family, specifically Harper. I haven't seen much of Harper in the past few years, but that wasn't entirely my fault."

Shaking my head, I said, "Not to doubt you, but she never mentioned having a friend named Ben. Again, I'm not trying to be rude..."

He sighed sadly. "I can believe it. I think she spent most of her life trying to forget me, but I never forgot her. I would have thought she had forgiven me after all this time. She must have, or she wouldn't have sent me here. Please take the envelope. It is meant for you."

I licked my suddenly dry lips and said, "I can't accept the envelope, Ben. First, I don't know what's in it, and second, as an employee of the Sunrise Retirement Home, it's against the rules to accept gifts from residents, past or present. As you say, you're here on Harper's behalf. So this would be considered a gift from her, or whatever this is. I am sure you understand; I have to follow the rules." That wasn't entirely true, considering the gifts Harper had given me for Marisol, but I didn't want to offend him.

Ben's wrinkled face reddened, and his faded green eyes were moist with unshed tears. He had a head full of hair, but I could tell he wasn't in the best of health. In this line of work, I had learned to pick up on these things pretty quickly. "Harper said you would be the one to help her find Jeopardy. It was her last wish, Miss Poole."

I didn't correct him on calling me Miss, but my face reddened too. "I have every intention of doing my research, Mr. Hartley, but I can't accept money."

"It's not money. It's the keys to Summerleigh and the caretaker's cottage. I used to live there. The cottage is still in working order. If you'd like, I can have it cleaned and updated before you arrive."

"I think there's been some mistake, sir." A nervous laugh escaped my lips. "I am not going to Summerleigh. Harper never asked me to move to Mississippi."

"How else will you find Jeopardy? You can't do that from a desk in Virginia. No, hear me out. All of the Belles are gone now, even little Loxley. There is no one left, no one to carry on the search." His shoulders sagged, and although I felt horrible for bringing him any discomfort, I had to be honest with him. I was nothing if not honest.

"What about the sheriff's department or a detective agency? I've never looked for a missing person before. Harper was my friend, Ben. She helped me through the most difficult time in my life. I am not exaggerating when I tell you that I loved Harper like a mother. I think it's a great tragedy, the disappearance of her sister, but I don't know why she believes I can help bring her home. I'm not a family member."

"Sometimes blood isn't thicker than water, Miss Poole. It's about the ties of the heart, not your genetic makeup. And I am sorry for your loss."

Not half as sorry as I am, I thought. I peeked inside the envelope. Sure enough, there were two brass keys inside and a slip of paper with an address written on it.

"Would you mind if I visited the restroom?" he asked politely. The phone rang in and surprised the heck out of me. Only Anita knew I was in here, so I knew it must be important. I picked it up hurriedly and covered the receiver.

"Of course, Ben. It's just around the corner to the right."

"Thank you." His southern drawl was very apparent now. Funny how I didn't notice it at the beginning of our conversation. It was almost as if the more tired he appeared, the thicker his accent.

"Yes, Anita?"

"I have the funeral home on the line. They have some questions for you—they say they can't wait. Can you take their call now?"

"No, let me wrap this up and I'll call them back. I mean, surely they can wait five minutes."

"Alright," she said and hung up.

I rolled the chair back to the table and picked up the envelope again. How long had Harper been planning this, and how in the world did her old friend Ben Hartley know she'd passed away so quickly? No way he made the drive up from Mississippi in just a few hours. I tapped on the desk as I waited for the return of the mysterious Mr. Hartley. How exactly did he know Harper? It sounded like something serious had passed between them. How could I politely ask such a question? *Curiosity killed the cat.* After a couple of minutes, I walked out to the office and waited in the hall. Anita raised her dark eyebrows at me.

"Where did he go?"

"The old man?"

"Yes, Ben Hartley."

"He left five minutes ago."

"What? He left his stuff in here." I walked back in the office and was surprised to see that his leather bag was gone but not the two envelopes. With shaking fingers, I opened the larger envelope. I couldn't believe my eyes. This was Harper's Last Will and Testament.

I read the document aloud just to make sure I wasn't losing my mind.

I, Harper Belle Hayes, hereby bequeath all my worldly possessions, including my home, Summerleigh, to my dear friend, Jerica Jernigan Poole...

Chapter Seven—Jerica

I parked the SUV in the driveway and sat for a minute; how amazing was it that I'd actually made it in one piece? I'd never been an adventurous person, and except for my senior trip, this was the first time I'd left the state of Virginia. And I'd certainly never been the one to do the driving; Eddie always commandeered the wheel for any day trips we went on. But look at me now. Here I was! I got out of the vehicle to stretch my legs. Driving for two days had left me feeling stiff all over. I slammed the car door and dug my hands into my back pockets as I stretched my back.

Summerleigh had undergone recent repairs. Even from just halfway up the length of the driveway, I smelled fresh cut lumber and sawdust. And I knew sawdust. My foster parents had owned a lumberyard, and I had spent many a happy day playing with blocks and piles of dust. The historic home had five columns that lined the front porch. Yes, there were two one-story wings flanking either side of the two-story main house, exactly as Harper had described it. The wing to the left needed some roof repair, and a massive tree branch lay next to it. *That must have been the culprit. They say this area of the south has incredible summer storms. Someone will have to trim some of these trees back because a few of those limbs look a bit dangerous.*

Besides the roof damage to the west wing, Summerleigh needed major siding repairs and a fresh coat of paint from top to bottom. That was just what I could see from the exterior. I noticed a wisteria vine loaded with purple blooms wrapping around the porch railing. Fat bumblebees were taking an interest in it too, and although the purple flowers gave the place a "lost in time" vibe, the vine would have to go. Or at least be cut back from the wooden railing.

Dad's words came back to me: *"You have to protect the wood, Jeri."*

See, Dad, I listened sometimes. You would love this place. I wish you could be here to see it. I protected my eyes from the glare of the sun with my hand as I stared at the top-floor windows. No glass had been broken, even though no one had called the place home in nearly thirty years. Still, the punch list was growing. The roof repairs, then a paint job, and who knew what I would find inside. The front lawn had been cared for, thankfully. Back when Harper first arrived here, the front yard looked like a jungle. Someone had obviously taken pride in keeping up with the gardening. Dark-leafed camellia bushes bloomed in neat flower beds in front of the house, and the white blooms gave the place an inviting look, like a postcard. The front porch light fixture had been replaced recently too. A grand black pendant light hung over the white porch below. Was I really doing this?

Well, Harper. I'm here. Now what?

I climbed back in the vehicle and drove to the back of Summerleigh. The back of the house was not as impressive as the front. A forlorn-looking circular courtyard was behind the house, and several gravel pathways disappeared into unkempt gardens. I followed the driveway around the courtyard and down a short drive that led to the caretaker's cottage. If you could call it that. The cottage was a smaller replica of Summerleigh, without the wings. Now this place was beautiful! It was a two-story home with painted whiteboards and two columns, one on each end of the front porch.

Anita, you're never going to believe this.

I immediately sent my friend a text and snapped a picture to go along with it. Like me, she could hardly believe Harper's generosity, but she'd supported me every step of the way since my decision to leave Sunrise. After the mysterious Ben Hartley's visit, everything in my life fell apart. Or maybe it fell into place.

Nightmares of the accident returned, and Eddie vandalized my vehicle several times. The detective couldn't locate him, but no matter where I hid out, Eddie always found me. And that was heartbreaking because I really wanted to help him—even after all the heartache. Losing Marisol had just about destroyed us both, but I'd managed to pull myself back up, thanks to my work. Eddie couldn't do that, and for whatever reason, the drugs, the grief, whatever...he blamed me for all of it. As if I were responsible for what happened to my baby, my only child. Guilt rose unbidden within me, but I immediately forced my mind to focus on what was in front of me. No, I wouldn't travel down memory lane today. This was my life now. The only regret I had was leaving my daughter behind.

Naturally, I had to give up my job. My employers weren't happy about the inheritance, and I certainly couldn't tell them that Harper wanted me to find her sister. But again, thanks to Harper, I had several thousand dollars in the bank with more to come later and a house that needed my attention. Not to mention a mystery that needed solving. Would I really be able to find Jeopardy Belle? What if I couldn't? If that was the case, I wouldn't stay. I couldn't do that in good conscience. I thought perhaps some heir would appear to claim the family home, maybe one of Addison's or Loxley's children. But nobody did. No one wanted Summerleigh. Nobody cared that Jeopardy had never been found.

So here I was in southern Mississippi, far away from home, and I felt invigorated. I hadn't expected to feel this level of "rightness," and it was a pleasant surprise. This had been the right thing to do. A raindrop hit my face and shook me out of my daydreaming. I grabbed my purse and hurried to the front door. I had a car to unpack, but it could wait. I slid the brass key in the door of the cottage and stepped inside. I was immediately met by a blast of cold air. Thank goodness the air conditioner worked in here. It was a bit too cold, though, I thought with a shiver.

"Wow," I said as I walked further into the inviting front room. The place had lovely hardwood floors, and there was a quilted rug in front of the wicker sofa. A beautiful window along the side of the room made the perfect picture frame for the greenery beyond. The sun was still partly shining, and rain had begun to fall softly. I spied a small patio and a barbecue grill too. On the other side of the room were built-in oak bookcases, and I immediately went to check them out. I was impressed by how well made they were.

A small dining room was on the other side, with a kitchen just beyond that. The kitchen was small, but everything looked perfect. A vintage gas stove was against the far wall, and it looked neat and tidy. I loved the metal cabinets. Someone certainly had done a masterful job of keeping the place vintage but up to date. I opened the fridge; it was so clean it almost sparkled. I'd have to go to town today to stock the pantry. I doubted that anyone delivered out here. *What's upstairs?* Probably the bedroom and a full bath. A half bath was across the hall from the kitchen. As I set foot on the stairs to scamper up and check it out, I heard a polite knock on my door.

I opened it without worry. Eddie would never find me down here. Nobody knew where I was, except Anita, and she'd die before she told him anything.

"Hi, may I help you?" A striking man stood on my doorstep. He wore a handyman's clothes, and his welcoming smile was brilliant and warm.

"I was wondering the same thing. I was working in the potting shed and thought I heard someone pull in. You must be the new lady. Do you need any help?"

"Jerica Poole," I said as I extended my hand to him. "And so far, so good."

He didn't shake back, showing me his dirty palms. "You probably don't want to shake hands with me. My friends call me JB."

"Hi, JB. You been here long?"

"Yes, it's been awhile. You plan on sticking around? I was sad to see Ben go. It will be nice to have someone here to watch over the place."

"It's my privilege. I can't believe how beautiful this place is, and I haven't even been in the main house yet." I smiled, wondering if I should invite him in for a glass of... *Wait, I have no groceries.* "I'd invite you in for a glass of tea, but I haven't made it into town yet. Where's the best place to shop?"

"Up the road. Lucedale has a Piggly Wiggly. They'll have everything you need."

"Great. Well, JB, I'm sure I won't be as handy as Ben, but I'll try. Will I be able to find you if I need to ask you a question? Is there a phone number where I can reach you, or do you have a schedule or something?"

"No, I don't stay in one place long enough for a phone—or a schedule—but I am usually wandering around here. If you need anything, you'll probably find me in the potting shed. Just up the path there, toward the pond."

"There's a pond?" I asked incredulously.

"More like a mud hole, but we call it a pond," he joked with me.

"Great. I'll see you around, then."

He paused at the bottom of the steps and smiled once more before he walked away, a pot of dirt tucked under a muscular arm. He glanced back at me one more time, and I waved politely. The rain had stopped; even though I was on the front porch, I felt so cold that my teeth were nearly chattering. *God, I hope I'm not coming down with something.* Rubbing my arms to warm myself up, I decided this was the time to get my boxes moved. Hmm... why hadn't I asked JB to help me? Dummy. Oh well, I could handle it. I'd packed it all, taped it and loaded it up. I could certainly unload my own car.

It was dark before I finished, and I was too tired to investigate Summerleigh. Unlike the cottage, which was bright and cozy, the main house was completely dark. Not a light shone from any of the dusty windows. Was the power off? Well, I'd have to worry about that tomorrow.

I stowed the last of my stuff inside, unpacked a few boxes and decided I couldn't ignore my stomach any longer. Driving into town seemed like such a chore now. Strolling into my clean kitchen, I opened a few cabinets and found them stocked with basic grocery supplies.

Ben must have done this! In fact, I noticed he'd posted his phone number on the refrigerator with a Campbell's Soup magnet. I reached for a can of soup, quickly found a can opener and warmed the contents on the stove. Chicken noodle soup and a glass of water would be my supper, and that was all I needed. I cuddled up on the couch with a small quilt I found, white and pink with roses all over it. I loved it. With my stomach full and my back slightly sore, I drifted off to sleep.

And then Harper was there.

Chapter Eight—Harper

Even though Jeopardy and I were the oldest, Addison rode in the front seat of the Master DeLuxe this Sunday morning. Addie had a tendency to get sick if she rode in the back seat for any length of time. I didn't care much about who sat in the front seat, but Jeopardy did, and I could see her point of view. Jeopardy was a young lady now, the oldest of the Belle sisters, all of fifteen. And who wanted their friends to see them riding in the back seat? *It's the baby seat*, she complained quite loudly as we loaded up. It didn't matter to her that she didn't want to go to church to begin with. But she was here now, and I squeezed her hand once to reassure her before she snatched it away. I didn't know why she was so mad at me, but I was determined to make her smile again.

Come to think of it, making Jeopardy smile had been my lifelong ambition, at least when Daddy was away. Just think, in another week, he'd be home again. I had begun to count the days off on my dime store calendar, the one with the puppies on it. Of course, I didn't show it to anyone. The subject of Daddy's arrival seemed off-limits right now, and I couldn't understand why.

Momma was behind the wheel, complaining the entire time and honking her horn every few minutes. Loxley slept between us in the back seat, despite the noise. Here we were, in our Sunday best. Even Jeopardy wore a dress this morning, but I noticed she'd forgotten to wear a slip, which to our mother's mind wasn't ladylike at all. I hoped Momma didn't notice that oversight. We pulled into the driveway and waited for the dust to settle before we got out. Momma checked her teeth in the mirror and shot Jeopardy a disapproving look before she opened the door and stepped out.

Just as she did seven days a week, Momma looked like a movie star with her short blond hair and pretty features. Despite having four children, she had a trim waist and a perfect figure. "Come on, girls. Church is about to begin. Now remember, no sleeping or looking around like a wide-eyed calf. Are you listening, Loxley?"

"Yes, ma'am." Our sleepy sister took Momma's hand, and the rest of us walked behind her. I always loved coming to church, mostly because of the music. Sometimes the pastor told funny stories, and I liked those too. I got lost in the "thees" and "thous," but even that was entertaining.

Most Sundays, Jeopardy frowned the whole time, doodled on paper when she could and always, always did a lot of people-watching. Daddy never said anything to her, but things were different now—Daddy wasn't here. Unfortunately for Jeopardy, Momma settled herself between her and Loxley and didn't mind pinching Jeopardy's arm if she let herself get distracted. Momma didn't pinch me often, but it could hurt worse than a fire ant. And that was pretty bad. I fell in a fire ant bed once; I had bumps for weeks and would never forget the pain. Never.

We'd gotten through "Bringing in the Sheaves" with no incidents, except Jeopardy wouldn't sing and didn't care that Momma was cutting her eyes. She cracked gum instead, and I thought for sure she'd get backhanded for that. Sister Sheryl Sellers—she liked being called "sister," as did most of the church ladies—half-turned in her pew to see who the gum-cracking culprit was but didn't say a word. She did give Momma an offended look, though. As soon as the heavyset woman's head was turned, Momma held out her hand and waited for Jeopardy to spit out her gum. With a petulant expression, she dropped her gum in the waiting tissue.

The choir began singing again. *Do Lord, oh do Lord, oh, do remember me...* Loxley and I sang loudly, and Addison's soft voice obediently sang too. Jeopardy alone refused to praise the Lord even though Momma offered to share her red-backed hymnal with her. *Please, Jeopardy, behave yourself.* I kept my eyes in front of me, but I sensed impending disaster. So did Addison; she clutched her stomach, but I couldn't comfort her right now. I kept singing but silently prayed to the Good Lord for help.

Where is Aunt Dot this morning? She never misses Sunday Service. Please God, send Aunt Dot to church this morning. Help Jeopardy, God. Please save her, Jesus.

I called on the Father, Son and Holy Ghost, but the tension rose on our uncomfortable wooden pew—and we were surrounded by a church full of witnesses. Pastor Reed had just begun his sermon on the Garden of Gethsemane when Jeopardy let out a yelp that shocked the entire congregation.

"Sit down!" Momma whispered like a freight train, but my sister wasn't having any of it. She was on her feet, her face like a dark cloud.

"Jeopardy," I whispered as she climbed over me with tears in her eyes. Momma hadn't gotten up yet, but she would in a moment if Jep didn't come back. She didn't.

Soon, all of us Belles were streaming out of the church and Momma and Jeopardy were having a shouting match in the parking lot. I didn't understand half of what they were saying, but my sister was yelling, her face red, and her bare, bruised arms gave evidence of Momma's cruel pinches. I didn't look back at the church, but I had a feeling that all fifty of the congregants were watching us from the arched windows of the First Baptist Church of Desire, Mississippi.

Loxley cried as Momma threatened to beat Jeopardy; Addison held her hand over her mouth as if she were going to throw up. Then like an angel from heaven, Aunt Dot pulled into the parking lot and scampered toward us. Her perfect bob bounced as she ran in heels toward Jeopardy, who was a screaming, crying mess.

"What in the world?" Aunt Dot asked as she gathered Jeopardy into her arms. "Ann, have you lost your mind arguing in the church parking lot? Oh great, here comes Augustine." Aunt Dot yelled to her, "Thank you, Augustine, but we're all fine here."

"She's incorrigible," Momma cried behind her handkerchief. "She'll ruin us all, Dorothy! Even Father says…"

"Ann, please. Don't say something you will regret later. I'll take Jeopardy home."

"She'll ride home with me, Dot. She's my daughter!"

Jeopardy sobbed on our aunt's shoulder. "No, dear," Aunt Dot answered calmly, "I think you need a break. You must be under so much stress with John Jeffrey gone. I will take Jeopardy home now. Have a cigarette or take the girls out for a soda. We will see you at Summerleigh." Aunt Dot didn't wait for an answer; she left with her arm around Jeopardy's shoulders.

Momma was silent as the grave on the drive home. We didn't stop for a soda, even though Addison whined about it until Momma popped her bare leg. I was suddenly glad that I wasn't in the front seat this morning. I blinked back the tears so Momma wouldn't see me cry. I couldn't be seen as taking sides, not if I wanted to smooth things over. If that was even possible now.

To my surprise, Aunt Dot's car was in the driveway when we got there. My sisters and I raced through the kitchen to avoid the coming battle. The Daughdrills rarely argued, but when they did, it was usually an epic event, although they never laid a hand on each other. I lingered outside the door for some morbid reason. Aunt Dot accused Momma of being cruel to Jeopardy; Momma called Aunt Dot a nosy spinster. I couldn't take any more of the accusations. I decided to tend to my sisters. They would need me, I believed. But Loxley didn't want a hug and instead went out the front door to go find one of her kittens. Addison headed to bed for a lie-down.

The only Belle missing was Jeopardy. She wasn't downstairs, so I knew she had to be in her castle room. I hated walking up the stairs, but today I would have risked walking through the gates of hell to help my sister. Why did it have to be this way? I vowed right then and there to write Daddy a letter. He had to know that his daughters needed him. Surely the Army would let him come home. I'd heard of soldiers coming home for emergencies before.

Jeopardy met me in the hallway. She'd shed her sundress and was wearing a pair of capris and a tank top; these were obviously some of Aunt Dot's hand-me-downs. Momma rarely bought Jeopardy an outfit, and Jeopardy hated the things Momma bought her and was quite vocal about that. Yes, she looked quite scandalous for a

Sunday. Her hair hung loosely now, and over her shoulder was her crocheted purse. I pretended I didn't see a pack of Momma's cigarettes peeking out between the stitches. "Where are you going?" I asked in surprise.

"I'm going to the river. I'm meeting some friends there. If you care anything about me, you won't rat me out."

"I would never, Jeopardy. I never have!" I was offended at being accused of disloyalty. She should know that hurt me down to the bone.

She tilted her head and said, "Then come with me, Harper. Just for the day."

"What if Momma comes looking for me?"

"What if she does? Are you my sister or not?"

"Okay," I agreed without thinking it through any further. Jeopardy had challenged my loyalty, and I had to prove it to her. "I need to change, though."

"I'll meet you behind the potting shed. But I'm only waiting five minutes. If you don't come, if you chicken out, Harper, I'm gone."

"Alright. I'll be there."

Jeopardy and I tiptoed down the stairs, and she left out the back door to avoid another battle with Momma. Momma and Aunt Dot were still going at it, so I took advantage of the distraction and went to my bedroom and quickly changed into a checkered shirt and blue jean shorts. Grabbing my tennis shoes, I left Summerleigh, happy to leave the heated argument behind me. Loxley had her favorite kitten in her lap. She wouldn't miss me.

I ran around the house, avoiding the kitchen window, and found Jeopardy waiting for me by the shed. My rebellious heart had never felt freer. Jeopardy smiled at my bravery and offered me a cigarette. I refused but smiled back. So this was what it was like to be Jeopardy...carefree and adventurous! I had never been either of those things. No wonder Momma didn't like her; Momma wasn't carefree or adventurous either. But I loved my sister, and it felt good to see her smile. Even if it meant we were about to get into major trouble. I'd never done anything like this before, but it was too late to turn back now.

We held hands and ran all the way to the river.

Chapter Nine—Jerica

Something woke me from my dream, but I had no idea what it could have been. Nevertheless, I was wide awake and feeling quite perturbed. One minute I was running free with Harper and Jeopardy, an invisible witness to their family troubles, and the next I found myself staring up at a white painted ceiling. Sunlight filtered through sheer white curtains, and the sounds of birds surprised me. Oh, yes. Now I remembered. I was in Desire, and this was Summerleigh, or at least the cottage at Summerleigh. Imagine me, Jerica Poole, here in south Mississippi, the new owner of an old mansion.

My heart broke for Harper, but I needed to think about what I had seen. I wandered into the kitchen and hoped that Ben had been kind enough to have purchased coffee. He had! I would have to call him later and thank him. He'd really saved me by thinking ahead. Still, I would have to make that trip to the Piggly Wiggly in Lucedale sooner rather than later. As I loaded the filter and coffee into the white coffee machine, I thought about the silence. There were no sirens out here, no horns honking or rowdy neighbors yelling across balconies at one another. It was really like another world. A slower world.

While the machine sputtered to life, I sauntered upstairs to finish arranging my toiletries in the bathroom. I loved the fractured glass windows and the tidy tile job. The fixtures weren't showroom new, but who was I to look a gift horse in the mouth? And I had so much space. I arranged the towels and filled my medicine cabinet. My two missing prescriptions were a concern, but maybe I could postpone finding a new doctor awhile. After washing my face and brushing my teeth, I headed back down to grab that cup of coffee. My watch told me it was three o'clock. *That can't be right. Shoot. Don't tell me I killed another watch battery.* Watches and I never got along, but I had loved this one so much I figured I'd give it another shot. Well, maybe there was a battery place in town too.

I noticed for the first time that there was a squeak on the third stair down. That was slightly irritating. I would have to take a look at that. Might be just a loose board. As I checked out the suspect piece, I heard a light tapping on the back door. It was so light that I had to really focus to hear it. Yes, someone was here for sure.

"Coming!" I yelled, hoping it was JB. The back door was between the kitchen and the laundry room if I remembered correctly. I rubbed my eyes and wished I'd bothered to brush my hair. "Almost there," I said pleasantly. The clock on the wall told me it was eight. Man, I had slept late this morning. That never happened.

Unlocking the dead bolt, I opened the door with a friendly smile, but there was no one there. No one at all. "Hello?" I called out. No one answered, but arranged neatly on the bottom porch step was a small bouquet of flowers. Not the hothouse kind but wildflowers, purple, yellow and pink. The only one I recognized was the black-eyed Susans.

Marisol...

Who would have left these here? Someone very shy, apparently. Maybe JB had children or I had a neighbor closer than I thought? I hurried back inside and went to the kitchen. Grabbing a mason jar from the cabinet, I filled it with water and put the flowers in the window above the sink. Okay, I needed coffee. I sipped the black brew and enjoyed the flowers. It must have been one of JB's children who left them. Had to be. I didn't see any other houses around here. Trespassers didn't normally leave bouquets on your doorstep. I touched one flower and smiled at the sweet offering.

Now, what was my plan? For sure I needed a shower, but Summerleigh waited for my exploration. After another few swallows of hot coffee, I grabbed the keys and headed to the house. The cottage was about fifty yards from the main house, and it was a lovely morning for a walk. Instead of going through the back door, I opted to make it official and go around to the front. It all looked so familiar. Just like Harper showed me in my dream, just as she had described many times in our conversations.

"What a beautiful place, Harper," I said as I nearly tripped over a stone. What in the world?

Who would put a marker this close to a pathway? Clearly, this wasn't some random rock but a stone marker with some inscription hidden under the grass. *That's funny*, I thought. The rest of the garden was so overgrown, that was true, but it had some order to it. This marker appeared to have been completely forgotten. Or at least overlooked. I squatted down and scooped away leaves. A tiny brown spider scurried away. Good thing too. Spiders were not my favorite creature.

In Loving Memory of a Lost Soul

Loving memory...so this was a person? I had thought perhaps a pet, but a person? This seemed an odd place for a memorial stone. How horribly sad.

Jeopardy! Could this be for Jeopardy Belle?

"Sorry, Jeopardy," I said as I lovingly touched the stone. And I didn't know why, but I added, "I'll bring you home...I promise." The wind fluttered my hair around me, and the sound of footsteps behind me made me stand up and look around. I saw no one.

I decided it was best not to linger here and allow my imagination to run away with me. I'd done that before, and look where that got me—medicated. I journeyed on to the house, walked to the welcoming front door and slid the key in. Some thoughtful person had wisely painted the porch floorboards a dark green. That was an excellent shade for hiding dirt and whatnot. I opened the front door and stepped inside Summerleigh for the first time. I remembered the mixed emotions Harper felt, and I experienced something similar. The porch and exterior had appeared so welcoming, except for the obvious roof disrepair, but there was nothing too welcome inside.

This would be what people would have called the Great Room when it was built. There was a sweeping staircase on the left side of the room that led to a windowed landing. Just before it and to the right were two evenly spaced wooden columns that gave you the feeling you'd stepped inside a Greek temple. In the center of the columns on the back wall was a large fireplace surrounded by built-in bookcases. *What a strange place to put a fireplace. Or maybe not. What do I know about south Mississippi architecture?* Not a lot, but I knew about wood. Whoever built this place spared no expense from what I could see, such beautiful oak and pine. Summerleigh must have been a beautiful place in her heyday, but happy? I had my doubts. I shivered again, wishing I had worn something besides shorts and a t-shirt.

To the left was an open door that presumably led to the kitchen and parlor. I remembered from Harper's time that the right side of the Great Room would lead to the bedrooms. At this moment, that area of the house felt dark and forbidding. Were the trees covering the windows? For a split second, I heard footsteps. I made the mistake of calling out, "Hello?" only to have the echo scare the snot out of me.

"Good Lord, Jerica. Get it together." I shoved the key in my pocket but decided to leave the door open. This place could use a good airing out. I went into the parlor; the faded burgundy area rug and matching couches were all too familiar. Only the radio was missing. I passed through the parlor and headed to the kitchen. As I stepped through the doorway, I had the urge to cry. Everything I had seen in the dream, the farm sink where Harper had filled the peach pot, the once shiny white stove, the family table, it had all been real. And because it was all real, the weight of my promise hit me hard. I was here to see justice done, not just for Jeopardy but for all the Belle girls. Yes, my dreams had all been real, and my promise!

Before I could take my thoughts to their expected conclusion, the front door slammed so hard the dishes in the kitchen cabinet shook. "Dear God!" I said as my knees buckled a second.

And then I heard footsteps.

A child's footsteps from the sound of them.

They were running up the stairs, and I took off after them.

Chapter Ten—Jerica

As I raced up the stairs and across the balcony, I paused briefly before clearing the last set of stairs. An entire unexplored floor stretched before me, but I was leery about adventuring too far from the staircase. Not because I was tired but because I had come to my senses. What was I doing chasing phantom footsteps across questionable flooring? And then the footsteps stopped just above me, and I heard the floorboards creak as if someone were standing on the top balcony looking down at me wondering why I was taking so long.

"Alright, just slow down," I said to no one in particular when I heard a whisper from above. I could tell it was a child's whisper, but for the life of me, I could not hear what she was saying. Was that a little girl? Or something that wanted me to think it was a girl?

With my pulse racing, I carefully climbed the last staircase and stood in the decrepit hallway. *Boy, this place hasn't seen any love in a long time.* The hallway wallpaper was in tatters, strips of the dry rotted paper had come off the walls in many places. There was a thick coat of dust on the floors and moldings. As I stood at the top, I counted four rooms on the top floor and a narrow door at the end of the hallway. Where did that go? The attic, of course—Jeopardy's castle room! "Hello?" I asked, praying that my own echo didn't come back in a frightening way. "Is anyone up here? I thought I heard...you."

Nothing. Not even a whisper now, but the air was electric as if I stood in a lightning storm that was ready to start popping at any moment. Then I heard a strange sound.

Thump. Click, click, click.

I waited and heard it again.

Thump. Click, click, click.

Off the top of my head, I couldn't say what that sound was, but it sounded familiar. I knew I'd heard it before. It was coming from the last room on the right. I passed the two empty rooms, one to my left and one to my right. There was no furniture up here and certainly no lost little girl. Maybe that was it? JB's kids? They liked to play in here. That had to be it. If this big old house stood empty, it seemed natural that some curious child or teenager might want to check it out. Funny, I hadn't seen any vandalism or other evidence of kids hanging out, no empty soda cans or candle stubs. Nothing except the flowers on my porch.

I now stood in the doorway of the largest room and waited. I couldn't make myself step into the room, not yet, but I heard the sound again. *Thump. Click, click...* I stepped inside expecting to see someone. Anyone. But I found a room that was empty except for an old wooden rocking horse, empty bookcases and a rolling red ball on the floor.

And a set of old metal jacks.

Oh, God, oh, God, oh, God! I immediately ran back down the hallway and cleared the staircases in a matter of seconds. The front door didn't want to open at first, but I kept tugging on it until it finally opened. Once I got into the yard I could breathe again.

That was the sound I heard! Someone was playing with the jacks. Loxley? Was Loxley's ghost here? *Oh, God! I can't do this.* I looked up at the empty window, but there was no one there. Wasn't that good? Did I want to see a ghost girl hanging out at the window?

Heck no. I walked around the house and headed for the caretaker's cottage. I had to think about this, or not think about it. I decided to get a shower after I locked the doors. Now was the perfect time to go to town. No sense in delaying my supply run. Thirty minutes later, the SUV was turning onto Highway 98 West. According to my GPS, Lucedale was only twenty minutes away. I could go to Mobile, but since JB had suggested the Piggly Wiggly to me, I thought I'd check it out.

I decided to take the town's Main Street and instantly fell in love with the charming little mom and pop shops that lined it. There was more than one shabby chic consignment furniture store (I'd have to check those out later for inspiration), a health food store, a clothing store, various specialty shops and a few restaurants. I liked it. After driving around for about ten minutes, I felt a bit disappointed that I hadn't found the Piggly Wiggly; however, there was another grocery store, as well as a big chain department store that had a grocery too. But now that my stomach was rumbling, I decided I'd rather stop at the diner I spotted, a little place called Ricky's Country Diner.

I pulled the SUV in and went inside to grab a bite to eat. Maybe someone in here would know how to get to the Piggly Wiggly. The place was packed. I hadn't expected that from the number of cars outside, but then again, some of these patrons were probably walk-ins. I found an empty table at the corner of the restaurant near the grill.

"Good morning. What can I get started for you?" This was no teeny-bopper waitress but a muscular man with intense dark eyes, dark hair and a deep voice speaking to me. I had not expected him either.

"Um, I have no idea." I handled a laminated menu but couldn't narrow down my choices. "It's my first time here. What do you suggest?"

"It's pretty close to breakfast, and we're still serving. The breakfast platter is a winner. The most popular dish is the Double Slam. How do you like your eggs?"

"Over medium."

He nodded. "And what to drink, ma'am?"

"Orange juice, please."

"Alright, I'll get that started."

I couldn't help but watch him walk away. *Wow, he's...*

"I know, he's a bit of eye candy, isn't he? But don't let that body fool you. Jesse Clarke has more brains than most. Hi, I'm Renee, but my friends call me Ree-Ree. Jesse is my cousin; we own this restaurant. You're a new face. First time here?" She smiled politely.

"Hi, Renee, Ree-Ree. I'm Jerica. Yes, first time here. I wasn't staring. It's just I wasn't expecting to see..."

"Oh, no need to apologize. Everyone stares at Jesse...he's just that handsome. Just passing through? Headed to Leakesville, maybe?" Without an invitation, Renee sat in the chair opposite me. I didn't mind, but I was a bit surprised. She got busy wrapping silverware, a fancy task for a small diner such as this one.

I smiled politely but hoped to change the direction of this conversation. I hated that I got busted ogling the waiter. "No, I live in Desire now. I was told that the Piggly Wiggly was a good place for groceries, but I'm kind of lost."

"Lost in Lucedale?" She chuckled and finished up her silverware, depositing the last one in a plastic tub. "And there's no Piggly Wiggly here anymore. Hasn't been in about five years, I'm guessing. Hey, Humble. When did the Piggly Wiggly leave?"

"2012," an old man answered her. He hardly missed a bite of his food.

"Yeah, that's what I thought. 2012. Someone sent you on a wild goose chase, Jerica. But we do have a Wayne Lee's. And of course, there's the big blue store that everyone hates but goes to anyway. What were you drinking?"

"Oh, orange juice."

"Be right back." Renee had long dark hair that she wore in a tight ponytail at the back of her head. She wore plenty of makeup, especially black mascara, but she didn't really need any of it. She had lovely skin, like her cousin Jesse. I stole another peek at him as she returned with my drink. He was actually the cook, not just the waiter. I guessed it made sense since he was one of the owners. He caught me staring, and I pretended to look at the menu. *Good Lord, Jerica. You're not a teenager.*

"Here you go. So, you rode over from Desire? Not much left of that little town, if you could ever call it that. Did you know that their old downtown area is nothing but a ghost town now? I guess you've seen it. Just three or four empty old buildings. Kudzu vines all over the place. It's sad. Where you staying, on the river? They've got some cute fishing cabins over there."

"I've never been fishing," I confessed. "I'm actually staying at Summerleigh."

"Summerleigh?" I couldn't help but notice that a few eyes were on me now. Including Renee's wide brown ones. "Why would you stay there? That place is..." I thought she was going to say haunted, but she caught herself and said, "falling down."

"Actually, I'm in the caretaker's cottage, but I do have plans to fix up the house. It's not that bad inside, but it does need some repairs to the flooring for a start. Do you know a good handyman? I have some skills with a saw, but I could use an extra pair of hands on this project." Jesse arrived with my breakfast plate, two eggs, bacon and a pile of grits with a biscuit. My stomach rumbled at the sight. I didn't often eat grits, but these looked delicious. "Thank you," I said.

"You're welcome."

Renee blurted out, "This is Jerica, and she's staying at Summerleigh."

Jesse wasn't impressed, but he didn't sound surprised either. "You plan on restoring it?"

"Yes, I do. I would like to make some basic repairs to start with. I promised Harper I would tend to a few things. I guess you know she passed away."

Renee shook her head at hearing the news. "I hadn't heard that. How sad. That whole Belle family, such a sad ending for all of them. But then again, I guess you'd expect that. They were a wild lot, by all accounts. Wait, are you a Belle?"

"Oh no, I'm not. Just a friend of Harper's."

"Shoot. Looks like Humble is ready to go. I'll go check him out. Hey, Jesse, she's looking for a handyman. Might be one way to get your boat fixed. You'll never make the money you need slinging eggs here."

Renee excused herself, but her cousin lingered. "That true? You need some help up at Summerleigh?" He tossed a semi-clean white rag in his hands a few times before he slung it over his broad shoulder.

"Mostly carpentry work to begin with. As I was telling your cousin, I know how to work a saw, but it would be nice to have an extra pair of hands. I wouldn't want to take you away from your work here, though."

"What work? Carpentry is my second love."

"Oh, what's your first?" I asked curiously. "Cooking?"

"No. I'm just filling in for Norman. That would be writing. I've done quite a bit of research on

Summerleigh and the disappearance of Jeopardy Belle."

"Really?"

"Yes, but I should let you eat your food before it gets cold. I've got a few orders to cook."

"Um, okay," I said, totally curious about his research on Jeopardy. "Why don't you ride up to the house later? Maybe take a look at what I'm talking about. It's a pretty big job, and I'd feel better if you knew what you were in for." *And I'd feel better if you could show me you could actually handle a board.*

"Sounds great. I get off at three if that's okay."

"Great, I'm in the caretaker's cottage in the back. You can't miss it."

"I'll be there about four. I'd like to get the aroma of food off me first."

"Four it is, thanks."

As he walked away, I didn't question what I was doing. Even if he wasn't interested in the work, I was interested in him. I mean, interested in his information.

I ate a few bites of my plate and left. I had a lot to do before four o'clock.

Chapter Eleven—Jerica

When I opened the door, I was surprised to see that I had two visitors standing on my doorstep. Before I could greet either of them, Renee waved and said, "Surprise! I couldn't let him come without me. I'm dying to see the place. I hope that's okay."

"Sure, the more the merrier. Come in, please."

I was glad I'd opted for jeans and a fresh t-shirt instead of that sundress. This was supposed to be a business meeting, not a date. But Jesse Clarke was even better looking without his stained apron. He too wore blue jeans and a soft t-shirt. *Get it together, Jerica.*

"Do you guys want something to drink? I have some tea made."

"None for me," Jesse and Renee said almost simultaneously.

"Let me get the key and we can take a look at the house." *Well, this wasn't how I thought things would go, but hey, I guess you have to learn to roll with the punches. Does Renee think her cousin needs a bodyguard or something?*

I grabbed the keys off the rack, and we left the cottage behind. I made it a point to show them the memorial stone. "I nearly tripped over this yesterday. Any ideas what this stone is for? I assume for Jeopardy Belle, but I can't be sure."

Renee shivered in the sunlight. "I don't know. What do you think, Jesse?"

"Could be." He squatted down and examined the stone closer, rubbing the concrete. "Doesn't look all that old, as far as monuments go. I guess it could be for Jeopardy, but then again, there's been a lot of tragedy here—even a murder or two, with the Belles and the McIntyre family before that." He got up, and the three of us continued on toward Summerleigh. Like my earlier trip, I decided to go around to the front of the house. Going through the back door felt like I was intruding.

"Who was murdered? One of the Belles?"

"Nobody knows what happened to Jeopardy; she disappeared in the summer of 1942, not long after her father died. That was a tragedy, but the murder I mentioned was Mariana McIntyre. She lived here long before the Belles, in the late 1800s. She died on her sixteenth birthday. The story goes, she went upstairs to change gowns during her birthday party. When she missed her grand entrance, someone went up to check on her and found her dead. Someone had cut off all her hair and stabbed her with her own sewing scissors. It was a gory murder, and quite shocking for 1870s Desire, Mississippi. So shocking that the town almost folded after that. Then Bull McIntyre, that was Mariana's father, had a stroke. Not long after that, he died too. Mariana's younger brother inherited the place, but he went crazy. Gosh, I can't remember his name. Bull McIntyre had been the mayor of Desire, but there was a lot of speculation about his role in his daughter's death. The place stood empty for a while, then it was sold a few times, but nobody really tried to make it a home until John Belle won Summerleigh in a poker game."

"I heard the story about how he won this place," I said with a laugh. "He must have had quite a hand."

"Full house, from what I hear."

"You know quite a lot about the house. Have you ever been inside?"

"Yes, but not legally."

Renee touched my arm. "He wrote a book about this place. If you ever want to know anything about Summerleigh, he's the guy to ask. Jesse is obsessed with old houses. And not just this one."

"Well, here we go." My mind was full of bloody scenes. To think, a girl had been murdered in this house, and then not a century later, another vanished. Maybe it was the house.

I opened the door and we stepped inside. It felt better in here now, although the staleness hadn't improved. I didn't hear any footsteps, thankfully, but I wasn't any more comfortable than I had been earlier. As if the dust knew I had a thing for it, I started sneezing.

"Bless you," Jesse said.

"Thanks. This dust has me sneezing my head off."

"Ugh, that's a horrible thing to say in this house," Renee said.

I blushed. "Sorry."

Jesse strolled around and examined the flooring. "The flooring in this room looks pretty good. Have you been under the house?"

"No, I have a thing about spiders," I confessed with an awkward shrug.

"I can do it. Which floors are you concerned with the most?"

"I think the parlor just to the left here might have some issues, and the upper balcony and some of the stair treads need replacing." I walked toward the parlor with Jesse in tow, but Renee was walking the other way. "You coming, Renee?"

"If you don't mind, may I wander around? I won't touch anything."

"Um, sure."

Jesse shook his head and said in a low voice, "Renee thinks she's some sort of psychic. I guess I should have left her at the diner, but she really wanted to come. This place is kind of a curiosity to the locals. Not many folks have been inside.

Your friend Harper was pretty protective of the place."

"Psychic, huh? I wouldn't have thought that, but then again, I've never met a psychic before."

"You'll find the Clarke family a strange bunch. Hey, I see what you mean." He looked up at the ceiling. "Yeah, looks like you might have had a leak at one time."

"Sure, that makes sense. I noticed the roof damage when I drove up but didn't put the two together. So, roof first over here and then the floor. I don't suppose you can do roofs too."

"No, but I know an excellent roofer. With all the summer storms we have down here, you learn to have a roofer on speed dial."

Hearing footsteps again, I glanced at the door. "You sure she's okay?"

"Yeah, what about the kitchen?"

"Alright."

We went from room to room and found plenty of things that needed the attention of a few competent pairs of hands. By the sound of it, Jesse Clarke knew what he was talking about. There was evidence of rodents in the kitchen, the parlor floor was damaged, and some of the windows in the west wing needed replacing before they fell out. "It's all lead paint, anyway. They'll have to be cleaned and repainted. But overall, I'm surprised there's not much more damage. It's never good for a house to sit empty. I don't mean to be nosy, and I'm not trying to discourage you—God knows I need the work—but are you sure you're up for this? This is going to be one helluva project, and a long one, not to mention expensive."

"One step at a time was my Dad's motto. Mine too. I'm willing to try."

He smiled, but it didn't last long. I could see that Jesse was more on the serious side. "That's all I need to hear. Let's check out the upstairs."

"Did I hear your cousin say you own a boat?"

"No, I own the hull of a boat. I have plenty of work ahead of me. Just like we do here."

I tucked my hair behind my ear, suddenly very conscious that I had skimped on my makeup and hair care today.

Renee met us on the stairs; her face was pale, and her worried expression bothered me. "I'll be in the truck, Jess."

"What's wrong? You look like you've seen…"

"I have, and I don't want to see another one. I'll be in the truck." We both stared at her as she walked out of the house and slammed the door behind her.

"Um, should we go after her?"

"No. Like I said, Jerica, we're a weird bunch." For the first time today, he used my name. I liked hearing that. "Is this the floor?" Neither one of us talked about ghosts, and I didn't hear any jacks or footsteps, thankfully. We finished our tour of the house and walked to the front porch. Did I really want to work so closely with someone I didn't really know? Jesse was right, this was going to be an expensive project. I mean, Harper had been very generous, but it wouldn't be hard to drop that hundred grand here. I'd been so shocked to receive the life insurance check in the mail. I'd never imagined Harper would make me her sole heir! Again, the responsibility of it all weighed on me. Yes, I had to be wise about this. One step at a time, I reminded myself.

"Well, let's start with the roofer. If you could call him and maybe have him come out Monday? I hate to get anything started at the end of the week. Then we'll start on the parlor floors. Let's get the bottom floor tended to and work our way up. What are your hours? I'll be happy to work around them."

"I'm all yours. I mean..." He cleared his throat. "I mean I was only helping out at the diner temporarily. I'm an owner, but I don't work there all the time. I can go at this full time if you need me."

"Let's start Monday, eight o'clock. We'll see what the roofer has to say and go from there."

"That sounds like a plan. Hey, I'm playing at a benefit tomorrow night at the Community Center in Lucedale. Why don't you come out and meet some of the locals?" We walked down off the porch and stepped into the hot sunshine.

"Maybe, what time?"

"Starts at seven. It's a fish fry for a young lady who needs medical funding. A friend of the family."

"I might surprise you," I said with a smile. "Thanks for the invite." We went back to my cottage and found Renee sweating in the truck.

"Renee, you could have waited in the caretaker's cottage," I said. "It's too hot to wait out in the heat."

"I'm okay. I just want to go home."

Jesse frowned at her but cranked up the truck. Before I could ask her anything else, she rolled up the window and the truck lumbered away.

As they passed the corner of Summerleigh, Jesse turned his head my way and waved once, and I waved back.

That's when I saw Ann standing at the kitchen window. She didn't look happy to see me. I ran into the cottage and locked the door.

Chapter Twelve—Harper

Daddy's homecoming parties had always brought the Belle family together, until this one. Momma didn't cook Daddy's favorite dishes. Aunt Dot was unofficially banned from Summerleigh, at least until Momma said otherwise. No one from the church called to inquire about any party for Daddy—usually, some of the First Baptist ladies came by to bring a dessert or something. Even Miss Augustine begged off tonight citing the horrible weather, which was strange because Momma left early in the afternoon in the Master DeLuxe. I thought for sure she was spending the day with Miss Augustine, maybe going to the beauty shop before Daddy got home. And now it looked like she hadn't even gone to the bus station to pick him up. Someone must have dropped him off at the road. At long last, he walked up to the house, arriving drenched and grim-faced. If I had known he needed a ride home, I would have ventured out on the road myself in his old truck. I'd faithfully cranked it for him every week, just like he'd asked me to in his one and only letter to me.

Loxley opened the front door wide and danced on the porch as he approached. "Daddy's home! Daddy's home!" Addison and I clapped our hands too. The three of us couldn't stop smiling. Yes, Daddy was home, and all would be right again.

All would be right!

I looked around for Jeopardy; she was normally the first one out the door. At previous homecoming celebrations, she would declare, "I'm the oldest," as she grabbed Daddy's hand first, but she was nowhere to be found this evening. I knew she was here, probably creeping around in the attic. She'd taken to staying up there. Even though I took a belt for going with her to the river, it had been worth it. I'd seen a whole other side of my sister. She was popular and smiling when she was with her rebellious crowd, and there wasn't a boy there that didn't call her name or whistle at her when she splashed around in the water. Even Troy Harvester made goo-goo eyes at her, but she acted like he wasn't even there. That was strange because she used to kiss her pillow like a movie star and call his name to make me laugh. I knew she liked him. Or she used to.

"Jeopardy," I called once before I helped Daddy bring his bags inside. I couldn't imagine why she'd miss this. Addison helped me carry his things in while Loxley climbed up into his wet arms and cried.

"No crying now, and you'll be wet through if you don't let me change my clothes. Where's your mother? I waited for her for hours."

"She left this morning," Addison said as she wiped at her nose. I closed the door before she got sick again. "We thought she was bringing you home."

He kissed each one of us on the top of our heads and removed his hat before he went to the phone. He made a few calls, but nobody seemed to know where Momma had gotten to. I couldn't hide my worried expression. There was so much I wanted to tell Daddy, but now I just couldn't.

"Where's Jeopardy? Did she go with your mother?"

"No, Daddy, I think she's upstairs."

His smile disappeared, and he kissed me on the top of the head again. He glanced up at the ceiling and then said quietly, "Addison and Loxley, do you think you two could manage to haul my bag to my room? It's very heavy now and very wet."

"Yes, Daddy." They beamed and scrambled out the door to make Daddy's wish come true.

"What's happening, Harper? Are you girls okay?"

A fat tear fell on my cheek, and I pawed it away as I fell into Daddy's arms. I didn't care that his clothing smelled damp and sweaty. Everything tumbled out of my mouth at once. I told him about the falling out between Aunt Dot and Momma, about Momma and Jeopardy fighting at church and…I even told him about the few nights that Momma slipped out when she thought we were all asleep. I told him more than I should have; I could tell by the way his jaw popped when he looked at me.

"Daddy, are you going to stay home now? Please, stay home."

He hugged me tightly but didn't give me the answer I wanted. "Harper Belle, I love you. It's going to be alright. I need you to be strong just a while longer. You think you could do that?"

"Yes, Daddy."

"You got something in the fridge you could heat up for supper? I'm hungry, and it's been a long time since I ate anything."

I thought about it for a minute and wiped the tears away. "Yes, sir. There is some rice and gravy left over from supper. I can make you some biscuits too."

"No biscuits. Rice and gravy is plenty. Did you girls eat yet?"

"Yes, sir. I made the rice and gravy."

His jaw popped again. "I'm going up to see your sister. I'll be back for that delicious meal. Thank you, Harper." I loved how Daddy always treated me like a grown-up. Always. Even when I was really little, he talked to me like I was big. And now I was.

I heard Daddy's footsteps on the stairs as he went up to see Jeopardy. I couldn't help but be nosy. I snuck to the bottom of the stairs and waited to see what kind of welcome he got. She'd been so moody lately, so angry at me. Maybe now that our father was home, she'd feel better about Momma, Addison and Loxley. And me.

My two little sisters caught me spying, but they didn't tell on me. They waited too. We heard Jeopardy crying her heart out. Loxley smiled up at me, her blue eyes moist, her lips quivering. "Daddy's home now, Harper."

"Yes, he is. Why don't you two help me get his supper ready? Daddy needs food and lots of it. He's been fighting the enemy, and he's probably really hungry."

"I'll help!" Loxley ran into the kitchen first and began to set the table. Addison arranged a jar full of wildflowers in front of his plate. I'd seen her out picking them earlier. It had been nice to see her out of doors, even though I worried that she'd get sick afterward. So far, so good. I smiled when I noticed she had a healthy pink glow in her cheeks. She smiled back. I poured a tiny amount of water in the saucepan to heat up the rice and poured the gravy into a smaller pan. There were also fresh peaches, so Addison and I peeled some and tossed them with sugar and cinnamon for Daddy's dessert. We were beginning to wonder if he'd ever come downstairs when we heard Momma's Master DeLuxe pull into the drive. Addison's eyes widened, and Loxley sat quietly in her chair as the back door opened. Momma walked in with shopping bags in her arms. She deposited the wet paper bags on the counter and peeled off her rain hat and coat. It was then that she noticed Daddy's hat on the table. She didn't say a word, but the smile vanished from her face as she hung up her coat on one of the hooks behind the door. She must have forgotten all about Daddy's homecoming.

"Loxley, go wash your face. Addison, how are you feeling, dear? Your cheeks are so pink." She laid the back of her hand on Addison's forehead and clucked once. "I hope that's not a fever you have coming on." Addison sniffed in response and touched her own forehead. "Harper, cat got your tongue?"

"Girls, go upstairs." Daddy was in the doorway now. I flicked off the burners and glanced at Momma, and in that moment she knew. She knew I'd betrayed her and told Daddy her secret. She knew I'd told Daddy everything. And what had Jeopardy told him? "Now, Harper."

"Yes, sir," I whispered as I exited with my sisters. We did as he told us and scrambled up the stairs, at least as far as the landing. We could hear dishes breaking in the kitchen and furniture getting slung about. Momma screamed at Daddy and called him a name we were all forbidden to use. Daddy's voice rose, but not as high as hers, and as far as I could tell, she wasn't getting the best of him.

"How could...Ann...I'm never...police...now!"

"I didn't know...JB...I swear..."

They continued to quarrel, and Daddy was in the Great Room now, Momma running behind him. Clearly, he wanted to leave again. "You'll shame her if you do that, John. You'll shame her in front of everyone."

"The shame is on you!" He stomped out of the house and slammed the front door with a big boom. I heard his old truck crank up, and soon Daddy was gone. All of us were crying now. Momma didn't come up to see us or check on us. Nobody went downstairs again that night. We didn't know what to do. Momma was crying pitifully, and a part of me wanted to comfort her too, but right now I had to think of Addison and Loxley...and Jeopardy.

"Come on, Belles. Let's go see if Jeopardy will let us in." We walked down the long hallway and tapped on the attic door. "Please let us in, Jeopardy. Daddy is gone, and we don't want to go downstairs."

She opened the door, her face a swollen mess, her hair a pile of tangles. She'd been crying, but at least she didn't look at me like she hated me. She stepped back and let us into her sanctuary. *So this was where all the spare blankets and pillows had gone to.* Who all was sleeping up here? Nobody talked. We were all confused, it seemed. All disappointed that Daddy had left us. All except Jeopardy. She was almost peaceful as she lit a candle for us and then a cigarette for herself and dropped the matchstick in an empty soda bottle. Nobody scolded her. We all found a place to lie down and waited for Daddy to come back.

That's where Aunt Dot found us the following morning; a tangle of arms and legs, all of us Belles sleeping on one big pallet. And then she told us the horrible news. Daddy was dead, hit by another vehicle on Bloody Highway 98. The rainy roads had kept anyone from finding him until it was too late. He'd bled out and was gone.

The day after we buried him was the first time Loxley saw his ghost.

None of the rest of us ever saw Daddy again.

Chapter Thirteen—Jerica

Arms were around my neck, sweet, young arms. They hugged me tight, and I felt the lightest whisper of a kiss on my cheek. My hand went to brush her hair, as I always did, but she slid away from me. My eyes blinked open, and I saw that I was alone. Again.

It took a few moments for the heartbreak to come, but it did not fail to arrive. And with it came the realization that my Marisol would never hug me again.

Marisol...baby girl.

And I remembered the horrible dream—the complete and utter loss of John Jeffrey Belle. Harper's loss. It would be something she never got over. I could feel that now.

Oh my God! This was JB—John Jeffrey Belle was the very same man I met when I came to Summerleigh.

He was no gardener but a ghost! Was he the one who left me the flowers? No. That was something a child would do, not a grown man. Not a tough hero like John Belle. I sat up on the bed trying to wrap my head around it all. And how was any of this getting me closer to finding Jeopardy Belle? Why was my daughter here? I swung the quilt back and decided there was no time like the present to get started on my mission. I'd fallen in love with this place. I wanted to see Summerleigh restored, not just for me but for Harper and all the Belle girls, but that act would be empty without finding Jeopardy and bringing her home to Desire. Where to get started? I'd pick Jesse's brain later; he seemed like a guy who knew quite a bit about local lore. But in the meantime, I was going to that potting shed to find out for myself if the man I had seen was actually Harper's father. What would my therapist say about all this?

Ghosts aren't real, Jerica. They are extensions of us, our emotions, unresolved feelings, but they aren't real. Marisol is gone, and you have to forgive yourself. Let her go.

And that had been the last time I'd seen Dr. Busby. What was the point? He didn't believe me when I told him I saw Marisol. I knew I wasn't responsible for my daughter's death, but I think for some strange reason Dr. Busby believed otherwise. I knew for a fact Eddie blamed me. Yes, I'd been in the car when the train hit us, when the metal twisted and my baby screamed for her mother. That had been me, but I had done all I could do. It wasn't my fault that the truck behind me pushed us onto the tracks. I smothered a sob and forced myself to keep moving.

Keep moving, Jerica.

I recognized this feeling. Not only was I knee-deep in grief again, but I was coming down with something. Hopefully not the flu. I didn't mind taking care of others but had no patience for being sick myself. I simply had too much to do.

I threw on some work clothes and my beat-up tennis shoes. With a heavy heart, I headed outside to look for the potting shed. Taking the gravel path to the left of the cottage seemed intuitive, so I followed it around and found a dilapidated shack not far in the distance. As I cleared a copse of trees and stood before a small potting shed, my heart sank. Windows were missing, many windows. A tattered blue tarp hung from the side of the roof, a clear indication that this building was probably now in complete disrepair. With a sigh, I opened the door and stepped inside. My heart sank even further when I saw that the shelves held nothing more than pots of old soil, weeds and rusty gardening tools. Nobody was here, and nobody had been here for a very long time.

"JB? Are you here?"

I stood in the middle of the potting shed, my hair crackling on my neck. And as each moment passed, the feeling that someone watched me intensified. I asked again, "JB? John Jeffrey Belle? Are you here?"

No one answered. Did I expect him to pipe up and say, "Yes, I'm over here?" Not really, but then again Summerleigh had proved to be a kind of magical place in that regard. As I walked around the shed, I was discouraged by the shape it was in but found an interesting book half hidden in a clod of dirt on a rickety potting table. *Neat handwriting*, I thought as I held a page up to the light to read the faded pencil markings better. A former gardener, possibly John Belle, had taken the time to write down the names of plants, the days they had been planted and other notations only a plant lover would understand. I flipped to the back of the book for more clues and was surprised to see that it didn't belong to John Belle after all. This book had clearly belonged to a McIntyre. I squinted at the first name but couldn't make it out.

Interesting bit of history. I'm sure Jesse would love to see this.

The laughter of little girls brought me back to the present. I ran to the window in front of me. The glass was broken, and I was careful not to place my hands in any of the panes. I almost fell to the ground when I saw the back of two girls clearing a group of trees in front of me, one with blond braids and the other with brown hair, like mine.

Marisol! Like a madwoman, I ran down the path after them. "Marisol! Wait!"

I heard the pair giggling again and even detected footsteps on the gravel not far ahead of me, but I could not catch up with them. No matter how fast I ran, they ran faster. Marisol and Loxley—that had certainly been Loxley—were always just out of my reach. I didn't realize how far back I had traveled onto the property, but I had managed to navigate my way to the banks of a river. Was this Dog River? I'd read that this was a tributary of the Escatawpa, but I couldn't be sure.

I traveled the banks for a while, walking up and down. I found evidence that this had once been a popular party place, but solid footprints of two little girls were nonexistent.

"Don't let this be my imagination. Not again! I can't do this again!"

As if she heard me, Marisol peeked her head around the trunk of a live oak tree. My hands flew to my mouth as I muffled a surprised yelp. I whispered her name, but she just smiled and vanished. I raced to the tree, but my daughter had disappeared. The sound of footsteps running away told me I would not catch up with her. Nor did she want me to, for some reason. I collapsed under the tree and cried my eyes out. I cried like I hadn't cried in two years. *Why is this happening now?* When I finished my crying jag, I got up and wiped my sweaty face with the back of my hand and walked back to Summerleigh.

I had things to do today, and it was looking less likely that I would make it to Jesse's benefit. I couldn't trust my emotions, and I was pretty certain a serious bug had a hold of me. After hiking back, I spent the next hour arranging my meager belongings in the caretaker's cottage and then took my camera and headed to the main house.

I had already seen the ghost of my child, so what else was there to be afraid of? I was going to go inside and explore every inch of Summerleigh. I was a woman on a mission. I had to find Jeopardy Belle. If I found her, maybe Marisol would stay. Why else would she be here but to encourage me in my search?

As I walked through the yard to the back of the house, I said aloud, "I'm coming, Jeopardy. I won't let you down."

Chapter Fourteen—Harper

Momma insisted that we eat dinner together at the supper table tonight. I couldn't think why. My sisters and I had been living off sandwiches or dishes prepared by various church ladies for the past month since Daddy's passing. For the first week after the funeral, Momma had kept to her room, crying night and day. Like all of us...except Jeopardy, who didn't cry at all anymore. I knew her heart was breaking; I'd heard her crying the night after Daddy died, but nothing since. Even Aunt Dot tried to talk with her, but she wouldn't speak about Daddy. Or anything, really. The only thing she did was sneak out of the house, smoke her stolen cigarettes in the potting shed and draw or doodle on paper. Once, I saw her shove a note into a chink in the attic wall, but she wasn't pleased that I'd spied on her; when I snuck back to read it, the note was gone.

She did strange things nowadays like wear bright lipstick and smudge mascara on her eyes. Momma never said a word to her, but she noticed. I could see her raise her eyebrows, though she said nothing. Feeling inspired, I dabbed on some of Momma's palest pink lipstick one afternoon and got the back of her hand on my mouth. "Isn't one whore in this family enough?" she asked me as I lay sprawled out on the ground.

I never wore lipstick again. Not as long as she was alive.

Miss Augustine had cooked tonight's supper, chicken and dressing. It was loaded with onions and I hated every bite, but who knew when we would eat again? Even picky Addison swallowed a few bites. Momma surveyed us all between her neat spoons of food.

Loxley ate like a hungry bear when she wasn't giggling at something, something or someone none of the rest of us could see.

"What in the world is so funny, Loxley Grace?"

Her eyes widened as she focused her attention on Momma now. "Nothing, Momma," was her sweet answer. It was an obvious lie, as she continued to giggle and spew Miss Augustine's horrible cornbread dressing everywhere.

"What do you see?" Jeopardy asked as she leaned next to Loxley.

Loxley didn't speak but played with her food.

"Yes, Loxley. Who are you making such faces at? If it's that funny, I want to know too." Momma's sweetest voice was always a trap that Loxley fell into. I tried to kick her under the table as a warning but missed. Addison yelped in pain.

"Sorry," I muttered.

"Daddy. Daddy is making funny faces, and he makes me laugh."

Only Jeopardy smiled.

Momma rose to her feet, and Loxley shrank down in her chair. "You stop telling lies, Loxley Grace! Go to your room. No more supper for you."

She snatched my sister's plate away, and the youngest Belle practically crawled out of the room. Momma put the near-empty plate in the sink and stared out the window into the dusky Mississippi evening. Fireflies were bouncing around already, and some of them hit the window. They looked like fairies that wanted permission to come inside. I could see them clearly.

When Momma spoke again, it was a strange sound, like measured steel. "Jeopardy, Dr. Leland wants some of those jars of peaches we have in the laundry room. You take him three or four after supper. See that he pays you, though. At least a dollar a jar."

Jeopardy's fork hit her plate, and her eyes narrowed.

A dollar a jar? Who in their right mind would pay a dollar a jar for some peaches?

"It's almost dark, Momma. Can't she go in the morning?" Addison asked nervously. Addie hated the dark and still slept with the lamp on every chance she got. She didn't like the idea of any of us being in the dark now. Hadn't Daddy died venturing out in the dark?

Jeopardy crossed her bare arms and said, "No."

Momma turned around and put her hands behind her on the sink. She looked perfect, like a catalog model, but right at that moment, I knew something was wrong with her. She was like a mannequin, perfect to look at but without a soul. Yes, that was it. Her soul was gone. Or something.

"I'll go, Momma. I'm not afraid of the dark, and I can walk really fast. I don't mind going for Jeopardy," I offered as an alternative.

Momma smiled at Jeopardy. "Should I let your sister go instead?"

Jeopardy was on her feet now. "You wouldn't send her. You wouldn't dare!"

Momma's left eyebrow lifted slightly, but she never shifted her gaze from Jeopardy's pinched face. "Wouldn't I?"

Jeopardy threw her plate on the floor, and cornbread splattered all over the tile. Addison crept out of her chair and stood by the door that led to the parlor. I couldn't move. *What do I do? Daddy? Are you here?*

"You can't do that! You wouldn't do that!"

"I would too. You do what I tell you, Jeopardy. We need the money."

Jeopardy slammed her chair under the table and stalked into the pantry to retrieve a few jars of peaches. She stuffed them in a cloth bag we kept hanging next to Momma's purse and keys.

"Can't we drive over there and drop them off? I could take Daddy's truck," I offered as one last idea to avoid whatever disaster lay ahead of us.

"No, we don't have the gas for that. Jeopardy can take the peaches; you clean up this mess, Harper." Momma lit a cigarette as the screen door slapped closed. Jeopardy was gone. I obediently cleaned up the mess while I smothered my tears. Momma left the kitchen to listen to Amanda of Honeymoon Hill on the stand-up radio.

It got dark fast. By the time I dried the last dish, it was well after eight and there was no sign of my sister. I snuck Loxley a sandwich and a glass of milk before I went in to bed.

I waited up for Jeopardy, hoping to hear that she was safe and sound, but my tired eyes let me down. I closed them only for a moment. And when I opened them again, the sun was up and Loxley was sleeping beside me.

I wondered if Jeopardy ever made it home. No one else was awake except Momma, who was busy putting on her face. I could hear her humming to herself like she always did when she got dressed in the mornings. I'd have to cook breakfast soon, but I had enough time to slip upstairs. Whether Jeopardy liked it or not, I was going to invade her castle.

The door wasn't locked. I didn't have to knock or beg for permission to come in. Jeopardy was there, sleeping in nothing but her slip. I gasped at the sight of her. From head to toe, Jeopardy was covered in bruises.

She never opened her eyes, but she must have detected I was there. "Get out, Harper."

"Jeopardy, what happened to you? Did you fall in a ravine?"

She finally opened her eyes and said something I would never forget as long as I lived. "The devil got a hold of me, Harper Belle. He put his hands all over me. Now get out." She rolled over and turned her back to me. I wanted to hug her, help her, but I could see it would do no good. She would talk to me when she was ready to and not until then.

As I went downstairs to cook breakfast, I couldn't help but think about what she said. What could that mean?

The devil got a hold of me, Harper Belle...

Chapter Fifteen—Harper

Addison and Loxley played a hand-clapping game on the front porch. It was a familiar song, Miss Mary Mack. Loxley did all the singing because Addison had a sore throat, but even the littlest Belle knew to keep things toned down today. The quiet tension rose, and it didn't help that Jeopardy was stomping around upstairs; I could hear her footsteps as I passed through the Great Room. Fortunately, no one else had yet.

Momma lounged in the parlor with Miss Augustine. The two of them were flipping through magazines and gossiping about Bette Davis' new movie, The Man Who Came to Dinner. They'd driven all the way to Mobile twice to see it, and both times came back with something negative to say about the big-eyed actress. According to Desire's cultural department, the two women in our parlor, Bette Davis was a sourpuss with no acting skills whatsoever. I tried not to snort. I'd never seen a Bette Davis movie, but since these two didn't like her, I figured I probably would.

And the debate raged on. Lana Turner was hands down Momma's favorite, while Miss Augustine preferred Rita Hayworth or Gene Tierney. "Lana Turner is too hoity-toity for my taste." The two women rarely argued about anything except important matters like who should get top billing in Hollywood's latest film or which actress had the most beautiful penmanship or some other nonsense they'd fight to the death to have the last word about. Before Daddy left us, Momma used to teach Loxley how to walk and wave properly, just in case she landed a pageant, but not anymore. Loxley didn't seem to mind. Momma used to win pageants when she was young. Lots of them.

"Really, Ann. You go too far!"

Today was one of those days. Miss Augustine made an offhand remark about someone's bathing suit photos in the tabloids, and Momma exploded. Luckily for Miss Augustine, Momma took her home and didn't make her walk, but our mother came back in an even greater huff than the one she left in. Everyone got quiet when her car pulled into the driveway. We waited for her inner storm to abate, all except Jeopardy. She kept walking around upstairs, and a few times I thought I heard her talking to herself. Once Momma got settled into her chair again, I said, "The Lady Detective Show is coming on. Should we listen to it?" Addison clapped her hands gleefully and came in off the porch, to which Loxley made a raspberry sound at her back. I noticed she came inside too, though. Momma's eyes went to the ceiling; she must have heard Jeopardy, but she didn't care enough to ask about her. But then someone knocked at the front door.

After fussing with her hair for a moment, Momma went to the door with all us girls except one trailing behind her. I couldn't believe who was standing there, complete with a bouquet of flowers in his shaking hands.

It was Troy Harvester, looking nice and smiling nervously at Momma. "Good afternoon, Mrs. Belle. I'm here to see Jeopardy, if I may."

Addison gave me a wide-eyed look, which I answered with a shrug. To my surprise, Jeopardy came down the stairs and paused at the bottom. It was clear she didn't know Troy was coming. For the first time in a long time, I saw Jeopardy's cryptic smile appear on her narrow face. Her cheeks turned pink, but she didn't come any closer. She wore her pink romper today, the one that had the cherries at the bosom. It was really too small for her, showing way too much leg. In fact, I remembered Momma telling her to hand it down to Addison, but she never did. She liked it, and the pink color made her tanned legs look long and slender, or so she said. I was definitely too tall for such a thing.

Jeopardy stood on the bottom step and leaned her back against the wall. She didn't come to the door or act like she cared at all that Troy was here, but I knew she cared. She always cared about Troy.

"I know why you're here. You came sniffing. Boys like you always do. Get out of here now! Before I call your mother and tell her..."

"Hey!" Jeopardy yelled as she rushed toward the door. "You can't send my friend away. He came to see me."

Momma simultaneously slammed the front door and slapped Jeopardy to the ground. "You little whore! So that's who you've been taking up with! I should have known you would pick up with the trashiest boy in the county," she screamed as Jeopardy managed to crawl away and didn't waste any time getting to her feet. Loxley began to cry, and Addison clutched her stomach.

I stood between the two of them but kept my head down, in case Momma decided to rain down her fury on me. "Run, Jeopardy!" I whispered, and she ran up the stairs.

Momma didn't slap me, but she twisted my arm and warned, "You mind your own business, Harper Louise!"

"Momma, please!" I squealed as I twisted away. It was alright, though. Jeopardy had escaped, and I heard the door slam behind her. Momma headed up the stairs after her, but not before she grabbed her brush with the red handle from the parlor side table.

Loxley cried furiously now, and I squatted in front of her. "You and Addison go outside. Go to the potting shed. I'll come find you. Okay?"

She poked out her bottom lip. "Is this like Hide and Seek?"

"Exactly like Hide and Seek, but you might have to count to a hundred before I come, okay?"

"Okay, Harper."

"Take care of her, Addie." Addison nodded and wiped her tears away as the two of them went out the back door and into the yard. I wouldn't be able to stop Momma from beating Jeopardy, but maybe my presence would deter her, at least a little. I really didn't know what I would do except try to stop the inevitable, horrible ending.

I prayed as I bolted up the stairs, "Please, God, don't let Momma hurt Jeopardy. Daddy, if you're here, help us. Send a whole army of angels to help us." I moved quickly across the first landing and then on to the next flight of stairs. Momma banged on Jeopardy's castle door with her hairbrush, they shouted swear words at one another, and all I could do was cry. I stepped into the hallway and nearly fell backward.

A lady all in white swooshed in front of me, passing from one door to the one across the hallway. I could hardly believe my eyes. There were only six rooms up here, and two of them were closets, but she was moving between them. Her face twisted, and her dark hair flowed behind her. She appeared to be a young woman in a white dress with a faded gray rose between her breasts. Her hair hung down her back in ringlets, and her hands were clutching her stomach. I froze. There she was again!

She passed from one closet to another and then slid straight down the hallway toward Momma, who was standing at the top of the attic staircase. My mother didn't notice the woman in white. She rammed her left shoulder against the door, striking it repeatedly and obviously hoping to knock it down.

"Open this door, Jeopardy! You open it now!"

"No! Go away! I hate you! You killed Daddy, and now you want to kill me!"

I watched in horror as the woman sailed on toward her target. Just at the last moment, Momma swung around with her brush. She must have thought it was me coming up behind her. Her face was a mask of terror as she swung through the invisible woman. She fell forward down the staircase in a heap with a terrified scream.

And then the woman was gone.

Chapter Sixteen—Harper

The days after Momma's fall were a blur. The ambulance came about a half hour after my call, and she remained unconscious until they arrived. I don't think she immediately remembered any of what happened, but she must have recalled the horrific moment by the time she got home with her face bruised and her arm broken. The Lady in White put the fear of God in Momma. She never spanked any of us again after that, and Jeopardy, who knew nothing about that ghost (or so I then believed), enjoyed new freedom. And so did I.

Aunt Dot moved in for a while to help take care of her sister and largely left us to entertain ourselves. School would start soon, and for the first time ever we had new clothes to wear, thanks entirely to her. These weren't just church hand-me-downs either. Aunt Dot bought me two sweaters, one pink and one blue, matching skirts and two pale yellow shirts. I loved every item, as did we all. Even Jeopardy got new clothes, and I saw her hug our aunt more than once.

"Come on, Harper. Let's go," Jeopardy said when she appeared in my doorway one day. She usually spent all her time in her castle whenever she was home, but since Momma was incapacitated, my sister visited my room too. Loxley spent a lot of time on the second floor; she claimed to be playing with Daddy, and I didn't doubt her. Summerleigh had become a house of spirits. I ventured upstairs once after Momma's accident in search of the lady. There was no trace of the ghost, except I thought I saw the trailing edge of her skirt as it slipped away into a closet. That could have been my own imagination, but it was enough for me. I pried Jeopardy for information about the ghost to no avail.

"Where are we going?"

"To the river. I want to swim."

I flipped the pages of my magazine and pretended to be bored by her offer. Loxley and Addison were attending a birthday party today. Connie Loper had picked them up about an hour ago, so there wasn't much to do. I didn't have to do all the chores like before; Aunt Dot did most of them now. I wondered how long that would last. "I don't have a bathing suit."

"You don't need one. Come on, Harper Louise. Stop being such a stick in the mud."

"You two come back before dark, please." Aunt Dot paused in the doorway with a basket of folded laundry in her arms. "Or thereabouts. Augustine Hogue is coming over tonight to visit your mother, and I thought that would be a great time for us to go get some ice cream."

"Okay, Aunt Dot," Jeopardy agreed with a wrinkled nose and waved at me to come on.

Aunt Dot rolled her eyes at the sound of Momma yelling her name. "Coming, Ann. Patience, my dear."

I slid on my tennis shoes, grabbed a towel and followed Jeopardy to the back door of Summerleigh. I had never experienced liberty like this! It was dreamlike and somehow felt dangerous—and I never wanted it to end. For a split second, I saw a face on the top floor in the window closest to Jeopardy's castle room.

Daddy!

That was no woman but clearly a man—a man in uniform. Could it be Daddy?

"Did you see that?"

"Let's go, Harper. Stop dawdling." Jeopardy grabbed my hand and dragged me away without listening to a word I said.

"I swear I saw Daddy. And the night Momma fell...you have to know the truth! She didn't really fall, Jeopardy. The Lady in White pushed her down those stairs. Well, Momma took a swing at her and then fell. It all happened so fast, but the ghost was definitely there. I think she was trying to help you."

"Too little, too late," she muttered. "No more talk about ghosts, Harper. You shouldn't be afraid of ghosts. It's the living you have to worry about."

"I'm not afraid of Daddy if that was him. But the other one...she could have killed Momma."

Jeopardy stopped to light a cigarette and frowned. "She didn't. No more ghost stories. Let's run the rest of the way."

"You can't run and smoke, Jeopardy," I said with a grin.

"Come on, pie-face. I can outrun you with two cigarettes in my mouth." She took off, and I chased her with a faux growl.

"You know I hate that nickname!" We laughed all the way to the river. With every pump of my legs, I felt the weight of the past horrible months melt away. For once in my life, I was going to be a girl my age. Whatever that meant.

There were more kids at the river than I had ever seen before, at least twenty teenagers. Some were smoking, and most were swimming. Jeopardy sauntered up like she owned the place, her wild hair tumbling down her back. Why she didn't bob her hair, I would never know, but the wildness suited her. My sister was the most beautiful girl in the world, and the saddest.

Except for now, except for this moment. The Harvester boys were there, all three of them. The oldest, Tony, strolled over and kissed her cheek. She kissed him back and took the soda he offered her. He had a nice car with a swanky radio that played Count Basie's *I Want a Little Girl*. How strange that we would hear that song today. Daddy used to dance with us girls every Christmas. At our last Christmas together, this had been our song. I suddenly had the urge to run back to Summerleigh, back to Daddy.

"Jeopardy, we should go home." I touched her elbow, but she cast me that look that said, *Get lost*.

One of the girls from school, Arnette Loper, walked over. "Hey, Harper. You'll be in the ninth grade this year, right? Me too. Maybe we'll get the same teacher. I hope we get Mr. Dempsey. He's dreamy." Another girl, I couldn't remember her name, giggled.

"Mr. Dempsey? Is he the one with the sad eyes?" I asked as I glanced at Jeopardy, who was guzzling her drink.

Arnette giggled and took my hand. "Yes, and boy, howdy. I wish he'd make those sad eyes at me. You want to go swim?"

I looked at Jeopardy again. Seeing as she wasn't in a big hurry to hang out with me, I said, "Sure."

"Come on, then. It must be so neat having Jeopardy Belle for a sister. Did she really kiss Tony Harvester after church last spring?"

"I don't think so," I said honestly. "First I've heard of it."

"Good, because he's going to be mine one day. Unless you like him," she added suspiciously.

"Uh, no thanks. I think I'll hold out for Mr. Dempsey."

We traveled down the hill to the river and eased into the warm water. Arnette carried on with her gossiping, and I agreed with her on most points as we splashed. I wasn't in the water five minutes before Jeopardy came down. To my complete surprise, she stripped off her shirt and shorts and dived into the dark blue-brown water wearing only her underwear. Every eye was on her, including Troy Harvester's. He was pouting, his arms crossed, staring at her with his big blue eyes like a hound dog that'd been banned from the porch. I knew he still loved her, or something, even after Momma's bad behavior.

Jeopardy didn't come up from the water right away. Just when I began to worry, she reappeared a good ten feet away, rising out of the water like a siren. Her face was turned toward the sun, and her hands were above her head. She swam toward me. "Hey, pie-face." She kissed my cheek and dived under again. I forgot all about frog-faced Arnette and played with my sister. We ducked and dived, trying to grab each other. This was the most fun I'd had with Jeopardy since we were just small kids.

And then Troy was there.

He'd shed his shirt but still wore his blue jean shorts, thank goodness. If any of these boys took off their clothing, I'd have to go home. I wasn't prepared to see a naked boy.

Jeopardy bobbed back up and splashed back in surprise when she noticed him. The three of us were alone now, since Arnette and her blond friend were trolling the other two Harvester boys. I felt like a third wheel, but I wasn't about to leave Jeopardy alone swimming around in her underwear. The two of them faced one another; Jeopardy's tan face glistened in the setting sun, and Troy's blond hair poked up as it quickly dried in the heat. It looked like cotton.

"I want to know something, Jeopardy Belle."

"What's that, Troy Harvester?"

"Why don't you ever kiss me? You kissed my brother just now. Right in front of me. I thought you liked me, but you don't kiss me. Why is that? I know your Momma hates me. I heard her call me trash."

She backed away from him but didn't go too far. She tilted her head and watched him as she continued to tread water. Her hazel eyes were hard and full of hurt. "I don't kiss you because I like you, Troy. And I don't care what my Momma says."

He wiped the water from his face and kept treading water. "Then stop kissing everyone else."

"You don't know a dang thing, Troy Harvester. Why don't you go find someone else to kiss on? Come on, Harper. It's time to go."

She was angry now. She splashed out of the water, ignoring the stares as she got dressed, and together we left the party. I guessed that was a party. I didn't have any punch, but it felt like a party. Kind of.

As we walked, her mood darkened. She smoked, and I walked beside her. I had to ask her the same question. "Why don't you kiss Troy, Jep? Is he gross or something? Got stank breath?"

"No, it's nothing like that."

"Then why?" I laughed as I tried to smooth my drying hair with my hands.

"Because Troy Harvester deserves a better girl than me."

I didn't know how to answer that. We didn't talk the rest of the way home.

Chapter Seventeen—Jerica

When I got out of bed Sunday, I felt like a truck had run over me. My sheets were sweaty, and my teeth and skin felt filmy. The reflection in the mirror didn't do much to boost my morale. At least I felt somewhat normal now. Moving slowly, my sore back muscles screaming, I stepped into the shower and washed away the remnants of whatever germ had held me prisoner for the past few days. During those feverish days and nights, I had dreamed.

The Lady in White had pushed Ann down the stairs! Was she protecting Jeopardy, or was she merely a spirit bent on bringing harm to anyone who crossed her path? Was this Mariana McIntyre?

And then I remembered Jeopardy's notes, the ones she crammed into walls and floorboards. Harper had never found them, but I had to. My stomach growling, I stepped out of the steamy shower feeling almost human again. I kept things casual with shorts and a tank top. I was so hungry, I could eat a bear, as my friend Anita used to say. Where was a good bear when you needed one?

Nothing in my refrigerator appealed to me, so I settled on a few fried eggs and some toast. But before I could get the skillet out, I heard a knock at the front door. It was Jesse's cousin, Renee.

"Hey, Jerica. I hope you don't mind me coming by, but I was in the neighborhood with a casserole..." She grinned at me.

"I don't mind at all, and perfect timing. I hate cooking for myself. Not to mention I'm not too good at it."

"Great, lead me to the kitchen."

"I'm glad you didn't come by yesterday. I've been a bit under the weather."

"I figured it must be something. I thought for sure you'd come hear Jesse play."

"Why would you think that 'for sure'?"

"I don't know. Just a feeling, but honestly, you didn't miss anything," she said as she pulled a plate out of the cabinet and served a slice of what looked to be a chicken casserole.

"Poor turnout?" I asked as I offered her a glass of tea.

"None for me, thanks. No, we had a great turnout. Poor playing. Jesse is a lot of things, a talented carpenter, even a good short-order cook...but a guitar player, he is not."

I laughed to hear that. "Oh no. I'm glad I stayed home then."

"Feeling better today?"

"Sure am. And luckily, I'm a nurse."

"Well, if you ever need a good doctor, go see Dr. Leland. He's the best doctor in George County, as far as I'm concerned."

"Leland?" That got my attention. This had to be a relative of Jeopardy's peach-loving doctor.

"Yeah, he's with that group in town. Nice guy. He went to school with my older sister, Rebecca. I think he had a thing for her, but nothing ever happened between them. So, what are your plans for today?"

The casserole was delicious, so much so I was tempted to ask for the recipe...but who was I kidding? I probably wasn't going to ever cook such a dish. "I'm probably going to explore Summerleigh. May I ask you a question?"

"Sure. I'm an open book."

"What scared you the other day?"

She shook her head. "That's really one of the reasons I came by, I had to tell you the truth. Someone shoved me. I felt a hand in the middle of my back, forcing me out of the master bedroom. I got the distinct impression that it was Ann Belle. She doesn't like you being here, or me, for that matter."

"I can totally see that being the case. She was not a nice lady. How in the world did she ever land a guy like John?"

"There are rumors about Ann; she was rough on those girls. But at one time she was the loveliest lady in George County. She even represented the state as Miss Mississippi, but her pageant days were cut short. In those days, unmarried and pregnant disqualified you from a lot of things."

"Wait, what?"

"Yep. That's the rumor, and Jesse verified it with his research. Either Jeopardy Belle was born three months early or something else happened."

"Oh, that explains a lot. She must have really resented Jeopardy." I sipped my tea and then asked, "What about John? Did he ever raise any questions about his oldest daughter?"

"He never did. John Jeffrey Belle is a town hero, even though he didn't die in the war. Before the accident he earned many awards, including one for bravery, what do they call it? I can't remember, but he was such a beautiful man. Did you know they have a statue of him right off Main Street?"

"No, but I don't know much about the area. Virginia seems a long way away now."

"You'll do fine. Want some more?" She gestured toward the casserole.

"No, I'm stuffed. Did JB win the house from a McIntyre? What do you know about Mariana McIntyre?"

"JB? You mean John Belle? No, I don't think he won Summerleigh from a McIntyre. They all died out at the turn of the last century. However, it can't be hard to figure out who owned the house before the Belles. It stood empty a lot of years before John claimed it. Jesse probably knows, but darned if I can remember. As far as Mariana goes, John became kind of obsessed with the family history. When he wasn't fixing up the place, he was at the library digging up information."

"Information about what?"

"Girl, that was before my time."

"Way before your time, of course. Want to walk with me? I'd like to check out something in the attic at Summerleigh, and honestly, I'd feel better if I had someone with me. Would you think I was crazy if I told you that I've seen Ann?"

"Nope. Not crazy at all. And I don't blame you. Just from my short survey the other day, I knew there were spirits lingering around. Summerleigh has never been a happy place." I couldn't hide my worried expression. "Oh, I mean until now. You'll make it a wonderful place. I'm sure of it."

"What else did you see the other day? Anything?"

"No, that was it. I didn't see a thing, but I felt that hand as sure as I'm sitting here. The touch of those cold fingers freaked me out. I mean, I knew the place was spiritually active. It had to be; it's so old and all, and so much tragedy has happened here, but I wasn't prepared for that."

"Do you think Jeopardy Belle is in that house? I'm only asking because I made Harper a promise. I promised I would find her sister, and I've been having these..." My face flushed. Imagine telling a near stranger that I'd been dreaming about Harper as a girl, about ghosts, and that I'd seen my dead daughter here at Summerleigh.

"Go on, Jerica. You can tell me. What have you seen? Have you seen a girl?"

"I've seen a lot of things but not Jeopardy's ghost. I'm not sure she's here, but I have to find out. I know this sounds strange, but I think she left clues. Notes in the walls and floorboards of the attic."

"What makes you think that?"

I bit my lip and then took a sip of my tea. "Because Harper told me." I got up to put my plate in the sink when a wave of dizziness came over me. "Whoa," I said as I waited out the spiraling scene.

"Hey, you better sit down. I don't think you're up to a field trip today. In fact, I'm not sure it's a good idea for you to go back into Summerleigh alone. Not in your current state. They say negative entities tend to latch on when we're physically weak. I know for a fact there is at least one negative spirit in that house."

"How do you know so much about this stuff?" I asked as she took the plate from my hand and helped me back to my seat.

"I grew up seeing spirits, hearing voices. My family all thought I was crazy until my uncle came back from the grave and told me where he'd left his truck keys. Nobody's given me any crap since then."

"Really? That happened to you?"

"Yeah, but it was a long time ago. Nothing as amazing has happened since, but I still see and feel things from time to time."

"And Jesse?"

"Ha! No way would he admit it, but I have my suspicions." I laughed to hear about it. "May I suggest something?"

"Sure."

"I have a friend, Hannah Ray. She's the best psychic medium I know. Why not let her walk Summerleigh with us? She might be able to tell us who is in there and who's not."

"I don't know, Renee. No offense to you or your friend, but I've never believed in any of that stuff."

"I'm not offended, but I am surprised. How can you not believe in what you've seen yourself? And you have someone with you all the time. A child, I think. I can only see her outline, but she's always near you. And from time to time, she touches you. I've seen you turn your head in her direction when she's close. Is she a relative?"

I burst into tears, and when I could stop crying I told Renee the complete story. By the time she'd left, she'd called Hannah and made an appointment for tomorrow.

"If anyone can contact Marisol, it is Hannah. I am sorry for your loss, Jerica, but I am glad you are here. Why don't you try to get some rest?"

"I think I will. Let me walk you to the door first, though."

"No need, I can find my way out. I'll see you tomorrow at eleven."

"Bye, Renee." I heard the door close and crawled onto my wicker couch to sleep. I didn't have long to wait.

Chapter Eighteen—Harper

A month later, Aunt Dot still hadn't left us despite Momma's increasingly obnoxious behavior. For all her ugly ways, I felt sorry for Momma and spent time with her a little while every day now that she could move around. Weeks had gone by before we had been allowed in her room; I think she didn't want us to see her with those bruises on her face. But I had great news today, and as she had made it all the way to the parlor, I had to tell her. Maybe she would be proud of me.

"Momma, guess what? I got voted into the Harvest Queen Court. Isn't that wonderful?" I asked nervously as I held her hand.

"You did? I am delighted to hear that. I knew you could do it, Harper. Of all my girls, you are certainly the smartest." I noticed she didn't say loveliest, but if smartest was all I could get, I would happily receive it. "Tell me all about the competition. Were there many girls vying for a court spot? That horrible Loper girl, the one with the frog face, is she in this court?"

"No, ma'am. She didn't make the cut." I didn't mean that in a mean way, but Momma thought it was hilarious. She laughed and gossiped about Arnette's mother for a few minutes. I smiled politely even though my subconscious warned me that by befriending Momma I was betraying Jeopardy; I knew it, but I could not help myself. I craved Momma's approval more than anything in the world. Except maybe Jeopardy's friendship. How unfortunate that those two things were in direct contrast to one another. After I provided my mother with all the details, she excitedly instructed me to pick a gown from her closet. I would need a nice one.

Aunt Dot joined our merry conversation, and between the three of us, we found a dress that would be suitable for such an important event. Of course, it was a formal gown and for the life of me, I had no recollection of Momma having ever worn such a beautiful, heavenly gown. It was light blue with shimmering rhinestones all over it.

"A fairy princess!" My aunt clapped her hands in approval.

"Oh, but her shoes, Dorothy. We will never get those size nines into my size sevens. Never ever, and without the right shoes, she will be a laughingstock." Was Momma changing her mind? Would she take the magical gown back?

Aunt Dot chewed her lip. "I know where to find the perfect shoes. I saw them in a store on Main Street. We'll go pick up a pair this afternoon, Harper. Why don't you come with us, Ann? It would be good to see you get out of the house for a while."

"No, I think I'll try to wash my hair; it's an absolute mess. But you girls have fun." Momma left my room and went into her own, closing the door behind her. I hated that our pleasant time had ended, but at least she had lent me her gown. Aunt Dot and I chatted about jewelry, but a knock at the front door put a pause in our conversation.

Aunt Dot opened the door, and my heart sank when I saw our visitor. It was Deputy Lonnie Passeau. He swung his key ring on his finger and gazed down at Aunt Dot as if she were a bug he'd like to squash. Or something. I'd seen him around the school a few times; apparently, some boys had spray-painted the outside of the gym and had gotten expelled for it. And now he was here. That couldn't be good.

It could only mean one thing. Jeopardy was in trouble.

"Good afternoon, Deputy. How may I help you?"

"Well, good afternoon, Miss Daughdrill. May I come in a moment?"

"Actually," Aunt Dot said as she stepped out on the porch and closed the door behind her, "my sister isn't really up to visitors right now. Is there something I might help you with?"

"Maybe so, maybe so," he said as he flipped his key ring around. "The sheriff is really interested in cleaning up the riffraff that tends to congregate around the river on the weekends. Those kids go down there drinking, smoking and doing God knows what, and it has to stop before someone gets hurt...or otherwise damaged. Now, I don't consider any daughter of John Jeffrey Belle's to be riffraff—the man was a war hero—but his oldest girl, Jeopardy, she's been participating in some shocking behavior as of late. I thought it best to tell her mother, in hopes that she could encourage Jeopardy to behave in a more ladylike fashion."

"No, sir. I can't believe my niece would do anything like that." Aunt Dot was lying; she knew Jeopardy smoked and had even tried to discourage her a few times to no avail. Jep would do what she wanted to do, no matter who said anything to her. "And as far as the river goes, it's a public swimming hole, isn't it?"

Passeau answered in his deep voice. He was clearly losing patience with Aunt Dot. "Perhaps you aren't the one I should be speaking with after all. Since you don't have any children of your own, you may not understand how crucial it is to be a good example to a child. When would be a good time for me to speak to Ann, I mean, Mrs. Belle?"

Aunt Dot's voice shook. "I couldn't say. I will tell my sister you stopped by when she wakes up from her nap. I am sure she will call you if she has any questions."

"I need to have a word with Jeopardy," he said as he shoved his keys into his pocket and tucked his hat down over his eye. I think he spotted me behind the lace curtain, and I ducked down to avoid further detection.

"No, I think that can wait. I'll speak to Jeopardy, Deputy."

He nodded and stepped down off the porch. "I'll hold you to that, Miss Daughdrill. If I find her misbehaving at the river, she will have to spend some time in the back of my squad car. Good afternoon now." With a grin, he walked back to his car, and Aunt Dot came inside looking like she'd lost all the blood in her face.

With her back against the door, she said, "Harper, warn your sister to stay away from that man." And that was all she said. She went into the kitchen and called someone on the phone, but I couldn't hear her muffled conversation.

Just then, Loxley tugged on my hand. "I found a treasure, Harper. A real-life treasure. You want to see it?" Her eyes were gleeful, and she was jumping up and down with excitement.

"I hope you haven't been plundering Momma's jewelry boxes, Loxley."

"No, these treasures belong to the lady upstairs. You want to see them?"

I swallowed at the mention of the Lady in White; that had to be who Loxley was speaking about. I glanced at the doorway, but Aunt Dot was still on the phone. "Yes, show me." We made our way up to the top floor, and Loxley opened the door of the attic. "Jeopardy won't like us being in her castle, Loxley. We should go now."

"Oh no, I haven't gotten into any of her things, not even her notes. Did you know she leaves notes for the ghosts?"

"Does she?" I had seen her once depositing a note but had been unable to retrieve it. "Have you read any of them?"

"You know I can't read." She frowned at me as if I were stupid. "The treasure box is over here, Harper, but you cannot tell anyone that I showed it to you. Not even Jeopardy. She doesn't come to this side of the attic."

"Okay, mum's the word."

We tiptoed through the many boxes and strange finds until we came to an old trunk. *It must be old*, I thought. I studied the lock and saw the numbers *1870* and some letters engraved near the opening. The letters were scratched, so I couldn't tell what they were. Two M's, maybe? "Is it locked?"

"No, it's open. I found this treasure; does that mean it's mine?"

"I don't know, Loxley. It must belong to someone. What's inside?"

We opened the trunk, and I was amazed at the contents. A ruffled pink gown caught my attention first. We carefully removed it, and I immediately held it up to myself and asked, "What do you think?"

"It's my treasure, Harper." She poked her bottom lip out at me, and I put the dress to the side.

"Alright, if it doesn't belong to anyone else, it is your treasure."

"Do ghosts own treasures?"

"I'm not sure. Why?"

She dug around in the trunk, obviously looking for something. "She wears that dress sometimes. Only it's all white when she wears it."

I spun around and stared at the dress. She was right! The Lady in White had worn that dress the night I saw her on the stairs, when she scared Momma nearly to death. "Oh, Loxley. I think you need to put this back. This isn't our treasure. It's hers."

"But she won't mind. She likes me; she smiles at me all the time. And look at this." She held a tiny snow globe in her hands. Shaking it up, she held her palm out so I could watch the snow fall.

"Let me see," I said, ignoring her pout. She didn't want to part with any of this stuff, but I could tell she had laid claim to this prize. I held the snow globe up to the light. The water was slightly cloudy…how old could this be? In the center of the "snow" storm stood two tiny figures, a man and a woman. They were dressed for an old-fashioned Christmas. The man wore a plaid coat, and the lady a plaid hat. Their mouths were open in perpetual song, probably a Christmas carol judging by the tiny hymnbook they held.

I could hardly believe it, but the man in the plaid coat looked exactly like Daddy. Daddy and the Lady in White were standing in the snow together singing their silent song! The room became cold, and I had never wanted to leave a place more than I did right now. "We have to go, Loxley. We have to go now." I tossed the dress back in the trunk and snatched the globe away from her and placed it back inside the trunk.

"No, Harper! That's my treasure. It's okay that I have it. She doesn't mind!"

I took her hand and ignored her complaint. To my horror, the attic door was closing. Even Loxley gasped.

"It's just the wind, Harper. It does that sometimes. It's just the wind, right?" Her whispering gave my goose bumps goose bumps.

"Hush," I warned as we tiptoed to the door. I put my hand on the doorknob and slowly began to turn it.

And then we heard the floorboard outside the door squeaking. Someone was out there. I let go of the doorknob and watched in terror as it began to shake, as if someone wanted to get in. We stepped back a few steps, Loxley's little arms went around my waist and she closed her eyes.

"Make him go away, Harper. Make the boy go away."

I held on to her and closed my eyes. The shaking stopped, and we collapsed on Jeopardy's pallet, waiting until we felt safe to leave. We didn't have long to wait; the door opened about five minutes later, and Jeopardy yelled at us.

"Don't come in my castle when I'm not here. What are you doing? Snooping through my things?" She cut her eyes to a plain wooden box in the corner near her pillow, but we both shook our heads.

"No! Loxley found a treasure, over there, but I told her to put it back. And then when we tried to leave, the door started shaking and we couldn't get out. We didn't touch a thing! I swear!"

"Swear!" Loxley repeated, raising her hand as if she were ready to pledge on a stack of Bibles.

"Fine, but don't come back up here without my permission. I have traps in place, and you'll get hurt."

"Fine," I said, aggravated at her lack of compassion. Didn't she realize a ghost could have gotten us? Loxley took off out of the room, but I lingered a moment.

"Deputy Passeau came by today looking for you. He says you've been behaving badly down at the river. He's going to arrest you, Jeopardy Belle, if he catches you doing bad again."

"Is he?" She struck a match and smoked a thin cigarette. Likely one of Momma's. "Did he tell Momma?" She smiled gleefully.

"No, he told Aunt Dot, and she wasn't happy about it."

"I wish he would have told Momma. That would have been better. I wish he would have told her. I would have loved to have seen her face."

"Why do you do this, Jeopardy? Why do you always have to make trouble? Why do you hate Momma so much? Why can't you let sleeping dogs lie?"

"Get out of my castle, pie-face! And don't come back." She got in my face and poked my chest with her finger. I was a full foot taller than her, but it didn't matter. She was stronger; she was always stronger than me. "If you side with my enemy, then you're my enemy too, Harper."

"I have never been your enemy, Jeopardy," I said as my heart broke and the tears came unbidden. "Please go to Momma. Tell her you're sorry. We can be a family again. Daddy would want us to love each other."

"Get out!" she screamed angrily.

And I did, suddenly unafraid of any ghost or spirit. The only thing I had been afraid of, losing my sister's friendship, had happened. I had crossed the line, and she would never forgive me.

Never ever.

Chapter Nineteen—Harper

Aunt Dot left a trail of sad faces behind this morning. I think all of us Belle girls had halfway hoped that she'd make the change of address permanent, but it wasn't to be. In the end, Aunt Dot looked tired, too tired to continue caring for Momma, who had obviously decided at some point that she didn't need her sister's help anymore. She'd dressed and decided to go to the ladies' auxiliary meeting at the church. Augustine Hogue would be there too, and thankfully, I wasn't asked to accompany them. Jeopardy had come home early this morning silly-giddy. I suspected she had been drinking, but I didn't ask her. I don't think our other sisters noticed.

"Hey, I have an idea. Let's have a party," Jeopardy said with a giggle.

"Like a birthday party?" Loxley asked expectantly. "Whose birthday is it?"

"Nobody's birthday, silly goose. It's just a party. You can have a party for no reason at all if you like. Let's turn on the radio and dance."

Addison coughed up a storm but didn't object. When she finished hacking, she said in her perpetually squeaky voice, "We don't know any dances. Show us some of your dances, Jeopardy."

"Okay, but you have to be my partner, Addie. No, you have to try. Now stand like this." Loxley and I giggled as Jeopardy showed Addison how to properly hold her partner; her left arm around Jeopardy's waist, her right hand in hers. They looked like the top of a wedding cake, except with two girls, not a bride and groom. Even Addison laughed as they shuffled through the waltz. "It's hard to teach you when you won't stop laughing," Jeopardy complained good-naturedly.

"Teach Harper, Jeopardy. She's going to be the Harvest Queen at school." Loxley clapped and then strutted around the room waving as if she'd won the award herself.

"Really? First I heard of it."

"I'm not the queen, and it's no big deal," I said defensively while casting a warning eye at Loxley.

"Oh yes it *is* a big deal. You should see the dress Momma gave her to wear. It's blue with star sparkles all over it. She looks like Miss America." Loxley ignored my warning stare and offered more waving and an over-accentuated prissy walk. Addison roared at her antics.

"I don't walk like that, Loxley!"

"Who's taking you to this dance, Harper? Not one of those Harvester boys, I hope."

I shook my head. I knew who she was talking about. How could she think I would go to a dance with Troy Harvester? I alone knew how she felt about him. Our conversation from our walk home from the river rang in my head. "Nobody. I am going solo, Jeopardy. Is that so bad?"

"Yes, that's terrible," she said with her hand cocked on her hip. "Don't y'all think that's terrible?" Our sisters agreed with Jeopardy.

Loxley quickly added, "Maybe you could invite Ray Loper from church? I am sure he'd look fine in a suit."

"Yuck. No thank you."

"Loxley's right. You should tell Ray to take you. He would. I know he would. I'll talk to him if you like," Jeopardy said with a cryptic smile.

"Can we talk about something else? I don't want to go to the dance with anyone."

Jeopardy's smile disappeared. "Liar, liar, pants on fire. Let me teach you some moves, Harper, so you don't embarrass us all."

"Fine," I said as I surrendered to Jeopardy's tutelage. We must have lost track of time because before we knew it, Momma's car was pulling in the driveway. I thought maybe Jeopardy would run upstairs since she hardly spent any time in Momma's presence anymore, but she didn't. She walked in behind us with her arms crossed.

"You girls hungry? My, you all look so pink-cheeked. What have you been doing?" Momma unpacked a casserole and took the tea pitcher out of the refrigerator.

"Dancing! Jeopardy has been teaching us." As always, Loxley volunteered too much information. She couldn't help it, I knew that, but I wished she'd shut up from time to time.

"Just the waltz," I added. "Can I help you with something, Momma?"

"Get the plates, Harper. Why don't you collect the silverware, Jeopardy? Addison can pour the drinks."

We all set about our tasks; even Loxley folded napkins. For one moment, I pretended we were a normal family; I enjoyed the feeling, but those moments never lasted very long. Actually, they were quite dangerous. They lulled you into believing that all was well. It never was. Not at our house.

Momma put the dish on the table, along with some bread. I knew right away Jeopardy wasn't going to touch it. It was spaghetti with stewed tomatoes. If there was anything Jeopardy hated, it was a stewed tomato. Raw ones off the vine or sliced with salt and pepper were okay, but not slimy, stewed ones. She'd gotten sick on them years ago and never forgot that sickness. Even today they made her gag. Still, Momma slopped a big old pile of the pasta and tomatoes on Jeopardy's plate and plunked it down in front of her. Jeopardy flashed her an *I-hate-you* look and then sat back in the cane chair with her arms still crossed.

"Harper, you say grace, dear." Momma bowed her perfect, pretty head and folded her hands. Everyone followed suit, except Jeopardy, who continued to bore holes into the top of our mother's head.

"Dear Lord, bless our food. Make it nourish our bodies, in Jesus' name. Amen."

Whenever asked to say grace, which wasn't often, I always used Daddy's prayer. I couldn't help but think about Daddy now. He loved to slurp his spaghetti noodles. He didn't cut up his pasta and eat it politely. Spaghetti nights at our house had been fun, once upon a time. And completely free of stewed tomatoes. Jeopardy ate the bread and then started to get up when Momma put her fork down.

"Where do you think you're going? I haven't excused you yet. There's been far too much laxity of decorum around here while I've been down with my arm. Aunt Dorothy must have let you all run wild. Have you forgotten your manners completely, Jeopardy Harris Belle?"

Jeopardy didn't speak but wiped her face with her napkin. She wasn't shaking in her boots, not like me. Addison was drinking her tea and looking green. Loxley alone enjoyed her feast, but even she ate with wide eyes as we watched the expected argument unfold.

"I asked you a question, Jeopardy. Have you forgotten your manners?"

Jeopardy banged her fist on the table. "Yes, I have. Do you want me to tell everyone when I lost my *manners*, Momma? Would you like the details? All those details? Maybe I should tell my sisters all about it too." She banged the table with both fists now and stood up threateningly.

Momma leaned back, surprised at her oldest daughter's outburst. I didn't know why she would be surprised, but she sure acted like it.

"Don't speak to me in that tone, girl! Do you all hear how disrespectful she is to your poor mother? All I tried to do was bring a nice dinner home from the church, and this is my thanks." Nobody answered. The three of us, Addison, Loxley and I, kept our eyes on our plates as Jeopardy huffed in frustration at us—no, at me. What did she want from me? I couldn't help her. What could I say that would help? Momma wouldn't beat Jeopardy anymore, not since her accident, not since she saw that ghost, but she would certainly beat me. And I had a dance to go to. In that moment, I realized the horrible truth. I was teetotally selfish, as selfish as selfish could be.

"Harper?" Jeopardy whispered hopefully, but I wouldn't look up. All my promises to stick with her, to stay by her side, disappeared like fog on the water. The only sound you could hear in our kitchen was the sound of Momma's chewing. She carried on with her dinner like Jeopardy was a rude stranger she hoped to ignore.

"Addison, please pass me the parmesan, dear." With shaking hands, Addie obeyed and the rest of us sat and waited for the storm to either pass or explode.

With a sob of betrayal, Jeopardy left the kitchen. I heard her footsteps running up the stairs to her castle. Momma acted like she didn't hear a thing. She dabbed the corners of her mouth with her napkin and smiled at Loxley. "Eat up like a big girl."

"Yes, ma'am." Loxley toyed with her food and cast a convicting glance in my direction. I couldn't stand it. I had to go see about Jeopardy. We'd gotten so close over the past few weeks, and I'd let her down. What if she hurt herself? I couldn't have that on my conscience.

"Momma, may I be..." Before I could finish my sentence, the radio in the parlor came on at full volume. It was Count Basie, playing *I Want a Little Girl*. Momma ran to the parlor to scold Jeopardy for playing with her radio, but she wasn't there. Nobody was there. Jeopardy had gone upstairs anyway. How could she be in two places at one time?

The room was empty, and the air was icy cold.

Loxley stiffened beside me. Momma was talking to herself, accusing us of playing with the radio when she knew with her own eyes that was impossible. We were all here, in the parlor with her.

And we had all been in the kitchen with her before that.

"Daddy's here, Daddy and that lady. Something bad is going to happen," Loxley shouted. Then she began to cry.

Momma lost her temper. "Shut up with that caterwauling, Loxley! You girls go to bed. I've seen enough of your faces today. Go on now." Momma stood with her hands on her hips, her face filled with fear and confusion, and we did as we were told. I stayed with my younger sisters that night. Something was going on here, things were happening that I couldn't see or understand, and no amount of persuasion would convince Loxley to stop crying and tell me. It didn't matter. I had a duty to protect my sisters from whatever bad thing Daddy was trying to warn us about, for surely that was why he was here. He watched over us still, but he would need my help.

Oh, Daddy! Why can't I see you? Help us! Help us all!

And later, when everyone was asleep, I would go upstairs to see Jeopardy. I had to tell her that I loved her.

That I was sorry for abandoning her, for being afraid, for not taking her side.

I stayed up for hours, waiting for Momma to go to bed. It was hard to pretend you were asleep when someone was watching you. Momma watched me for a full minute, even whispered my name, but I ignored her and hoped she wouldn't drag me out of the bed as she sometimes did. She didn't. God had at least heard my prayers tonight. Later, when the house got quiet, I crawled out of the bed and crept up the stairs, praying again for protection. *Please, God, keep the ghosts away unless it's Daddy*.

When I got to Jeopardy's door, I found it slightly ajar. I pushed it open, but she wasn't there. My heart dropped as I walked to her open window. The air smelled like dirt and rain. Yes, it would certainly rain tonight, and it would be here soon. One thing you could be sure of around here were evening storms. It would be that way until fall truly arrived, and then it would be dry and windy.

I opened my eyes just in time to see my sister running through the backyard. And she wasn't alone. A boy ran beside her, but who? I wanted to yell her name, but the risk was too great. What would happen if Momma knew Jeopardy had been off with a boy?

I shuddered at the thought. I heard footsteps in the hallway and became afraid that I wasn't alone. What if the door-slamming ghost showed up again? I tiptoed out of the room and back downstairs.

There was nothing I could do about Jeopardy tonight, but maybe tomorrow. Yes, tomorrow I would call Aunt Dot. I would tell her that horrible things were happening here and how much we missed her. She would know what to do. Someone had to help us with Momma.

I walked into my room and found my borrowed dress removed from the closet and spread out on the bed. The beautiful dress Momma had lent me was torn to shreds like someone had taken a knife to it. No, scissors. A big old pair of silver-plated scissors were lying beside the destroyed garment. I'd never seen those scissors before. Who would do such a thing? Jeopardy? Momma?

What would I wear to the Harvest Dance now?

Jeopardy, how could you be so cruel? I didn't mean to let you down. I was coming to apologize. My teenage heart felt heavy, and I cried myself to sleep clutching the blue fragments. Nothing would ever be right again.

Chapter Twenty—Jerica

Strange to think that the first social event I had at Summerleigh would be a ghost hunt. I wasn't sure what else to call this...it certainly wasn't a séance or anything like that. I kind of felt silly about the whole thing now, but it was too late to change my mind. Hannah, Renee and Jesse were here, although Jesse remained outside with the roofer, who had come to give me an estimate on the east wing. I was kind of glad he'd stayed out there.

Despite my reservations, I greeted the ladies politely and welcomed them into the old place. Hannah's eyes grew big. "Wow, so this is Summerleigh. I can see why you'd want to fix this place up. What a grand old lady! What will you do with her when you get the job complete? Will this be your family home, or do you have something else in mind?"

"I'm not sure, honestly. I'm not much for planning too far ahead anymore."

Hannah was tall, taller than me, with large eyes and a thin figure. Simply dressed in a blue and white dress, she had an old-fashioned purse on her shoulder that she clutched like someone might steal it. Maybe it was her lucky talisman and comforted her. Maybe it held her lucky charms. I had no idea.

Hannah touched my arm sympathetically. "You made a promise to someone. Someone who lived here." I nodded in agreement. She let me go and walked around the Great Room, stopping at the corner near the fireplace. "She was young back then, but she was old when you knew her. I can see her. She's with us."

"Yes, that's right," I said as I glanced at Renee suspiciously. "Harper Belle was a friend of mine."

"I didn't tell her a thing. I swear," Renee whispered.

"Your friend is not the only one here, and I don't think she stays here all the time. She comes and goes, but there are others who never leave." Birds began chirping on the front porch; I had noticed a nest in the porch roof earlier. Their chirps created a strange echo through the empty house. Hannah walked toward me. "Would you mind if I walked by myself for a little while?"

"Are you sure you want to?" I asked her.

"I'll be okay. If you could stay here, that would help me focus on the other energies here at Summerleigh rather than the one that follows you."

"Follows me? You mean Harper."

"Oh no. This isn't Harper Belle. This has to be a relative of yours. She looks very much like you, especially her eyes. Maybe a sister or a...oh, dear. I'm sorry. She's your daughter. Mary? No, that's not it." Hannah closed her eyes and appeared to be listening. "Marisol, what a lovely name."

"Yes, she was...she is my daughter. Is she here? Can I talk to her?" I tried not to cry.

"We can certainly talk to her, but there are others here, Jerica. We will come back to Marisol." I couldn't hide my disappointment, and she held my hands briefly. "I know you are eager to communicate with her, but that's best not done in here. You don't want to attach her to this place. No, you don't want that. It's best to leave the communication with her for later, at your own home so she won't be confused about where to find you when she feels she wants to connect."

"Okay," I said breathlessly as I blinked back tears. Hannah touched my arm again and continued her survey of the room.

"Yes, there are too many others present," she said, but I had no idea what she meant. "I'm coming up now," she called up the stairs. "I'm not here to take anything or to harm you." She paused at the bottom of the staircase and waved at us to stay back. "I'll be back in a few minutes."

"No, I want to go, too. As the homeowner, I can't let you get hurt. I won't say a peep, but you have to let us come with you. I know I'm not supposed to say anything but what I know—I mean, I guess that's the rule—but there is a lady. She caused Ann Belle to fall. I wouldn't want anything to happen to you."

"Alright," Hannah said, "but ask Marisol to stay down here. You don't want her getting involved in this."

I shivered at her words like a rabbit ran over my grave. "Marisol? Honey? Stay down here, okay. Don't come up the stairs. Listen to Mommy." I waited, unsure if she'd heard me or if she was even here. How would I know? What if Hannah was playing some cruel joke on me? Renee was friendly and all, but I didn't really know her. She might be the sort of person to arrange such a prank. A horrible, cruel prank.

"Okay, I feel her leaving. Let's go upstairs and see who's waiting for us." The three of us slowly climbed the squeaky staircase. "This used to be such a beautiful place," Hannah said absently as she ran her hand over the wooden railing. "There was another house here before this one. It was smaller but just as grand." As we reached the landing, Hannah glanced down. I thought I heard something, like the shuffling of papers downstairs. Maybe it was Jesse? I hadn't heard him come in, but he could have come in the back door.

Renee whispered to us, "Did you hear that? Sounded like scratching or something."

"Like papers shuffling," I said.

"Yes, like someone was flipping the pages of a magazine or a newspaper in a quiet room. Oh, I can see her. She's not a very nice lady. She doesn't like our being here. And she doesn't like you at all, Jerica. She knows why you're here. Oh yes, she's angry. I think she's following us. Let's go upstairs quickly. She doesn't like it up here, so she won't come up. The others are up here."

"How many ghosts are in this place, Hannah?" Renee asked excitedly.

"So far, the one downstairs, the lady who looks like Grace Kelly. She's so angry, so full of hate. She tries to keep others away, the ones who want to come here. She has a secret, many secrets, but there are more energies here. A man, a child—a boy, I think—and another lady." We were walking the hallway of the second floor now. "The boy has been here longer than any of them. He's strong, and he's...evil. He stays mostly in this room."

I recognized the room as Loxley's playroom. "How can a child be evil?" I asked.

"I don't know, but that's what I feel. He's disappointed because there are no kids to play with. Oh, God. Don't let kids in here, not until he's gone. He won't tell me his name. He wants to know where the girl is, the one he used to play with in here. They played these kinds of games..." Hannah closed her eyes and clapped her hands, and I couldn't help but think of Loxley.

"Hand-clapping games? He played with one of the Belle children, Loxley."

"He wanted Loxley to do something bad, and she wouldn't play with him anymore," Hannah said. "What is your name?" she asked the boy aloud. "Tell me your name."

I heard nothing, and Hannah frowned. Obviously, she didn't hear anything either. Apparently, this boy wasn't willing to share any information with her. Although sunlight filled the room, it felt clammy and unwelcoming in here. I hadn't noticed that before. A board squeaked near the window. *Must be the house warming up. Boards creak from time to time, Jerica.* I didn't want to be here anymore and wished I hadn't insisted on coming along.

"Stop that," Hannah warned him. "You can't hurt us." She frowned again and turned away from the window where she'd been lingering. "I don't think we can help him. He's not in his right mind. Let's keep moving." Renee looked frightened as she took my hand.

As we stepped outside, Hannah caught her breath. "It feels better out here. Ah, I see a man, a soldier. He has a handsome face and expressive eyes. He's looking for someone. I can't hear him, but I can see him quite well."

"That has to be John Belle. He must be looking for his children, maybe Jeopardy. He tried to protect her, I think, but he was killed in an accident." I couldn't help but blurt it out. If Hannah was a fake, she was a good one. There was no way she could know about Loxley and her hand-clapping games. No way at all.

"John? Are you John Belle? My name is Hannah. This is Jerica and Renee. Why are you still here, John?" Hannah clutched her cheap white purse and stared at the empty hallway. "Where are you going? John? We're here to help."

Then the attic door slammed shut, and Renee and I nearly jumped a foot off the ground.

"I think he wants us to follow him." Hannah's light blue eyes widened as she took off down the hallway to the attic door that led up the short stairs to Jeopardy's castle. "Yes, he definitely wants to show us something."

"What do you think, Jerica?" Renee whispered. "Should we go up there?"

"John wouldn't hurt us. I think it's safe if it's him." I didn't bother telling them about how frightened Harper had been up here, how the Lady in White had nearly scared her and Loxley to death. *Maybe it wasn't her. What if it was the angry boy?*

We followed Hannah up the stairs and into the attic. The place seemed so desolate now even though it was stuffed to the brim with boxes and junk. *Where did all this come from?* I brushed my fingers across the top of a dusty box. Did these things belong to Harper? "Jeopardy's bed was over by the window. She liked to watch the moon before she went to sleep," I said to no one in particular. "Jeopardy loved this room. She called it her castle."

"You have a gift, Jerica. Why have you been holding out? How do the visions come to you? When you're awake or asleep? When did they start?"

I swallowed guiltily. "Asleep, mostly, but I have seen a few things awake too. It used to happen a lot when I was little. I used to dream all the time, but then it stopped. When Marisol...left."

"I hardly ever dream, but I think I would prefer dreams sometimes. Hey, why don't you talk to John? He likes you; I can feel it."

My pulse raced at the thought. "You think I should? I really don't know what to say."

"Try it. What's the worst that can happen?"

I could think of a dozen terrible things that could happen, but I didn't voice them. "JB? Are you here? It was nice meeting you the other day. Do you remember me? I'm Jerica Poole."

I heard a soft whisper, but no words were clear to me. Was I hearing things? Hannah said softly, "He remembers you. Can you hear him?"

I shook my head and said, "Not really." I walked to the window and looked down just as Harper had in my dream the other night. She'd seen Jeopardy with someone. Who had it been? The boy looked a bit like Ray Loper, but she hadn't been sure. "JB, I want to find Jeopardy. I know you tried to protect her. I know you tried to protect them all. Let me help you both. What is it you want me to know?"

Then we heard a strange noise, like scratching. The sound was made by something larger than a rodent. Scratching, clawing. "What is that?" Renee asked breathlessly. Nobody moved for a few minutes. We waited, listening to the scratching, and then it quit. It sounded as if it came from the far wall, near a patch of exposed brickwork. I squatted down and watched in amazement as a small brick tumbled out of the wall. I could see something behind it. I picked up the brick and without thinking poked my fingers in the hole. I couldn't believe it! There was a folded piece of paper in here. No, several papers folded together, like a letter.

I put the brick back in the hole and gazed at Renee and Hannah, who were as amazed as I was. This note belonged to Jeopardy Belle.

Chapter Twenty-One—Jerica

Another shuffling noise surprised me. I ran my hand over another brick and quickly discovered it was loose too. Wiggling it out easily, I found another folded note. Five minutes later, Renee, Hannah and I had recovered five small bundles of paper. As I began to unwrap the first one, I said, "Thank you, JB."

Hannah said quietly, "Wait, I think we should leave now. I am sensing another energy, a young woman, someone different from the woman downstairs. John's presence is waning, and I'm not sure this other one wants us here. In fact, I have a creeping suspicion that she doesn't. Let's leave now. I could use a glass of water anyway."

"Alright." I clutched the bundles protectively as we left Summerleigh. I felt nothing now, nothing except a kind of sad emptiness. Renee breathed a sigh of relief when we stepped outside.

"That whole experience was intense. Thank you, Hannah, and thank you, Jerica, for allowing us inside. I have never experienced anything like that in my life, and I've been to more than a few spooky places."

"You're welcome," I said anxiously. I was ready to get home and read the notes again. It wasn't to be just yet. Jesse was making his way to me. "Hey, what's the word on the roof?" I asked him.

"You called it. It needs to be replaced, and from what I hear from Roger, the other wing needs some serious repair too. What do you have there?"

"Notes, I think. We found them in the attic. They belonged to Jeopardy Belle, I'm sure of it. We're just about to go read them."

Jesse's brown eyes narrowed at hearing my news. "That's incredible. Kind of sorry I missed the investigation now." His phone rang, and he answered it immediately. "Hey, Norm. Yeah, she's right here. You need her?"

He handed the phone to Renee, who frowned at him as if to say, *Couldn't you say I wasn't here?*

"I'm here," she said, walking away from us to take her call. Hannah stared up at the house, her eyes fixed on the nursery window.

"I think at some point you may have to do a cleansing. That boy isn't going to go easily, and he's no less dangerous now than he was in life."

"What boy?" Jesse asked her, giving me a puzzled look.

"I've got to go," Renee said with a sigh. "Norman caught the kitchen on fire, and I've got a mess to tend to. Hannah, if you're riding with me, I'm afraid we'll have to leave now. I've got the fire chief at the diner."

"I'm ready," she said as she tore her gaze from the window. "If you ever need me, Jerica, call me. Don't be afraid to talk to your daughter. She's always near you—just keep her out of Summerleigh."

I couldn't hide my disappointment. I really wanted to ask her more about Marisol, to talk with her at length. "Maybe I could take you home. I don't have anything else to do."

"Yes, you do," she answered cryptically. "But we'll continue this conversation. I promise. We'll talk soon."

Jesse called after Renee, "You need me to tag along?"

"No," she yelled back. "You should probably keep this job at least. I'll call you when I know more."

"Alright," he called back. It was just the two of us now. Even the roofer was leaving.

"Where's he going?"

"I told him to come back after lunch. I have to show you these numbers, and there are a couple of decisions you have to make. We've got to choose a roof color and shingle styles, but I can see you've got other things on your mind."

"Kind of, yes. I'm dying to read these notes. Indulge me a minute or two? I've got some sweet tea in the fridge."

"I'm curious too, and tea sounds great."

Five minutes later, Jesse and I were sitting at my kitchen table carefully unfolding Jeopardy's notes. The ink was a faded blue but not so faded that I couldn't easily read them. Jeopardy's handwriting was slightly slanted except in a few places where the words jumbled with emotion. I began to read the first one, an undated note addressed to her father.

Dear Daddy,

A bluebird sang outside my window today and I threw a rock at him. I couldn't believe it, but I hit that bird. I felt bad when he fell out of the tree dead but not as bad as that bird made me feel singing when you're dead and gone, knowing that I probably killed you by telling you about the Horrible Thing. I am sorry, Daddy. Down to my soul, I am sorry. I wish someone would throw a rock at me!

I buried the bird in a shoe box near your potting shed where you can find him. Maybe you can watch over him, maybe you can bring him back to life and he'll sing for you instead of me. I don't deserve a happy song.

I mean it, Daddy. I wish someone would hit me in the head like that bird. Knock me out cold so I could wake up and be with you every day. I'm not brave enough to do it myself. Carter Hayes' uncle shot himself, but I don't have a gun and I think Momma sold yours. I swim too good to drown. I don't know how I could do it.

But then I worry about what the preacher said and what if dying by your own hand would really send my soul to hell. I would surely never see you again, for you have to be in heaven. Aunt Dot says you are in heaven, all heroes go to heaven, but Loxley says she sees you all the time. I wish I saw you too. I guess you like her more now because she hasn't done any Horrible Things.

I wish I had never told you, I wish I had died instead, Daddy. Maybe Momma's right, I am a Lost Soul.

I need you, Daddy,

Jeopardy Belle

"This is so heartbreaking, Jesse." My hands were shaking as I handed him the note and unfolded another one. "How can she believe that she caused her father's death?"

"Kids think differently. What I want to know is, what's the horrible thing she's talking about? Let's keep reading."

"Okay." I sipped some tea and began to read the second note.

Dear Daddy,

Please come get me, take me where you are! I can't live another day here in Summerleigh. Momma is going to send me to him again, I know she will! And I don't want to go, but she says she will send Harper instead if I don't obey her. What do I do, Daddy?

I thought about something else. What if I killed him so he could never do Horrible Things to anyone again? Wouldn't that be the right thing to do? God would forgive me, I know he would. I have a friend. His name is Troy. You probably remember him...he had the blue spotted hound that used to tear up the garden digging for moles? Well, he's my friend, Daddy, but not my boyfriend even though I know he would like to be. Anyway, he's my friend, and I think he would help me if I told him about the Horrible Thing. He would help me do the deed, but I am afraid. Will I kill him too if I tell him?

Daddy, please answer one of these letters. I have written you so many times, and I don't know what to do. I can't tell Harper or Addison, they'll hate me for sure. Loxley is too little to know about such things. Aunt Dot would never believe me—she always sides with Momma even though Momma hates her too. I don't know what to do. If you don't write me soon or let me see you like Loxley sees you, I will talk to Troy Harvester.

Forgive me, Daddy.

I love you,

Jeopardy Belle

"Troy Harvester? I wonder if she's talking about the old man who owned the tractor supply store in town. He's got to be in his nineties now. I know his granddaughter, Paige. She was part of the Kayla Dickerson benefit I was working with."

"I'm sorry I missed it, but I think I had a heck of a bug." I chewed my fingernail nervously. "I would love to talk to Troy and ask him what he remembers. Hey, come to think of it, how well did you know Ben Hartley?"

"You mean the fellow who used to live here? Not too well, but he was a nice old man. I thought he died a few years ago."

"Well, that's not possible. He's the one who gave me the keys to this place. He came to see Harper the day she died."

"I could be wrong. You know, I might have heard that he moved to the northern part of the state. I'm not sure. You want me to call Paige?"

"Yes. I'll keep reading."

With a nod, Jesse scrolled through his phone and found the number he was looking for. "Hey, Paige? It's me, Jesse. Yeah, I know. Long time no hear from. Renee has kept me busy at the diner." He looked embarrassed but stayed with me. I tried not to be a Nosy Parker. The rest of Jeopardy's letters were much the same as the other two. Whoever this man was, the one who did the "Horrible Things," her mother knew all about it and made every effort to put Jeopardy in his path. I felt sick to my stomach. Who could do such a thing to a child?

"I am working on a story about Jeopardy Belle. I understand your grandfather knew her. I was wondering if my research partner and I could have a few minutes of his time." He waited while she asked.

"Yes, I know it was a long time ago, but it would mean so much. Sure, I'll wait." A minute later, Jesse hung up the phone and said, "Tomorrow at eleven. His place is just outside of town. Anything else in those?"

"Wow, you're good at that. No, and thanks for making that call. I've never been a research partner before," I said with a smile.

"Well, you are now. Or vice versa."

Just then, the roofer pulled into the driveway, and we left the kitchen and Jeopardy's notes to answer his questions. And of course, I had to sign a check. Roger and his crew would come back in the morning to begin working on the roof. I didn't want to go back in the house right now. I needed to work on something, to think about something besides lost Jeopardy and the Horrible Thing she had endured.

"Hey, you want to help me with a small project?"

"Sure, what's that?" Jesse asked curiously.

"I want to clean out the potting shed."

"Okay, Renee will call me when she needs me. Until then, I'm all yours."

I couldn't help but smile at the expression. I wondered what it would be like to be all his...

"It's this way," was my answer. No need to add fuel to a fire that was already burning, at least on my part. It felt good to remember that I was still in the land of the living.

Chapter Twenty-Two—Harper

I expected Momma's fury when I showed her the remnants of her dress, but strangely enough, she didn't blame me at all. She said nothing and gazed up at the ceiling. Jeopardy! Of course she would blame her. But then again, hadn't I? Momma collected the pieces of her dress without a word and left me alone. She didn't offer me another dress, and who could blame her?

"Harper? Why don't you wear the lady's dress? The one from the treasure box in the attic upstairs. I can get it for you if you want me to," Loxley whispered from the doorway.

"That's not my dress, and it wouldn't be right to wear it." Loxley began to cry, and I immediately took her in my arms. "There now, it's not the end of the world. There will be other dances," I lied to her. I never planned on going to another dance again. And if anyone ever nominated me for anything, I would flatly refuse to participate.

"I'm sorry, Harper. I didn't mean it."

"You didn't mean what? What's wrong?"

"Heads up, you two. Aunt Dot is here, and she's got something for you, Harper," Addison's squeaky voice sang happily.

"What do you mean?" I asked Addie.

She leaned against the doorway with her arms crossed. She looked proud of herself, and for the first time in a long time she didn't have pinkeye, a runny nose or a cough. "I called Aunt Dot this morning and told her what Jeopardy did to your dress. She bought you a new dress, a pink one with a little jacket and everything."

"You lie!" I said with a smile.

She crossed her heart as she always did whenever someone accused her of telling a fib. "I never lie. That would send me to the flames. Come see for yourself."

The three of us walked across the Great Room and into the parlor. Aunt Dot was chatting away to Momma, who wasn't saying much. "There she is! Look what we got you!" It was kind of Aunt Dot to pretend that Momma had contributed to this gift. I knew better, but it was a pleasant fiction and I wanted to believe it.

"Oh my goodness! Your hair! Well, we have a few hours to get you fixed up. Try on the dress first. I'm dying to see how it fits."

I couldn't stop smiling as I scurried off to my room and stepped into the satin and tulle dress. I raced down the hall to look in Momma's full-size mirror, and what I saw made me catch my breath. The gown had a sweetheart neckline, and I swear I'd seen one just like it in my magazine. With my head held high, I walked into the parlor and accepted all the compliments. Momma looked mildly pleased as she raised her head from her magazine once or twice, but my sisters were delighted.

After an hour of doctoring my hair and helping me into my stockings and shoes, Aunt Dot clapped her hands at her handiwork. "Now, Cinderella, it's time to head to the ball."

"I'll take her, Dot," Momma said in a dry voice as she stubbed out her cigarette butt in the ashtray. "She's my daughter, after all." My stomach fell, and I couldn't hide my disappointment.

"Oh, I see. Well, alright, but I really didn't mind, Ann. I thought it would be fun."

"No, I think I'll take her. Are you ready, Harper Belle? Where's your jacket? The pink one that Aunt Dot so kindly bought you."

"It's here, Momma."

"Let's go, then. We don't want to be late. Girls, I'll be back soon. Clean up the kitchen. Goodbye, Dot."

"Bye, everyone." Aunt Dot sniffled as she grabbed her hat, gloves and purse and made to leave us. Addison kissed my cheek, but Loxley stayed away as if she were afraid to say goodbye. I walked in a fog, trying to navigate what was happening right now. Later, I would look back and say, *Aha, this is when the warning came*, but at that moment I knew nothing.

"Aunt Dot, you should take her," Jeopardy called from the stairs. Then she headed toward the front door but didn't get too close. She wore her wild hair loose and was dressed like a bohemian, as Momma liked to call her when she wore blue jeans and t-shirts. Tonight she wore a dress and a pair of white high heels she'd borrowed from Momma, no doubt without her permission.

"You have a lot of nerve showing your face tonight, Jeopardy Belle. First, you destroy your sister's dress and now you're trying to ruin her special night? Go to your room!"

The natural smudges under Jeopardy's eyes darkened as they always did when she felt some sort of strong emotion. "You lie! I didn't touch her dress. You probably did it, you mean old..."

"Jeopardy!" Aunt Dot warned her as she scooped up Loxley, who was crying again. "Don't speak to your Momma like that. If you didn't do it, then I believe you, but we don't need to argue and name-call."

"Aunt Dot, don't you let her take Harper anywhere. You have to take her! Please!"

I glanced from her to Momma, unsure what to do—Aunt Dot wasn't sure either. She didn't move, and the five of us stood around the Great Room.

Until we heard the footsteps above us.

I wondered how long we would listen to the sound of heavy footfalls crossing over us. Finally, Momma squinted her eyes at Jeopardy. "You have a boy up there, don't you? Is that who's stomping around upstairs, Jeopardy Belle? That Harvester boy?"

"I ain't got no boy up there, Momma. That's another damn lie!"

Momma's hand flew to Jeopardy's face, and she slapped her hard. Aunt Dot yelled, "Don't hit the girl, Ann!" but it was too late. Jeopardy didn't strike back, just screamed in anger and was gone. She raced through the parlor and then the kitchen. I could hear the screen door slapping behind her.

Momma sagged a little as if it had taken all her energy to slap Jeopardy. "You take her, Dorothy. I'm going to rest a little while. This whole experience has been terrible, just terrible. You see how she treats me! Has any child ever been more disrespectful? She blames me for her father's death, and I just...I don't know..." She began to sob, but nobody moved to help her. Even Aunt Dot didn't try to comfort her.

Aunt Dot whispered to us, "Come on, girls. Let's go." In dramatic fashion, Momma began to weep as she made her way to her favorite parlor chair.

We were in Aunt Dot's car and headed down the road in just a few minutes. That would be the last time I ever saw Jeopardy Belle.

I never even had a chance to say goodbye.

Chapter Twenty-Three—Jerica

"Thank you, Mr. Harvester, for meeting us."

"You're welcome. My granddaughter says you are doing some research about Jeopardy Belle. Do you know how long it's been since I heard anyone say her name? Are you trying to find her?"

"Yes, we would like to find her, Mr. Harvester. I know you cared about her and wanted to help her. I found some notes that she wrote. She mentioned you a few times." I held Jeopardy's faded note in my hand, but he didn't try to take it from me. He didn't say anything at first, but then a sob suddenly escaped his lips.

"Grandpa? Are you okay? Uh, I don't think this is such a good idea. He's been through a lot lately, what with my mother's passing."

"I'm fine. Stop fussing over me like I'm a child, Pat."

She shook her head. "I'm Paige, Grandpa. Pat was my mother."

"You know what I mean. Stop confusing me and make us some coffee, please," he asked her politely in a slightly irritated voice.

She slapped her knees as she got up and said, "Fine. I'll put some coffee on. You guys want some?"

Jesse and I both said yes, and I reminded myself to take my time with this interview. Perhaps I should let the local historian take the lead. I was a nurse and a hobbyist carpenter but certainly no historian. I looked at Jesse as if to say, *You take the lead here.*

"Jerica owns Summerleigh now. Harper left her the house and asked her to continue the search for Jeopardy."

Troy Harvester's eyes were damp with tears, but that news caught his attention. "That's a big place for one person. Do you have a family?"

"Not anymore."

"Oh, I see. I don't have much of one anymore either. Except for Paige. She's a good girl if a little overprotective. Hand me that book there, please." I retrieved the dusty blue vinyl book and handed it to him. He flipped open the photo album and tapped on a black-and-white photo. I recognized Troy's young face beaming back from the picture. "This was my wife, Elise. We went to school together, but I never even noticed her until our senior year. She never held that against me, and she had a way of loving you completely that made you forget everything else. It was a healing kind of love. Elise had a beautiful voice and an infectious laugh I will never forget. I loved her, I truly did. We had a good life together, better than what I deserved."

"Your granddaughter sure seems fond of you," I said with an encouraging smile.

"She is a feisty young lady like her grandmother was when she was her age." He sighed and shook his head. "You two must think I am an old fool talking about love, but I've been thinking about it a lot lately. Even before I heard you were coming."

"No, we don't," Jesse and I said simultaneously. Mr. Harvester leaned back in his worn cloth recliner and nodded at both of us appreciatively.

"I will never forget that whole horrible year. 1942 was the year Jeopardy disappeared. There she was one moment, larger than life, and then gone. Her disappearance sealed the fate of this town. You see what's left of it. Not much. The war took away many fathers and brothers, and what was left...well, we were a broken community. Desire, Mississippi, didn't amount to much after the war. Most families moved to Mobile for work at the shipyards and others to Lucedale for other types of factory work. My father was a railroad man. He didn't serve in the military long because he had an accident that left him with a limp, but he could still work. Now Mr. Belle, Jeopardy's father, he was a nice enough man, but he could never hold down a job. Back in those days, they didn't label veterans with PTSD and the like. There was no medication. Just booze and whatever mischief you could get into. I think Mr. Belle saw too much. He had those empty eyes, like a lot of men did. I could never understand why he couldn't keep a job. Like I said, he was a nice man, but he was not one to stick to anything. When he won Summerleigh in a card game, he must have thought his luck was changing. He loved those girls of his. He died not long before Jeopardy vanished."

Nobody spoke for a while after that. Troy had poured out a lot of information in lightning fashion, and I was on pins and needles. I wanted to know so much, but Mr. Harvester obviously wasn't going to be rushed.

"Mr. Harvester…"

"Call me Troy."

"Troy, the night Jeopardy disappeared, did you know that she had a fight with Mrs. Belle? She mentioned that something horrible happened to her, a Horrible Thing, she called it." I slid the note toward him hoping he would read it. Again, he didn't try to. Troy closed his eyes and whimpered again. I hated that I would be the one to bring him such pain. It had to be painful to remember all this.

"Yes, the Horrible Thing." His eyes flickered open, and he licked his lips. Paige came in and set a tray of cups, spoons and a sugar bowl on the table. She couldn't hide her worried expression, and she didn't stick around. "I remember the first time I knew I loved her. We were at the river, my brothers and I. My oldest brother, Anthony—everyone called him Tony—he liked to ride to the river after church on Sundays. Harry and I didn't want to be left behind. It was a rare thing for a teenage boy to have a car in our small town, and it was nice to be noticed. Tony was a popular boy. The girls were always circling around him...that day was no exception. That particular day he tried putting the moves on one of those Taylor girls, but she wasn't having any of it. I got tired of watching him act stupid.

"Harry and I were in the water when Jeopardy came down the bank. I don't think she noticed me at all. She walked into the water wearing a white dress like she was headed to a baptism. After she waded out about waist deep, she closed her eyes like she was saying a prayer and then sank down in the water until it covered her head. I don't know that anyone else saw her, but I did. Everything stood still as I waited for her to come back up. Do you believe in magic?"

I nodded, and Jesse did too.

"That was some kind of magic. I will never forget the sight of her. I watched and waited, and just when I thought the worst, that she drowned herself in Dog River, she burst out of the water like some kind of siren, slinging her hair behind her. Her hands slid over her face and brushed the water away, and then she stared at me with those sad, hazel eyes and said, 'What exactly are you staring at, Troy Harvester?' I could hardly believe it—she knew my name! From that day to this one, I have loved her with all my heart."

"Oh, Troy, she loved you too," I blurted out. "I know she did."

"In her way, perhaps. Jeopardy Belle was a summer storm, and I was a trusty rock that she battered against when she needed someone, which was rarely. I was so young; I didn't know how to help her. All I knew was I loved her."

I sighed hearing Troy's account of Jeopardy, and then he surprised me by adding, "I saw her that night after she left Summerleigh. I never told anyone that, but I should have. She came to my house and stayed with me. I went to sleep, and when I woke up, she was gone."

"What? You saw Jeopardy that night? I don't remember reading that in the police report," Jesse said. "Are you sure, Troy?"

"Yes, I saw her. No one but me."

Paige reappeared with a pot of coffee, which she placed on the trivet in front of me. Eyeing us suspiciously, she disappeared to the kitchen again. I knew she was listening. I would too if I were her.

"I was already asleep when she tapped on my window. My room was over the garage, but she didn't come up the stairs. She climbed up the wisteria vine like a wild creature. My brothers had gone to the school dance, but I stayed home.

I didn't have the courage to ask Jeopardy to go, and I didn't want to see her dancing with either of my brothers. She liked to kiss Tony on the cheek; I used to think that was because she knew it bothered me. I don't know. Sometime that night, I heard fingers tapping on my window. It was Jeopardy, soaked to the bone. I thought I was dreaming. Imagine seeing the girl you loved with all your might tapping on your window.

"'What are you doing here, Jeopardy Belle?' I asked as I rubbed my eyes to make sure I wasn't dreaming. She didn't answer me, and I held my hand out to her to help her in. I closed the window behind her, raced to the rocking chair for my extra blanket and wrapped it around her.

"'Warm me up, Troy Harvester. I'm so cold,' she said.

"'What are you doing here? Are you alright?' I asked. I pushed her wet hair out of her face. I wondered if she'd had a fall or something; she had a purple bruise on the side of her face.

"'No, nothing is right. Nothing at all, Troy.' She laid her head on my shoulder. I don't know how long we sat there. Then she asked, 'Do you have any food? I am so hungry.'

"I told her I could make her a sandwich and asked if she liked peanut butter. She said yes, so I told her to stay there and dry off. 'Where else am I going to go?' she asked.

"I raced down the stairs and into the main house to make Jeopardy a sandwich. My grandmother was in the front room listening to her radio program. She saw me but didn't think my ransacking the kitchen was strange. My parents were already in their beds, and my brothers wouldn't be home until much later. A few minutes later, I hurried back to my room. I was so worried she would be gone, but she hadn't gone anywhere. During my absence, she'd helped herself to a pair of my jeans and a jersey that was far too big for her. Her wet dress was draped over the back of my desk chair. I stepped inside with the sandwich and brought it to her like her obedient servant.

"'Don't forget the milk,' I instructed her politely. She ate half the sandwich, chugged down the milk and crawled into my bed. I didn't know what to do. I'd never had a girl in my room and certainly not one in my bed. I picked up the plate and glass and put them on my desk.

"Without being asked, I crawled back in my bed and lay on my pillow uneasily. Jeopardy curled up to me with her head on my chest. That was the happiest moment of my life. She smelled like sweat and rain, like cotton and peanut butter. God, I loved her.

"Then she said, 'A Horrible Thing happened to me, Troy, and it's going to happen again. Pray with me. Pray that Daddy comes and takes me away.'

"I said to her, 'Your father is gone, Jeopardy. You can't go with him; that means you'll be dead.'"

I had to ask, "What horrible thing was she talking about, Troy?"

I wasn't sure he heard me because he didn't answer me. He said, "I don't know why, but I suddenly had the courage to tell her how I felt. I was completely unaware of how much she needed me. I just blurted it all out without fear. I told her, 'You know I love you, Jeopardy. I have always loved you. Don't you kiss another boy from this moment on, you hear? You climbed up into my bedroom, and now we're here together. You're my girl, Jeopardy Belle. Promise me we'll always be together.'

"'I promise, Troy Harvester,' she swore as I held her close and she clung even tighter. We didn't do anything beyond that; she didn't need me pawing at her. When I woke up, she had changed her clothes and left my jeans and shirt behind. And I never saw her again. Never, and I waited every night." Troy burst into tears. "She needed me, and I let her down. I knew she was in trouble, and I couldn't help her. Now she's gone!" He covered his eyes with one hand and sobbed as Paige came back.

She said softly, "I'm afraid you'll have to leave. That's enough, please."

"I am so sorry, Troy. Yes, we'll leave, Paige. Thank you."

We walked out of the Harvester home and drove back to the cottage in silence. Jesse and I didn't talk much on the way, and he didn't stick around to chat. He had to meet Renee, something to do with the fire damage.

I politely thanked him for the ride and went inside.

Someone was waiting for me.

Chapter Twenty-Four— Jeopardy Belle

Troy Harvester slept through my kiss. I didn't want to leave him, but I couldn't stay here and bring my misery down upon him. Troy was right—I was his girl. I always had been, but I couldn't tell him anything. He didn't deserve it. When I came to the Harvesters' house, I had every intention of asking Troy for a gun. Just a small gun that I could use one time, and then I'd give it back to him. But then he told me he loved me, and how much he loved me, and all that changed.

I loved Troy Harvester almost as much as I loved Harper and Daddy and Addison and Loxley. Too much to get him into trouble. When I shimmied down the wisteria vine, I had no idea what I would do. All I could do was go back to Summerleigh, maybe sleep in Daddy's potting shed until I could sneak back into the house. When I didn't have to see Momma, when I knew she wouldn't come after me.

She'd hated me all my life, and I didn't know why. I couldn't understand it. For a long time, I did everything right. I said ma'am and please, I made good grades in school, cleaned my room, tended the garden...but it didn't matter. She never saw any of it, so I quit. I quit trying and she noticed me then, but she still didn't love me. Not even a little bit.

What made it worse was she wanted Daddy to hate me too. She wanted everyone to hate me. I think most everyone did, but I didn't care. Daddy loved me until the day he died. He told me he did; he promised he did even when I told him about the Horrible Thing.

He was so mad, but not at me, he said. "You're my daughter, Jeopardy Belle. You always will be. I'll make this right. I'll take care of this, Jeopardy."

"I'm sorry, Daddy. I didn't mean for any of this to happen."

"You don't have a thing to be sorry about." He held me as I cried out my heart and soul. I remembered how strong he felt. He kissed the top of my head and told me to wait for him. "I'll be back soon."

"Okay, Daddy."

But he never came back, except as a ghost.

No, I wasn't sure what I would do when I began walking down Hurlette Drive, down to Summerleigh, but then I saw a white rock in the road. I remembered the bird I'd killed accidentally. Maybe if I hit Grandpa Daughdrill with a rock, he would die too. I picked up the rock and put it in my purse. Yes, that's what I would do. I would hit him, once, twice, maybe three times if need be. And then everyone would know what a Horrible Man he was and what Horrible Things he did to me.

I was almost home now. The sun would be coming up soon. And then I saw the lights coming down the road. Those were the lights of a Master DeLuxe. Grandpa Daughdrill had one, and so did Momma. They bought them together, and I think Grandpa gave her the gift in exchange for me. He never told me that, but he promised me many things and he always gave me money afterward. I hadn't spent any of it, except to buy cigarettes.

How strange that I wasn't allowed to call him Grandpa until after the Horrible Thing. "None of your sisters can call me that. Only you, sweet Jeopardy. My special girl. Just like your Momma. She was always my favorite, like you."

I cried as he told me these Horrible Secrets. And then he pawed at me and I floated away and thought about swimming in the river until it was over. And now he was coming again. That had to be him. I dug my hand in my purse and held the rock.

My grandfather pulled up beside me and rolled down the window. "Get in the car, girl. Your mother is worried about you. What do you mean running out of the house like that?" I didn't answer him but obediently got into his car. I started to get in the front seat, but he shook his head and clucked his tongue. "No, you ride in the back seat. I am afraid you'll have to be punished, Jeopardy."

"I haven't done anything wrong," I said with my hand still on the rock. Panic rose in me. I didn't want this! Why had I gotten in his car? I couldn't have run from him; he was too tall and big and strong. I started to cry, and he began to scold me and threaten me. Suddenly, I took the rock and banged it against the window and glass shattered everywhere. I was getting out of this car one way or another.

He swore at me and the car stopped. I reached my hand outside and opened the door. I tumbled out but not fast enough; Grandpa Daughdrill was grabbing me off the ground, and I started to scream. His hand clasped my mouth, and I kicked and punched him. I'd lost my rock but managed to grab it again before he carried me off into the woods behind Summerleigh.

"No! You won't touch me again!" I screamed behind his hand. I even bit it. He snatched his hand away because of the pain, and I screamed at the top of my lungs, "Daddy! Help me!" I hit Grandpa Daughdrill in the head with my rock, and he hit the ground.

But he didn't stay down. He got back up, and I began to cry as he staggered on his feet. "You little bitch! You'll pay for that. I'm done with you, Jeopardy Belle. It's time to find a new favorite!" He hit me like a man and knocked me out. When I woke up, I was bound and gagged and in a sack. I must be in the trunk of his car. I heard a woman's voice too. Was that Momma? I kicked around in the trunk of the Master DeLuxe and screamed through the gag. Nobody could hear me, but I had to try.

Finally, when I grew tired, I heard the voices again, outside the trunk now. "It was an accident, Ann. She went wild, there was no reasoning with her. I think she was drunk, or something. She fell and hit her head. She's dead."

"No, that can't be right. She can't be dead. I never meant for her to die. Father, how could you do this?"

"Now, now, Ann. You know your father would never do anything to hurt you or Jeopardy. Trust me. I'll take care of her body, but you have to keep quiet, no matter what."

"Okay, Father. I will let you handle it."

"Good girl, Ann. Now go home. Go home and take care of your girls. Jeopardy is mine."

I twisted and kicked in the bag, but nobody heard me. Then the trunk opened, and light filtered through the rough burlap bag I was in. Grandpa Daughdrill picked me up and took me somewhere. Where? I could smell pine and rain. I kicked, but he said, "Shh...it's too late now. You are a great disappointment to me. I have something to tell you, Jeopardy. You aren't a Belle at all. You're my daughter. All mine. That man, John Jeffrey Belle, he was nothing to you. I was your father, all the time. I wanted you to know that before you die."

I cried and screamed but couldn't talk. My mind screamed at him, railing against him, but then I heard the gun cock and I knew what was about to happen. My prayers had been answered. I was about to die, and it wouldn't be by my own hand. Grandpa thought he was punishing me, but he was really setting me free. I would be free to be with Daddy. My own Daddy!

I didn't hear the gunshot. Suddenly, I wasn't in the bag but standing beside it, watching Grandpa's grim face. He picked up the bloody sack, tied rocks to it with ropes and carried me out into my precious Dog River and sank me beneath a log.

I didn't feel sadness. I felt free, and I wanted to go home now. Home to Daddy. I walked along the road, and nobody saw me. I walked up to the door at Summerleigh, but I could not get in. The door wouldn't open! I walked around to the back door too but couldn't get in there either.

A little boy was in there, an angry boy. He told me my Daddy was here at Summerleigh, but he was his Daddy now. He wanted me to go away. He was strong, so strong that he could keep me out forever. And he said with an evil smile that Momma would die soon too, and he would make sure she would never let me in. He laughed at me, and I walked toward the potting shed. I turned back once and saw my Daddy upstairs. He couldn't come to me, and I couldn't go to him.

I didn't think dead people cried, but I did. I cried because even after everything, I couldn't be with Daddy.

We would be apart forever.

***

I woke up immediately and called Jesse. It was after eleven o'clock, but who else could I tell? "Hey, Jesse. I had a dream. I saw Jeopardy Belle...I know who killed her. I know where she is."

"I'm on the way."

Five hours later, the George County Sheriff Department was searching for her body. It took them only four hours to find her. I cried the whole time. Jesse held me, and I didn't care that I hardly knew him. He was here and I needed him, just like Jeopardy needed Troy.

When it was over with, we went home and Jesse persuaded me to eat by whipping up his famed Double Slam. I didn't eat much, but it was nice to have someone care for me. I needed it.

I walked outside after supper and stared up at the attic window. "I wonder if he's there right now, just watching and waiting for Jeopardy."

"She's not far. She's in the potting shed."

"We have to bring them together, Jesse. We have to!"

"I'll call Hannah and Renee. Let's bring them in, and they can tell us how to do it."

"Okay, sounds good to me."

Jesse hugged me, and I loved every second of it. "You're amazing, Jerica Poole. You found her even when everyone else had failed. You did it."

"I think it was just time, and Harper helped a lot. All I had to do was put the pieces together."

"So, is your work done here?"

"No, we're just getting started. There are two other ghosts at Summerleigh. They deserve to be at peace. All we have to do is…"

"I know, put the pieces together. Do you do this all the time, Jerica?"

"No, I'm a nurse. Not a psychic or anything else."

"You're a mom and a sensitive, I'd say. Are you sure you aren't a cook too? We could use a hand at the diner," he said with a wink.

"Definitely not," I replied with a laugh. "One more thing, Jesse Clarke. I like you."

"I like you too, Jerica. I'm hoping to get to know you better."

I liked hearing that. I smiled and said, "Well then, stick around. We're just getting started."

Epilogue—Jerica

"Now, Jerica. Tell her what you know," Hannah said as she held my hand firmly. "We have to reveal her secret or she'll never leave."

"Ann Belle, I know—no, we know—what you did. I know what you did to Jeopardy." The dusty red velvet couch shifted a few inches. "Did you see that?"

"Don't let her scare you. Stand your ground, Jerica. This is the only way Jeopardy and John will ever be reunited. Ann has to move on," Renee said in a soft voice. I glanced at Jesse, who watched me protectively. At least I wasn't doing this by myself.

"Okay," I said as I held hands with Renee and Hannah even tighter. "I'm sorry for what was done to you, I am sorry your own father was such a horrible man. I know what he did, but what you're doing isn't right." The couch bumped again, and I heard footsteps upstairs; they sounded like heavy boots. Hannah looked troubled, but I pretended not to notice. I kept talking. I had to get through to Ann. She had to let Jeopardy come home!

"Ann, you can't change what you did in life, but you can change what you're doing right now!"

The front door flew open, and an evil wind blew in blasts of wet leaves. "Keep going," Hannah encouraged me.

"Ann, the secret is out. All the secrets. You can't hide them anymore!" The chandelier above us began to sway, and the footsteps upstairs sounded louder and close. Were they coming down the stairs?

"You can't hide it anymore! We know the truth!" Tears streamed down my face now. Images of Marisol flashed through my head. My baby's smiling face as I stuck my tongue out at her in the rearview mirror that moment before the crash. Her cries for me when the truck struck us, the absolute silence when the train hit us. My own Horrible Thing.

"I know the truth, Ann. You can't always protect your children, even though you want to more than anything." The door slammed shut, and the leaves fell around us. I closed my eyes, determined to stay focused. "But you can't blame Jeopardy for what happened to you. I know if she could, she would forgive you, Ann. She would forgive you with all her heart."

And suddenly everything stopped.

"She's gone. You did it, Jerica. Ann is gone."

I opened my eyes again, and everyone except Jesse was crying; he was staring at something over my shoulder. "Holy heck! That's John," he said.

We all looked at the staircase, and sure enough, an apparition appeared. It was solid for a few seconds, then it faded, but I could still see him standing there waiting for something. No, someone.

The front door of Summerleigh opened slowly. No more wind, no more leaves and swaying chandelier. Everything was calm now. I didn't see her, but I could feel her.

Jeopardy Belle was home! A warm breeze pushed past us, and my hair fluttered as the breeze blew up the stairs. The strips of wallpaper fluttered with her passing. They were together now, Jeopardy and her Daddy. The place felt lighter, and it was easier to breathe.

They would always be together.

The Ghost of Jeopardy Belle

Book Two

Ghosts of Summerleigh Series

By M.L. Bullock

Text copyright © 2018 Monica L. Bullock

All rights reserved

Dedication

To all the broken ones.

The lady sleeps! Oh, may her sleep,
Which is enduring, so be deep!
Heaven have her in its sacred keep!
This chamber changed for one more holy,
This bed for one more melancholy,
I pray to God that she may lie
Forever with unopened eye,
While the pale sheeted ghosts go by!

Excerpt from *The Sleeper*

Edgar Allan Poe, 1831

Prologue—Harper Belle

Desire, Mississippi
October 1942

"Momma, Loxley is talking to her ghosts again," Addison announced sourly. The three of us girls were in the parlor reading the magazines that Mrs. Hendrickson gave me after her granddaughter left them behind when she returned to Mobile, but Addie was in a bad mood. Mostly because Loxley refused to move out of her current spot on the couch. Their bickering frustrated me. I wanted to finish this article about dreamy Frank Sinatra. I loved all his songs, especially Stardust, and I thought it might be a hoot to start a fan club right here in Desire. Other girls liked him too, but only I knew all his songs by heart. Whenever one of Sinatra's songs came on the radio, I sang it with all my might. I'd been saving up to buy a few of his records, maybe a whole album, but my record player would need a new needle soon. Aunt Dot gave me her RCA Victor because she bought herself a Wellington record player and radio for her birthday. It played three speeds and had a shiny wooden case. That was the last time I'd seen Aunt Dot, weeks ago. I missed her.

"Addison, stop," I warned her again in a whisper. My sister rubbed her nose with a hankie, but it didn't do much good. Her nose ran perpetually nowadays. Probably because it had rained for a whole week straight. Any kind of mold made her sick, and there were plenty of moldy spots in the old plantation we called home. Although I felt sympathy for her, I wished she would heed my warning. Instead, it appeared that her ill mood and Loxley's mischievousness would put us all in harm's way.

"No, I wasn't, Momma," Loxley called out innocently. "I was talking to Lenny, my pet."

"You girls keep quiet in there," Miss Augustine barked at us as she and Momma continued their gossiping and gin drinking and card playing at the kitchen table. I peeked around the corner from my spot on the floor. No, Momma wasn't moving, and she looked terrible today. Ever since Jeopardy's disappearance, something about her seemed wrong. Ann Marie Belle had always been a proud, pretty woman, beautiful like a model. Not anymore. She wore too much makeup, so much that it bordered on clownish, and she often had lipstick on her teeth. Her blond hair showed dark roots, and today she was still wearing her robe and pajamas. That was unheard of around here. Momma had always been the first one up in the morning and always dressed to the nines like a proper lady, especially on Sundays. But we didn't go to church anymore, and no one from First Baptist came to visit us. It was as if we were living on an island here at Summerleigh.

"Want to see my pet, Addison? I'll show you he's real." Loxley hopped off the loveseat but didn't budge from in front of it. With a perfectly innocent smile, she held out a pocket of her pinafore and offered Addison a peek inside.

Addie rubbed her nose again and waved her away. Her pale face crumpled miserably, and although she spent much of her time in bed, I thought perhaps she really needed to go for a lie-down. "Take your pet outside and give me my spot back, Loxley."

Loxley poked out her bottom lip and stomped her foot. "It's not your spot. I don't see your name on it. Isn't that right, Harper?" I didn't offer her any help. She was only making matters worse. I flipped the page of the magazine and tried to ignore them both. "Don't you want to see Lenny, Addison?"

Before Addison could reply, a green tree frog with big red eyes hopped out of Loxley's pocket and onto Addison's shoe. Addie screamed, and before I knew what was happening Momma stormed into the room with Miss Augustine in tow. Momma grabbed me first, picking me up by my hair, uncaring that I had nothing to do with the hoopla. Miss Augustine scolded her, "Now, Ann. Calm down. Remember what the doctor said about your nerves." But Momma didn't listen. She swung at my behind with her free hand, striking me not once but three times before she let me go. I yelped in surprise and pain while my sisters scrambled up the stairs.

"I told you to keep those girls quiet! Why don't you ever listen to me, Harper? You never listen!"

"I'm sorry, Momma. I'm sorry!" I yelled back, shocked at her violent attack. Miss Augustine stepped back and watched us from the doorway as if she too were afraid of Momma. Momma stomped toward me while I tried to back away. It was no use. There was no sense in fighting her, and I couldn't bring myself to raise a hand back. I closed my eyes and waited for the blow, thinking she'd slap me across the face. She liked doing that when I spoke an ill word to her. Or what she considered an ill word. A knock on the door put a stop to her intentions, and she squeezed my arm one good time before releasing me and tidying her robe. Without waiting to see who had arrived, I raced up the stairs to hide. The creaking floors moaned at my steps, but that did not slow me down. It was at that moment I decided Jeopardy's castle would become my castle, at least until she came home.

I ran up the attic stairs and closed the door behind me, tears streaming down my face. I didn't know where Addison was, but Loxley sat on Jeopardy's pallet crying for all she was worth. Her pretty face was streaked with dirty tears; her usually tidy braids were sagging in the heat of the attic.

"I'm sorry, Harper. I didn't know Lenny would jump out. He's never done that before. He's a good frog. Honest he is." I collapsed on the pallet and covered my face with my hands. My broken heart weighed heavy in my chest like a ton of lead. Even though she was the baby of the family,

Loxley held me as I cried. After a few minutes of stroking my hair, she said, "I'm sorry, Harper. Really, I am. Did she hurt you real bad?" Her eyes were fearful and full of tears.

For her sake, I lied, "Not too bad." I sat up now and did what older sisters were supposed to do. I comforted Loxley, and we held one another a few minutes. "Loxley, tell me the truth. Do you ever see Jeopardy? I have to know. Is Jeopardy here...is she a ghost?"

Loxley slowly shook her head. "I never see Jeopardy, but I look for her, Harper. Honest, I have tried. Daddy comes sometimes, but he doesn't talk to me. I can see his mouth moving, but I can't hear him. He looks sad now. And he doesn't smile anymore."

"Is he...does he look like he always did?" *He's not bloody, is he? Tell me he doesn't look like a bloody fiend.*

"Yes, he looks the same." She wrinkled her neat blond brows and said, "But he's not the only one here."

"The lady ghost? Do you see her?"

"Not much, but the other night I heard tapping on my window." She tapped at the air. "It was real soft, like how Jeopardy used to tap on your window when she wanted to come inside. But when I got up to look for Jeopardy, it was just the boy, the mean one who comes around sometimes. He used to stay upstairs, but now he goes all over the place, even outside. He has black eyes, Harper, and he scares me. He scratches me sometimes."

I didn't have any sisterly advice, so I just nodded thoughtfully, and suddenly her eyes brimmed with tears again. "He...he made me cut up your dress, Harper. I'm so sorry. He said I had to do it or something horrible would happen to you. He gave me the scissors."

Stunned at her confession, I held her and said nothing else. All this time, I had believed that Jeopardy had destroyed the dress Momma had let me borrow for the Harvest Dance. I believed that Jeopardy wanted to hurt me, and she'd been innocent the whole time. Loxley and I both gasped as the attic door creaked open, but it was only Addison who stepped inside. I waved at her to join us on the pallet.

She didn't say, "I'm sorry." Addison rarely apologized, but just her being here was proof of her repentance. I held her too, and the three of us sobbed together until we were all cried out. I opened the window to cool the room, and soon my sisters and I fell asleep. No one came to look for us. Not like the day Aunt Dot came to tell us that Daddy had died. I shuddered to think of him bleeding out pinned inside his old truck. Momma didn't like coming up here, not since that ghost pushed her down the stairs. And I knew it was a ghost because I'd seen her with my own two eyes. The door hung open for a while and didn't move again. But just as I closed my eyes, I saw the door open wider.

"Jeopardy?" I asked as sleep took me under. It was then that I saw him. I hovered between sleep and wakefulness, and I was unable to move or speak. I couldn't cry out or warn my sisters. It was as if I were paralyzed. At first, I saw a black form—blacker than a crow's wing, blacker than the darkness that enveloped the attic. But then the blackness became something else. It was a gray mist and had a shape, a boy's shape. And now, by some strange magic, I could see him clear as day.

He stared at me with perfect hatred, and then a black smile crossed his face.

Chapter One—Jerica Poole

Present Day

Sawdust floated in the sunlight that shone through the new parlor windows. The roof repairs were finally finished, but I was a long way from completing Summerleigh's restoration. The combined scents of fresh paint and new wood thrilled my soul, and I pretended that the progress made the Belle home feel lighter. Happier. But I knew I was only fooling myself. Despite the activity, the constant stream of people coming in and out of the old plantation, I couldn't shake the feeling that we weren't alone here...and we weren't wanted. I couldn't understand it. Jeopardy and John Jeffrey Belle were together now. Together and free from the sins of the past. Why would they linger at Summerleigh?

And now Ben Hartley was standing in the Great Room, and he wasn't happy. "Please, Jerica. Please reconsider what you're doing. You have done enough here. Harper never expected you to do all this. She wanted you to bring Jeopardy home, and you did that. Take what's left of the money—she wanted you to have it—take it and go home."

I couldn't believe what I was hearing. I wiped the sweat from my brow and tugged off my gloves, shoving them in my back pocket. "I don't understand, Ben. I thought you would want this. You love Summerleigh...I know you do."

"I loved Harper, Jerica. Not this place. I never loved this place," he confessed as he cast his eyes around the room and then at the ceiling. Yes, I heard the footsteps too, but it was only Jesse checking out the floors on the second level.

"Is it the money, Ben? I'm staying on budget, and there's plenty left to complete the repairs."

"It's not that. You can do what you want with the money, as that was Harper's wish. But what happens after you finish all this? Do you plan to stay here at Summerleigh? Raise a family? What are your intentions?"

Before I could respond, Jesse walked through the front door with his new helper, Emanuel, trailing behind him. If Jesse wasn't upstairs walking around, who was? I gulped as Ben stared back at me, obviously hoping for an answer.

Get a grip, Jerica Poole. There are people all over the place in here today.

"I'll be honest, Ben. I don't have an end game, but I need to do this." I waved my hands at the construction happening around us. "I want to honor Harper's generosity, leave a legacy in her name. And I don't want the Belle girls to be forgotten, not Harper and not Jeopardy. None of them. They deserve better than that."

Ben shook his head sadly and sighed. He clutched his old-fashioned hat in his hand and flinched at the sound of the nail gun going off in the other room.

"Come in the kitchen. You have to see what we've accomplished." I hoped showing him our progress would appease him or at least make him happier. I hated seeing him upset. Ben had been Harper's friend, and I cared about him. I didn't quite understand their relationship and was certainly curious about it, but I wasn't one to pry. "The original Wedgewood stove couldn't be saved, but Jesse helped me find this replacement. It's modern but looks close to the original; it's gas, but the connectors won't corrode. I didn't want a bunch of chrome in here, so I went with the original white enamel for the stove and refrigerator. Pretty neat, huh?"

I lived in Ben's old home now, the former caretaker's cottage, and I knew he loved vintage kitchens. When I moved into the cottage, I'd been amazed at the neat metal cabinets and mid-century modern table and chairs.

"Yes, it's all very nice. I should go now. Thank you for your time. If you don't mind, I'd like to go for a walk in the garden and maybe visit Jeopardy's new memorial stone before I head back to the hotel. I'm leaving for Jackson in the morning."

I didn't want to cause him more hurt, but I didn't understand his sadness. "Of course, Ben. You're always welcome here."

He opened the door and paused. "Goodbye, Jerica," he said. "I wish you the best of luck."

Why did that sound so foreboding?

"Bye, Ben." Then I had an idea. "Why don't you stop by the cottage before you leave? It's almost four o'clock, and we'll all be knocking off for the weekend in a few minutes. I've got to pay everyone, but maybe we could talk after?"

Without looking back, he said, "We'll see," and then he closed the door behind him and left me standing in the newly renovated kitchen by myself. That sounded exactly like something my father would have said—and it always meant no.

"Okay," I called to him through the closed door. I was mystified by the entire exchange.

"Am I interrupting anything?" Jesse's deep voice surprised me, and I smiled as I spun around to face him. Jesse Clarke was a handsome man, that was for sure. In the three months I'd been here, we'd become close. We were nothing more than good friends, although there was always the temptation for more, at least on my part. Of course, twenty-six-year-old Jerica was much more careful than the Jerica who had gotten married right out of high school.

Jesse had proven to be a skilled carpenter, and I was glad to have his help with Summerleigh. I'd yet to see his boat—or more precisely, the hull of his boat, as he described it—but he'd asked me to join him for a bite to eat tonight. He wanted to try out some new steakhouse on Highway 98. I tried not to think of the dinner as a date; we'd eaten lunch together a few times, but we'd always talked about some project related to the house, so I'd never considered those dates.

"No. Just talking to myself. Ben just left, and he didn't seem happy with my decision to stay at Summerleigh."

"He told you not to stay?"

"He thinks I should leave. I get the feeling that he thinks I'm doomed if I stay," I replied with another nervous laugh. "Am I missing something?"

Jesse leaned over the shiny new farmhouse sink and stared out the window. "I'll talk to him. Which way did he go?"

"He said he was going to visit Jeopardy's memorial, take a walk in the garden. He's acting pretty strange."

"Huh, he must have been moving pretty fast because I don't see him now. Well, that's Ben for you, Jerica. Don't take any of what he says to heart. He's probably like a lot of people; he thinks the place is...unlucky."

"You started to say cursed, didn't you?" I shuffled my feet and shoved my hands in my blue jean pockets. "Is Summerleigh cursed?" Again I felt the sensation that someone was standing behind me, but I didn't turn around.

"No. I don't believe in curses, and neither should you."

"I know you believe in ghosts. We didn't dream that up."

"No, we didn't. Ree-Ree is my cousin, remember? So of course I believe in the supernatural. But like I said, I wouldn't put much stock in anything Ben said. He's an unhappy old man. Summerleigh is just a place, a dot on a map. Like any old house, it has seen its share of tragedy. What you're doing here is a good thing, Jerica. I'm happy to be a part of it. It's been a dream come true for me. I've always loved this place, and working in here, seeing it come back to life...I can't tell you how lucky I feel to be a part of it."

I smiled at hearing his words, but his confession also worried me. What if Jesse's affection for me wasn't really for me? What if it was because he loved this house so much? *God, what are you doing, Jerica? Stop overthinking it.* He was right. I was letting Ben's moodiness affect me, and I really shouldn't. Things had been going so well. I got word that my ex-husband was right where he needed to be, in jail, and my friend Anita was planning to drive down and visit me for Christmas.

"What do you know about Ben and Harper? I mean, what's their connection? I get the feeling that for Ben, she was the one that got away. Am I right?"

He smiled slyly. "I'll tell you all about it tonight. Pick you up at seven?"

"Sure, you can pick me up, but wouldn't you rather I just meet you there? I would hate for you to come all this way when you live so close to the restaurant," I said as I locked the back door.

"I'm not sure how the dating scene is in Virginia, Jerica Poole, but here in Mississippi it is customary for a gentleman to pick up a lady," he replied with a playful wink.

"Oh, it's a date-date," I said softly as my stomach flip-flopped from either nerves or excitement.

Jesse leaned back against the sink and crossed his arms. That was his move when he was unsure about something like my choice of stain or my idea for the new spindles on the staircase. "If you think it's better that we don't call it a date, I'll understand. Or if you want to cancel, I'll understand that too."

By the tone of his voice, I knew neither was true at all. And I didn't want to cancel. "I'm not canceling anything, Jesse Clarke. I'll be ready at seven o'clock, but I'd better go pay the guys. Will you make sure nobody is left upstairs? I thought I heard someone stomping around up there earlier."

"Sure, I'll do a walk-through, pack up the equipment and lock up the place."

"Great," I said with an awkward smile. "I'll see you later."

I tried not to skip out of the kitchen like a silly teenager.

Chapter Two—Jerica

Ben never arrived at the cottage; I hadn't really expected him to, but I worried about him nonetheless. I didn't see any extra cars in my driveway, but Summerleigh was a big place. At least there were a lot of woods around here to hide a vehicle. I walked to Jeopardy's monument between Summerleigh and the cottage but didn't see Ben anywhere. Not on the bench under the oak tree and not strolling the graveled walkways. I'd replaced the previous obscure marker with something more appropriate. The new monument read, "Jeopardy Belle, Beloved Daughter of John Jeffrey Belle. Together Always." Rumor had it that Ann Belle had placed the former stone there in memory of her lost daughter, but I couldn't be sure. I believed the ghost of Jeopardy Belle visited here from time to time, though her body now rested next to her sisters. Once in a while, I thought I heard her young, raspy voice, a voice I would know almost as well as my own or Marisol's. But I never saw her.

After walking to the potting shed and down the path a bit, I decided that Ben had most certainly left, and I hurried back to my cottage to get ready for my first official date with Jesse Clarke.

Me? Dating again? I couldn't believe it. While my hair dried, I ransacked my closet for something appropriate. Should I stick with blue jeans or wear a dress? I settled on the latter. I'd bought a few dresses from a boutique in Lucedale, and now I had the chance to take one off the hanger. The dress was made of a soft material, mossy green with a scoop neck and cap sleeves. I had strong arms, and after all the work we'd been doing, I was proud of how toned they looked.

The phone downstairs rang, which was so rare that I had to think about what it was I was hearing. I hurried downstairs to answer it. "Hello?"

"Hello, Jerica? This is Hannah Ray. Do you remember me?" Of course I remembered Renee's friend, the psychic who helped us connect with Ann and John Jeffrey Belle. During the process of helping find justice for Jeopardy Belle, I discovered that my daughter was close by. In fact, it was Hannah who let me know that Marisol lingered near me often and listened to me whenever I spoke to her. After setting things right for Harper, contacting Marisol was all I could think about. Talking to my baby again seemed like a dream come true, but the past few months I had dragged my heels about contacting Hannah. Renee had brought her up to me once or twice, but I hesitated. I guessed a part of me was afraid that if I did communicate with Marisol, she would leave me forever. Didn't I want her to be at peace and happy? Yes, but I had to admit that I was selfish enough to want to keep Marisol close to me. Yes, I could admit that, even if only to myself.

"Of course, Hannah. Glad to hear from you. I've been meaning to call you, but…"

"Jerica, I have to warn you," she blurted out. "There's a shifting occurring at Summerleigh. I can feel it, and I'm hearing disturbing things, to put it bluntly. Very disturbing. Have you been experiencing any activity there?"

"I haven't seen any ghosts, if that's what you're asking. I think Jeopardy and John Jeffrey Belle are at peace now, Hannah. You said it yourself. I haven't seen any sign of them."

"It's not about the Belles..." Her voice crackled on the phone.

"What? I can't hear you, Hannah. Are you on your cell phone?"

"It's really important that you listen to me, Jer... I don't know what's causing this disturbance, the renovations or something else, but things are stirred up. Spiritual things. I am concerned that—"

And then the phone went dead.

I stared at the receiver of the old-fashioned Princess phone and clicked the button up and down, but there was no sound. Not even a dial tone. I hung the phone up and picked it up again, but still nothing. The knock at the door pulled me away from the strangeness of the moment. It was Jesse. I recognized his knock. He always knocked three times, and it was always a firm, confident knock. Strange that I would know that.

Opening the door with a forced smile, I said, "Hey, Jesse. Come in. I was just on the phone with Hannah, but the line died. Give me just a second." I picked up the phone again and this time got a dial tone. Whatever happened, the phone company had apparently corrected it quickly. I flipped through the little phone book next to the phone, searching for Hannah's number, and dialed her back. She quickly answered.

"Jerica, thank goodness. I was just about to drive over there. I thought...never mind. Do me a favor, stay out of Summerleigh tonight. Don't go in until I get there."

I turned my back to Jesse to hide my growing apprehension. "I'm not going to be here, Hannah. I have a date with Jesse. Is there something I should know about? What's going on? Tell me plainly, please."

"I will, but I have the feeling that I need to talk to you face-to-face. Are you gonna be home later tonight, or should I come in the morning?"

"Morning works for me. How about around nine o'clock? Come to my place, the caretaker's cottage."

"Sounds great, but remember what I told you. Please, stay out of the house tonight."

"Okay." She hung up the phone, and I put the receiver down.

"What's up?"

I turned to face him and forced another smile, despite the fact that the hair on my arms stood up a mile high. It was then that I noticed he was carrying a bouquet of wildflowers, which were my absolute favorite. "Hey, are those for me?"

He gave me a curious look. I knew he wanted to know about my phone call, but I wasn't going to go there. I'd already set our date off on the wrong foot by running back to the phone to call Hannah. Why make it worse?

"Nope. I found them outside."

"Are you for real?"

"Of course not. I bought them for you. Unless you don't want them. I guess I could give them to someone else."

"You wouldn't dare," I said as I grinned back at him. And then I asked playfully, "How is it that you, master carpenter and five-star hash slinger, are still single? Is it because you like to play guitar on your first date?"

"I see my cousin has been bragging about my musical skills. I'm not the best guitar player in George County, but I enjoy playing even if I do hit a wrong note every now and then."

I laughed, happy to think about something besides that phone call. "I'm sure Renee's exaggerating. I bet you are a stellar performer." I accepted the flowers and went to put them in the sink, but Jesse caught my hand and gently pulled me back.

"I might be rushing this, but I've been thinking about it all day. Hell, I've been thinking about it for months. I'd like to kiss you, Jerica." He was so close to me I could smell his skin. It smelled clean and had a touch of cedar to it. His hand was warm in mine, and he looked a sight in his gray dress pants and charcoal gray dress shirt.

Clutching the flowers, I looked up at him. "What have you been thinking about?" I asked as I stepped a little closer to him. There were only a few inches between us now.

In a husky voice, he pulled me closer and whispered, "This." And then his soft lips were on mine. It wasn't quite a chaste kiss, but he didn't push himself on me. It was sweet and warm and a kiss that I would probably be thinking about long after this night was over.

Without moving away, I bowed my head a little. I just couldn't meet his eyes yet. I didn't want him to see how much I enjoyed it. "I have to admit I've thought about it too."

He asked even more softly, "Should we do it again?"

"If we do it again, I'm not sure we will actually make it to dinner. And I think... I think..." And then I caught a glimmer of light out of the corner of my eye. "What is that?" I pulled away from Jesse and walked to the window. The light flashed through the window again, but it wasn't coming from my house or the yard.

The light was low and steady now. And it was coming from the attic of Summerleigh.

Chapter Three—Jerica

"You did the walk-through, right? There weren't any lights on when you left, were there?" I asked Jesse, keeping my eyes on the light that was pulsating in the attic. The colors changed subtly, first white, then blue, and then the light took on a strange purple hue and turned white again. It was almost as if some disco ball spun around up there.

A weird, otherworldly disco ball.

"Yeah, like I always do." He was beside me now, both of us staring at the attic window. "I'd better go check that out. It's possible that I missed one, but I don't know what the hell could make that kind of light. Maybe one of the guys is having a joke on us, but I'm pretty sure I would've seen any light when I pulled up. Might be that we have an intruder."

Or it might be something else. No way was that a burglar. Then I remembered Hannah's admonition. *Stay out of the house tonight.* Jesse walked to the front door as if he had every intention of going up there this very minute to see who might be plundering around in the attic.

"Wait. When Hannah called, she warned me that there was a strange energy at Summerleigh tonight. She warned me not to go inside. She's coming over tomorrow to talk to me about what she knows."

"What? What do you mean she warned you?"

"That was her on the phone when you came in. She wanted me to stay out of the house until she could go with me. There's something happening, Jesse. She was pretty adamant that I stay out of there." I chewed my bottom lip and twisted a strand of hair around my finger as I talked.

"I would never call Hannah a thief or a criminal, but it seems awful convenient that she would ask you to stay out of the house and now we see a strange light in the attic. If you don't want to go inside, that's okay, but I should go check it out. I mean, I am the general contractor on this job."

Was he pulling rank on me? I was never going to go for that. "If you go, I go." I grabbed my keys and turned off the lights. "It's probably just some..." No. I had no explanation for it. "I don't know." I really didn't know, but I was about to break my promise to Hannah. I locked the caretaker's cottage, and we walked past Jesse's truck down the gravel path to the back door of Summerleigh. Walking into the house through this door always felt like an intrusion, but the front porch still needed some work in a few places. So for safety's sake, this was the best option.

Before Jesse could take out his key, I put mine in the lock and turned it. The new lock was silent as the grave, and the new door didn't squeak or make a sound. Without turning on any lights, we eased the door shut and hurried through the kitchen and into the parlor. I held Jesse's hand as we waited to hear evidence of an intruder. We didn't have long to wait. Footsteps raced up the second-floor stairs, and I could hear someone running down the hall.

Those weren't the footsteps of a man or woman. Those were the footsteps of a child. We paused at the bottom of the stairs.

"Why don't you stay down here?" Jesse suggested. "Just in case."

"In case what? If there's really someone here, I want to know about it."

"Let's move quietly, then. Take off your shoes."

I kicked off my high heels and quietly set them out of the way. Together, Jesse and I climbed the stairs, pausing after every squeak the old floors made. We'd replaced some of the wood, but most of the staircase was actually in good shape. We stopped at the landing and waited again. We heard nothing now. Whoever was up there had to know we were coming because they didn't make a sound. *And we have no weapons!* Still holding hands, we stood on the top-floor landing. The long hallway stretched in front of us, but sure enough, there was a low light shining from beneath the attic door. There was movement in the light, as if someone were silently walking back and forth. I clutched Jesse's hand tighter, and he glanced at me reassuringly with a finger to his lips.

This was wrong. It felt wrong. There was such a heaviness in Summerleigh now; it felt much heavier than earlier. The place had felt off for days, as if someone were watching every move I made. But now it was like the entire focus of the house was on Jesse and me, and that focus was deadly.

With faux bravado, I blurted out, "Who's there?" To my shock, the movement stopped and the light faded. Jesse released my hand and eased down the hall, leaving me behind. His dress shoes were quiet, but the grit on the floor made a light crunching sound beneath them.

Ugh. I wish I could wash my feet before I put my shoes back on. The doors to all the rooms were open, and blackness poured out from all of them. But I wasn't fooled by the apparent emptiness. We were not alone. I could feel the presence of someone else here. Someone who wanted to remain hidden. Someone who didn't believe we belonged here. I didn't dare call out again since the element of surprise was no longer on our side. We hurried to the door and I reached for it, but Jesse shook his head. He leaned his ear against the wood and listened.

Nothing. We heard nothing at all.

I put my hand on the old-fashioned doorknob and turned it with the slowest of movements, but the door wouldn't budge. Because my eyes had adjusted to the darkness, I could see Jesse's face clearly. He shot me a curious look, so I removed my hand and he gave it a try. No luck. It was as if it were locked from the inside. And there was no key to it. Who had locked the door? He turned the chipped enamel knob again, rattling it furiously now. The sound echoed through the empty hallway.

"We know you're in there. Open this door," Jesse said authoritatively as he knocked on it.

Nobody answered. But then I heard the sound of a long, heavy breath in my ear. And with the breath came the moving of air. Every door on the top hallway began to slam shut. Not together, as you might expect if a blast of wind blew through the house. No. They closed hard, slamming shut one at a time until there were no doors left open. And suddenly the attic door swung wide open and Jesse nearly fell into it. I ran after him and we stood in the attic room, our hearts pounding as we looked around wildly, but there was no one and nothing to see. Nothing except some trunks, a half-dozen stacked crates, an old wooden rocking horse with an angry face, a rusty birdcage and a turn-of-the-century mannequin. There was more junk in here than I remembered from the last time I'd been up here, and certainly more than when Jeopardy Belle claimed this place and dubbed it her castle room.

"Hello? Who's in here? We saw your light. Don't hide from us." Still not a word, but then my left hand felt cold as if some unseen person had grabbed it. I caught my breath and lifted my hand to look at it. Now my entire arm was cold—no, it was freezing. "Jesse. Something's touching me. I can feel it."

With a worried expression, he said, "I better get you out of here. Come on, let's go. I've got a flashlight in the truck. I can come back and..." His words trailed off as he stared down the hallway.

My eyes followed his, but at first I didn't see what he was looking at. Then the strange light reappeared, illuminating the little figure. Yes, I could see him now. The little boy from my dream, the one Harper saw.

The light vanished, and only the boy remained. He wore knee britches and a fitted jacket with black socks and boots. His hair was black and combed carefully to the side. His face was pale, but his eyes...oh, his eyes were horrible and as black as two endless wells. And then he opened his mouth as if to scream, only no sound came out. His mouth was so wide, and it was black too. There was no doubt that what we were seeing was not a human child. This creature was a ghost, a phantom.

As I stared unblinkingly, I noticed that he did not move a muscle but stared back, his head bent down a little further now.

His dark eyes focused on me. He wanted me to die. He wanted Horrible Things to happen to me. I clutched Jesse's hand again and felt him grabbing at mine. As long as we were together, if we stayed together, we would be okay. I wanted to believe that, but the thing was not moving. His head bent even lower and he squatted on his haunches as if he would pounce on us like a wild animal. Suddenly all of the doors began slamming, opening and shutting furiously. The movement was so violent I feared they would fall off the hinges. What if he tore the place apart and brought Summerleigh down upon our heads?

From somewhere deep within me, a scream erupted. "No! Stop it!" And suddenly, he vanished.

The attic door swung silently closed and we were alone again, but the air crackled still. My cry had stopped him, but I did not believe he would be gone forever. We had to go, and we had to go now. Hannah Ray had been right. We should never have come here.

Jerking Jesse's hand, I yelled at him, "Come on!"

Together we raced down the hall. I prayed that the boy would stay away and not pop out at us or try to stop us. Before running downstairs, I paused to look behind me, and that's when I saw the other one.

The ghost of a young woman, a teenager, wore a long white dress with a faded rose at her bosom. The front of her gown was marred with dark stains, and her dark hair fell over her pale shoulders as she hovered near the attic. *Oh God! She had no feet. She has no feet!* She reached out to us and began to move slowly toward us.

"Run!" I screamed at Jesse as we hurried out of Summerleigh. I forgot my shoes and didn't remember to breathe until we got into his truck. I was pretty sure the gravel had cut my feet, but I didn't stop to look at the wounds. We sat panting in the vehicle, but this wasn't far enough. We had to go farther; we had to get out of there. I glanced up at the attic, which was dark now, and imagined I could feel the boy's dead black eyes watching us.

"Get me out of here, Jesse."

"Where to?" he asked as he cranked the truck and made the trip around the circular drive.

"I don't care. Anywhere."

We didn't talk again until we made it to Lucedale.

Chapter Four—Harper

Momma spent most of her days sleeping because she spent most of her nights drinking. Even Miss Augustine hadn't been to the house in weeks. Knowing Momma, they'd gotten into a big row over some silly thing like who would become the next Miss Magnolia or what the preacher's new wife would wear to the fellowship Sunday next. Not that we would attend. We hadn't been to church in so long.

Loxley spent all her time creating "art" on the floor of her room and the porch and anywhere she found a blank canvas. I'd been happy for her when Mrs. Loper surprised her with a box of chalk for her birthday, but it quickly became a source of contention around the house. Momma didn't like it when she drew on the floor. I didn't either, but I didn't think it merited a spanking. Not Momma's idea of a spanking, anyway.

We were stretched for school clothes this year. Addison and I had both had a growth spurt, and our skirts were shorter than they should have been, which would no doubt land us in the principal's office if I didn't fix them soon. Mr. Alfred was a notorious stickler for proper skirt lengths. In fact, it was said that he kept a measuring tape in his desk at all times. Only Loxley appeared locked in time and hadn't grown an inch, except her hair. One night, I spent my time letting out the hems of our skirts and giving my sisters haircuts. Loxley cried at the idea of cutting her hair, but I bribed her with a peppermint stick, one I'd kept since Christmas, and I had to promise to cut no more than an inch. Before tucking her into bed, I braided her hair, and she drifted off to sleep soon after. Her sweet face was all sticky when I kissed her cheek.

Every night when we got home from school, I hoped I would see Aunt Dot pull into the driveway and come to our rescue. But there was no sign of my aunt, and since the phone had been disconnected, I had no way of calling her to let her know how dire our situation was. Just last night the power went out, and I had a sneaking suspicion that this was further proof Momma was not paying the bills and was spending what little money we did have on gin and cigarettes. I'd scrounged up some candles in a bureau drawer, but that wouldn't last long. I didn't look forward to taking cold showers either.

After I finished fixing our skirts, I was just about ready to go to bed when I heard someone tapping on the front door. It was almost nine o'clock, and we didn't have callers this late unless it was something serious. I pulled my robe around myself to cover up my flimsy nightgown. I even took the trouble to button the top four buttons. Luckily, I hadn't set my hair yet. The visitor tapped again. *Maybe it's Aunt Dot? Or Jeopardy?*

"I'm coming." I was suddenly happy at the possibility of seeing someone I loved. I hurried down the hallway before stepping into the Great Room.

I saw no sign of Momma, which meant she hadn't heard the door. The house was so dark without any electricity, and I regretted not bringing a candle with me. With my hand on the door, I felt a sudden sense of dread and said, "Who is it?"

"Mr. Daughdrill. Open the door, Harper."

I almost never saw my grandfather, and for him to visit our home without Momma preparing us first was highly unusual. I opened the door but kept the screen door latched and said, "Yes, sir?"

"Where's your Momma? She's not answering my phone calls; the operator says the phone has been disconnected. Is that true?" My grandfather was a tall man, probably the tallest man I'd ever seen. He wore a loose gray suit and no hat. Mr. Daughdrill had salt-and-pepper hair, which he kept short, and he was always neat. Even his fingernails were neat. You'd never see dirty nails on him, not like Daddy, who always liked working with his hands. I wondered what Mr. Daughdrill did for a living, but I never had the courage to ask him.

Almost happy to relay the negative report, I answered him, "Yes, sir. The phone is out, and we don't have any electricity. I'm sure it's an oversight on Momma's part. She's been so upset, what with Jeopardy being gone and all."

"Open the door, Harper."

As I flipped the hook up, I noticed I didn't have to stand on tiptoe anymore to open the latch. I stepped out of the way as Mr. Daughdrill walked inside Summerleigh. For the briefest second, I thought I heard footsteps overhead. But it was probably just my imagination, the old house settling in the autumn heat or some such thing.

"Where is your Momma now?" He pulled off his suit coat and hung it on the bare coat rack.

"I think she's in her bedroom. Do you want me to get her?"

"No. That's not necessary. My, you've become a beautiful young woman, Harper Louise. So much like your Momma." His cool hand touched my face ever so briefly. "You go to bed now," he said, smiling at me in the half-light.

I shivered but smiled back politely. I rarely received compliments, and to be compared with Momma was certainly a compliment.

"All right, Mr. Daughdrill. Good night."

"Harper?"

"Yes, sir?" I paused in the doorway of the Great Room that led to our bedrooms. He was only a few feet behind me now.

"I wouldn't mind if you called me Grandfather. I wouldn't mind it at all."

I smiled again and answered, "Yes, sir. Grandfather. Good night."

I hurried off to my room and closed the door behind me. My heart was pounding in my chest, and I heard my grandfather's footsteps travel down the hall to Momma's room. He didn't yell at her, but his voice was loud and stern at first. I couldn't quite make out the words. Momma cried and argued with him, but the house soon grew quiet and I fell asleep.

I woke before dawn, surprised to find that Momma was up too. She wore one of her favorite dresses today, the blue and white checkered one that she usually wore only when Daddy was coming home. It broke my heart to see it. Despite her attempt to put on a happy face, she still wasn't quite together, but at least she was not wearing a robe and didn't have lipstick on her teeth. Her hair still needed to be fixed, but she wore a smattering of makeup and had taken the time to put on pantyhose and her newest heels. She had a ladder in her hose, but I wasn't going to be the one to tell her that.

As I walked into the kitchen, she smiled sweetly at me and said, "Good morning, Harper Louise. I made y'all some scrambled eggs this morning. Would you like some toast with your eggs?"

I stared at her, not believing what I was hearing and seeing. Momma never made us breakfast. She rarely cooked dinner, and for her to be up and ready to take us to school was just too much of a coincidence. I attributed her change of behavior to my grandfather's visit last night.

"Yes, ma'am. I'll go see if Addison and Loxley are ready yet."

"You do that. I'll get that toast going." I stared at her as she sliced hunks of bread from the stale loaf and placed them on a baking sheet. We didn't have a toaster, so we had to make toast the old-fashioned way in our house. She smiled up at me and said, "Don't dawdle, Harper. Get going. I don't want you girls to be late. And don't forget to put on pantyhose. You're too old to go around with bare legs."

"Yes, Momma." I hated wearing pantyhose. In fact, not many girls wore hose anymore except for formal occasions. Bobby socks were all the fashion, but I didn't have any of them or any saddle shoes. Maybe one day, if I was smart enough to find a job, I would have my own money and could buy the clothes that I dreamed of, like the ones in the magazines. What girl wouldn't want the latest styles? One day, I would own a whole collection of floral scarves to wear around my neck and hair.

Addison felt ill, but she usually did before any kind of social activity. It was her nerves, I reminded her, and I coached her through her many worries. Loxley dressed quickly and hurried off to the kitchen to enjoy her breakfast. Addison had another spell of retching, but I helped her clean up. When I walked into the kitchen with her, I was surprised to see my grandfather sitting at the table as if he intended to take breakfast along with us Belle girls. I didn't like that he was sitting in Daddy's chair, but nobody else seemed to mind so I kept silent.

Momma should say something! She should ask him to move! I glanced at my mother's face and could hardly believe the transformation in her. But no matter how hard she tried, I would never trust her again. The memory of my mother striking me and picking me up by my hair was still fresh in my mind, even though it had happened weeks ago. I wondered what my grandfather would think about her behavior.

"Good morning, girls," he said politely to us as he opened his newspaper and placed it beside his plate.

In unison we replied, "Good morning." He smiled at us all but winked at me. Momma saw it but didn't say a word. She kept her eyes on her plate and didn't eat anything at all.

"Eat your food, ladies. You need a good breakfast to do well in school. I hear you'll be graduating in a few years, Harper Louise. Tell me, what are your plans for when you graduate? Are you going off to college?"

I scooped up a forkful of eggs and said nervously, "I would like to, but I don't know if we can afford that, Grandfather." I popped the eggs in my mouth as my Momma's eyes widened. She drew in a sharp breath and sat up straight in her chair staring at her father and me. Addison and Loxley eyeballed me but kept eating. None of us girls were allowed to call him Grandfather, none except Jeopardy, but now I had that privilege. I instantly regretted using the term.

"You leave that to me, dear girl. If you want to go to college, I'll make sure that you do." He reached for my hand and squeezed it. His hand felt clammy and cold, and I wasn't used to being touched. There weren't many hugs administered in this house, not since Daddy died. Once upon a time, Jeopardy had been one to hug you, to show affection in sudden and wonderful ways, but before she disappeared, those spontaneous hugs had become as rare as Momma's.

"Girls, let's go now. It's time we were off to school." Momma still hadn't eaten a bite but sipped her coffee quickly and stood, straightening her dress.

"Oh no, dear. You can't go out looking like that. Just look at your hair, Ann." He clucked his tongue as Momma's hands flew to her unbrushed locks.

"I'll wear a scarf, Father."

"I don't think a scarf will help. I'll take these girls to school and come back when I'm done. I think it would be good for us to have a chat about Harper's future. Don't you?"

I saw Momma's hands clench by her sides in tight fists, and she wobbled in her shoes. Would she faint? Her face reddened, and she did something I had never seen before—she defied Mr. Daughdrill. "I'll take my girls to school, Father, and I'll be right back. Hurry up, girls. Let's go."

Loxley whined about not finishing her breakfast, but she grabbed her toast and followed behind Momma. I cast an eye behind me to my grandfather's face. He was clearly furious, but it was the silent kind of fury, the kind I'd seen on Momma's face so frequently. And then he called out to us, "I will be picking you girls up. Look for my car after school." Momma didn't argue back but took me by the hand and led us out of the house and to her car.

I expected her to say something to us, something about the weirdness of our grandfather being at our kitchen table this morning. Perhaps an apology or some declaration of how things would change and how she would try harder to be a better mother to us all, but she said nothing. She clutched the steering wheel so hard her hands were white, and I noticed she wore no gloves. *Momma always wears gloves when she drives the car.* She pulled up in front of the school, and even though we were thirty minutes early, we got out of the car and watched her pull away. Momma looked at me with an expression I could not interpret and then left us behind. She was gone by the time I thought to ask her for lunch money, but luckily for my sisters, I had fifty cents in my purse.

We waited on the bench outside the front door of the school until the principal arrived and unlocked the door. He was polite and made a sweet comment about us being anxious for classes to start. Other teachers arrived a few minutes later, but none of the adults said a word to us about Jeopardy. I could tell they were curious—or perhaps they felt sorry for us. I wasn't sure.

The day did not go as planned. My hose kept falling down, and I had to retreat into the ladies' restroom to pull them back up more than once. I finally gave up about halfway through the day and went into a bathroom stall and removed them completely, shoving them in my purse. My bare legs felt cool, and the strange defiance of going without hose thrilled me slightly. I would never be as defiant as Jeopardy, but I was learning in my own way how to show the same kind of bravery she did.

How I miss you, Jeopardy Belle!

Thinking about being at school without her was too much. I didn't return to class that period but stayed in the stall and cried until the bell rang. I ate lunch with Addison, but Loxley was in the other building. The elementary kids were kept separate from the rest of us. They played separately, learned separately and ate separately. Knowing Loxley, she was having a fine old time. She was never one to go without a friend for too long, and I suspected that the smaller children were not as curious about Jeopardy's disappearance as were my own schoolmates. It was so strange that nobody mentioned her name. Actually, no one spoke to me much at all. It wasn't until after lunch that Arnette Loper came walking beside me. Jeopardy used to call her frog-face behind her back. She never cared for Arnette too much.

"I've been meaning to tell you for weeks, I'm so happy for you that you got voted into the Harvest Queen Court. And you looked real pretty at the dance, too. Of course, I'm sorry I didn't make it on the Court, but maybe next year. Older girls have a better chance, they say. I can't wait." Arnette ran on and on and then finally saw the sadness in my face as I remembered the night my sister disappeared. She said, "I'm real sorry about your sister. Jeopardy was..."

I stopped in the hallway, ignoring the impatient crowd behind me. They could walk around. "You mean Jeopardy *is*, Arnette. She's not dead. She's just missing."

"Oh, I didn't mean to imply that she was dead. Sorry, Harper." She clutched her notebook to her chest and looked up at me. I was a full three inches taller than Arnette; I was probably the tallest girl in the ninth grade.

Her voice dropped to a whisper, "Is it true that she ran off with a carnie? You know, the good-looking one who looked like Dean Martin. What was his name?"

"What are you talking about, Arnette? Jeopardy didn't run off with anyone. She's just missing." We started to move toward our biology class. The bell would ring soon, and I was glad because I really wanted to get away from Arnette.

"Well, Harper, she can't just be missing. She's got to be missing on purpose. I mean, someone would have to be taking care of her, right? It makes sense that she went off to get married, and that would be so like Jeopardy Belle. She was nothing if not romantic."

I hadn't thought about that before, and it certainly was a possibility, but a carnival worker? No way. If Jeopardy was gonna run off with anyone, it would've been with Troy Harvester. And where was Troy? His brother Tony held court in front of his locker before last period, but I hadn't seen Troy in a while. It was like he'd disappeared too.

"Anyway, I'm real sorry." She walked away and found a seat at the front of the class while I chose one at the back. Last year, I would've been right up front with Arnette, but not this year. I wanted to be as far from the spotlight as possible, plus she'd given me a lot to think about. What if it was true? What if Jeopardy did leave me behind? Would she have done that? I shook my head as I opened my notebook and prepared for the long boring biology speech I was sure Mr. Dempsey was about to give us. Mr. Dempsey might be dreamy, according to Arnette, but he loved nothing better than to talk on and on about nuclei and cells and other boring things. As he talked, I pretended people weren't looking back and staring at me like they'd done for weeks. I avoided their eyes and wrote Jeopardy's name about a hundred times before the class ended. I'd never been so glad to be out of school before, but every day without Jeopardy was just awful.

Arnette caught me in the classroom doorway. "Hey, why don't you ride with us? We're going to Lucedale to the soda shop."

"Hey, Harper," a boy with a shiny round face and cropped blond hair said with a nervous smile. I'd seen him before but couldn't recall ever speaking to him. He didn't say anything to Arnette, who merely stared at him with her bulging green eyes. The boy didn't shuffle away but stood with us as if he'd been a part of the conversation from the beginning.

"Um, hello. Benjamin, right?"

"Only Dempsey calls me that. I'm Ben or Benny. Hartley." He was sweating pretty good but extended his hand to Arnette. She shook it.

"Benny, I was just telling Harper that some of us were going for a soda after school. You game?"

"Sure," he said with a grin as he pulled his book strap up on his shoulder. "I've got a car. I'll be glad to drive you, Harper. And you..."

"Arnette," she said with an amused smile.

I shook my head. "No, thank you. I appreciate the offer, but I'd better go home. I think my grandfather is picking me up." Arnette smiled good-naturedly, and I instantly liked her again. I know she didn't mean to hurt my feelings or insinuate that Jeopardy was some kind of fast girl. Arnette was just being Arnette. Benny looked disappointed, but I gave him a polite finger wave and he perked back up.

"Goodbye, Harper."

"Ciao," Arnette called after him. That was her new thing. She'd seen it in some movie with Ava Gardner or some glamorous star like that. When was the last time I had been to the movies? I glanced back one more time at Benny. Nope. Still didn't recall him.

Addison waited for me at the front door, and together we walked out into the sunshine.

"Who was that boy?" she asked between sneezes.

"Just a friend." I handed her my one and only handkerchief. I dreaded the ride home. I didn't like my grandfather at all, and it seemed strange to me that he would want to be a part of our lives now that Daddy and Jeopardy were gone. We stood outside, and Loxley ran toward us holding up a piece of paper. In class today, she got to glue macaroni onto paper. Before I had the opportunity to compliment her on her artwork, a horn honked. To my sheer joy, I saw Aunt Dot sitting in her convertible. She waved at us and called my name.

We all ran toward her. Maybe today wouldn't be so bad after all. Maybe it would end with some laughter and happiness. Aunt Dot always brought sunshine with her. We hopped in the car as she drove away, and I pretended that I didn't see my grandfather's Master DeLuxe just four cars back. He honked at us, but none of us paid attention. Addison finally looked back and tapped me on the shoulder, but I touched my finger to my lips to encourage her to keep quiet. She nodded back with wide eyes. Loxley had taken the front seat today, but Addison and I didn't complain.

For the first time in a long time, I felt joy. Real joy. It wouldn't last long.

Chapter Five—Jerica

I woke up feeling groggy, but then again, I'd stayed up much later than I normally would. Since leaving the third shift at the Sunrise Retirement Home behind, I'd gotten used to going to bed at a decent hour. Despite last evening's frightening beginnings, my date with Jesse went well. Instead of going to the new steakhouse, we drove through the Sonic, ordered a bunch of junk food and went back to his place. Nothing intimate happened beyond some handholding on his front porch swing, but it had been a nice evening, especially after the terror we experienced at Summerleigh. For the first time in a long time, my first thought of the morning was not imagining the arms of my daughter around my neck or the sound of her footsteps running to my bed. I felt a tad guilty about that but whispered, "Good morning, Marisol," as I always did. I listened quietly for a response, knowing that there would be none. The only sound I heard was a bird fussing in the live oak outside my window.

As I waited for the fog to lift, I recalled with perfect clarity the strange little boy Jesse and I saw standing in the hallway of Summerleigh last night. We had talked for hours about it but were no closer to understanding what forces were at work. The little boy was clearly not a Belle; we assumed he was a member of the McIntyre family, but since that was so long ago, we had no real way of identifying him. One thing was for sure, though—whoever or whatever he was did not like the repairs and improvements we were making. I rolled over and stared at the clock. It was already eight, and Hannah was scheduled to be here at nine. The hard work of the past week left me feeling tired and sore, but it felt good. I'd forgotten how much I loved working with my hands and the pure exhaustion that came with intense physical labor. I used to save lives, and now I saved houses.

Or at least I was trying to save the house. I wondered if I should have so readily ignored Ben Hartley's warning. Maybe I shouldn't stay. But how could I just leave? This place felt like home, and Marisol had followed me here. What if I left and she didn't come with me?

Maybe I'll call Ben today and insist that he tell me what he knows. Maybe he's seen the boy too. Yeah, that's what I'll do, I promised myself.

The hour flew by, and Hannah knocked on my door promptly at nine. "Good morning. Come in," I greeted her with a smile.

Hannah was tall, taller than most, and she seemed really self-conscious about that. As always, she clutched her purse close to her like a life vest. She didn't appear nervous or frightened as she had been when she called last night.

"Would you like something to drink? Maybe a cup of coffee?" I asked as I led her into the kitchen.

She politely declined and took a seat at the table. "You went to Summerleigh, didn't you?"

I finished pouring my own cup of coffee and took a seat across from her. I smoothed out the tablecloth and shrugged. "I had no intention of going over there, but after you called, I—I mean, we—saw a light in the attic. Jesse was here. And since we had equipment and materials in the house, we couldn't ignore it. How did you know that there would be activity?"

Still clutching her purse, Hannah tilted her head and looked past me thoughtfully as if trying to figure out how to best answer my question. "Ever since I visited Summerleigh, the energy there has kind of stayed with me. It's like I have this weird connection with it now. That happens sometimes; it's a risk that psychics take, and it usually doesn't amount to anything, but this time was different. I'm always careful, but I left Summerleigh with a heaviness, an attachment for lack of a better word. I'm positive it originated from something in that house. My alarm bells went off, and I couldn't stop thinking about Summerleigh. When I saw your daughter, it kind of clicked. I think she came to warn me."

"Marisol? You saw my daughter?"

"Yes. She was worried about you, Jerica. I think she's trying to protect you."

Tears filled my eyes, but I blinked them back. Hannah offered me a tissue from her purse. I dabbed at my face as she continued, "I'm not like a lot of psychic mediums, meaning that I don't commune with spirits the way some psychics do. I sense energy more than anything, not usually ghosts directly, so that's why it surprised me to see Marisol and get those impressions about the house. I can sense when energy builds and dissipates. Right now, I know energy is building. The spirit world is stirred up, and there are many eyes concentrated on this place. How about you? Are you feeling anything unusual? You have a rare sensitivity, Jerica. I think that's why Harper picked you."

"I've had a few things happen, but I didn't think much of them because Jeopardy Belle has been found. We recovered her remains."

"But Harper...you still see Harper," Hannah said wide-eyed. It wasn't really a question.

"Yes. I have dreamed about Harper a few times recently. Her grandfather, the man who murdered Jeopardy, is coming around again. But if he'd done anything to Harper, I would've known about it. She would have told me. We were friends, and if she suspected he had anything to do with Jeopardy..."

Hannah reached across the table and held my hand. "When you're dealing with the supernatural, it's really important that you don't assume anything. I know that's hard when your emotions are involved, but it may be that Harper wants you to know something. Something that will help you." She patted my hand one last time and sat up straight. "I think we should take a walk, Jerica. Let's go check out the house."

"I don't want to put you in further danger, Hannah."

"It's the only way I can help you, and I have my protection now. I have no one to blame but myself for that last incident. I know better than to walk into a place like Summerleigh without preparing. Lesson learned. Let's go check it out. Unless you want me to go by myself?"

"No way. You should know that Jesse and I both saw the boy with the black eyes last night. He was on the top floor, and I got the distinct impression that he did not want us there." We rose from the table, and I put my cup in the sink. I locked the back door, and we stepped out the front into the warm sunshine. I hadn't noticed how chilly it had become in the cottage.

"Tell me what happened, and don't leave anything out," she prompted me as she pulled her purse higher up on her shoulder.

"Jesse and I were in the kitchen, and we saw a light moving in the attic. It wasn't like a flashlight beam, more like a strange disco light. There were different colors; first white and then blue and purple and then white again. And it moved around, so it kind of looked like someone was having a party in the attic. I told Jesse what you said about not going in the house, but like I said, we couldn't ignore it." I closed the front door behind me and locked it before we walked down the gravel path toward the front door of Summerleigh. I could avoid going through the back door in the daylight.

"And?"

"We heard what sounded like a child's footsteps, so we went up to check it out. When we got to the end of the hallway on the second floor, we could see the light shining under the door, and you could see the shadows of someone passing through it. While we were busy trying to open the door, the boy appeared at the end of the hall. The doors started slamming—I mean they were slamming so hard it sounded like they were going to be ripped off the hinges. I won't lie; I was scared out of my mind. I don't know what I would have done without Jesse. The sound kept getting louder and louder." I put the key in the door of Summerleigh and turned it slowly. "I couldn't take it anymore, so I screamed. I said, 'Quit it!' or something like that, and it all stopped. Jesse and I didn't waste any time getting out of there."

"Interesting. He listened to you. He must know that this is your place now. Still, I can't imagine he'll go without a fight."

We stepped inside the Great Room. I left the door open because the air was so heavy that it felt like it might smother me. "I almost forgot, Jerica. I made this for you." Hannah dug inside her purse and retrieved a necklace. After untangling the chain, she handed it to me. It was a silver chain with an odd blue pendant. "This will protect you while we're here. Let's go upstairs to the center of the activity. Funny, though, I don't feel any of the Belles in here. Not even John, the father."

As we walked toward the staircase, I sighed sadly. All of the happiness and goodwill that I felt earlier this week, all the hard work we put into restoring Summerleigh, seemed so worthless now. Perhaps Ben Hartley was right. This place was cursed.

"Oh yes. The boy is here. Such an unhappy entity. Definitely human, so at least there are limitations to his power. But I get the sense that he is..." Hannah paused on the stairs and looked behind her.

"What? What is it?"

"It's just a voice, a droning in my ear. Don't you hear it?"

I shook my head but listened for a minute. The hair all over my body crept up. "Let's keep going. I'll see if I can communicate with the boy, but if he's anything like last time, I'm not sure how successful I'll be. If we can figure out what he wants, maybe we can help him move on."

I remembered something important from a dream I had recently. "I forgot to tell you, Hannah. Loxley, the youngest Belle girl, admitted to Harper that she was the one who cut up her dress with the scissors. She said the boy wanted her to do it...and in fact, he was the one who gave her the scissors. And I remember Jesse mentioned once before that Mariana McIntyre was murdered with a pair of scissors. I'm not sure if that means anything, but I figured I'd tell you."

Hannah nodded as she clutched her purse and whispered to herself. With nervous hands, she removed a small electronic device from her pocket. She clicked the button, paused on the top stair and then slowly began to move down the hall, looking through each open doorway as she went. I followed a few steps behind her.

Was she praying? Maybe I should pray too?

Hannah said, "Little boy, I know you are here. We're not here to harm you, but you cannot harm us either. We need to know, are you a McIntyre? Was Mariana your sister?" She waved her recorder around and then walked into the room that the Belle girls always referred to as the nursery. It was as silent as the grave. We waited but heard nothing except the sound of scurrying somewhere. *Oh great, please don't let there be mice in here.*

"Oh yes, you like it in here, don't you? This was your own little kingdom, wasn't it?" I heard a bumping sound coming from the nearby closet, but Hannah didn't react to it. She continued to walk around the room and finally put her device in the window. "This lady owns this house now. This is not your house anymore. There are no children here for you to play with. You should go, be with your family." Another bumping sound came from the closet, and I was feeling less comfortable by the second. "Why are you hiding from us? I'm not opening that closet door. We're not playing with you. You need to leave." The door handle on the closet began to shake as if an invisible hand tugged on it. I stepped back and stood in the corner of the room, my pulse racing and my hands sweating. Hannah extended her hand behind her and waved at me to calm me down. I tried to keep cool, but it wasn't working. She waved at me again and looked back at me, lifting her chin to prompt me to speak.

"My name is Jerica Poole. Summerleigh is mine now. I don't want you here." The door to the closet flung open, but there was nothing inside. Not a strange boy with a hateful stare. No lady in white. Not even a coat hanger. All I could see was a dust-covered floor.

Hannah stepped up beside me. "Let's go, Jerica." As she went to retrieve the device from the window, it flew across the room and smashed against the opposite wall. I shrieked and did a side step, but Hannah didn't flinch. We both raced over to examine the damage. Hannah retrieved the batteries that had flown out the back. It didn't look like anything else was wrong with the machine. She popped the batteries back in, slid the back on and turned on the power. "It's still working," she said to me with a frown. Then she said loudly, "That was not very nice. We're leaving this room, and you cannot follow us. Remember, we are protected." Hannah made the sign of the cross, and I did the same. We walked out of the room, leaving the bone-chilling cold behind.

"You okay?" she asked as she patted my shoulder.

"Yeah. Just startled me."

"Let's head toward the attic. I think we should leave him alone."

"Does that happen a lot?"

"Some ghosts are intelligent, meaning they know what's happening. They may not understand that they are dead or that they exist in a different time, but they are intelligent nonetheless. I've found that most are not mean, but some are. I have the feeling that if we could ever discover his name, it would help us. He respects you, for some reason."

I whispered to her, "Is this other one, Mariana, intelligent also?"

"I'm not sure yet. She's intelligent enough to want to avoid us, but she might tell us what we need to know. There is certainly a residual aspect to her haunting, meaning she does the same thing over and over. She likes visiting the same places; she feels at home." We walked to the attic, and to my surprise, Hannah stopped and knocked softly on the door.

"Mariana? My name is Hannah Ray. My friend Jerica is with me. May we come in?" I reached for the doorknob, but Hannah touched my shoulder. "No. We can't go in." She stepped back and stared at the door.

"What? Why?"

"Let's leave. I think I need some air."

"Okay," I said as we walked back down the hall. I purposely did not look into the nursery as we passed by. I hurried down the stairs probably quicker than I should have and nearly tripped on the last step, but Hannah caught me. "Thanks." We walked outside, and I locked the door behind us. It felt good to stand in the sunshine. Hannah began to walk away from the house, and I caught up with her.

"Nothing can follow us. No one can follow us."

Okay, that's worrying. "It's not good, is it?"

"I'm going to go home and review this recorder to see if there are any clues as to who this child is, if he is a child."

"What do you mean if? I saw him. It was a boy."

Hannah shook her head and said, "Some very intelligent entities like putting on faces that are useful to them. If there were children in this house, it would make sense that he would appear to them as a child. Or if there is a mother missing her child..."

My heart sank. "Oh, I see." I rubbed my lip with my finger. "But you said that it was definitely a human."

"Yes, but it may not be a boy. It could be a man or a woman. Who knows?"

"I have to know, Hannah. Why did you stop me from going into the attic?"

"I'm not sure. It just felt like the wrong time to go in. I'm sorry, Jerica. I don't mean to sound so mysterious, and I wish there were more I could tell you. It's just not how things work. Summerleigh is a very active place, and although most of the Belles appear to be at rest, there are other spirits here. They need to be dealt with too. I'd like to come back and bring a few friends with me. People with similar gifts who know more than I do."

I sighed and tried to fight the frustration that threatened to overwhelm me. "My crew is coming back Monday, so tomorrow would be okay."

"Tomorrow it is, then. I'll call you with the details as soon as I hear from my friends. In the meantime, Jerica, go for a walk. Spend some time outdoors. That's where you'll find your strength. And stay out of Summerleigh. I don't care how many lights you see. Don't go in there by yourself." Hannah paused on the pathway before getting into her car.

I wrapped my arms around myself, suddenly feeling very alone.

"You haven't asked me about her."

"I know she's here. That's enough for now." The truth was I wasn't ready to say goodbye to Marisol. And for some reason, I believed that if I did truly connect with her, I'd never see her again. Ever.

Hannah closed the door and rolled the window down. "When you're ready, just ask." Then she drove away.

I brushed a tear from my eye and decided not to wait for that walk. As my father used to say, "There's no time like the present." I stuffed my cold hands in my pockets and kicked a rock in my path. With a glance at the looming mansion behind me, I turned away from the house and tried to ignore the feeling of eyes watching me.

I didn't shake the feeling until I reached the river.

Chapter Six—Harper

I pleaded with Aunt Dot to let us stay the night at her house, but I didn't quite come out and explain why. What would I say? *Mr. Daughdrill makes Momma cry and wants me to call him Grandfather now. Like Jeopardy used to.* As always, my sunny aunt didn't want to hear anything negative about her sister, but then again, Aunt Dot was a glass-is-half-full kind of gal. Even though we couldn't stay the night, she did take us shopping; I didn't get the exact outfit that I saw in the magazine, but Aunt Dot bought me three scarves and two new skirts. Addison and Loxley got new dresses and shoes. With a trunk full of packages, we headed down Highway 98 back home to Desire.

The closer we got to Hurlette Drive, the more Addison rubbed her stomach and the whinier Loxley became. Couldn't Aunt Dot see how upset we were?

"Let's sing a driving song," she said to me with a big smile in the rearview mirror. I wanted to smile back but didn't have the energy to summon one. "The wheels on the bus go round and round, round and round, round and round." Nobody joined in. Aunt Dot's smile disappeared, and for the first time, I understood that my aunt was nervous too. She didn't want to leave us at Summerleigh any more than we wanted to go.

With a sigh, she eased into the slow lane and said, "Girls, you know I would take you all home with me if I could. But I can't. What about your Momma? She's a handful at times, but she has a good heart. I know she's moody and unreasonable, Harper, but you have to remember she's lost a husband. And with Jeopardy being gone, Ann is a broken soul, and we've all got to be patient with her."

I didn't bother answering her; she'd made up her mind not to see the bad things. Not to know that we were hungry and hurting. She didn't want to see how completely abandoned we all felt. It was easier that way, I guessed. Still, despite her naivety—I never believed I'd ever use one of my vocabulary words in a sentence—I didn't hate her. One could only love sweet Aunt Dot. I gazed out the window at the trees as we rushed past them. The shadows were gathering, and it would be time for supper soon. I wondered what I'd find in the refrigerator, if anything. There were some jars of tomatoes in the pantry. Maybe I could whip up some tomato gravy and biscuits. We had flour; I knew we had flour.

"Harper, are you listening, dear?"

"Yes, Aunt Dot," I lied as she talked about how things were going to get better, how things would turn around for us Belle girls. She wasn't fooling anyone in the car. Except maybe Loxley, who joined her in singing "When We All Get to Heaven."

"How about I pick you girls up for church on Sunday, if your Momma is still too ill to go? You haven't been in almost a month of Sundays." She chuckled as if she'd made the biggest joke ever. I didn't have the energy now to appease her determined sense of humor. I suddenly remembered that I wasn't wearing my hose. I'd stuffed them in my purse at school and forgot to put them back on. I hoped Momma didn't notice. It would be bad if she did.

"That would be fine, Aunt Dot." Addison glanced back at me as if she were expecting me to say something too. I couldn't. I was too busy counting. The car turned down the drive. I counted the seconds from the turn. It was twenty seconds from that turn until the first glimpse of Summerleigh. As we got closer, I felt sicker. Despite the presents and the renewed friendship with Arnette Loper, I wasn't any happier than I had been when I left home this morning. Funny how I'd almost become accustomed to the gloom that had fallen on Summerleigh, how differently I felt about the place now that Daddy would never return to bring her back to life. And I missed Jeopardy with all my heart.

Momma wasn't alone at the house. Thankfully, Mr. Daughdrill's car wasn't there, but a rusty red truck sat in the driveway. Aunt Dot's car crept to a stop, and she turned off the radio. She slid the gearshift into park and stared at the vehicle and then at the brightly lit parlor. *Wait a minute. I recognize that truck.* It belonged to Dewey

Landry, Aunt Dot's sometime sweetheart! The curtains were open, and I could see Momma and the dark-haired man sitting on the couch together. Momma's legs were curled up under her dress, and she was smoking and laughing like everything was hunky-dory.

"Who is that? I can't see his face," Addison said to no one in particular.

I knew, and apparently so did Aunt Dot. She didn't take her eyes off the window, and all four of us watched as Momma whispered in Dewey's ear and he slapped his knee at her joke. I was completely shocked. Jeopardy had always claimed that Momma had "friends" coming to the house at late hours, but I'd never seen one myself. It wasn't that late now, but it was Dewey Landry. What was she thinking? With his slicked-back brown hair, plain white t-shirt and blue jeans, Dewey was practically naked in our parlor. I didn't know which I found more troubling, Momma entertaining Dewey like she was a teenage girl and he her high school crush or my aunt's teary-eyed expression.

Aunt Dot opened the car door. "You girls stay here. I'll be right back."

"Yes, Aunt Dot," we said in unison. Count Basie blared from the radio in the parlor, and Momma's laughter escalated like it always did after she'd had a few drinks. I knew this song, "Take Me Back, Baby." We weren't allowed to listen to it at home, but the kids at school loved it. Tony

Harvester liked playing Basie as loud as he could on his car radio. For the hundredth time today, I thought of Jeopardy. What would she think about seeing Momma in the house with a man who wasn't Daddy? *I told you so, Harper. Momma ain't nothing but a w-h-o-r-e. Wait until I tell Daddy.*

"Harper? I'm afraid," Loxley whined as she poked her head over the back seat for a better view.

"That's Dewey Landry," Addison declared finally. "What's he doing here?"

"Maybe he's here to fix the refrigerator. He is a repairman," I lied to my little sister too easily. Addison sneezed again in the front seat. I watched in horror as Aunt Dot cleared the distance between the car and the house and walked right into the parlor. Clearly, she was yelling at Momma and Dewey, but I couldn't hear her over the radio. Like a cornered wildcat, Momma sprang to her feet and threw her glass on the floor. I'd have to clean that up, and the carpet. And then Dewey was up, his hands in front of him as if he believed he'd be able to control the situation. What a fool he was to think he'd be able to calm those two. Next thing I knew, Aunt Dot and Momma were tussling. I couldn't tell who threw the first punch because Dewey blocked my vision. He was still trying to break them up.

"We have to stop them, Harper!" Addison was out of the car without waiting for an answer. Loxley began to cry beside me, and I held her, still too shocked to move. Seeing Addison running through the yard clutching her stomach stirred me—I couldn't just sit here like a bump on a log and let her get hurt. That's when I saw another car roll up behind me. I knew the shape of the headlights immediately. This was none other than Mr. Daughdrill in his Chevy Master DeLuxe.

"Holy smokes," I said as I tried to sink down in the car. I don't know why I tried; it was impossible to hide from those lights, which shone like two white suns. Mr. Daughdrill wasted no time running to the porch and ordering Addison to stay outside. He stepped inside just in time to see Aunt Dot slap Dewey across the face as Momma collapsed on her red velvet sofa in a crying heap. In a few steps, Mr. Daughdrill crossed the room and unplugged the radio, then slung Dewey Landry out of the house. Both of his daughters stood up and faced him, screaming words we weren't allowed to say, being Baptists and all. Then Mr. Daughdrill struck Momma across the face, and she hit the ground. He grabbed her by her blond hair, just like she'd done to me, and struck her again. I had never seen such violence. Aunt Dot crumpled back, obviously too frightened to intervene.

Before I knew it, I was screaming, "Momma!" I ran to the house with Loxley in my arms. I don't know how I managed to climb out of that back seat holding her, but I did it. She'd peed on me as she cried, but I couldn't stop and change her clothing. Addison trailed behind me as we raced inside. Loxley was weeping loudly, and she ran to Aunt Dot as soon as she saw her.

From some place unseen and unknown within me, anger exploded and I yelled at Mr. Daughdrill, "Don't you ever hit her again!" I picked up the poker from the fireplace and held it in my hand. I was no small girl, and I had quite an arm on me. He might be six inches taller, but I would strike him as sure as I was standing here if he hit Momma again. "Get out of our house now! Get out of here, you mean old bastard!" I'd never used that word before, and it shocked everyone into silence. Except Aunt Dot.

"Harper Louise," she said in a steady, quiet voice, "Put the poker down. It's all over now."

"Girl, don't you ever threaten me again. I see now what a horrible mother you are, Ann. Here you are, rollicking like a harlot with a two-bit grease monkey, and now your children disrespect me. I will not tolerate this any longer. There will be order." He grabbed Addison's arm—for what intention, I did not know, but his words broke me. That was the last thing Mr. Daughdrill said to me because I struck him hard across the opposite arm. He let go of Addison, who scrambled to Aunt Dot. Every feeling I had, all the grief and sadness, exploded into uncontrollable anger, and I struck him not once or twice but at least a half-dozen times.

And nobody moved to stop me.

"That's enough now, Harper," Momma said in a whisper. She lifted her bruised face to me. I couldn't discern her expression. Was it relief? Anger?

My hands stung, and I could see that I'd bruised them. I dropped the poker. It landed on the carpet with a thud, and I backed away from the sight of Mr. Daughdrill bleeding on the parlor floor.

"Look, he's breathing," Addison said as she craned her neck to see him.

"Girls, get in the car. We're leaving," Aunt Dot whispered as she held Loxley tighter.

Momma began to cry, but she didn't argue about it. I don't think she was crying because we were leaving. I felt sure she was crying because I almost killed her daddy. Or something. Or maybe she was crying because we saw her fooling around with Dewey. I couldn't be sure. Whatever the reason, I couldn't leave her alone. Not now.

"I can't go, Aunt Dot. I have to stay and take care of Momma," I said in a wooden voice. I couldn't believe my own ears. What was I saying? I'd been praying for weeks—no, months—to get away from Momma, to leave Summerleigh forever. Now here was my chance and I couldn't do it.

Aunt Dot's mascara ran beneath her eyes, and her hat was crooked from the earlier melee. "No, you don't have to stay. I'm sorry I didn't listen before. Come with me, Harper Louise. I won't let you go through this another day."

With all my heart, I wanted to leave with her. I wanted to burn Summerleigh to the ground, along with every sad memory I had of this place, but I couldn't leave Momma. She'd have no one if I left. No one at all.

"I'm sorry, Aunt Dot. I can't go." To my surprise, Addison took my hand. She didn't speak, but I squeezed it back.

"All right," Aunt Dot said sadly. "Ann, I'm leaving with Loxley. I'll make sure she gets to school."

Momma nodded and reached out her hand to me. Her beautiful face was the picture of sadness, as if all her hopes were now pinned on me. Aunt Dot and Loxley left, and I heard the car pull out of the driveway.

The blood around Mr. Daughdrill pooled, but he was still breathing.

I took Momma's hand and helped her to her feet. She fell on my shoulder and cried like I was her best friend, but I knew better than that.

I wasn't her friend. I was her prisoner.

Chapter Seven—Jerica

John Jeffrey Belle had been right. The pond was nothing more than a glorified mud hole except for a few ducks that called it home. I walked farther, deciding that I would go down to Dog River and look at the water there. Jeopardy Belle used to love going down to Dog River. I remembered Troy Harvester's description of her rising out of the water "like some kind of siren." I wanted to see it for myself again. I'd been down there once before and had seen my daughter briefly. She'd been playing with Loxley Belle. In retrospect, I think Marisol wanted me to know that she was happy here at Summerleigh. She liked that I was here, but now I wasn't so sure. I didn't feel her like I used to. I didn't see her, and I couldn't understand why she was being so elusive.

And then it dawned on me. Maybe the boy with the black eyes forced her to leave Summerleigh. Maybe he was keeping her away from me. Maybe he wanted to keep me all to himself. Yes, that could be it. Marisol was scared and hiding from him. All the more reason to get rid of him.

"Marisol, honey," I said with my eyes closed and my face turned up to the sun, "I'll never let anything happen to you. Never again. I failed you once before, my baby, but I'll never do it again. Trust Momma, please. Can you hear me?"

Then as clear as a bell I heard a splash in the water. Not a fish jumping or a pebble plunking into the water but a splash as if someone had jumped in. I twisted around on the rock and looked over in the water just in time to see a spray of bubbles appear. I waited and waited, but nobody emerged from the murky water. I looked around and stood up on the rock to see if I could locate anyone near me. I searched for any evidence that someone was down here on this part of Dog River besides me but couldn't see a soul. Scanning the banks again, I checked for clothing or a boat but saw no one. And then the water stopped bubbling, the ripples ceased to move, and it was as if it never happened.

I know that just happened. I know someone dived in. I heard it with my own two ears. Oh, God! What if he was in trouble?

Without taking off my shoes or emptying my pockets, I dived in. Fear and urgency overwhelmed me. I swam with all my might, and when I got to the spot that I believed I'd seen the splash, I dived down in a panic.

Beneath the surface, the water wasn't as murky as I expected, but it was much deeper than I had believed. Under the top layer of brown water, the bottom part of the river was clean and crystal-clear and fast moving. I swam about, looking for someone, anyone to rescue. I was running out of air, so I swam quickly back to the surface and sucked in a breath, then dived again and swam down a few feet. For one fleeting moment, I thought I saw a figure, but then it was gone. Someone *was* down here! My lungs burned, and

I breached the surface again to catch my breath. I had every intention of diving back down until I saw a man standing on the shore.

The sun was behind him, so I couldn't see his face clearly. "Hey! Help! I think someone is drowning," I shouted. An icy-cold chill passed over me, and I slunk down in the water a bit. I peered hard at the man, but he didn't seem to hear me.

Oh no. I know who he is, but that can't be possible! It was Mr. Daughdrill, Harper's long-dead grandfather! I raised my hand to my eyes to shield them from the sun, but I still could not see his face. I had no desire to swim to shore and see the ghost face-to-face. *What do I do? I can't swim to the shore as long as he's standing there. How is this possible?* Treading water furiously now, I thought about my options. I could swim downstream and then find another way home. Or I could stay in the water until someone else showed up. Surely someone else would come.

"Marisol!" I whispered. "Stay away." The man didn't move. The wind blew, but his hair and clothing did not. He wore the same loose gray suit that I'd seen him in before, in Harper's memories. Yes, that was Daughdrill. Who else could it be?

And that's when I felt the tug on my foot. A strong tug. I screamed in surprise and tried to swim away. That was not a branch or a piece of debris—that was a hand grabbing me! I screamed, but the scream was choked out with water as I was plunged beneath the surface of the suddenly violent waves. *Let me go!* I tried to yell, but no one could hear me. I thought I would drown as the hand gripped my ankle tighter. The last thing I wanted to do was see who or what had me, but I had no choice other than to swim down. I had to get free! With my last bit of oxygen, I released a bit of air and dived down to face the bloated white face that met mine.

This was the boy with the black eyes, the one from Summerleigh!

He was here in the water, and he wanted to drown me. He wanted me to die. I kicked at him so hard with my other foot that I felt his slippery skin move beneath my foot. I gagged at the sight of pieces of his flesh floating away in the water. He let me go and disappeared as he fell down further into the river. I launched to the surface, breathing in air as quickly as possible. A scream erupted from my lips, and I swam to the other side of the river, screaming and crying all the way. I had to get away from the boy. I prayed as I swam. Looking over my shoulder once or twice, I realized that no one was there. Daughdrill was gone.

I eased up on the muddy bank of Dog River and held my ankle in my hand. It was clearly bruised but not broken. I was a nurse after all; I knew what breaks looked like. I got up on my feet as quickly as possible—I had to get away from this hellish river.

I thought I would have a peaceful day out here, spend some time in nature and get away from the ghosts of the house. Maybe see Marisol again. Unfortunately, the ghosts had come looking for me.

Hannah was wrong. I was not protected, and the boy with the black eyes was not going away easily. And he had an evil friend. I left immediately and began walking along the opposite bank until I came to a bridge that would lead me back to the other side of the river. The road was lonely, and I suddenly realized this was the road where Jeopardy had gone missing. This was the road where Daughdrill had done his last Horrible Thing—he took Jeopardy's life right here. I paused, feeling sick. I heard a car approaching but didn't stick around to see who it was. I hurried through the woods back to the cottage.

The sick feeling morphed into something else. I was angry. Angry that children had been hurt. Angry that Daughdrill thought he could harm me by sending that demented child after me.

I understand now, Harper. I know what you want me to know. You were a fighter. You were never a quitter—you never gave up on Jeopardy or any of your family. Not even your Momma. I know this about you because you never gave up on me, either. And you knew that I'm like you. I am a fighter too, Harper.

And this isn't over yet.

Chapter Eight—Harper

For a long time, none of us said a word. After I helped Momma to her feet, she sat on the couch and stared at Mr. Daughdrill, who hadn't moved an inch. It was Addison who spoke first. "I think you killed him, Harper. I think he's dead for sure. Truly I do think it."

"No, he's not. I can see him breathing, Addie." I did see him breathing, didn't I? Or was I imagining that? I felt sick all of a sudden and panicked. "I'm sorry, Momma. I didn't mean to do it."

And then I heard him moaning and murmuring, "Ann, help me, girl. Ann..." His eyes were open, but he couldn't move his mouth. Had I broken his jaw?

Momma stiffened her back and sat up straight on the couch. She tucked her feet beneath her, posed as pretty as any picture, without making a move to help him. She stared down at her father, and we all watched him move his fingers. Yes, he was starting to move now. He might even be up and moving in a few minutes. She said, "Girls, you get cleaned up and get dressed for bed."

"Shouldn't we call a doctor or someone?" Addison asked in a small, scared voice.

Momma shook her head once and tilted it as if she were posing, just like one of her old photo shoots. All the tears and desperation I saw on her face had been replaced with something else.

Something cold and calculating, something ladylike and calm. I think I would've rather had her tear my hair out than behave so calmly.

"You just leave everything to me, Addison," she said as she rose from the couch and smoothed her pencil skirt. Neither one of us girls moved. All we could do was stare at her. Had she lost her senses? We needed to call the police. I'd probably be arrested. "Do as Momma tells you now. Both of you."

In unison, we said, "Yes, Momma." Addison took my hand and led me out of the parlor, into the Great Room and into the hallway that led to our rooms. "Stay with me tonight, Harper. I can't sleep by myself."

"All right, Addie," I said as I sat on her bed and stared off into the distance. My body shook, my hands hurt, and I could see bruises on my fingers. I couldn't stop staring at them. These were proof that I had it too. I had the same rage Momma and her father had. Even Aunt Dot had it. I saw that tonight. Deep inside me, the Daughdrill rage had lain hidden all these years, but it was there. And now I would go to prison. People who kill people, people who beat people, they send them to prison. I'd probably die in prison.

Addie was talking to me, but I couldn't hear her. Then she put her hand under my chin and stared into my eyes. "Harper, can you hear me?"

"Yes, I hear you. I'm so tired, Addison. I just want to sleep."

"You heard Momma; we have to get ready for bed."

"I just want to lie down," I murmured, feeling so lightheaded I feared I might actually faint. My hands and head throbbed.

I lay on her pillow and drew my legs up to my chest. Without another word, Addison removed my shoes, covered me with her worn but heavy quilt and crept in beside me. I stared at the wall for a few minutes, but it didn't take long to fall asleep.

"It's all right, Harper Louise. I won't leave you. It's okay. Go to sleep now." Addison sniffled as she scooted up to my back.

I tried to say, "Thank you, Addie," but I found that I couldn't speak. I was too tired. I fell into a black, dreamless sleep.

I woke up feeling cold and realized that the quilt had been pulled off me. I reached behind me, thinking that Addison had stolen it in her sleep, but it wasn't there. The quilt was not on the bed. I sat up and looked for it. We must have kicked it off because it was lying on the floor at the foot of the bed.

Get up, pie-face.

I sat up in my bed straight as a board, like one of those old dolls whose back refused to bend because of age. "Jeopardy!"

You coming or what?

"Jeopardy Belle?" A smile stretched across my face because I knew that voice. Addison stirred beside me. She reached for me, but I was already on my feet. I heard Jeopardy's light steps traveling down the hall toward the Great Room.

"Harper? Where you going?"

"Come on, Addison. It's Jeopardy!"

"Really?" Addison was by my side now, and I held her hand as we hurried down the hall following Jeopardy's footsteps. This was a dream come true! Was I dreaming? I had dreamed so many times of Jeopardy's return. But I knew I was awake—I could feel the cold floor beneath my bare feet, and my lungs burned because the air all around me was cold. I glanced back and saw Addison's pale face. Her teeth were chattering.

I could hear Momma's radio playing in the parlor. It wasn't loud, not like earlier when she was entertaining Dewey Landry, but low and quiet. She was talking to someone, but who? Surely not Jeopardy. There was no love lost between those two. I paused to eavesdrop on her conversation. No, she was on the phone. I could tell by the tone of her voice. I wondered if I would see Mr.

Daughdrill lying on the floor dead if I peeked into the parlor. There was no time to consider that. As we tiptoed through the near-empty Great Room to head up the stairs, I heard an odd sound. A thump. No, two thumps. Momma wasn't on the phone after all!

A man murmured in the other room. Was Dewey Landry back? Knowing that someone else might be in the house, I raced up the stairs with Addison in tow. We had to find Jeopardy and keep her out of sight. Way out of sight. I'd have to warm up Momma before I told her that Jeopardy had returned. Unlike Addison and Loxley and me, Momma had unpredictable moods. She might not be happy that Jeopardy had returned. But why? I'd never understand it.

And after what happened tonight, perhaps it was me Jeopardy should be afraid of. I nearly killed someone. But he wasn't dead, was he? Momma said he wasn't. I was sure he was hurt pretty bad, though. I forced the memory out of my mind, and Addison moaned behind me as she stubbed a toe on a worn step.

"Quiet," I whispered to her as we hurried up the last of the steps. We were on the second floor now, and if I thought it was cold downstairs, it felt like the freezer of the soda shop up here.

Addison hugged me and said, "Harper, I'm afraid. What are we doing up here?"

"I heard Jeopardy's voice, and so did you. Jeopardy is here." And then as if she were hurrying us along, the attic door slowly began to open. It squeaked on its hinges as it opened wide inch by inch, like Jeopardy was welcoming us inside her castle room. There was nothing but blackness in the attic, but I had to go on. I had to see Jeopardy Belle. I wanted to hold her in my arms and never let her go. My heart pounded as I thought about finally telling her how sorry I was that I had wrongly blamed her for destroying my dress. How sorry I was that I didn't do more for her. And if she wasn't happy at Summerleigh, we'd run away. The three of us. Jeopardy, Addison and me. We would leave Desire, Mississippi, behind and go explore the world. We were all smart and hard-working. We could make our way in the world.

"Come on, Addison," I said, smiling back at her as we raced to the attic.

But what about Loxley? I argued with myself. Addison whined again. What was the matter with her? We stood in the doorway now, peeking inside.

"Jeopardy Belle, where are you?"

She didn't answer, but I could sense that she was watching us from the darkness. "Come on, Addie." I hurried into the cluttered room. It wasn't as cold in here, and Jeopardy had been kind enough to light a candle. It wasn't much of a candle, only a few inches of white stub, but it was enough to illuminate her makeshift bed. I laughed to see it.

"Jeopardy? Why are you hiding? Come out this instant." I laughed at her playfulness. But then Jeopardy did not emerge from the shadows. Addie clutched my hands and stood in front of me. She put her pale face near mine. I didn't realize until that moment how tall she'd gotten; she was almost my height, and I was nearly as tall as Momma.

"Harper Louise, we can't stay here. Jeopardy isn't here. You were dreaming."

Dumbfounded, I blinked at her. I didn't dream any of this. I heard Jeopardy! She called me pieface. "I didn't dream that candle, Addison. I didn't dream her voice; I know it like I know yours. It was her, all right. She's here, but she's being ridiculous. Jeopardy, if you don't come out right now, I'm going back downstairs. I mean it." I waited. Still nothing. "All right, you give me no choice. I'm counting to three—no more games. One...two..."

At the far side of the room where the junk was stacked the tallest, where there were trunks and crates arranged haphazardly on top of one another, I saw Jeopardy. But only for the briefest of seconds. It was as if a shaft of moonlight had hit her, revealing her hiding spot to me. She still wore those clunky white shoes, the one she'd taken from Momma. Her wild hair was around her shoulders, and she looked as pale as a sheet of paper. She even had her purse on her shoulder, which I knew was impossible. The sheriff's deputy had brought the shoes and purse to us the day they found them. Then she vanished. There was no more light, except for the candle.

And then I knew the horrible truth.

Wherever she was, Jeopardy was never coming home. I hadn't seen her at all, not living and breathing Jeopardy Belle. This was not her, just her shadow. Wild and brave Jeopardy was gone forever, and I'd seen her ghost. Addison saw her too because she was crying now. And then as quickly as I understood the horribleness of it all, I felt myself falling.

I welcomed the darkness.

Chapter Nine—Jerica

To my dismay, Hannah's phone went directly to voicemail. I hoped that meant she was communicating with her paranormal investigator friends and trying to pull together a few who might help me clear Summerleigh of its unwanted residents. The events of this morning left me feeling desperate, and I never wanted to swim in Dog River—or any other river—ever again. I left Hannah a message about my encounter at the river and immediately called Jesse.

"Hey. You busy?" I asked.

He paused, and I feared that he'd say yes, but he didn't. "Let me set this down." I heard a thud, and then he said, "What's going on?"

I paced the floor, twisting a strand of hair in my hand as I talked. How would I say this without sounding like a lunatic? "Do you think the boy and Mr. Daughdrill are connected somehow?"

"What? I don't think so. The McIntyre family was gone from Summerleigh in the 1870s, and the house was vacant for a long time before it was sold again. It wasn't until John Belle won it that Daughdrill came around. He wasn't hurting for money. The man owned several homes and hundreds of acres. Why?"

I plopped down on the couch and sighed. "You're not going to believe what happened to me this morning." I told him everything. Jesse knew there were ghosts at Summerleigh, but they were different now. It seemed they weren't limited to the house but were stalking me around the property.

I could hear the worry in his voice. "That's not good, Jerica. That's not good at all. Listen, I know this might sound inappropriate, but I really wish you'd spend the night here tonight. I've got the guest room, and I wouldn't mind the company. I could use a skilled helper. This boat isn't going to build itself."

I smiled at that. It did sound like fun, and I'd never worked on a boat before. But the nagging feeling that I shouldn't go was strong. I glanced around my kitchen as if I would see Marisol pop up at any moment. She'd be the only reason why I would stay here. What about my daughter? What if I wasn't here? Would she be able to fend off the boy? "I'd love to help you with that project, I really would, but I don't want to take advantage of our friendship. And I know this sounds crazy, but I need to be here."

"I'll bunk out at your house, then. Just for tonight. I mean, surely you know I'm not trying to be pushy. I'm really concerned. If that boy tried to drown you, who's to say he won't attack you again? I don't want you to be by yourself there."

I leaned back and looked around the corner into my living room. No way was big, tall Jesse Clarke going to make a comfortable bed for himself on my wicker couch. But I did see an air mattress in the upstairs closet. To be honest, I liked the idea of someone else being here. I just couldn't leave Marisol. What if she didn't follow me?

"That sounds great. Would you mind? And bring whatever information you have about the McIntyre family. Maybe if we dig a little deeper, we could find something to help us identify this boy. The thought of those two working together is more horrifying."

The phone line began to whine, and there was a strange crunching sound like the connection was breaking up.

"Jesse? Jesse, can you hear me?" And then the phone went dead. *Okay, that's just weird.* I had to call the phone company about this. Twice in one week could not be a coincidence. I felt my phone vibrating in my pocket. It was a text from Jesse: *I'll be there in fifteen minutes.* I breathed a sigh of relief and texted him back a smiley face.

I made some sweet tea, cleared my kitchen table and plundered the refrigerator for something I could whip up for lunch. A light tapping on my back door drew me away from my search. No one ever used the back door, no one but Marisol and Loxley. *Marisol!* I hurried to open it but didn't see any little girls running away. There was no one there, nothing except a lone bluebonnet. I picked up the dark blue flower and held it. *Marisol. Thank you.* I went back into the house and found a small bottle to use as a vase. I filled it with water and put the flower on the kitchen table. We needed some good luck. I stared at the flower and experienced all sorts of emotions waiting for Jesse to arrive. True to his word, he showed up promptly with armloads of books, an overnight bag and a plastic crate of folders.

"Goodness. You came prepared. Let me help you." I grabbed the plastic file folder bin, surprised at the weight. "You weren't kidding when you said you had a heck of a lot of research." He shook his head, and I admired the glasses he was wearing today. "Hey, those look good on you." He gave me a half grin, and we walked into the kitchen and deposited all of the materials on the table. "Would you like a glass of tea?"

"Sure. Sounds great. Did you hear anything from Hannah yet? I guess you know Ree-Ree is all over this. She's gonna come over sometime today. She happened to be at the house when you called and overheard everything."

"It's no bother. I like your cousin. I just hope it's not unsafe to have people around. I mean, my God. I would never have imagined anything like that happening to me. It was like something out of a movie. A horror movie." I shivered at the memory of the boy grabbing my ankle and pulling me down into the river. If I wasn't such a good swimmer, if I wasn't determined to live, I wouldn't be standing here right now. *No, I'd be with Marisol. Is that such a bad thing?* I walked over to the refrigerator and poured Jesse a glass of tea. I set it down in front of him and watched him arrange stacks of papers on the table.

"Where do we start? Tell me what you know about the McIntyre family, in a nutshell."

"Mariana McIntyre, the young woman who was murdered, her father's name was Robert 'Bull' McIntyre. And just like his name suggests, he was a force of nature all by himself. It was strange that anyone would want to build a mansion out here in the middle of nowhere, but he was determined to do it. Rumor has it that there used to be another house on this property before Summerleigh, but it burned to the ground. The records from that time—probably in the early 1830s—are not reliable, and there isn't much information about who owned this property then. So as far as official records go, we can only go back to the McIntyre family. Mariana had just turned sixteen when she was found dead. Let me see if I can find a copy of the actual newspaper clipping. I have it here somewhere." Jesse shuffled through his records until he found what he was looking for. "Ah, here it is."

He slid it to me, and I silently read the headline: McIntyre Mystery Murder Friday Night. I read and reread the tiny article, but there wasn't much information there except for Mariana's age and a mention of her brother and father.

"Is that it? Did they ever find her killer?"

"I haven't found any record of anyone being charged with her murder. I found nothing in any of the papers. To make matters worse, Summerleigh was full that night. It was her birthday celebration."

"God, she died on her birthday?"

"Yeah," he said. "After that article, I don't find even a mention of Mariana again. But Bull McIntyre went downhill fast. His lumber mill burned, and he was accused of all types of crimes, arson, murder—two men died in that mill fire. He refused to help their families afterward. He accused them of arson and even threatened lawsuits against their widows. The women gave up their claims, but the damage had been done. All of George County turned against him. People had nothing to do with him after that, and everyone pointed at him anytime something went wrong in Desire."

"Do you think he did it? Could it have been him I saw at the river?"

"I don't know, but we shouldn't rule out Mariana's brothers. She had two, a younger one and an older one. The younger one's name has been lost, but I do know both boys' names started with the letter J. Military records indicate that a Jameson McIntyre enlisted in the Mississippi militia around the time of Mariana's death, but he was never seen or heard from again. But you have to remember that times were different then. If people wanted to get lost, they could."

"So he disappeared after her murder?"

"I can't be sure. It's pretty close, as far as timelines go."

"This other McIntyre, the younger boy, I wonder what his name is. Hannah told me that she believed I had some authority with the ghost because I own the house now. She thinks if I knew his name, I could command him to leave. Any chance we'll find it in here?"

"I've looked for years," he confessed as he opened a folder. Seeing my expression, he quickly added, "But today might be my lucky day."

I accepted the folder and skimmed through the lists of births and deaths. Geesh, Jesse had put in a lot of time on this. After a few minutes of paper shuffling, I sat back and closed my eyes. This wasn't the time to get a headache, but I could feel one coming on. The house was quiet except for the ice cracking in Jesse's glass. I half expected to hear that light tapping again at the back door. For a moment, I wondered what it would be like for Jesse to meet Marisol. Would she like him? Surely she would have. He was kind and loving, just like Eddie used to be before the drugs sucked his soul dry. And then my house phone rang. I gasped and put my hand on my chest. "Excuse me. That must be Hannah." I picked up and said, "Hello?"

"Jerica, this is Ben, Ben Hartley. I'm on my way to Summerleigh. I have something to tell you. Please, promise me you'll wait for me to arrive."

"Wait for what, Ben? Are you okay?" I looked at Jesse, who raised his eyebrows.

"It's something I should have told you a long time ago. I'm driving down. Be there in about an hour." And with that, he clicked the phone down and the line went dead.

"Ben?" I held the phone up and put it back on the base. I turned to Jesse and said, "You're never gonna believe this, but Ben Hartley is on the way here. He says there's something he has to tell me."

"Well, I guess we might as well keep plowing through. There is a chance I missed something. I mean, this is a lot of information. You ready to dig deep?"

My stomach was growling, but my fear was growing too. I chewed on my bottom lip, wondering what in the world Ben wanted to tell me. And why couldn't he have told me on the phone? Or the other day? There was nothing to do but wait. I took my seat beside Jesse and began shuffling through the papers, looking for any reference to the McIntyre family that I could find. This might be the slowest hour of my life.

I suddenly snapped my fingers. "Wait a second. That book. I found a book in the potting shed, and I've been meaning to show it to you. I think I put it in the bookcase."

"What book?" Jesse looked up from a land owner's record he was flipping through.

"I found it a few months ago and forgot all about it. It was the day I heard the girls giggling outside the potting shed." I rifled through the bookcase in the living room and found the dusty old book in a drawer. "Here it is. The writing is faint, but I think the name inside is McIntyre."

I leaned over him as he examined the cover. There was no title, and the cover appeared a bit worse for wear. It wasn't a large book, more like a journal. He flipped it open and laid it on the table in front of him. "Hey, turn that light on. You're right, this ink is pretty faded."

"I think it's some sort of record. Maybe for plants? Was Mr. McIntyre a botanist?"

"Not that I know of. I wish I understood all these notations. Look, there are several columns, but the headings are too faded to read. Maybe these are flower species? I need a magnifying glass to make this out."

"I don't have one." I peered closer. "The more I look at it, I don't think those are flower names. Aren't those usually Latin? That one there," I said as I pointed at the page, "that's C-L-A-U-D-E-T-T-E something or other. And that one there, A-R-, is that an I? Or an L? It could be A-R-I-C-E-L-I. Grab a pen, Jesse. Hey, I'll use my phone to magnify the writing."

"Brilliant," he said as he slid the book to me and reached for a notebook.

Surprisingly, the hour didn't drag by. By the end of it, we were looking at a list of names, places and strange descriptions. At the very back of the book, we found the faint signature of Jameson P. McIntyre.

At least we'd solved one mystery and confirmed the name of one of the McIntyre sons. Little did we know that things were about to get even stranger.

Chapter Ten—Jerica

Jesse and I were still waiting for Ben to arrive. So far, he was a no-show. The afternoon was burning away; we were losing daylight, and I began to feel anxious. Not just at the idea of going into the house at night but because Ben had seemed so frail when last I saw him. I couldn't understand his change of heart. He'd done everything he could to make sure I came to Summerleigh, leaving me those keys and walking out of the Sunrise Retirement Home without another word. If he hadn't shown up, I would never have fallen in love with the place and the long-lost Belle family. Now he wanted to send me back to Virginia?

Yeah, color me confused. I checked the clock again. It was after four now. If he was coming from Jackson, he should've been here an hour ago. I turned to Jesse, unable to hide the worry I felt.

"Does Ben have any relatives in the area that you know about? Someone we could contact?"

"No. I can't think of anyone. But you know how Ben is, Jerica. He'll be here soon, and if he's not, we can contact the state troopers or somebody."

Someone tapped on the front door, and I hoped and prayed that it was Ben Hartley. Instead, it was Hannah. I'd been so worried about Ben that I completely forgot about her. She was here with two people I didn't know, so I gathered she'd gotten my voicemail that I wanted to move forward with our investigation into Summerleigh.

"Hey, Hannah. Please come in. I'm so glad you could make it."

Hannah clutched her purse as she always did and smiled nervously before introducing me to her friends. "Thanks for inviting me. These are two of my colleagues, Amy Whitehead and Rex Nylund. Both have a lot of experience in the paranormal field. Amy's here to help me with the technical aspects of our investigation, and Rex has other skills. He's a sensitive." Amy nodded, and Rex extended his hand. I shook it politely and invited them into the kitchen where Jesse was tidying up our research to make room for them.

"Hey, Hannah," he said, glancing over his shoulder. "Hey, y'all," he said politely to Rex and Amy as he arranged his papers in the plastic bin and slid it out of the way.

"Jesse, I didn't know you were here," Hannah said, giving him a sunny smile. That was a rare thing—she was friendly but not one to smile much. I invited everyone to have a seat around the table. Since we were one chair short, I pulled the extra one up from its usual spot near the Princess telephone.

Rex said, "I hear you have a negative entity at Summerleigh. I can't say I'm surprised, considering all of the history that's happened on this property. What is it you hope we can do for you, Jerica?"

"I'm hoping to get rid of him. I mean, if he were the peaceful sort of spirit, I wouldn't mind him being there. But slamming doors and scaring people? I can't have that happening all the time."

"Hannah told us that the activity ramped up when you guys began to renovate. That's not uncommon. Any particular hot spots?" Amy asked in a soft voice as she whipped out a notebook and pencil.

"Yes, that is correct. The house was empty for quite some time before I got here. I was hoping to change all that. I think most of the activity happens on the second floor, in the nursery and the attic."

Rex leaned forward and rested his chin on his folded hands. "I want you to understand that I am a sensitive, but I'm not an exorcist, so I don't have any special skills for ousting ghosts. But I will be glad to lend whatever skills I do have to help you navigate this situation. I understand it can be frightening to have that activity happening around you."

Jesse nodded in agreement. "The doors on the top floor slammed so hard I thought the place was going to fall in. It was the scariest darn thing I've ever seen. If I hadn't seen it myself, I'm not sure I would believe it. We've been working in that house for weeks and have not had any problems. But now, it's straight-up dangerous. Jerica, tell them what happened to you today at the river."

All eyes were on me, and I fought the urge to kick Jesse under the table. Since he brought it up, I told the group what happened earlier and then concluded, "And Mr. Daughdrill was standing on the bank watching. Like he wanted me to drown, like he expected me to die. I guess I can understand why he would want to come after me. At least Harper went to her grave not knowing what a monster he really was, but I know him for who he is. He was never the kind of man who liked it when a woman had the upper hand on him. I know the type." I avoided looking in Jesse's direction. I hadn't meant to drop hints about my past like that.

"That's not quite true. She knew. Harper knew," a voice from behind me whispered. I spun around to see Ben Hartley standing in my kitchen drenched with sweat.

"Ben! I didn't hear you come in. Please have a seat. Would you like something to drink?" Ben's face looked pale, and his lips were colorless.

"Yes. Water, please."

"What happened to you, Ben?"

"I had a flat, and I'm not as spry as I used to be."

I handed him a glass of water and said, "These are my friends, Ben. This is Hannah, and this is

Amy and Rex. They're here to help me with the house."

With shaking hands, Ben sipped the water. "I don't think you understand, Jerica. Some of those spirits can't be pacified, and no amount of pleading with them is going to change that. They are dead and gone, and there's nothing more you can do for them."

The kitchen was so quiet you could hear a pin drop. I didn't want him to get worked up again, not after what he'd been through already. In an attempt to steer the conversation in another direction I asked, "What do you mean, Ben? What did Harper know? Did Mr. Daughdrill die that night?"

Ben put his empty glass on the table and buried his face in his hands. He sobbed, and I put my arm around him. What was it about this man that made me want to protect him? He seemed so broken, but I had no idea why. Hannah, Rex and Amy excused themselves and hurried off to the living room to give us some privacy.

Jesse grabbed some tissues and handed them to him. Ben said, "I'm so sorry, Jerica. I don't mean to blubber like a child. And I know it was a long time ago, but it doesn't make it any easier. You understand."

I nodded. "Tell us what happened. What did Harper know?"

"Daughdrill didn't die that night. She told me about it later, after we had become better friends. She and Addison were like my own two sisters. I admit I had a bit of a crush on Harper back then. Maybe I still do. Old man Daughdrill hated me. He'd complain to Mrs. Belle when I came around, but she didn't say a word to Harper. I think she was proud of her, thankful in her own twisted way, but she would never say so. Oh no. She was never the kind of woman to admit she needed anyone. But really, she was needier than everyone."

"Go on, Ben. Tell me more about Harper."

"Mr. Daughdrill started coming around the school to see Addison. He would bring her presents like jewelry, but she never left with him. Harper was always there, running defense. But he was a master at manipulation, and he succeeded in driving a wedge between them, at least for a little while. Before he died, he practically moved into the house and took over. Her mother didn't say a word." Ben began to tear up again. "Harper wouldn't want you to be in danger, Jerica. Please promise me you'll stop the renovation. Let sleeping dogs lie, Jerica. Go back home and have a happy life."

Jesse couldn't hide his surprise. "Why, Ben? You haven't given her a reason except to say bad things happened to the Belle girls. We know that. Don't you think it's time to let some sunshine into the place? Let Summerleigh breathe again?"

"You can't see it. You see the house and want to love it, but nobody is happy there. Nobody is ever happy at Summerleigh. John Belle thought he could fix the place up. Look where it got him. Jeopardy, Addison, Harper...they're all gone. You don't understand. You haven't seen what I've seen." He sobbed again.

I cast an eye at Jesse and nodded my head toward the living room. Thankfully, he got the message and immediately left to apologize to Hannah and her friends. I heard the front door open and close as they left. I'd have to call her later.

More than anything, I wanted to know who that little boy was, but it wouldn't be today. Ben Hartley was in no shape to drive home, and I couldn't in good conscience ignore his wishes. Not while he was here, anyway. I sat quietly and waited for him to regain his composure. Jesse returned and sat at the table with us. I was glad to have him there.

"Now tell us everything, Ben. What have you seen at Summerleigh that makes you so afraid?"

"I've seen the devil there, Jerica. And he's not going to leave. It was his place before they ever built Summerleigh. This is old land. Lots of deadly things happened here. Even the local native tribes avoided this patch of land. I tried to warn Harper. I told her what I knew, what my grandfather told me, but she didn't listen. Not until it was too late." Ben sounded confused, and it set off alarms in my nurse's brain. *I know these symptoms, don't I?* "At least she made it out alive. I am glad for that. I loved Harper Belle, you know. It broke my heart when she married that Hayes fella, but it is what it is. Water under the bridge." He wiped at his eyes again. "When I lived here, I woke up to find flowers on my doorstep every now and then. How about you?"

I glanced at the flower on the table. It had withered a bit but was still a vibrant shade of blue. My heart sank. I wanted to believe Marisol had brought me those flowers. Had I been wrong?

"Yes, I've found flowers a few times."

"Ah, but you never know who's bringing them. Be careful what you invite into your home, Jerica Poole. Be really careful. Some things aren't that easy to get rid of."

Jesse stared hard at the old man, and I could see the uncertainty on his face. Ignoring the icy-cold feeling I had, I glanced at the clock. Suppertime. That's what Ben needed, food and some rest.

"Jesse, how do you feel about grilling some pork chops? I've got some in the refrigerator. Are you hungry, Ben?"

"Yes, but I thought you wanted to hear everything."

"I do, but right now I want to eat. Why don't you get freshened up while Jesse and I whip up some grub?"

"That would be lovely. Thank you. I'll do that." He wandered off to the bathroom. Of course, he didn't have to ask where it was. He'd lived here. He knew this house inside and out. And he knew Summerleigh.

Jesse touched my arm. "I hope you don't intend to let him stay here. Something seems off about him. I know you want to see him as a sweet old man and everything, but I can't shake the feeling that something is wrong."

"I agree. But the less he hears about the house, the better off he'll be. I don't think Ben is well. I really don't. Let's cook supper and go from there. Thank you for being so patient with him. And me."

Jesse grinned down at me and said, "Just show me the way to the grill."

"Just out back on the patio." I kissed his cheek playfully. He paused, like he wanted more, but Ben came back into the kitchen.

"I'm not interrupting you all, am I?"

"Not at all, Ben. Have a seat while I prep these chops."

And for the next few hours, nobody talked about Summerleigh or ghosts. It was nice to pretend that everything was okay. Unfortunately, it was just the calm before the storm.

Chapter Eleven—Harper

"Loxley wasn't at school today, Momma. Can't we go see her?"

A haze of cigarette smoke swirled around my mother's face, and she wore her usual lost expression. She always looked like this when she'd spent the previous night drinking, and she did that more and more as of late. "She's better off with Dot. In fact, you'd all be better off." And she was still drunk.

I hung up the phone and stared at the back of her head. Her hair was unbrushed and unwashed. She wasn't dressed either. Addison and I would have to hoof it, and quickly, if we were going to make it to school on time. One more tardy and I would face Mr. Alfred's wrath. And possibly his paddle. Too bad he couldn't paddle Momma.

"Where's Jeopardy this morning? Jeopardy?" It of course wasn't Jep but Addison. She came into the kitchen wearing new shoes, and her hair was brushed and tidy.

"Morning, Momma. What's for breakfast, Harper?" she said as she frowned at the empty table.

Am I the only sane one around here?

"You don't have time for breakfast, your majesty. We're walking to school this morning," I said as I picked up my books from the table and slung my purse over my shoulder.

"I can't walk to school in these shoes. They're brand new!" she whined as she pursed her pouty lips. "Grandfather would be so mad if I scuffed them up before he saw me in them."

That woke Momma up from her stupor. She rose to her wobbly feet and put her hands on the table to steady herself. "What did you say? Who's buying you shoes, Addison Lee?"

Addison backed away from Momma, and I pushed her behind me as I reached for the back door. "We better go, Addison."

"Okay," she said as she scurried out of Summerleigh. "Bye, Momma." I could hear her voice breaking up as she sailed down the back steps.

"Addison, you get back here!" Momma shouted after her.

I closed the door and left Momma to stew in her own juices. I caught up with Addison around the corner of the house. The overgrown hydrangeas made the perfect hiding spot. "Come on out, Addie. She's too drunk to follow us to school. Take your shoes off if you're worried about getting them dirty, but the walk might be hard on your feet."

Addison clutched her notebook to her chest and looked down at her shoes. "These are the nicest shoes I've ever owned." She didn't take them off, and we walked together down Hurlette.

I smiled at her. "Yes, they're very nice."

Addison smiled back, but her expression changed. Daddy always said she would make a horrible poker player. She could never hide her emotions. "I'm sorry, Harper." She grabbed my arm gently. "I tried to get you a pair too, but you know how Grandfather is. Maybe if you apologized to him, he'd like you again. I tried to explain it to him, how hard it was to live with Momma, but I think...I think you really hurt him. I mean, you did beat him with that poker."

I couldn't believe my ears. It was too early in the day to be stupefied twice. "He was beating Momma, Addison. How can you take his side? You're my sister."

"I know, and I love you, Harper, but you can be so strong-willed sometimes."

"Where did you hear that?" I asked suspiciously. I needn't have wondered. Mr. Daughdrill pulled up in his long black Master DeLuxe and rolled his window down.

"Would you like a ride to school, Addison? I'm going to town. I'll be happy to take you so you don't get caught in the rain."

"Sure," she said, but then she looked at me. "But can Harper go too? Like you said, it might rain and all."

He cast a steely look at me. Now, Mr. Daughdrill would have made a fine poker player. You never knew what he was thinking. Never. "Of course, dear. Hop in, girls. You wouldn't want to be late. That's not the Daughdrill way. Your mother was never late for school. Not one day."

"We're not Daughdrills. We're Belles," I murmured as I walked to the car. Addison shot me an ugly grimace, and I rolled my eyes. I climbed in the back seat and listened to the radio as we pulled up into the schoolyard. I immediately began searching for Aunt Dot's convertible but didn't see it. I wondered if Loxley would be in school today, but I didn't dare ask Mr. Daughdrill. When we arrived at school, I got out of the car and gave a half-hearted thank-you.

"Harper, a word of advice." He waved me toward him, but I didn't step any closer. "Don't ruin things for Addison. She has a real future; she's such a lovely young lady. It's not attractive for a girl to be jealous of her sister."

"I'm not jealous of my sister. And I have three of them, remember?" Cars were pulling in behind his, and I took another step back.

"Stay out of trouble, Harper. We can't afford another scandal. I'll see you girls after school. Make sure you are here and ready to go home."

I stared after him as he pulled off. Addison was already in the schoolhouse; she'd left me behind, probably anxious to show off her new shoes. I guess I really couldn't blame her. We rarely had new things. But at what cost? Why would he do that? I couldn't imagine Mr. Daughdrill doing anything that didn't benefit him directly.

The day dragged by. The only bright spot was a surprise invitation to go fishing with Benny and his little cousin Angie. I agreed to meet them at the river at four o'clock but had second thoughts later. I hadn't been to the river since Jeopardy disappeared. Why was it nobody said her name anymore? I had that deputy's phone number somewhere, and I made up my mind then and there to call him. Momma wasn't going to do it, and I wanted my sister to come home.

I waited outside the school after the bell, but Mr. Daughdrill didn't show up, and neither did my sister. It would be very much like him to leave me behind as a way to teach me a lesson. Yes, very much like him.

"Hey, Arnette?" I caught my friend as she walked out with her steady, a tall, skinny kid named Roger. "Have you seen Addison?"

"She left a few minutes ago. With your grandfather, I think. Did you see them, Roger? I ducked inside to get my sweater."

Roger squinched his eyes and said, "You know, I think she did leave in that big black car. The new one."

"Was she alone?" I asked.

He shook his head. "No, her friend Bobbie Ann was with her. Need a ride? Did they leave you behind, Harper?"

"Yes, please. I guess she forgot all about me."

Arnette rolled her eyes. "Sisters. I'm glad I have Roger here. Let's take Harper home. It's on the way to my house."

"Sure thing, sweetie."

Arnette shook her head. I could tell she didn't like his nickname for her, but at least he was a nice guy. The ride home was long, not because the company was bad but because I was worried about my sisters. Loxley was with Aunt Dot, absent again today. Addison was off with our grandfather, and Momma was probably drinking herself to death. And God only knew where Jeopardy was. I didn't want to believe she was really a ghost. That would mean she was dead, right?

We pulled into the driveway, and I got out of the truck before it stopped. "Thanks, you two. I'll buy you both a Coke sometime."

"Sounds great. Bye, Harper," Arnette said with a smile.

"Bye," I said as I walked up the steps of Summerleigh. I rarely came in the front door, but it was unlocked and I walked right inside.

I walked through the Great Room into the parlor. My grandfather was lounging in the red velvet chair, the radio on low, the newspaper in his lap. He sucked on his pipe and smiled at me. I didn't return the smile. "Where's Addison?"

As if she'd heard me, Addie walked into the room from the bedroom hallway. "Hey, Harper. Just the person I'm looking for. What do you think? Pink sweater with the green dress or the blue one? I'm not sure. Grandfather says pink, but I kind of like the blue." She strutted around in her new dress and spun around for our grandfather, who complimented her on the color...and the fit.

"I don't know," I grumbled at her as I headed into the kitchen to find something to eat. Momma was on the phone, obviously with Aunt Dot, and I tried not to eavesdrop. When I opened the refrigerator, I almost passed out. It was loaded with food, a nice chunk of cheese, milk, butter and fruit galore. I couldn't help but notice that these were all Addison's favorites.

"You bring her home, Dot, or I'm going to call the police." She paused and then said, "No, he's not. I haven't seen him. Now bring me my daughter." She slammed the phone down and stubbed out her skinny cigarette in her seashell-shaped ashtray. "There you are. I've got some chicken laid out for supper. Are you up to frying it? I need to go lie down. I can feel a headache coming on."

"No. I already have plans."

"Well, those plans will have to wait. Someone needs to cook supper, Harper." She walked out of the kitchen with her hand on her forehead.

I sighed, but nobody heard me. *Same old, same old.* Just then, I heard Ben calling me from the screen door. "Hey, we've been waiting for you at the river. You ready to go?"

I reached for a few strawberries and put the pint back in the refrigerator. I wasn't cooking supper. I wasn't doing any of it. I was going fishing. "You got a pole for me?"

"Yep, and it's ready to go." Ben smiled and showed his missing tooth. I liked him more by the minute. "All right. Let's go."

We only caught two small fish, but it wasn't a total loss. Ben was quiet and his little cousin even quieter. It was a nice evening tossing lines in the water. We talked a little, more than I thought we would. I didn't come back until after dark, and I was bone-tired. I had homework, but somehow, it didn't seem that important anymore. They must have managed supper because although the kitchen was tidy when I came in the back door, I could smell the remnants of fried chicken. I opened the refrigerator hoping to find a piece, but there wasn't any left. Mr. Daughdrill must have stayed for dinner. I grabbed some more strawberries and headed to my room. But then I heard the pop of Momma's lighter and saw her face illuminated in the yellow light.

"Awful late, Harper Louise. I guess you were out with a boy."

"It's not that late. Only nine o'clock. I lost track of time is all."

"It's easy to do when you're in someone's arms," she said as she spat a stray bit of tobacco leaf out of her mouth and eyed me. She had her arm crooked over the back of her chair. I couldn't smell any alcohol, but I had to be careful. Any minute, Momma could turn on you. I glanced around carefully and spotted a skillet on the stove. She followed my eyes and tilted her head up.

"I wasn't in anyone's arms. I'm only fifteen, Momma. I went fishing is all."

She took a deep drag off her skinny cigarette and said in a quiet voice, "You'll have to sleep upstairs tonight. Mr. Daughdrill is sleeping in your room. I expect he will sleep in there for a few nights at least."

"What? Why is he here?"

She didn't answer my question. "I left you some blankets on the couch. I guess you could sleep on it if you don't mind the smell. It really needs to be cleaned, Harper."

"Why is he in my bed? Don't you remember how he treated you?"

"That's all over now, and I've forgiven him. And you should too, dear. It's what's best for us all. Now, don't make a fuss. Go to sleep. You have school in the morning, in case you forgot. I swear, you behave more like your sister every day."

I stomped my foot. "Good! I want to be like her. And why can't you say her name, Momma? Do you remember her name? Jeopardy! Why can't you say her name?" I was shouting now, but there was nothing I could do about it.

"Of course I do. You think I could forget her? You think I don't see her all the time? I wish...I wish a lot of things, but wishing don't make it reality. Go to bed, Harper."

"I'm not sleeping on the couch."

"You can't sleep with Addison. She's ill and can't be disturbed."

"So you want me to go upstairs and sleep with the ghosts, then?" I wasn't joking. The idea of sleeping in Jeopardy's castle room or any other room on that floor frightened me. Jep had always been braver than me.

"You know perfectly well your sister would never hurt you. Go to bed."

And in that moment, I knew Momma believed Jeopardy was dead. But why did she think that? I lay on the couch first, but it was so uncomfortable that I couldn't sleep. I could smell Mr. Daughdrill's pipe tobacco too, and the odor made me squeamish. I tiptoed to Addison's room. I could hear Mr. Daughdrill snoring in my room before I even got into the hallway. Addie was out like a light. I crept back down the hall and retrieved my blanket and pillow.

I felt like I was going into exile, like I was now officially banned from the family. I didn't fit in anymore. I wasn't wanted.

Was this how Jeopardy felt?

I haven't given up on you, Jep. I love you. You are the best sister a girl ever had. I'll bring you home. I swear, as God is my witness, I swear. With fat tears, I made the trek up the stairs and walked down the dark hallway to the attic. I heard nothing, I saw nothing, and I kept my eyes ahead of me.

It was as if the ghosts were expecting me and welcomed me. I was one of them now. Or I would be soon.

The attic door opened with a creak. I closed it behind me and stood in the dark trying to adjust my eyes to the dimness. Jeopardy's pallet was under the window. I tossed my blanket on top of hers and put my pillow beside hers. Absolutely exhausted, I curled up in a ball and clutched her pillow, which still held her sweet, wild scent. She smelled like sunshine and wildflowers and tobacco. She smelled like life...but not anymore.

Where are you, Jeopardy Belle? Why did you leave me?

I cried myself to sleep and woke up early as the sun was beginning to rise. My body was stiff and achy all over from sleeping on the floor. I missed my comfortable bed, but I doubted that I would ever sleep in it again. I could hear the signs of life in the house even before I opened my eyes.

Mariana, oh Mariana. Open your eyes. Open them. Open your eyes. Look what I have…

"What? Ben?" I heard a boy's voice, but I couldn't fathom who it could be. There were no boys in this house, especially not up here. I blinked against the sunlight that streamed through the window. I saw him for only the briefest of seconds.

It was a boy with large dark eyes, black hair and pale skin. He held a pair of scissors in one hand and a lock of my hair in the other. I screamed as he vanished, and my hand immediately went to my hair.

I couldn't believe it, but the ghost had cut a lock of my hair. It was gone. I looked around the bed and saw nothing. Had I cut my hair in my sleep? No, of course not. I didn't even own a pair of scissors.

I scooted away from the pallet and put my back against the wall, waiting for my heart to stop racing. There were indeed ghosts here. And one of them had a pair of scissors. Loxley had been telling the truth all along.

I ran as fast as I could out of the attic and down the stairs. I didn't stop until I found Addison. Instantly, she put her arms around me. "It's okay, Harper. You can sleep with me tonight. You can stay with me. You don't ever have to go upstairs again."

I would hold her to that promise.

Chapter Twelve—Jerica

I glanced at the clock, surprised to see that it was eight o'clock already. I could hear men's voices downstairs. *Must be Jesse and Ben.* I didn't wait for Marisol's hug. I'd given up on those. Instead, I clutched her purple bear to my chest and kissed it before climbing out of bed. It wasn't her favorite toy, but it was the only one I had left. Eddie had taken everything else. I suddenly felt the urge to call the detective handling his case to get more details on how things had turned out, but I resisted. Yeah, I wanted Eddie to rot under the jail, but as long as he was nowhere near me, I wasn't going to bother wasting any more time on him.

I found a white t-shirt and a pair of blue shorts to wear. It was going to be another hot day, and I had to get into that house somehow without upsetting Ben too much. I wondered how Jesse had fared on the wicker sofa. I heard a vehicle pull out of the driveway. Was that Jesse? Ben? I'd find out in a minute, but first I had to brush this hair of mine. I began brushing the knots out and was surprised to find a chunk of it was missing.

A sizable chunk.

Oh my God! Was I going bald? I searched my bed for the missing hair, but there was nothing there. I didn't know why I couldn't remember what happened to it. I hadn't had a drop to drink last night and couldn't remember the last time

I'd taken a pill, since I'd never found a new doctor to get those new prescriptions. But whether I remembered it or not, a good half-inch of my hair had been cut, and whoever had done the deed had chunked it up big time. No, wait. He'd cut several chunks of my hair. And now I had a fragmentary memory of the sound of heavy scissors.

"What in the..." Well, there were only two other people in my house. But would either Jesse or Ben pull such a prank? Was this some sort of south Mississippi joke?

"You guys, is this a joke?" I said as I walked into the kitchen, holding up my hair to show them the cut spot. The room was empty except for a note on the table written in Jesse's neat handwriting.

Taking Ben to town to buy a new tire. His spare won't make it home. I called Hannah. They'll be back over after Ben leaves. Made you some coffee and cinnamon rolls.

-J

He didn't say, "Hey, I took some hair," so I must be losing my mind. I poured a cup of coffee and marched back upstairs to try and do something with my mop. The struggle was real. I finally pulled on a ball cap and pulled my ponytail out the back. This would have to do until I could see a stylist about my unwanted haircut.

That boy, the ghost that scared Harper in my dream, didn't he have a pair of scissors? The creepy crawlies covered my body, but the sensation did not fill me with fear as it might have before. No, I was feeling something else now. I was feeling pissed off. First, he tries to drown me in the river, and now he cuts my hair off? What was wrong with this ghost? Did he think I was Mariana? Maybe he thought he screwed up the first time and wanted to come back to finish the job now?

I waited around for a few minutes and decided to take a walk to Summerleigh. I wanted some answers, and I wanted them yesterday. And by heavens, I was going to get them. I didn't know what I expected to learn, but I finished my coffee and walked out of the caretaker's cottage, leaving the door unlocked in case Jesse beat me home. I walked down the gravel pathway and went to the back door of Summerleigh. I knocked politely, as I nearly always did when I came in through this entrance. Nobody answered, of course, but for a moment I imagined I heard a chair slide under the table. *Am I interrupting breakfast, Harper?*

"It's me, Jerica Poole," I announced as I opened the door. I dreaded hearing the sounds of doors closing again in this breezy old house, so I propped a chair against the door to keep it open. "I'm not here to bother anyone, Harper. I'm still your friend."

Jerica...

Someone whispered my name. But who?

"Yes, it's me. I'm here by myself, Harper. Addison, Jeopardy. I'm here by myself. I'm going to walk through Summerleigh. I don't want to disturb you, but I need to find the boy. He cut my hair last night, and I want to know why."

And then I heard nothing but a breeze blowing in over the sink. Hey, wasn't that window closed? It had to be. I walked over to the window, and sure enough, it was closed. So where was that breeze coming from? We hadn't installed the new air conditioning system yet. I raised my hand above my head. No, this wasn't a draft. It was coming from the window. I could feel it up there too. What was that? There was a small stepladder in the kitchen, which I moved under the window so I could take down the curtains. Maybe the window wasn't sealed properly. Maybe air was getting in through a loose shim that we'd neglected to caulk. Anything was possible.

I stood on the ladder and reached above the window. Aha! That was it. It was breezy out, and this crack in the window seal was making the curtains flutter. I felt like a true paranormal investigator on one of the shows that Eddie used to enjoy watching. "Debunked," I announced proudly as I started to climb back down the short ladder.

But then I saw a face looking back at me from the other side of the window. It was the angriest face I'd ever seen. With red eyes in a shriveled skull, it bared its yellowed teeth at me. I knew who I was looking at. This was the very dead Mr. Daughdrill. With a scream of surprise, I fell backward and hit my head so hard that I saw stars.

And then I felt warm blood trickling down my neck. "Harper..." I whispered as everything faded.

Then I heard nothing at all.

Chapter Thirteen—Jerica

"Come on, Jeopardy. You'll make us late again." I heard a woman's voice behind me and recognized it as belonging to Jeopardy's Aunt Dot. I clutched her hand. Dot was so pretty, far prettier than her sister. Why couldn't anyone else see it, especially Dot?

"Please, I'm not Jeopardy. My name is Jerica, Jerica Poole."

"Jeopardy Belle, what did your Daddy tell you about lying?" Aunt Dot led me to the mirror in her room and pointed at me. The face looking back wasn't mine. I wasn't Jerica Poole anymore. I was truly Jeopardy Belle. Or at least I was her in this dream or whatever it was.

"John Belle, come see your daughter. She's playing that game again, you know, the one where she pretends she's somebody else."

John walked into the bathroom and leaned against the doorframe in his white overalls and a white t-shirt. He was as handsome today as he was the day I met him on the front porch of the caretaker's cottage.

"Please tell her, JB. You know who I am. You must know I'm not your daughter. I'm Jerica Poole." A gleam of recognition was in his eyes, but he couldn't answer me because Aunt Dot stepped in the way and closed the door between us.

"Jeopardy Belle, stop playing these games and get ready. We aren't going to have enough time to get you up to that school before Harper's big debut, and it's so important to her that you go."

No, this is all wrong. John Jeffrey Belle had already died when Harper went to the Harvest Dance. "Let me out of here. I have to go. I have to go now. I don't belong here." And then I saw that Aunt Dot had a pair of silver scissors in her hand.

"Dot? What are you doing with those?"

Aunt Dot's eyes were no longer a pretty soft blue, and her face had lost its feminine softness. Her eyes were dark, like two bottomless pits with no white at all. The woman—or whatever it was—was not Jeopardy's Aunt Dot.

She shouted, "Give me what I want! I must have it!"

With a scream, I pushed her away as I closed my eyes and waited for the blow. I had nowhere to run, nowhere to go. I was trapped in the bathroom with this blade-wielding entity. I threw my hands up instinctively to fend off the attack.

It didn't come.

"Mommy, come with me."

I looked up to see Marisol in the doorway. The door was open, but the boy, the one who had pretended to be Aunt Dot, was in my way. "I command you to leave me alone! I own this house. It's not yours!" He wasn't as small as I remembered. No, not at all. This ghost was much older than the boy Jesse and I had seen on the second floor of Summerleigh.

And then he vanished, but I got the sense that he was not far away. I might have repelled him for the moment, but he was strong and persistent. And he wasn't going to give up until he got what he wanted, whatever that was. I shivered at the thought. I stepped into the hallway and looked left and right. Just as I turned to the right, I saw my daughter's shiny dark ringlets sailing behind her as she ran up the attic stairs.

"No, wait! Marisol, don't go in there. Please!"

She turned back to me for the briefest of seconds before she opened the door and walked inside. I had no choice but to follow her. I had waited so long to see her, and I wasn't going to pass up the opportunity now. I walked to the attic door, which stood open, put my foot on the step and waited to hear something. *What if this is another trick?* It didn't matter. I had to go!

"Marisol?" I cried softly. "If you're in here, please tell Mommy. I need to hear your voice, baby girl."

And then I heard her say as clear as a bell, "Where are you, Mommy? I'm waiting for you." As I stepped into the attic fully, I said a silent prayer. It was the same kind of prayer I had heard Harper pray so long ago. "Dear God, please don't let her be terrible. Please don't let my baby look like a monster. Please, God, help me."

There were many candles lit in the window near the place where Jeopardy's bed used to be. Jeopardy always liked candles. I knew that about her. Not many people knew it, but she enjoyed making candles. She'd spent many afternoons up here working with wax and wicks and molds, making her own creations. She had gotten quite good at it too, but like most things, once she mastered it, she got bored with it. But she loved this room; the ghosts never bothered her. And she loved her family, especially her sisters.

Yes, it was as if I could feel Jeopardy. I knew what she knew, what she felt. How strange that I would have this experience.

Jeopardy. You have to know I tried to help you. Harper tried too.

She didn't want to hear about that right now. She had something else on her mind, something she wanted to show me. She liked Marisol. Marisol reminded her of Loxley. And then I saw that my Marisol was sitting on the pallet with Jeopardy Belle. They were playing some sort of board game and having the time of their life. Marisol laughed as she tossed the dice and moved her blue piece around the board. I thought for a minute that they didn't see me, but I knew that wasn't true because I could feel and see and hear what Jeopardy felt and saw and heard. She knew I was there.

I didn't know what to do. Should I approach them? What if I walked toward them and then Marisol vanished? I couldn't live with that. Quietly, so I didn't disturb them, I sat on the floor a few feet away and stared at my baby's face. It was perfect and not broken at all. She was alive; her face was not pale, as it had been when I'd seen it last. It was sun-kissed, lovely and just as I remembered. My hands covered my mouth as I attempted to remain quiet. They wanted to show me something. Why didn't they just talk to me?

Jeopardy? You know I'm here. Just tell me what it is you want me to know.

She didn't answer. Instead, they began picking the pieces up and putting them back in the box. Was their game over already? I reached a shaking hand toward Marisol, but the air moved around me and I heard Jeopardy's raspy voice in my ear.

No. It's forbidden.

They wouldn't look at me or talk to me, except Jeopardy picked up a tiny book and let me see it before she put it in the Life board game box. They got up from the pallet and walked to the door with the game.

Marisol, please, honey. Look at Mommy.

She didn't, and I wanted to cry. I followed the girls as they left the castle room and went downstairs. To my surprise, they went not to the kitchen but instead to a small closet under the stairs. I don't think I'd noticed the hidden cabinet before, but now I wondered how I hadn't seen it. I was a carpenter's daughter, for pity's sake. Jeopardy put the game in the hidden door and closed it tight. She looked at me once more, then stood up and stretched out her hand to Marisol.

It was in that moment that my baby girl, my beautiful, perfect daughter, saw me. She didn't smile or frown. "Marisol..."

With a sad expression, she shook her head and spoke to me, but her mouth didn't move. "You can't come with me, Mommy. Not yet. Go back, okay? I'm okay, see? I'm with Jeopardy and Harper. Go back, Mommy."

I collapsed on the floor and cried my eyes out. After a few moments, I heard tiny footsteps approach me. My daughter put her arms around my neck, and I smelled her sweetness. I knew the feel of her skin, the smell of her hair. "My Marisol. I love you, Marisol. Mommy is so sorry."

And then she was gone. Those sweet arms around my neck vanished. It was a strange sensation to feel someone vanish beneath your fingers.

The next thing I knew, Jesse was there. The worried look on his handsome face caused me to worry. I smiled at him, in spite of the pain. "Marisol was here, Jesse. I saw her. She's here." And then I was out again.

When I woke up again, I was in a hospital room.

Chapter Fourteen—Jerica

"Hey, Jerica. You finally decided to wake up?"

I glanced over to see Jesse in the chair beside my bed and gave him a wry smile. "I'm awake now. Don't these people know you aren't supposed to sleep if you have a concussion? What kind of hospital is this?"

"The closest. And for the record, you were told not to go to sleep. You snore, by the way."

"Good to know." I squinted at the light. "What happened? The details are a bit fuzzy." My mouth felt dry, and I had one hell of a headache.

Jesse pulled his chair close to my bed. "As near as I can tell, you fell off the ladder and smacked your head on the counter. But maybe there's something I'm missing."

And then it all came rushing back to me. The breeze, falling, seeing Jeopardy and Marisol. I swallowed and said, "I saw them, Jesse. I saw Jeopardy and Marisol. They were in the castle room." I saw my baby! Grief overwhelmed me again. It always seemed to creep up on me. I missed her every minute of every day, but sometimes the pain just heaped up and swept over me like an ocean tide. This was one of those moments. I couldn't help but cry. "Sorry to be such a mess."

"Hey, don't apologize."

I covered my eyes with my hands and forced myself to breathe. "I saw her, Jesse, as plain as day. She wasn't a ghost, not like the boy. She was beautiful and happy, but she wouldn't look at me. Not until the end. They were playing a game together, her and Jeopardy. A board game."

He squeezed my hand. We didn't get far into the conversation before the nurse stepped into the room. Without missing a beat, she said, "Great to see you awake. How do you feel? Any nausea? How is your vision?"

"I'm not sick at all, and I see perfectly. I'd like to go home now," I said as I tossed the covers off me.

"Whoa, Nellie. One step at a time, Mrs. Poole."

"It's Jerica."

"Okay, Jerica. Let's let the doctor check you out first. He'll be right over."

I slung my legs over the bed and steadied myself. I had to get back to Summerleigh. I had to find that game. It wasn't just a dream. It couldn't be. "You have five minutes," I answered as I waved goodbye to her. She didn't like my answer, but I didn't care. I had bigger fish to fry.

Jesse chuckled and stood ready to help me. "I have always heard that doctors make the worst patients, but I think nurses might give them a run for their money. What's the rush, Jerica?"

"How long have I been out?"

"About half a day. You hit your head pretty hard. I think they want to keep you for observation. I'm no medical professional and wouldn't know what to do if you had a seizure or something. Shouldn't you stay?"

"I'm not asking you to take care of me, Jesse Clarke. I just want my clothes."

He handed me a bag from the closet and said, "And I'm just concerned about you. I don't understand why you want to leave so badly."

"I have to go to Summerleigh, Jesse."

"Why?"

"Let me get dressed first, okay? I feel a little strange talking to you in my underwear."

He laughed at that. The tension of the moment dissipated, and he stepped out so I could put my clothes on. My head felt like it was on a swivel, but I was determined to leave. What if Marisol was still at Summerleigh? Seeing her only made me want to see her again. I wanted to hold her, comfort her. Whatever I could do to be with her. But I didn't say that to Jesse.

Thirty minutes later, we were headed back to what used to be Desire, Mississippi. Mobile was a pretty place with lots of fine homes, but it wasn't my home. Somewhere along the way, Summerleigh had become home. I loved every inch of the green grass, even the stubborn weeds and the wild woods that grew beside her. I loved the mud hole, the potting shed and every nook and cranny. It had been Harper and Jeopardy's home, and it was now mine. The doctor was polite and reminded me to take it easy and look out for the typical symptoms that can accompany a concussion. He suggested that I stay, but of course I did not. I couldn't. And quite honestly, I didn't understand the urgency, but I felt it deep in my bones.

I had to do what I was going to do now. It couldn't wait. Jeopardy Belle had been waiting too long.

When we arrived at Summerleigh, we sat in the truck a minute. I felt like Jesse had something he wanted to say to me, so I waited. Maybe he was waiting for me to say thank you? I probably should. I forgot about things like that sometimes. I didn't usually have anyone to thank except Anita. I missed my friend.

"Hey, thanks for checking up on me. If it weren't for you, I'd probably still be lying on the floor."

Jesse smiled good-naturedly. Gosh, he was such a nice guy. He kind of felt too good to be true. "You're welcome, Jerica. You can thank Ben, I suppose. He was adamant that I get back here. He's really afraid for you to be here. I don't understand it, but that's how he feels."

"Where has he gone?"

"He says he's going back home, but I don't know if I believe him. I think he needs medical help. He's almost obsessive about you and this place. It's concerning. Like I said, I don't know much about diseases, but it wouldn't surprise me if Ben wasn't getting good blood flow to his brain. For a few minutes, he was talking out of his head. Acting like you were Harper. He even called you that once or twice."

"It happens when you get old. Harper used to call me Jeopardy all the time."

"Still, be careful. I know you have a big heart and you want to help him, but...just use caution."

I leaned close to him. It was a bold move, but I was making it. "I promise to be careful. Now let me thank you properly." I pressed my lips to his and kissed him with my hands in his. He felt warm and alive. Soon our tender kiss became more fervent. He was the first to break contact.

"Wow," he said. "That's some thank-you."

"Too much?" I asked with an embarrassed smile. "If so, I blame it on the concussion."

"It's not too much." He kissed me again, and I snuggled up next to him. "We should probably go inside. What is this you want to show me? Something about a game?"

"Yeah, I saw Jeopardy hide it under the stairs." I slid out of the truck and closed the door behind me. Summerleigh looked like such an innocent place, but it was all an illusion. "You think Ben was right? That this place had activity before Summerleigh was built? That this property was haunted from the beginning?"

"I don't know how much stock I'd put in any of Ben's stories. I know he loved Harper and she trusted him for some reason, but he's not quite all there. I have heard about the other house, but like I said, the names of those people are lost at this point."

We walked into the house, and for the hundredth time, I surveyed the place. Even though there wasn't a stick of furniture in the Great Room, the smell of new wood encouraged me and reminded me that we were making progress. We were making a difference. One day, Summerleigh would be beautiful again, and she would be my own.

"Over here, Jesse. I didn't even notice this section of wall before. I mean, I looked at it but never noticed it. See how the panel is hidden in the grooves?" I waved him to the staircase and squatted down to get a good look at the hidden panel. Sure enough, it was right there.

"I never saw it either. But Summerleigh is huge, and I was so focused on the stairs and floor that I didn't think to look for a hidey hole." He squatted down beside me. "You say Jeopardy hid something in there?"

"Hidey hole?" I laughed. "I've never heard of that before."

"Must be a local thing. All good southern homes have hidey holes. It's where you keep the real important stuff."

"Like the family jewels?"

"No, like the moonshine. Or your mother-in-law's body. I'll have to tell you about that sometime. So what is it you think is in there? A game?"

My head throbbed, but I stayed focused. "Yes, a board game. Jeopardy and Marisol were playing with it. Jeopardy tucked a book inside of it. She showed it to me."

Jesse pushed on the panel, which came off surprisingly easily. He grinned at me, and I couldn't hide my enthusiasm. "Hey, do you have your phone?" I asked. He eased the panel to the side and dug his phone out of his pocket. Hitting the flashlight app, he illuminated the small space.

"I see a stack of games, and there's some other stuff too, a metal box and something else. Is that an old hat box? Can you hold the phone?" I did as he asked, and soon Jesse handed me a small stack of old games including Monopoly, Life and a box of playing cards.

They were covered in a layer of dust, but I didn't let that deter me. I opened the Life game and sorted through the pieces. There was no sign of the book. I dumped the box out, and the book fell into my lap. Jeopardy had tucked it under the insert.

Jesse was amazed at our discovery. "Hey, this book looks familiar. Like it belongs with the other one. See the cover? It's similar to the one you found in the potting shed."

I flipped it open, and my eyes fell on a familiar name, Jameson McIntyre. "Oh my gosh! Look at this, Jesse." I handed the book to him. He strained to read the text without his glasses since it was getting darker by the minute in here. I didn't hear the usual footsteps, but you never felt alone at Summerleigh. "Why don't we take all this stuff to the cottage and go through it there?"

"Okay. You got that stack?" We hurried back out of the house and headed to the cottage. Jesse grabbed his glasses from the truck, and then we went inside to examine our find. "No way was that a coincidence. You really did see Jeopardy Belle, Jerica."

"I told you I did. Don't tell me you didn't believe me," I said as I reached for a cloth to wipe the dust off the games. Once again we were huddled together around the kitchen table.

"I'm not saying that..." He opened the metal box but then paused and said, "Maybe that is what I meant. All this is new to me. I have always loved history, but to have it come to life...I'm not good at processing all this. There's no denying that Summerleigh is haunted. But to have a ghost tell you where something is hidden and have it be true isn't something you hear about every day. Look, I believe you, Jerica, but I have a scientist's mind. If I didn't, I wouldn't be here. No matter how attractive you are."

If he thought an offhand compliment would melt my heart, he had another thing coming. I thought he was attractive too, but I wasn't the girl next door. I was a strong woman with my nursing degree, which I'd used to build a successful career. I wasn't some fawning teenager. I didn't say anything else for a minute or two. I picked up the book and opened it, carefully flipping through the pages. "I know you love Summerleigh. You have loved it for a long time, haven't you?"

He put the box down and examined the lock, which seemed to be rusted shut. "You know I wrote a book about the history of the house, about the Belle and McIntyre families. I hope you don't believe I'm here looking for material to write a new book. I think I'm done with writing books for a while. I have a few extras if you'd like one," he joked, but then his voice got serious again. "I mean it. I enjoy working in the house. It makes me feel connected to the people there. You have to admit they were interesting people. And bringing Jeopardy home, that meant something to me."

"Yeah, me too."

"I like you, Jerica Poole. I'm glad you're here."

"I like you, too. I'm glad you are here." I studied the book, still confused by the unfamiliar notations. At least I didn't have to strain to read them, even if I didn't understand them. The book had been well preserved in Jeopardy's hiding place.

"What in the world is this?" Jesse dumped out a bundle of strange braids and stacks of leather-bound books. He flipped open one of the books and whispered, "These are the lost books. These used to belong to John Jeffrey Belle. They're all about the McIntyre family. I knew it was true!"

"Get out of here! Really?"

"Yes, look. Here's his name. And this, this is all his research. Remember when I told you how obsessed he'd become with this place? Man, the answers we need about the boy might all be right here."

Looking at it with wide eyes, I added, "And Jeopardy wanted us to find this. She needed us to know. I think...I think she needs our help, Jesse. We have to help the ghosts of Summerleigh find peace with one another. This boy has to go. At least I know Jeopardy is staying close to Marisol. But where are John Jeffrey Belle and Harper?"

"They're at peace now, Jerica. They accomplished what they needed to do. Why would they be here?"

"But that means Jeopardy isn't at peace. She hasn't moved on. What have we missed?"

Jesse's face said it all. He knew the answer, and so did I. Jeopardy had been reunited with her father, that's true, but she didn't move on with him. Not yet. She wasn't resting with him. She had someone to look out for, someone to protect. Someone to watch over.

Marisol! Jeopardy was protecting Marisol!

Jeopardy Belle hadn't left Summerleigh because Marisol was here and the boy, the one with the black eyes, was too strong for my daughter. He would keep her away from me forever if he could.

"Jeopardy!" I gasped as the thoughts came together like puzzle pieces in my mind. "Jeopardy is here for Marisol." I started to shake. "Oh, Jesse. We have to find out who he is. We have to get the paranormal team back here."

Jesse was on his feet as quick as lightning. "We'll do it, Jerica. We'll do it, I swear. Let me get you your blanket. Your teeth are chattering." He raced out of the room to fetch my favorite throw blanket with the pink roses on it.

And then I saw the boy, reflected in the glass of the china cabinet. I turned around, but he wasn't there. No, he wasn't there anymore, but he had been. And he knew what we were trying to do.

Oh, Marisol. Sweetheart! Stay close to Jeopardy! Mommy is coming soon. I promise.

Chapter Fifteen—Harper

As I expected, Addison wouldn't wake up. "Get up, Addie. It's going to be light out soon, and we want to get to the river before sunup."

"It's too early, and my stomach hurts."

"Your stomach hurts because you need to eat something. You never eat anymore. Please, Addie. I have a basket of food. I baked us some blueberry muffins last night while Momma was at the Ladies Auxiliary. Come with me. Spending time in the sunshine would do you good, Addison. You'll feel better. I'll bait all your hooks for you. Don't make me go by myself, please."

It wasn't that I was afraid to go alone. Ben was nothing to be afraid of, but I didn't want to be alone with anyone, not if I thought they liked me. And I was pretty sure he did. I didn't like him like Jeopardy liked Troy. I wasn't opposed to having a friend who was a boy, but I would rather there be no confusion about my feelings. I had no intention of giving my heart away so easily, and certainly not to a boy who was younger than me.

"No, Harper. Now let me sleep."

I sighed in exasperation. I hated leaving her here by herself. What if Momma's mood took a turn? There would be no one to help Addison fend her off. But there wasn't anything I could do about it, and a promise was a promise. I had told Ben I would go fishing, and I tried to keep my word. He was my friend, after all.

To avoid any misunderstanding, I left a note for Momma on the kitchen table explaining where I was going and who I would be with. If she wanted to, she could ride down to Dog River and find me. We planned on fishing off the bank near the road. I'd be able to see her coming because there were no trees there.

I'd managed to rig Daddy's old fishing pole, and I did a pretty good job if I did say so myself. I'd left it by the potting shed along with the tackle box. I'd been willing to share all my goodies with Addison, but since she wanted to be Sleeping Beauty this morning, she'd just miss out on the fun. I snapped my fingers when I remembered I'd left my fishing hat in my bedroom. It was one of Daddy's that I'd found in a chest in Jeopardy's castle room. I'd raced up there yesterday to get it and saw nary a ghost. I couldn't believe my luck. I tiptoed back down the hall to my bedroom.

I heard Momma giggling and then a man's voice. There was a man in Momma's room, and he would be coming out soon. I could hear them both laughing, and he was saying things no man should say to a respectable lady. I pulled my hat down on my head to cover my ears and hurried out of the house. I was tempted to linger outside to see who Momma was entertaining, but I needn't have bothered. Dewey Landry had never been that smart. His parked truck was halfway hidden in the wild woods next to our house.

She was disgusting! Right here in our own house? What would Mr. Daughdrill say about that? I had a mind to tell Aunt Dot right this minute if I could get her on the phone. Maybe I'd steal Dewey's truck and drive it over to her house.

Feeling sick to my stomach now, I munched an apple to save the muffin for Ben. I walked down the gravel pathway and made a quick stop by the potting shed to retrieve my fishing pole and tackle box. Then I continued on to Dog River, relieved that I wouldn't have to hear Momma pretending to be a lady this morning. I expected to see Ben there when I got there, but he wasn't.

This had been his idea; he better not cut out on me. I have better things to do with my Saturdays, I lied to myself like I was someone important.

He was supposed to bring the worms, but after an hour I realized he wasn't coming. I used my apple core as bait but didn't catch a thing and succeeded only in losing the core. I had no shovel for digging up worms and no idea where to look for them anyway. I mean, I knew they were in the dirt, but according to Ben, worms liked certain types of soil. He should know—his older brother ran a bait business down at the Escatawpa. About ten o'clock, I decided to go home. Ben had stood me up, and we hadn't even been on a date. I put Daddy's pole and tackle box back in the potting shed. I'd try again later, even if I had to get my own bait.

I'd better go check on Addie.

I went inside and was amazed to find that Addison and Momma both were still in bed. Now Momma, I could understand. She'd been carousing all night; that's what Daddy accused her of once. I didn't know the exact definition of "carousing," but I was pretty sure it meant acting like a floozy. Momma used to call Jeopardy a floozy all the time.

I wasn't home ten minutes when George County's youngest deputy, Andrew Hayes, arrived at our doorstep. I touched my hair to make sure my bob was in place, but I could tell that this would be no pleasant visit. Sheriff Passeau—I remembered to call him Sheriff and not Deputy, since he'd just been promoted—was here too, and both men were holding their hats in their hands.

That was always a bad sign.

I opened the door and waited to hear the news. Had they actually found Jeopardy? Or had something happened to Aunt Dot and Loxley? Last I heard, Loxley had the chicken pox and had been out of school for nearly two weeks. Momma called daily, but Aunt Dot refused to bring her home. I was forbidden to call, but I'd already made up my mind to disobey Momma in this.

Now it might be too late. "May I help you, Deputy? Sheriff?"

Deputy Hayes' expression saddened. "I'm afraid we have some bad news, Miss Belle. We need to speak to your mother."

I opened the door and invited them into the Great Room. "I'll get her for you. I think she's lying down. She and Addison have been under the weather. Please excuse me."

"Thank you, Miss Belle," the deputy whispered to me as my face flushed. I nodded once and left the room and hurried to Momma's side.

"Momma, you have to get up. The sheriff and the deputy are here to see you. I think something bad has happened."

To my surprise, Momma wasn't sleeping. She was just lying there staring off into space. "What did you do, Jeopardy?" I could barely hear her whisper.

"I'm Harper, Momma. Please get dressed and come see the sheriff. Let me help you. You can't go in there in your slip."

"Get out, Harper. I'll dress myself, if you please," she snapped as she crawled out of her tangled sheets.

"I'll tell them you are coming."

I raced to Addison's room and woke her up. She immediately got up and got dressed. Apparently, she too believed there was big news. Had to be. Why else would they be here?

A few minutes later, Momma strutted into the Great Room with a lit skinny cigarette in her hand. These past few weeks had taken a toll on her elegance, but she was still a pretty woman. And even though she'd been misbehaving just a few hours ago, she was acting as polite as the Queen of England now.

"Would you like something to drink? Maybe some iced tea or coffee? Harper, where are your manners? Please, gentlemen, come sit in the parlor." They obeyed, but I made no move to put coffee on.

"Ma'am, we are here at the coroner's request," Sheriff Passeau said.

Momma's hand flew to her throat, and she gasped. I knew immediately that something was wrong. Momma could pose as pretty as any catalog model, but she was a horrible actor. I was convinced that whatever she was about to hear would come as no surprise to her.

"Ma'am, your father is dead. He was found this morning at his home in Barton. His housekeeper discovered him in his bed."

"What?" Momma said quietly. So this wasn't what she expected to hear after all. She thought they were going to tell her something else.

Like what? What did she expect to hear? My stomach soured, and Addison sank down onto the couch beside Momma. Of all the people in the world, Addison may have been the only one who cared about Mr. Daughdrill.

"I'm sorry to say he did not die of natural causes," Deputy Hayes said discreetly, "but you don't have to see him. The housekeeper gave a positive identification when we arrived. I think that's good enough for us, and we all know Mr. Daughdrill."

"How?" I asked, uncaring if I sounded morbid or not.

"He was stabbed multiple times in the chest," Sheriff Passeau said, placing his steely gaze on me. "With a pair of shears, presumably while he slept since there was no sign of a struggle. While nothing appears to be missing, we thought maybe you could come and check his property, Mrs. Belle. We may have missed something."

Momma rubbed her face with her pale hands. She looked very confused. "You say my father? My father is dead? He has been murdered?"

Passeau answered, "Yes, ma'am. He's dead." He glanced at the deputy as if to say something in their secret police language. I wished I knew it.

Momma stood to her feet slowly, and I thought she would fall over. Maybe she would faint. To my horror, she began to scream and sob, which made Addison do the same. And Momma didn't scream once but over and over again. No amount of talking to her would make her stop sobbing. And when she was done sobbing, she began to laugh and talk to herself.

Deputy Hayes said, "I'll send for a doctor, Miss Belle. She's going to need a sedative. You should call your aunt and ask her to come help with her."

The deputy had a point, but I didn't think Aunt Dot would pick up the phone. And then it occurred to me. Momma did expect something to happen. She'd prepared for it, daydreamed about it all morning. But this wasn't it. What, then? Suddenly, I worried for Aunt Dot. It was no secret that the Daughdrill sisters had tied up over Loxley and that Momma was furious that Aunt Dot hadn't brought her baby home. There were things going on that I didn't understand. To top it all off, Momma had been entertaining Dewey Landry. No, I couldn't fathom any of this.

"Deputy Hayes, I think my aunt's phone is out of order. Once the doctor arrives and I get Momma settled, would you mind taking me over there? I would like her to hear the news from one of us, if you please."

"Of course I will. Always happy to help a lady."

Addison was sitting with Momma now. Momma had her head on Addison's shoulder, looking at something none of us could see. Sheriff Passeau spoke kindly to her, which was something of a rarity for him. She continued to sob, her face a mess now with streaking black mascara and tear-stained powder. Soon, Dr. Leland arrived at the house with his black bag. With his encouragement, Momma went to bed and took a tranquilizer that would help her sleep. He left me a bottle of about ten more and warned me not to let her have the bottle.

"People experiencing grief do the unpredictable, young lady. See that you give her only one at a time, and only twice a day. I'll come back if you need me." He patted my shoulder kindly and left Summerleigh. He'd always been our biggest peach customer.

"I'll be right back, Addie. I promise." I kissed her cheek and noticed that she had stopped crying and hadn't said much at all. I worried about leaving her, but Momma couldn't be by herself right now.

Deputy Hayes pulled out all the stops for me. He used his siren and horn to get us to Aunt Dot's in no time. To my surprise, we weren't the first people there. A repairman was cutting out wood for a broken window. Aunt Dot ran to me and hugged me.

"What happened?" the deputy and I asked at the same time.

"Someone tried to break into the house this morning, not that long ago. I guess that's what he was trying to do. He shot my bedroom window all up." Her hands were shaking when she held mine. "Your sister slept through the whole thing."

"That sounds like Loxley," I said with a small smile. "I am sorry to come here like this, but I have more bad news to tell you."

"What is it, Harper? Is it Jeopardy?"

"No, ma'am. It's Mr. Daughdrill. He died sometime this morning. Someone killed him, Aunt Dot. In his own bed."

She sank slowly into her cane-back kitchen chair. "Any suspects, Deputy?"

"No, ma'am. We're just beginning our investigation, and with what happened to you, I'm even more concerned. Do you know anyone who might want to harm you? Someone who might want to kill you?"

Aunt Dot looked at me; her heart-shaped face was sad and kind of broken. "I never think about those things, Deputy. I wouldn't want to make a list like that."

"Well, I think you should come with us. Your sister is beside herself with grief."

Aunt Dot stood up and put her glass in the sink. "No, I don't think I will. And believe me, sir, my sister has all the comfort she needs now. Harper, tell Addison I will come see y'all soon."

"Ma'am, I don't think you understand. Mrs. Belle had to be given a sedative, and these young ladies are by themselves."

Aunt Dot brushed away a tear but shook her head stubbornly. "I'm sorry. I have to think about Loxley."

I looked at the deputy. "May I have one more minute? In private, Deputy Hayes."

"Yes, but I have to get back to the precinct after I take you home. We've got a lot going on today, Miss Belle." He shot Aunt Dot one last look of disapproval and walked out on the porch.

I turned to Aunt Dot. "May I see Loxley a minute? Is she feeling better?"

She smiled and accepted the tissue I offered her. "She's not contagious now. Of course you can see her. Her scabs are healing, and the doctor says she won't have any scars at all."

Just then, my sister walked into the kitchen, looking confused at all the hubbub going on around her. Aunt Dot said sweetly, "Loxley, look who's here."

"Harper!" She raced toward me with her black and white stuffed pony in her hands. We hugged, and I cried; I was so happy to see my baby sister. "Guess what?"

"What?" I asked.

She whispered in my ear, "I don't wet the bed anymore. There aren't any ghosts here."

"That is wonderful, Loxley. That means you're all grown up now. You'll be driving a car soon and getting a job as the world's stuffed animal zookeeper."

She laughed and said, "Do they have that?"

"No, silly. They don't."

"Then I'll be the first."

I hugged her again. "I have to go home now, but I'll come back to see you again soon. I promise."

She poked her lip out but didn't complain. She wanted to show me her room and all her dresses, but I had to leave. I couldn't stay another moment or I'd never want to return to Summerleigh. Aunt Dot's small cottage was so peaceful and quiet. You could feel the love in this place. I kissed them both and ran out of the house crying. This was what love felt like.

Accepting, healing and peaceful.

One day, if I was lucky, I'd have that kind of love too.

Chapter Sixteen—Harper

Momma wasn't going to be happy unless she was the center of attention at her own father's funeral. The First Baptist Church of Desire, Mississippi, turned out in a big way. Although Mr. Daughdrill didn't attend church regularly, he frequently pledged money to special causes like the girls' choir. He bought all their robes last year and even paid for their trip to Tennessee to sing at the Baptist Convention up there.

Oh yes, Mr. Daughdrill was something of a big deal in this community...still, there were whispers in between the speeches and testimonials about the fine citizen they were laying to rest. Since I was so plain and quiet, people talked in front of me like I wasn't even there.

Well, there was that time he'd been involved with that one incident.

Remember when he was asked about that girl?

Oh, that was so long ago, and he was young himself then.

No, his granddaughter. They questioned him about Jeopardy.

Oh, yes, they did. I heard it from...

And then the conversation broke off because the next person took the podium to make glowing statements about Mr. Daughdrill, a man many people secretly hated.

Momma had borrowed the fold-up chairs from the church and had them arranged in the Great Room. We'd lit the fireplace to make it look nice in here, even though it was as hot as Hades. I opened the back door to let some of the heat out. Even Mr. Daughdrill's makeup looked a bit shiny, as if it would slide off his face at any moment. Why she had to bring him here, I had no idea.

I stood in the back of the room near the open door drinking my soda through a straw when Aunt Dot came in with Loxley by her side. I'd refused to pay my respects and walk by his casket pretending to miss him. I'm sure Momma wasn't pleased with me, but I didn't care. I didn't want to see him again, and I was glad he was gone. I would have preferred a more peaceful death for him, but that was beyond my control.

Like Momma, Addison was dressed to the nines. She wore her shoulder-length hair pulled back in a ribbon and wore a dark blue dress with black sleeves. Such a stylish dress for someone so young. She placed a white rose on Mr. Daughdrill's chest and walked away.

She seemed to genuinely miss him, which gave me some relief. If he'd behaved inappropriately with her, she wouldn't be acting this way. She wouldn't be acting as if she had just lost the grandfather she loved. No, his death came at the right time. I don't know how I knew all this, but I did. Call it a young woman's intuition if you like.

Ben caught me at the door after the service. "Hey, I'm sorry about your grandfather, Harper." He stuck out his hand like he was meeting me for the first time. I couldn't help but notice it was bandaged up. Like he'd been in a fight with someone.

"What happened to you, Ben? You didn't show up for fishing, and you look like you put your hand in a wood chipper. Is it serious?"

"Did you say he put his hand in a wood chipper?" Addie joined us, chewing on a celery stick and smiling at Ben. She was clearly interested in talking with him, which suited me fine. I was still ticked off that he'd stood me up for our fishing date. Well, not date. I wasn't interested in dating Ben.

"No, that's not what happened. Excuse me. Hey, wait, Harper. Don't run off. I need to talk to you."

"Okay, so talk." I was getting anxious because I wanted to spend time with Aunt Dot and Loxley.

"Well, I can't talk to you here. Come outside. It won't take but a minute."

I tucked my cardigan around me and arranged my barrettes. I needed a haircut in the worst sort of way.

Once we got outside, Ben said, "I've been meaning to tell you this for a very long time, Harper

Belle. I know you barely know me, and you probably didn't realize that we've been in school together for almost two years."

"Really? Has it been that long?" *I really wish he would get to the point.*

"I mean to say, I know I'm young. And I know you're young. We're both young." Ben's dithering was getting on my nerves. And it was hot out here.

"Spit it out, Ben Hartley. We are at my grandfather's funeral."

He glanced around him and saw that a few people were looking in our direction. *Well, if he didn't want to be embarrassed, he shouldn't make a fool of himself.*

"What I am trying to say is that I love you, Harper. I have always loved you. And I hope you know I would do anything for you," he said, showing me his hands and looking at me with a serious expression, "and I do mean anything. Don't let my size fool you, because I got a heart as big as any other guy. And that heart loves you, Harper Belle." He took my hand and kissed it as if he was a knight and I was his lady. It was the most ridiculous thing I had ever seen.

I pulled back my hand and felt my cheeks redden to the shade of a vine-ripe tomato. I said, "Please, Ben. Go home." I paid no attention to the small gathering that had begun to watch us and even applaud. There was the tittering of laughter from some of the older women and good-natured guffawing from some of the men. Ben sputtered in frustration. Obviously, things had not gone the way he had planned them. He cast an evil eye my direction and stormed off the porch and down Hurlette Drive. I wasn't going to chase him. I had no idea where he was going. I resolved that I wouldn't go fishing with Ben Hartley, or any other boy I wasn't serious about, ever again.

"Not even eighteen years old and already breaking hearts," Deputy Hayes said politely.

"Oh, he's just a friend. Thanks for coming to the service." The deputy looked so much nicer today than when he wore his brown uniform. I liked him in blue. "It means a lot."

He ducked his head and walked away with a smile.

Aunt Dot appeared out of the crowd and hugged my neck. "He's right, you know. You're as lovely as your Momma."

"Bite your tongue, Aunt Dot. I don't want to be anything like her." I glanced in Momma's direction. She was sitting in the red velvet chair receiving a line of guests with a distressed look on her face. She caught me looking, but I quickly looked back at Aunt Dot. "I would give anything for you to be my mother."

Aunt Dot sighed and kissed Loxley on the forehead before she ran to our mother, who scooped her up in her arms and made a big deal of her. Loxley sat proudly in her lap as the mourners came forward and expressed their condolences to our family.

"Once upon a time, I would have scolded you for saying such things, but now I understand a little better. Having Loxley with me, I learned a few things. Your little sister is much more observant than you might believe. I was astonished to hear some of the things she told me. I'm sorry for all you had to go through, Harper. I want to make amends, if you'll let me. I want to make it up to you and Addison. You had to endure so much with no help from anyone, but that's going to change."

"You can't change it, Aunt Dot. No more than I can. All we can be is who we are. All we can do is play the roles that are assigned to us. We are not in control of our destinies."

She hugged me up and whispered in my ear, "I hope you don't believe that. I hope you never believe that. You have choices in life. I know things seem hopeless right now because you're young and still living at home, but that's not forever. It is gonna get better. As a matter of fact, I want you and Addison to come and live with me. I will make a home for us; we'll make one together. And I have it on good authority that neither your mother nor I will ever have to worry about money again. Your grandfather was generous to us at least at his death. You girls can go to any college you want, be anything you want to be. I will make sure it happens for you. Just come with me." Addison had joined us and leaned her head on Aunt Dot's shoulder even though she was much taller than our aunt. It was an awkward but sweet picture. And then Loxley came running to us, and I scooped her up in my arms and held her tight. I smelled her fresh, clean hair and her naturally vanilla scent.

"She'll never let me go, Aunt Dot. You know that."

And then Momma started to cry. She was standing by Mr. Daughdrill's coffin now, looking down at him holding his cold dead hand in hers. "Poppa, Poppa why did you leave me?" She cried and wailed and nearly fainted until someone helped her into the kitchen for a cup of coffee.

Soon, Miss Augustine barreled in my direction. "There you are. I've been looking everywhere for you, Harper Louise. Your mother is beside herself with grief. The least you could do is show some compassion. If you don't come now, I don't know what we're going to do with her."

Aunt Dot replied, "She'll be right there, Augustine."

Miss Augustine appeared to have a smart reply right on the tip of her tongue, but I waved my hand at her. "Tell Momma I'll be right there."

Aunt Dot held my hands and ignored Loxley's whining. "You don't have to do this, Harper. You do not owe her anything. She has it all wrong. She owes you everything."

I sighed, and my soul felt like a heavy anchor. "Without me here, I don't know what she'll do. She won't have anyone. She drinks all the time now. Until today, she wasn't even talking to Miss Augustine. She doesn't go to the movies anymore. And you know about the other things."

My aunt's eyes widened for a moment, and she nodded her head. "But you can't fix it, Harper. Someone else will step up into your place. Someone else will have to pacify her. You've done enough. I've already lost one of you girls because I waited too long. I can't lose another one. I love you all so much. Please come with me, Harper and Addison. Loxley wants to stay, and she wants her sisters with her."

With all my heart, I wanted to say yes. A part of me said, *Go now and pack your bag!* But I couldn't. Things had happened that I just didn't understand, and I needed to understand them. I needed to know how those scissors made it to my grandfather's house, for I felt sure it was no coincidence that he'd been stabbed to death with a pair of silver scissors. Had that spirit killed him? The little boy with the black eyes? And why did Momma act so strange when we got the news that Grandfather was dead? No, I couldn't leave yet.

The other shoe hadn't dropped yet. But it would. For now, I would stay with Momma. But knowing that I had options, that I had somewhere to go, set me free.

I would stay with her for a little while, but I would never again be her prisoner.

Never again.

Chapter Seventeen—Jerica

I rolled over in my bed and reached for Marisol's stuffed animal. It wasn't there. It must have fallen off the nightstand. I probably bumped it sometime during the night...I've been told I'm a wild sleeper. And I apparently snore. At some point, I'd have to search through my old albums to find a good picture of her and buy a nice frame, but I wasn't ready to do that yet. It was easier to not remember those lost moments.

"Good morning, Marisol," I whispered. The sunlight streamed into my room from the open window. Of course, I heard nothing and never would, but I couldn't spend the morning wallowing in self-pity. Hannah and her friends were coming this afternoon, and I had a whole host of chores to get done before then. My head didn't hurt too bad, and thinking about all the things that could have gone horribly wrong, I considered myself extremely lucky to have woken up this morning.

And then I thought about Harper. She had loved my daughter just like she was her own grandchild. At least I was still connected to Harper in some strange way. I never knew she'd had such a horrible upbringing, but it felt good to know she eventually had choices.

Poor Ben. I felt embarrassed for him, but he'd been young and in love...still, who tells someone that you love them at a funeral? He and Harper had apparently worked through that bit of awkwardness because he had been a dear friend of hers later in life, at least according to him. I still thought it was strange that she never spoke about him or mentioned him to me in the years that we'd known one another. I guess that proved relationships were complicated no matter what decade or century you were in.

I got busy tidying the house and doing mundane things like taking out the trash and mopping the kitchen floor, things I had neglected to do for the past week. How was I going to let the reconstruction crew back into the house knowing that I might put them in danger? I'd canceled work for today, but I couldn't leave the guys hanging forever. Seriously, I had to put an end to this—get to the bottom of who this kid was and get him out of Summerleigh. Not just for me but for everyone.

Time flew by, and soon I had guests arriving at the house. I was happy that Jesse was there first. Renee wasn't going to make it because she had some problem at the diner; since we didn't have to wait for her, we quickly got into his latest finds. I'd allowed him to take John Jeffrey Belle's research home, and by the looks of him, he'd pulled an all-nighter examining the material.

"This guy, this Jameson McIntyre, he was one troubled individual. It's a good thing his father got him out of Desire before the law caught up with him because I'd say he was the obvious choice for a suspect. He had this weird fetish, Jerica. He liked cutting things."

"You mean like stabbing people? I think there is a name for that."

"Up until the murder of his sister, there's nothing to indicate that Jameson McIntyre went around stabbing people, but he did like to keep souvenirs." Jesse put the box on the table and dug out the journal we found in the Life board game, the one Jeopardy showed me. "See, I figured it out. These notations aren't locations or clues to anything. They're just a record of his sick victories. For instance, beside the name Claudette, you see the abbreviation HR? It stands for hair. He cut this girl's hair. And over here, this abbreviation? RB? That stands for ribbon."

"I can't believe this. You're right, he was sick. But I thought you said Jameson was much older than the boy we saw. I mean, why would his younger brother be popping up everywhere if it's Jameson's malicious spirit wreaking havoc on the other ghosts of Summerleigh?"

Jesse put the journal back into the box and closed it. "All good questions, and I have no answers. Maybe Hannah's friends can help us. They should be here any minute. But thanks to John Jeffrey Belle, we have a lot more information than we did. He really took meticulous notes. Oh, I forgot..." He opened the box again and removed a small bundle. "Don't read this now. But when you get a chance later, I think you should check it out. It might explain a few things."

I accepted the packet of faded letters and ran my finger over the pale pink ribbon that tied them together. How could I resist diving into these now? I caught my breath when I saw the top envelope. It was addressed to Dorothy Daughdrill. I had no time to ask questions because there was a knock on the front door. No doubt it was Hannah, right on time as usual. I welcomed her crew in, and we shared with them the information that Jesse had just presented to me. I took a minute to deposit the envelopes in my nightstand drawer and raced back downstairs to lead the crew into Summerleigh.

"Wow, this place is amazing." Rex took a minute to take in his surroundings. He clearly appreciated all the work we'd been doing in the house.

"It's huge. How many square feet is this?" Amy asked.

"You know, I'm not really sure. With the upstairs and everything, probably close to 5,000. Maybe more. I know it's a lot of house to cover, but most of the activity happens on the second floor and in and around the attic."

"It's a good thing too because I only have four cameras with me. I'll make it work," she said good-naturedly as she carried cases up the stairs. While Amy set up cameras on the second floor, I showed Hannah the collection of books we'd found, the ones that John Jeffrey Belle used to write down the clues he'd found about the Lady in White and her potential killer. According to the journals, John Belle had seen the ghosts on several occasions and tried to communicate with them but had no luck. Hannah pointed out that there wasn't much in the way of paranormal investigation techniques in those days. Ghost hunting had not gone mainstream, and the chances that he could communicate directly with the spirits without some of these new devices were slim.

Jesse said, "It really frustrated him because he wanted to help Mariana McIntyre. He'd even considered holding a séance upstairs but didn't get around to it as far as I could tell. He died unexpectedly, as you know." Hannah nodded and began walking around the room, her favorite purse on her arm, as he continued, "From what John wrote, Mariana was a lot more active back when the Belles were here. And even then she wasn't harming anyone."

"She pushed Ann Belle down the stairs, Jesse."

"You saw her push someone?" Rex asked with some surprise.

I thought about it a moment. "Not exactly. More like she scared her so badly that she fell down the stairs. Broke her arm, but it stopped her from beating on Jeopardy."

Jesse said, "Mariana used to appear downstairs when the Belles first moved in here. She was often seen crying in the Great Room and said the name Jameson repeatedly. It's almost like she was a residual haunt but eventually retreated to the upstairs. I guess that would also make her an intelligent haunt."

"Sounds like you know a little bit about paranormal investigation," Rex said, grinning at Jesse.

Jesse shook his head and said, "Only what I've seen on TV. I'll leave that stuff to you guys."

"Hey!" Amy called from upstairs. "Can you guys come up here a minute?"

Alarmed, we hurried up the stairs and followed Amy's voice to the nursery. "What is it? Did you see something?" Hannah asked.

"No, but is that supposed to be here?"

I couldn't believe it. Marisol's purple bear was hanging from the broken light. Someone had tied a string around the toy's neck and strung it up there. It couldn't have been easy to do—the ceilings were eight feet tall.

"That's my baby's toy. I had it in my room on my nightstand."

"That can't be good," Amy said dryly as she walked over to it and pointed her flashlight up at it. "I want to take some readings before we take it down. Hey, Rex, would you mind getting the EMF detector? It's in my case right there."

"Sure."

I hovered in the doorway as they waved their equipment around the bear. They were apparently disappointed in the readings, and Amy declared it a mystery.

"Someone, a living someone, could have done this, you know. Does anyone else have keys to this place?" Amy asked as she and Rex worked to get the bear down from the light with the ladder Jesse had brought from the kitchen. She handed the bear back to me, and I shook my head.

"Who would do that? Nobody has keys to this place except Jesse and me. And he didn't know anything about that bear, what it signifies or who it belonged to. That was my daughter's toy. I keep it close, like I said, on my nightstand because..."

"You don't have to explain why you keep that." Hannah touched my shoulder gently, and I clutched the bear to my chest. Amy set up a camera in the corner of the room and asked a few more questions, and then the five of us headed to the attic.

Rex visibly shuddered as he approached the door. "Sheesh, it's cold up here. Heat normally rises. Who's got a thermometer?"

Amy tapped on her phone and handed it to him. "You know I have every paranormal investigation app there is. Try this one." She stepped inside and wandered around.

Hannah seemed hesitant about joining us but eventually did. "It feels so different now. Not like the last time. I do feel like there is some sort of battle going on here. Young and old. That's what I keep hearing, young and old." She wandered around, staring at the walls, the ceilings and the many nooks and crannies in the attic. Then she squatted down in front of a familiar chest, the one that Loxley had discovered. She opened it and immediately rocked back on her heels. "Oh my. Such a sweet presence. Such a sweet girl. She didn't deserve what happened to her. She never expected that he would hurt her. She loved him, and he turned on her. She never expected it."

I looked at Jesse, unsure how to process what was happening. Still clutching the bear, I hung back and listened. Rex leaned over to me and said, "This is a good thing. She's tuning in. That means the spirits are talking to her." I wanted to say to him, "I know what that means," but I kept my mouth shut and my eyes open. I had learned from experience, both mine and Harper's, that you could take nothing for granted in this attic.

Hannah was on her feet and pacing around the attic. "He doesn't like people being in here. He has a treasure somewhere here." She waved at a wall and then kept pacing up and down the floor.

"No, he doesn't. His buried treasure is here. He says the girls were too nosy. They like to plunder and look through his things, but those are his treasures." Hannah's hand flew to her heart, and she gasped in surprise. "He inherited those treasures. When his brother left, he gave them to him. They are precious to him. He doesn't want us here. We have to go! I think he's coming!"

Jesse put his arm around me protectively, and we all waited as if the boy would step into the room. Did they understand what this meant? The boy wasn't the one who killed Mariana! It was his brother—it was most certainly Jameson—but the boy wasn't leaving. Not without his treasure.

"What is his name, Hannah? We need his name," I reminded her in a whisper. But Hannah didn't move. She stared at the window over the place where Jeopardy used to sleep. "Hannah?"

"In the hallway. I'm hearing footsteps. Anyone else?" Amy retrieved her camera from somewhere and began filming the session. She nodded her head at Rex, and I strained to hear what they were talking about. It didn't take but a few seconds. Yes, there were definitely footsteps, and they were walking toward the attic. I took a step back, and Jesse came with me. Amy, Rex and Hannah did not move. I expected the door to slam, as they did so frequently on this floor, but nothing happened. The footsteps stopped outside the door, and still we waited. It would be completely dark in here soon, and I didn't fancy the idea of hanging out in this attic in the darkness. The room felt very different from the other day when Marisol and Jeopardy were playing their game. It had felt light and sunny, warm and inviting. Now, not so much.

And that's when I heard the whisper.

Run, pie-face!

Chapter Eighteen—Jerica

"Jerica!" Jesse called me as I snatched him by the hand and ran out of the attic. As soon as my foot hit the top step of the staircase, I felt a blast of cold air. "Jerica, wait!" Jesse pulled me close.

"We have to go. I heard Jeopardy's voice. She told me to run. You didn't hear her?" The rest of the team filtered out of the attic and joined us in the hallway. Jesse didn't have a chance to answer me. One of the devices that Amy deployed in the nursery was making a whirring sound. As the three of them entered the room, Jesse held me tight.

"We can get out of here if you want. They don't need us here to do what they're doing."

"No, I'm good." I stepped back and tucked my hair behind my ear. "But we had to get out of there." I could hear Hannah talking in the other room, and she wasn't talking to Amy or Rex. She was speaking to the boy. The hair on the back of my neck pricked up, and I froze as I listened to her. I didn't want to go into the nursery, not just yet. Jesse stood beside me as we heard her ask him to tell her his name.

"It's okay. We are not here to steal your treasure. We just want to know your name. We know your brother's name. Tell us your name." She whispered to Rex, "Do you have the audio recorder going?"

"Yes."

"We're not going to be here for much longer. You don't want to be forgotten, do you? You deserve to be remembered. Tell us your name and we will leave."

They waited a few more minutes, and I heard Amy say, "Let's play it back." I walked to the doorway but didn't go into the room. The atmosphere had shifted. It felt dark, even morose. I could plainly hear Hannah's voice on the recorder but nothing else. I heard her sigh.

"Any suggestions? He really doesn't want to talk." Rex sounded frustrated, which didn't encourage me. What if all I was doing was making things worse? What if Ben Hartley had been right? This suddenly seemed like a bad idea.

"Maybe we should try one of the other rooms. It looks like it's going to be a long night," Hannah answered, but she didn't sound dissuaded.

I was happy to leave them to their work because I was beginning to feel like I couldn't breathe. The air was so thick up here. Surely I wasn't the only one who noticed it. "Can we go downstairs? I'd like to get out of here for a little while."

Jesse agreed, and we walked down the stairs and left the paranormal investigators alone. Maybe they would have better luck without me around.

I paced around in the Great Room. I didn't want to leave Summerleigh; it would be irresponsible to leave people in here. I was the one who had suggested this, and I was going to see it through.

"You need anything, Jerica?"

Clutching the teddy bear, I shook my head. "No. I'm fine." I stopped pacing and stood beside him. "Thanks, Jesse." He hugged me briefly, and then it was his turn to pace the floor.

Then I heard the scratching sound. At first, I thought it might be a mouse or a rat scratching at some wood, but that wasn't quite it. And it was coming from the hallway that led to the bedrooms. I raised my eyebrows and looked at Jesse.

"Yeah, I'm hearing it too," he said. "Sounds like it's coming from in there."

"Should we go tell them?"

He shook his head and said, "No. I think we can handle this. Might just be a rodent."

"Okay." We headed toward the hallway as the scratching continued. It wasn't quite like a rodent, more like a smooth scratching sound. And it was coming from Addison and Loxley's bedroom. I knew that sound! I'd heard it before. Or at least Harper had. That was the sound of someone drawing with chalk on the floor.

Loxley! As we stepped into the room, I smelled the faint scent of vanilla. Yes, Loxley! It felt so much better in this room than upstairs.

"Look at that! Someone was just drawing in here. What does that say? You know I can't read without my glasses."

"It looks like 'Jacob.' Loxley did this...she gave us the answer we needed. That's his name—his name is Jacob!"

As soon as I said that, a loud thud smashed above us. "We have to go up there. We have to tell them." There was another thud, but not above us this time. The sound came from the wall. I didn't run or flinch. I walked out of Loxley's room, down the hallway and through the Great Room.

I know your name now. You can't stay here. You can't torment us anymore, and you will not harm my daughter.

Lightning illuminated the room in blue light. Thunder soon followed, and the house shook as if a sonic boom had crashed overhead. Jesse was right behind me, and we found the team in one of the other rooms.

"I know his name, and I know what we have to do," I said. I swallowed at the thought of facing off with this spirit again, but it had to be done. There was going to be peace in this house, one way or another. Time to let the ghosts of the past rest. Some part of me felt sorry for this boy, that he would inherit such a perverse treasure and that he would linger here long after his death to watch over it. Yes, I felt pity for him, and it grew stronger than my fear with every passing second. "Hannah, the boy's name is Jacob. He has to be Jameson and Mariana's younger brother. Loxley wrote his name on the floor downstairs." Thunder rolled over us, and the floor began to creak. Was it just the old house settling, or was something more ominous about to happen?

"That's great," she began as all the doors slammed shut at once. Even calm, cool and collected Amy jumped at the sound.

"He's here," I said as I held onto Marisol's bear with both hands.

"It's not going to be as simple as calling his name, not if he's attached to something in that attic. We need to find his treasure and move it. If we get it out of the house, he'll leave with it. We're going to need a distraction, though. Are you ready for this, Jerica?" Hannah asked with sincere concern. *What was she asking me?*

"Yes. What do we do?"

Hannah sent Jesse, Rex and Amy to the attic to search for Jameson's morbid collection. Jesse didn't want to leave me, but I assured him everything would be okay. "I'm in good hands."

The door opened without a fight. But when we entered the room, it closed behind us. And during the time my attention went from the door to the room, everything had changed. This wasn't an empty nursery anymore. There was a large, round blue carpet in the center of the floor. One large chair was positioned in front of the fireplace. Heavy blue curtains hung from the window, and there were three desks at the back of the room. I could see a large wooden toy box, a rocking horse and books that filled a bookcase I did not recognize.

"Hannah?" I whispered as she took my hand. "What's going on?"

"Talk to him, Jerica. I can't see what you're seeing, but I can feel him."

Talking to him was the last thing I wanted to do. He looked like something out of a horror movie with his white skin and black eyes. I couldn't see his face fully, but those horrible eyes were as plain as day. *How do you reason with something like this? Just kill some time, Jerica. Give them time.*

"I know your name now." The boy raised his head, and I swear I heard him growl. "My friend Loxley told me your name. She knows you. You used to play with her."

The rocking horse began to move back and forth, and the flames in the fireplace rose.

"My name is Jerica, and you're Jacob. I am not here to hurt you, Jacob."

"That's good. Keep talking, Jerica."

The horse rocked faster, and the clock on the mantelpiece began to make a horrible sound. I glanced at it and could see the hour and minute hands spinning wildly, like an unseen hand was manipulating them.

"Jacob, I know you want to stay here, but you can't. You have to go. Your time here is over, Jacob."

The boy took a step toward me, and I thought I saw a shadow dart behind him. A tall shadow. I heard Hannah yelp in pain beside me, but I kept my focus. She was still holding my hand, and I squeezed hers. She squeezed back to reassure me she was okay.

"Jacob, listen to me. I know that bad things happened in this house, that you saw bad things. I'm sorry that happened to you, but the bad things have to stop." The rocking horse flew across the room and broke into many pieces. I caught my breath and turned loose of Hannah's hand. I clutched Marisol's bear as if it were a life preserver. "I'm sorry about Mariana and Jameson, but it wasn't your fault. None of it was your fault. I don't know what happened to you, but I'm sorry."

The clock flew off the mantel and smashed on the floor, and a ball in the corner bounced furiously. The boy frowned and raised his face so that I could see him clearly. Yes, he was a terrifying sight, but at one time he had just been a boy. A boy who had been hurt by someone. A boy who had died here. The storm outside raged. Lightning smashed the darkness and illuminated the room in frantic flashes. But the thunder was strange, like it was happening in the house and not outside of it.

Now what do I do? What should I say to this angry creature? "Jacob, please believe me. Your brother's treasure is not yours to keep. You are not responsible for what he did; his crimes are not yours. I know you loved your brother, but what he did was wrong."

Leave here.

"I will not leave. This is my house now, along with everything in it. You have to go. I'm setting you free, Jacob. You don't have to stay and watch over Jameson's treasure anymore." He moved closer, but I stood my ground. "I promise you I'll take care of it. I won't let anything happen to it."

Hannah whispered beside me, "The energy is changing. He's used a lot of his strength. Command him to leave now, Jerica."

She was right; I could feel his power waning. Yes, I could command him to go, but my sympathy for him still grew. I got on my knees to get at eye level with him. "Jacob, you have to leave Summerleigh now. You can't stay here anymore. Go and take this treasure with you. It's my treasure, and I want you to have it." I held the stuffed animal out to him, my hands shaking, my heart pounding. Tears filled my eyes because I didn't really want to part with it...and I wasn't sure this was going to work. "It's okay. You can have it."

Everything got still. Jacob stepped closer to me. He was so close now that he could reach out and touch me if he wanted to. But he didn't. He touched the bear, and then he and the toy were gone. A quick flash of light filled the room, and then everything was as it had been. The room was empty and in need of repair.

Hannah was weeping, and I took her hand. The place was quiet. No more knocks and bangs. Even the wind outside stopped blowing. Somehow, we had achieved our goal. Summerleigh was finally free.

And so was I.

Chapter Nineteen—Harper

After the funeral, Addison and I spent the rest of the day cleaning up the kitchen in the parlor. Miss Augustine stayed for a little while, but of course she didn't lift a finger. She did, however, fill her plate multiple times before unceremoniously leaving it on the kitchen table for me to wash.

I gave Momma another one of the pills the doctor prescribed for her and once again told her that was the last one. I had to, or else she would want the whole bottle. I still didn't trust that she wouldn't hurt herself. Several times in the past few days she'd called me Jeopardy, and once I caught her talking to herself (or someone) on the second-floor landing. Addison stayed close to me, and as I promised her, I slept in her room that night. She questioned me about a few things, including Aunt Dot's offer to come live with her, but agreed with me that the best thing to do now was to stay close to Momma.

"Everyone is gone now, Harper. Daddy, Jeopardy and now Grandfather. Promise me you'll never leave me."

"I promise you, Addison Lee. Wherever I go, you'll go too. Okay?"

I had a restless night that night but eventually fell asleep. After years of training, it was hard for me to sleep late; as usual, I got up before sunrise. I dressed quickly and went to the kitchen. I put on the percolator, mainly for myself because Addison didn't drink coffee and I had a feeling that Momma would not want any this morning. She'd probably drown her sorrows in cheap wine again. At least her supply was running out, and there was no one to take her to the store or buy her more. We hadn't seen hide nor hair of Dewey Landry, thankfully, and Momma sold her Chevy Master DeLuxe last week for some reason. God only knew what she'd done with the money. But if Aunt Dot proved right, we wouldn't need to depend on Momma anymore. What would that be like, to have food in the house and new clothes to wear whenever we wanted them?

"Harper?"

I nearly jumped out of my skin. Ben Hartley was calling me from the window. "What are you doing out here, Ben?"

"I thought you might want to go fishing. I've got the poles and stuff."

I was surprised to see him, what with everything that had passed between us earlier. I was kind of glad to see him…just not this early in the morning.

"Shouldn't you be getting ready for church?" I asked as I unlocked the back door and opened the screen to let him in.

"You going?"

"No. I don't go much anymore."

"Me either. I just thought we could fish. You know, like before. I'm sorry."

"You mean you're sorry you said what you said?" I asked him with my hands on my hips. "We hardly know each other, Ben Hartley. Do you go around telling all the girls you love them?"

"No. I've never done that. Just with you. But I won't say it again, I promise. I want to be your friend at least. Please go fishing with me."

I shrugged and said, "Okay, but only if Addison goes with us. I don't want to get a reputation."

"Okay," he agreed with a gap-toothed smile.

Addie wasn't up yet, which didn't bode well. That meant she wanted to sleep late. I tried to talk her into fishing, but she wasn't interested. "Go fishing, Harper. I'll be here."

I sighed and put my sneakers on. "All right, but I'll be back by ten. There's food in the refrigerator. Please eat something, Addie."

She agreed, and I left at the sound of her snoring.

Benny and I didn't talk much on the way to the river, but I could tell he was deep in thought. I wondered if I had made the right decision. I said I wouldn't go fishing with him again, but here I was. Was I so desperate to have friends that I would break my own rules? Well, Benny was a nice enough boy. We made it to the river just after sunrise, and he offered to bait my hook.

"No thanks. My daddy taught me how to fish."

"Did you like your dad?"

"Yes. Don't you like yours?"

He tossed his line in the water. "Nope. Not really."

Our luck was better today. I caught a speckled trout, and he snagged a redfish. His specimen outweighed mine, but at least he didn't brag about it. Not like Jeopardy would have. *Jeopardy. Here I am, having fun, and you're dead. You must be dead, or else I wouldn't have seen your ghost.* It was getting warm, so we retreated to a nearby shade tree to take a break from the heat. Benny offered me some of his soda pop, and I chugged a few swallows before handing the warm drink back to him. At least it was wet.

"What do you think y'all will do now? You aren't moving, are you?"

"What do you mean? Were you listening in on my conversation with Aunt Dot? That's not polite, you know." I didn't tell him I did it all the time.

"No. Of course not. I mean, now that your grandfather is dead, would you have to move? I mean, I guess he was taking care of y'all."

I wiped the sweat off my face. Benny asked the strangest and most inappropriate questions. "He didn't take care of us, Ben Hartley. You have some strange ideas."

My stomach was rumbling, and I was toying with the idea of going home. I was getting tired of Benny's company. Not because I didn't like him but because I'd gotten used to being alone. I liked it much more than I could have guessed. You got stronger when you were alone. I think that was a secret Jeopardy knew too.

Again Benny acted like he wanted to tell me something, but I didn't hurry him along. I hoped he wouldn't tell me he loved me again. I'd have to end our friendship if he talked crazy. "You won't have to worry about him anymore, Harper. He'll never hurt y'all again."

I launched to my feet. I had the creepy crawlies all over me, just like when that weird boy ghost popped up at Summerleigh. "What are you talking about?" He got up too and wiped his sweaty hands on his jeans. He wouldn't look at me. He looked at the river, at the grass, everywhere but at me. And that worried me. "What do you mean? You think you know something? Out with it, Ben Hartley."

"Why do you always do that? You think you're better than me? All I've tried to do is help you, Harper."

A rare wind caught the leaves overhead, and a few fluttered down between us. If it had been any other moment, it would have felt magical. This wasn't magical. Benny was trying to tell me something, something I didn't want to hear. But I had to listen. I had to listen good.

"How? How have you helped me? What do you know?" And just like that, as if someone had snapped their fingers, I knew too. I had figured it out a long time ago, and I just didn't want to admit it. My grandfather liked to hurt people in ways no one should.

Momma most of all.

Benny didn't answer me. He reached for the dingy wrapping on his hand, and my stomach did a double clutch like Daddy's old truck.

"How did you do that to your hand? Let me see it." I stepped toward him. I loomed over him now. I hadn't realized how much taller I was than him, but he didn't back down.

"Fine. You want to see it?" He unwrapped it furiously and held it up so I could see the angry red gashes. "I didn't mean to do it, Harper."

"You killed him, Benny. You killed Mr. Daughdrill. Why?"

He sobbed, and his eyes shone with tears. "I love you, Harper. I know I'm not supposed to say it, but I do. I just wanted to talk to him, to tell him to leave you and Addison alone. Everyone knows, Harper. Everyone knows what he is, but they didn't do anything." He was shouting now, and I was afraid of him. I'd never been afraid of him before. "Don't look at me like that. I didn't mean for it to happen."

"You stabbed him, Benny. Where did you get the scissors?" Those creepy crawlies were on me like white on rice.

"I was just going to talk to him. I went to his house to talk to him man to man, but he didn't come to the door. I tried the handle, and the door was open. I remember opening the door and going in, but I don't remember nothing after that. I think he yelled at me, but it's like it was a dream. Next thing I knew, I was holding the scissors, and then they were poking out of his chest. Honest, Harper. You have to believe me."

"You killed him, Benny. You killed him. You're a murderer!"

"I did it for you, Harper. I swear I didn't plan on it. It just happened."

I took off running. I cried and screamed, hoping someone would hear me. I'd never been more scared in all my life. I was friends with a murderer. Ben Hartley killed Mr. Daughdrill. He might say he did it for me, but that didn't make it right.

"Harper, wait! Please, wait! I love you, Harper Belle!"

I'd never run so fast. By the time I made it home, my legs were burning and I couldn't hardly breathe. I raced past Momma and picked up the phone.

"Harper, what is it?" Addison asked as she came in from the parlor.

I dropped the phone because I was shaking so bad. Addison helped me to the chair while Momma got me a glass of water.

And in that moment, I knew I couldn't do it. I couldn't turn in my friend. He was no serial killer, no psychotic murderer. He was a boy who wanted to help me. He'd been influenced by this house, by the spirits here, and had become an unwilling vessel for their evil. I hung the phone up. I never spoke about it again to anyone, not even Ben when I talked to him years later. Things were settled between us. He had helped me with something that I would never have had the courage to ask. But I believed that Ben didn't know what he was doing that night.

The damage had already been done, but we were free.

The sheriff came back to our house again that day. At first, I thought it was because he knew the truth about Benny, but that wasn't it. Dewey Landry had been arrested for shooting up Aunt Dot's house and trying to kill her. He'd been caught trying to leave town with a stash of money in a black bag. There were rumors that Momma had put him up to it.

Momma denied everything, but six months later she was ordered to undergo treatment at Searcy Mental Hospital and I never saw her again. Aunt Dot agreed to move back into Summerleigh with us. The state made her our legal guardian, and for the next ten years, we lived happily together there. Then each one of us slowly drifted apart as we all made our own lives. Aunt Dot died not long after Loxley married and moved away. Loxley had been the baby Aunt Dot had never had. She loved us all, but we knew she loved Loxley a little bit more. And we were okay with that.

There was plenty of love in this house now. Plenty of peace. Plenty of everything.

Chapter Twenty—Jerica

Mommy, wake up. And I did. I shot right up in bed and immediately knew I was not alone in my bedroom. That's when I saw the dark figure sitting in the painted wooden chair near my door. He looked like a statue just sitting there watching me. Yes, it was true—Ben Hartley was sitting in my room. It wasn't quite morning yet, but I heard roosters crowing in the distance and the air had that strange kind of strawberry-colored glow that let you know the sun was about to appear.

How long had he been here? All night? I glanced at my nightstand and was relieved to see that there were no scissors lying there, but that didn't make me feel more comfortable.

"What are you doing in here, Ben? How did you get in?" That was kind of a stupid question since he lived here before I did. He must have still had a key.

He didn't answer me, not at first. "I tried to explain to you; I wanted you to know how important it was. You needed to leave, but you didn't listen to me. I told you to let sleeping dogs lie. It's not that I'm afraid of going to jail. I don't think I'll live another year, so what's to fear? It's just that I don't remember any of it. What I told Harper was the truth. One minute I was walking into Mr. Daughdrill's house, and then the next thing I know, I have blood on my hands. Not just his blood but mine too. I cut him so savagely that I cut myself in the process."

"Ben, you shouldn't be telling me this. Why are you here?"

Ben looked off into the distance, and I quickly grabbed my phone off the nightstand. He didn't seem to notice. I carefully pulled up Jesse's number and tapped on the screen.

"Everyone knew what he was doing to those girls. The whole town knew. And nobody did anything about it. I couldn't prove that he killed Jeopardy, but I saw him pulling up in that big black car of his and dropping Harper off at school. He wanted to do what he always did, but she fought back. I saw her do that and knew she was the one for me. She wasn't going to die, not like the other one. And I wasn't going to let it happen."

I could hear Jesse calling my name on the phone, and I surreptitiously turned down the volume. I said loudly so that Jesse could hear me, "Ben Hartley, you cannot be in my bedroom."

Ben got up out of his chair and walked over to me. He knelt down in front of me and took my hand. "I don't want to hurt you, Harper. I never wanted that. It's this place. Ever since I came here, I haven't been the same. When I used to live here, I would wake up sometimes and find myself walking the halls of Summerleigh. And I wouldn't even know how I got there. It's like it cursed me or something. It has control over me, and I don't want it anymore. I can't live with it anymore. I did the wrong thing, and I'm not even sure how I did it. I swear to you, Harper. I loved you then, and I love you now. Please forgive me for what I'm about to do."

I leaped off the opposite side of the bed and plastered myself against the wall. "No, Ben." I reminded myself to remain calm. "Don't do anything you're going to regret. Please, go home. Or go to the hospital, and I will meet you there. I'm a nurse, remember? You need help, and I can help you. Please, let me help you."

He smiled at me and shook his head. "There's no time for that now. I'm sorry, Harper. I will always love you." And then he left my room and I heard his footsteps going down the stairs. From my window, I watched Ben walk to Summerleigh, and he had something in his hand. What was it?

Oh God! It was a gas can! What was Ben planning to do?

I picked up the phone, surprised to hear Jesse still there. "Jesse! Ben has some gas, and I think he's going to burn down Summerleigh! I have to call the police!" I hung up the phone and immediately dialed 911.

"911. What is your emergency?"

"My house! Ben! He's trying to burn down my house!"

"What is your address?"

I gave the dispatcher the address but refused to answer any more questions. I could already see smoke pouring out of the bottom floor of the house. And Ben never came out.

I was in a pair of pajama shorts and a t-shirt, but it didn't matter. I had to get him out of there. He was out of his head—what if he killed himself trying to set the place on fire? I would never be able to live with myself if I let him die. I ran down the stairs and slid my feet into tennis shoes. I raced to the back door of Summerleigh, but Ben had locked it. I ran to the front door and found it was locked as well. I began to scream, "Ben! Open the door!" I could hear him crying and talking to himself or someone. I pounded and pounded, but he never came to the front door.

Now what do I do?

My eyes fell on a large rock. I picked it up and put it through one of the Great Room windows. Glass shattered everywhere, and I carefully reached inside and undid the latch. I slid the window up and climbed through without cutting myself too much.

"Ben? Please, come out now. Before it's too late."

I searched the entire bottom floor and found him nowhere. The kitchen was on fire, and one of the bedrooms—the one that had the mattresses stacked against the wall—was burning. Smoke was beginning to fill up the place, and all the windows had been closed.

I raced up the stairs searching for Ben. Suddenly, he was there in front of me and sloshed gasoline on the front of my shirt. "Jerica! You cannot be in here. You aren't supposed to be here. I wanted to save you. You must leave now!" And then he took off, running as fast as any man half his age. He ran up the steps of the attic, went into the castle room and slammed the door. I could hear it lock as I raced up the steps and banged on the door. I listened carefully and heard the gasoline sloshing around. If I let him do this, if he succeeded in setting the attic on fire, he would certainly kill himself.

Okay, Jerica. You are a nurse. You can handle this. Talk him down. Be calm and talk rationally.

"Ben, you have to open this door. If you don't, you are going to hurt yourself, and you're going to make it really hard for people like me to help you. Please, stop what you're doing." No reply.

Okay, forget logical. Forget rational. I was going to have to lie to him just to save his life. "Ben Hartley, Harper's going to be so mad at you when she finds out you did this. She loves this place, and if you destroy it, she is never going to forgive you."

Ben came to the door and opened it slightly. As he did, smoke poured out of the room. I had to get him out of there fast.

"Ben, you don't want to miss a chance to see Harper. She's waiting for you downstairs. Just come with me, and I will take you to her. No. Leave that gas can here. She wants to talk to you."

"Really?" His excited face encouraged me. "Yes, take me to her."

Smoke was beginning to fill the hallway, and I had a strong urge to cough. I put one hand over my mouth and reached out my other hand for Ben's. He allowed me to take his hand, and we both coughed as we walked down the hall quickly. Or as quickly as he would move with me. "Are you sure she's not mad at me?" He coughed his question out.

"No, she's not mad at you. In fact, I know she loves you, Ben. She's waiting for you."

"She loves me? She said that? She loves me?" He was smiling from ear to ear.

We were coming down the stairs now. Just a few more steps and I would have him out of the house. I could see that he had left the key in the front door. And that way had less smoke than the back, so it seemed an obvious choice.

"Where is she, Jerica? You said she'd be here. Where is she?" He became agitated very quickly, another sign of the Alzheimer's that I suspected he had.

"On the front porch, Ben. She couldn't wait in here because it was too smoky. Come on, just a few more steps." I tugged at his hand, but he pulled away. I was losing him. He didn't believe me, and even in the smoke I could see that the madness was taking him again. The horrible madness, the disease that had taken so many.

He shook his head. "You said Harper was here. I know where she is. I know where she always is. She's in the kitchen. Right? Is she hiding in the kitchen?" And then he bolted and ran into the fiery furnace he'd created.

I screamed his name, but it did no good. There was so much heat coming from the kitchen that I would not survive entering it. I was still screaming when Jesse ran into the house. He too tried to reach Ben, but the old man didn't seem to hear us.

He kept yelling for Harper until his calls became screams, and then we heard nothing else. We knew that Ben Hartley was dead. He had killed himself in the most horrible way, completely out of his mind. Covered in smoke and wrapped in an emergency blanket, I sat in the back of the ambulance and watched as Summerleigh burned. The Volunteer Fire Department of George County did a good job of putting out the fire. They came pretty fast to the scene, but the damage was done.

Summerleigh would never be the same, and it had taken its last victim.

I vowed then and there to do just as Harper had done. I would keep Ben Hartley's secret for the rest of my life. I would tell no one, not even Jesse. That's the way Harper wanted it. I knew that.

I didn't stay at the caretaker's cottage. I took Jesse up on his offer and spent several weeks at his house thinking of nothing and doing nothing except working on his boat. It was nice to pretend that we were a family.

Jesse and me...and Marisol. She liked this place too.

Epilogue—Jerica

"Are you sure you want to return to Summerleigh? It's a mess, Jerica. I didn't want to tell you this, but I went by there the other day, and it is truly a mess."

I sighed and kissed his cheek. "Yes, but it's my mess. I can't keep ignoring this. I have to see how bad it is. I've got some decisions to make, and I want you with me."

He kissed me back. "That's all you had to say. Let's load up. Put your work boots on, though. It's pretty bad in some places. Will you grab my camera? It's on the dresser in the guest room. Your room."

"Sure," I said with a smile. Yeah, I was ready to do this. I couldn't put it off forever. I'd gotten some emails from the insurance company, and from what I saw, they'd been pretty generous. So it would be possible to rebuild if that's what I wanted to do. But that was a big if. Jesse's camera was not on the dresser, so I opened the top drawer. Maybe he meant inside the dresser? Sure enough, it was there, and so was one other thing. I reached in and grabbed the camera and also the packet of letters tied with the pink ribbon. The letters addressed to Dorothy Daughdrill. I had brought them here from the caretaker's cottage but hadn't had the nerve to look at them yet. With shaking fingers, I untied the knot and removed one of the letters.

I slid the delicate paper out of the envelope. There was an address on the back, a military address, and I knew immediately that this letter was from John Jeffrey Belle.

Dear Dorothy,

I hope this letter finds you well, for it has brought me much hope to receive yours. To know that you love me no matter what your father says, that you love me above all others...well, it is more than I deserve. Ever since I first met you, I knew you were the one. You are the love of my life, and I will love no other. Not as long as I have breath in my body. I pray this war ends soon so that I can come back to you and all my Belle girls. I know you worry about Ann, you worry about your father, but you shouldn't. We love each other, and that's all that matters. If your father hadn't interfered in the beginning, none of this would've happened. Just think, it's taken us ten years to discover the truth of what happened that night. I believed that you stood me up, that you left me there at the altar. What a fool I was. I'm sorry, Dorothy. I'm sorry I didn't wait for you, but I'm going to spend the rest of my life making it up to you.

All my love,

John Jeffrey Belle

I stared at the letter and read it again and again. Jesse came in looking for me and found me reading the rest of them. I'd arranged them on the bed and read every single one. After the last one,

I leaned back on the pillow, closed my eyes and sighed.

"This is horrible. What Mr. Daughdrill put those girls through, it's unreal. All this time, John Belle had been in love with Dot. And he believed them—Ann and her father, I mean—when they said that Dorothy had rejected him. And that she didn't want Jeopardy. Jeopardy was really Dorothy and John Jeffrey Belle's daughter. That's why Ann hated her so much. And that's why she was so willing to allow Mr. Daughdrill…"

Jesse shook his head in disgust. "Yeah, all of that. Talk about star-crossed lovers. They didn't have a chance."

I folded up all the letters, put them back in a stack and tied them up with the ribbon. "Let's put this away and forget about it. And I can tell you what I'm gonna do. I am going to rebuild Summerleigh. It is going to be the most beautiful, happiest bed-and-breakfast that George County has ever seen."

Jesse smiled and said, "I like that idea. I like it a lot."

"Can't do it by myself. You on board?"

"Do you really have to ask?"

Fifteen minutes later, we were back at Summerleigh. I was surprised to see that much of the house remained intact despite significant fire and smoke damage. We walked around the building carefully and made a mental punch list of where we needed to start on this new project.

"Forget this. I'm never gonna be able to remember all this. Let me go to the truck and grab a notebook."

"I thought writers could remember everything," I joked with him.

He didn't even turn around when he replied, "No, that's why we need notebooks. Be right back."

I heard a sound to my right coming from the bedroom hallway. I walked into the hallway and immediately saw my daughter. Marisol wore a yellow dress with a yellow ribbon in her hair. In life, I'd never seen her wear anything like that. Clearly, someone was helping her dress. And then Jeopardy stepped out of the room and stood behind her. I stared at them both and smiled.

"It's okay, baby. You can go play with Jeopardy. Mommy is okay." She took Jeopardy's hand, and they turned away from me and walked toward the back wall and then right through it. I went to Ann's old bedroom. It was the only room that didn't have any fire damage, and the window there was intact. From the window, I could see the two girls running together, hand in hand.

And then they disappeared. And I knew I would never see Marisol again. Not in this lifetime.

And I was okay.

The Lady in White

Book Three

The Ghosts of Summerleigh Series

By M.L. Bullock

Text copyright © 2018 Monica L. Bullock

All rights reserved

Dedication

For Jeopardy Belle.

Oh, lady bright! can it be right—
This window open to the night?
The wanton airs, from the tree-top,
Laughingly through the lattice drop—
The bodiless airs, a wizard rout,
Flit through thy chamber in and out,
And wave the curtain canopy

Excerpt from *The Sleeper*

Edgar Allan Poe, 1831

Prologue—Harper Belle

Desire, Mississippi
November 1948

"Addison Lee, you look like a princess! A real princess." Loxley squealed beside me and clapped her hands before she raced to hug our trembling sister. Loxley was right. Addie did look like a princess, a nervous one with a handful of shedding buttercups, quivering lips and a worrisomely pale face. It was so like Addison to get a case of the jitters on her wedding day—had I expected anything less? Poor Addie had a lifelong relationship with her distraught nerves, but she never wavered in her determination to marry Frank Harlow. And for that, she had my utmost respect. In fact, if I were to be really honest with myself, I would have to admit that Addison was braver than I. The idea of leaving Summerleigh, of leaving Aunt Dot and the others behind, was too much to bear.

Addison was as beautiful as any of those girls in the magazines that we used to spend hours admiring. My younger sister surprised us with her wedding dress choice, a tea-length, scoop-necked, short-sleeved gown. But as it was an afternoon wedding, it seemed appropriate. Although I was no fan of the coral-colored bridesmaid dresses we'd been asked to wear, I felt stylish and pretty. And for sweet Addison Lee, I would wear chicken wire if I had to.

Just this morning, Aunt Dot surprised Addie with a pearl choker that now shook around her thin neck while Loxley and I gifted her with a pair of glistening hair combs. The four of us had a tearful moment then, but Aunt Dot never mentioned Momma. She didn't say how proud Momma would be of Addison or how much Momma must wish she could have made the trip, and I was thankful for that. We never talked about poor, crazy Momma locked away in the asylum far from Summerleigh. No. We never talked about her, and I did my best not to think of her. *Stop that, Harper. This is a happy day.* There were enough shadows here at Summerleigh without adding one more, especially today. After dabbing at her eyes with an embroidered handkerchief, Aunt Dot scurried out of Addison's bedroom, presumably to direct the caterers and waitstaff and even early guests who had begun to arrive at Summerleigh. The old house would be alive again today, at least for a little while. Aunt Dot had managed to turn the place into a comfortable home for us, but it had its cold spots. Its empty places.

The three of us were alone now; it was just us Belle girls. This was the first time we'd been alone in so very long. I could tell by my sisters' expressions that they were aware of the moment too and that they also felt the shadows of the ones who hadn't made it to witness this glorious day. None of us mentioned Jeopardy or Daddy, and we didn't have to. Addison's lip began to tremble, but I prevented her from speaking a sad word with a squeeze of my hand. I refused to allow the Belle melancholy to settle over us and intrude on this wonderful day.

"Addison Lee, you look every bit a dream. Frank Harlow is a lucky man. But never forget, even when you change your name, you will always be a Belle—and that means something special. To Loxley and to me." Loxley nodded and smiled broadly beside me.

"I will not forget that, Harper. I could never forget my sisters, and I won't be far away. You can visit me anytime you like, both of you. In fact, I insist on it. Promise me? Promise you will come next week for tea or for lunch?"

Loxley and I hugged her, and I clung to them so tightly it surprised me. How could I let either of them go when it had been my job to take care of them? I'd been doing it for so long. Just like Daddy would have wanted—and like Momma always expected me to. But Addison loved her Frank, and he most assuredly loved her.

Tall, skinny Frank with his horn-rimmed glasses and slight overbite. He owned a gas station in Lucedale and perpetually smelled of gasoline, but he was a nice enough young man. I wasn't surprised that he asked Addison to marry him, since he had been crazy for her for a long time, but I was glad that Aunt Dot had insisted that Addison graduate high school first. I think Addison was glad too. Now the only one left in school was Loxley.

I had been out for two years now but still hadn't left for college. For some reason, I dithered. I hesitated. In the back of my mind, I told myself that it was responsibility that slowed me down. *How could I leave Loxley and Addison without safely depositing them into their futures?* But that wasn't the truth. I hid myself away here at Summerleigh for entirely selfish reasons.

Because I didn't want to face a world without Jeopardy Belle in it.

And if I stayed here, I would never have to think about Ben's secret. I wouldn't be tempted to tell anyone. I could never do that.

As we hugged, I pretended Jeopardy was with us too, that she was holding us and smiling, her wild hair in an unruly cloud around her face. Maybe she was. I didn't see ghosts on a regular basis, not like Loxley, but I imagined Jeopardy hovering near us now as I often did. What silly thing would she say if she were here? What words of advice would she want to impart to Addison? I struggled for the appropriate words, the right encouragement to share with Addie, but I could think of nothing. Nothing that wouldn't make us all weepy at the prospect of being separated forever. And we would be. No matter what Addison said or how we all pretended otherwise, we would be separated forever. Marriage was a forever thing.

A tap on the bedroom door broke the spell of that poignant moment, and we fell back laughing and wiping away the odd tear. Mr. Foshee, the photographer, had arrived and wasted no time in ordering us about. Addison's small room had been beautifully decorated for the bridal photo shoot, but we were taking some photos outside too. That was worrisome, as it promised to be warmer than any of us had expected. November was normally much cooler than this, but I wouldn't complain. I would sweat and smile and be happy for Addison. Today would be perfect for her. It had to be.

I think I was the first one to hear the footsteps overhead. The photographer reminded me to smile, and Loxley glanced in my direction, her eyes immediately rising to the ceiling above us. My eyes met hers as Addie smiled and fluffed her dress on the settee. She clutched my hand, and I remembered to smile at the camera.

There it was again, clear as a bell. Footsteps. But not heavy footfalls, the sounds of high heels, a lady's footsteps. And I could see that Addison heard them too.

I said, "It's probably a guest, Addie. Someone's up there exploring is all." Loxley began to shake her head as if she disagreed with me, but I frowned at her in an attempt to remind her that we should think of Addison.

Ignore the ghosts, Loxley. Ignore them all.

I knew she couldn't hear me, but I couldn't bring myself to say the words aloud. Thankfully, Mr.

Foshee decided that it was time to go outside and take our outdoor photos. He glanced at his watch and reminded us that we would have to hurry. We didn't want to bring bad luck on the bride by letting the bridegroom see her before the wedding. We followed Mr. Foshee out of Summerleigh, but of course we were stopped numerous times along the way as everyone wanted to congratulate Addison.

With just minutes to spare before we had to spirit her away, we gathered beneath the large oak tree in the backyard. Fall leaves were everywhere, and it was a beautiful setting for a wedding photo. I couldn't help but smile at Addison's beautiful face lit with happiness at long last. Mr. Foshee snapped his fingers and reminded us all to watch him as he took the final photo. The light popped, and we all froze for a moment, laughing and smiling.

Everyone except me.

All I could do was stare at the girl who watched us from the attic window. She didn't move or try to hide from me. She didn't vanish as you would expect a spirit to do. This wasn't Jeopardy watching us from on high.

The pale face, even paler than Addison's, peered back at me, her expression sad and empty. Her eyes met mine, and I knew she wanted me to see her. She wanted me to know that she was there, that she watched us. And I knew who she was.

She was the Lady in White.

Chapter One—Jerica Poole

I woke to the sounds of a circular saw whirring. Obviously, Jesse was trying to get a jump on the crown molding that we were scheduled to install today, but I really wanted to sleep. No such luck since the guest room overlooked his garage where he was hard at work. I groaned and pushed my hair out of my face. The clock said nine, but it felt much earlier than that. *Too early, Jesse.*

I wanted to—no, I needed to sleep. Between the late nights we'd spent planning the renovation, my regular bouts of sleeplessness and my romantic interludes with Jesse, I felt like I'd never catch up on my rest. It was as if my biorhythmic schedule was completely out of whack. I felt drained and a bit cranky as I tossed around for one last minute before getting up to greet the day. For the first time, I didn't feel like bounding down the stairs and kissing him on the cheek. There would be no lighthearted chatter as we ran boards, taped them and loaded them on the truck. This morning, despite having genuine romantic feelings for him, I dreaded facing Jesse.

Why in the world would he ask me to marry him now? I told myself that it wasn't that he asked but how he did it that bothered me, but I couldn't be sure. Yes, Jesse Clarke was an amazing man. A skilled carpenter, a good friend and a talented lover. Yes, we were great together, but I guess I just didn't see it coming. I, Jerica Jernigan Poole, was blindsided. Again. And I didn't like it.

"I think Jerica Clarke has a nice ring to it. Just think, we wouldn't even have to fight over monogrammed towels."

"Tell me you're joking. I'm not the kind of girl who has monogrammed towels."

I'd tried to brush it off, joke about it, but I could see the hurt in his dark eyes. Our conversation moved on, and so did our lovemaking, but that halfhearted proposal hung between us like a living thing.

It's time to go home, Jerica. And that's what I planned to do. I wasn't mad at Jesse, at least I didn't think I was, but we needed to put some space between us. I mean, it wouldn't be a long space since we had work to do together, but at least I could have a few minutes to myself. I slid on my jeans and t-shirt and searched for my shoes. How was it that I, a grown woman, could lose my shoes so easily? I was worse than a child. I kicked them off wherever I landed and never remembered to put them in my closet.

And then I recalled last night's dream.

I dreamed of Harper and Addison and of course sweet Loxley; it had been so long since I'd seen them, at least a full six months. They were so happy and full of life, but the dream hadn't really been about the Belles. I hadn't been there to see them. It was someone else who wanted to be seen. Like Harper, my attention had been drawn away from Addison and her special day. Away from the coral crepe paper and the candles, away from the heavily frosted cake and the table of carefully wrapped wedding gifts. My attention had been on the ghost in the attic, the young woman we'd all believed was the murdered Mariana McIntyre. And now that I recalled the moment when our eyes locked, I remembered something else.

She spoke to me!

Just a few words; I heard them in my ear, but now as I woke, I couldn't recall them. And that filled me with sadness.

This wasn't the first time I'd thought about the Lady in White this week. Not once but twice I'd walked into the Great Room during our renovation work to find the space filled with an unusual floral scent. No one else seemed to notice the aroma, so I kept my observations to myself. It was certainly a flowery perfume, old and sweet and not one that I recognized. But it had been just as if someone left the room right before me. And that made sense; history had proved that the ghost of Mariana McIntyre liked to avoid the living as much as possible. Now that the Belles were at peace and nobody lived at Summerleigh—not yet, at any rate—the Lady in White was free to roam the house again.

And she was asking for something. Was it help? Yes, she'd spoken to me. My ear remained icy from the encounter. I rubbed at it while I wracked my brain.

I had to get home. I had to go back to Summerleigh.

Chapter Two—Jerica

"Hey, I'm headed back. I'll see you there, okay?"

Jesse pushed his safety glasses up and stared at me questioningly. "I didn't hear you. What's that, Jerica?" He turned the saw off and leaned back on the flipped-down tailgate. "You're leaving?"

I shuffled my feet awkwardly as I slid my hands into my back pockets. I had my overnight bag tossed over my shoulder and apparently forgot to zip it up all the way because some of my underthings fell in the dirt beside me.

Great, Jerica. Perfect timing.

Well, no sense in being embarrassed by the sight of my underwear. It's not like he hadn't already seen me in and out of them. Still, my face flushed as I squatted down and stuffed the dusty items back in my bag.

"Got to get back home. Need to put some laundry in and do a few other things," I lied. "I'll see you at Summerleigh, okay?"

Jesse didn't respond and didn't try to stop me as I walked away and quickly wheeled out of his driveway. As I glanced in my side mirror, I could see his questioning look become one of steely determination. He shook his head, marked another board and made another cut with the saw. I gave him a halfhearted wave, not that he was even looking in my direction, and headed down the street feeling like a Class-A jerk. With a sigh, I turned onto Highway 98 and blazed a trail toward Hurlette Drive. Except for a few turns, it was basically a straight shot back; there was very little traffic and nothing but pastureland for scenery. At least it wasn't a long drive and I wouldn't have to think for too long about what an ass I was being. This was all wrong.

Was I really mad at Jesse because he didn't get down on one knee and propose? What was wrong with me?

I turned down the drive and eased toward the house. Every time I drove up and cleared that last hedge, I caught my breath. Not because of the size of the house or the history it represented but because it was mine. Summerleigh was mine to care for and protect, and the responsibility of it all weighed on me.

I didn't bother pulling around back and parking at the cottage. This was where I was supposed to be, here at the big house. Mariana McIntyre wanted me to come here. She told me something important—why couldn't I remember it? And why did it feel like a matter of life and death? I put the vehicle in park and slid out of the seat. I'd been in such a hurry to get here that I hadn't even turned the air conditioner on, and I was sweating already.

My eyes scanned the newly replaced windows, but there was nothing to see. No ghosts stared back at me as they had in the past. Had I imagined last night's dream? Had I ginned up the urgency I felt to return to Summerleigh just to get out of an awkward conversation with Jesse? I hoped not. I walked up the front steps and slid the key in the door. There was no resistance, and as I stepped inside, no odd sounds. No ladies' heels clunked on the wood above me, but for a fleeting moment I caught a whiff of that strange perfume.

Then nothing.

I walked around the bottom floor for a few minutes, still amazed at everything that had been accomplished in the past six months since Ben Hartley's tragedy. And that's what it had been, a horrible tragedy. There were no more burn marks, no evidence of a deadly conflagration. Everything was new and fresh. I waited, my ears pricked up for any noise. Anything at all.

I whispered, "Harper? Are you here?" Of course, there was no answer. She was gone, at rest now. Right? As I put my foot on the stairs to go check the top floor, my phone rang and I nearly jumped out of my skin. I dug my phone out of my pocket and studied the screen. And that was the last name I expected to see.

"Yes, this is Jerica," I said coldly. Anytime I talked to Detective Michelle Easton, I always got bad news. Why would this call be any different?

"Hi, Jerica. This is Detective Easton. I have an update I thought you should know about. It's about your husband, Eddie. Did I catch you at a bad time?"

"Eddie is my ex-husband, Detective. What kind of update? Did you recover my stolen photos? Some of my property?"

Of course this is a bad time. I never like hearing from you, lady.

"Have you heard from Eddie at all, Jerica? Any calls from him? Have you noticed anything strange lately?"

"No. He doesn't have my phone number. Why are you asking me this?" My skin continued to crawl as the conversation dragged along. I felt an uneasiness growing in the pit of my stomach. I sat on the second step of the staircase and waited for the evasive detective to get to the true reason for her call. She went on and on about procedures and Miranda rights, and I wasn't really sure what she was getting at. "Please bottom-line it for me, Michelle. Do me that kindness, please."

"He's out, Jerica. Eddie is out. We don't know where he is, and I wouldn't be surprised if he's looking for you."

"What do you mean, 'He's out'? Are you telling me that Eddie isn't behind bars where you promised me he'd be? Remember that, Detective? You warned me that because he would be a three-time loser, he'd never get out. And I believed you. What the hell are you people doing?"

Detective Easton's voice was calm and reserved, but she couldn't hide that she was concerned and embarrassed by his untimely release. "Nobody could have predicted that this would happen, Jerica. It's just one of those weird things. A glitch in the system. I'm sorry I didn't catch it sooner, but we're looking for him now. And I expect we will apprehend him before he can make his way out of the state."

"Out of the state? And what do you mean it was a glitch? Somebody let him out on accident?"

Easton sniffed on the other end, and her voice dropped like she was trying to be quiet. "Kind of like that. He made some accusations about his rights not being read properly—it was all bogus, but the judge had to hear his motion. For a poor guy, he has one heck of a swanky lawyer. Eddie was being processed for trial, and someone entered the wrong code. It's as simple and stupid as that. That's not the worst part."

I began to pace the Great Room wondering if I really wanted to know what the "worst part" could be. "And that is?"

"He knows where you are, Jerica. He knows the address. It was on his paperwork. I'm really concerned for your well-being. I think it would be wise for you to go to the sheriff's office there. What is that, George County? Go tell them about this situation. Give them my number so we can coordinate our efforts. I'm sure we'll catch him soon."

I hung up the phone. She wasn't sure of anything. She couldn't be. She couldn't protect me or keep Eddie away from me. He hated me, that much was true, and he'd never forgiven me for Marisol.

I suddenly recalled Mariana's words to me.

You should run.

Chapter Three—Mariana McIntyre

I learned at an early age that my memory was quite superior to those of others. I could recall with near-perfect clarity the first song my governess ever sang to me. I remembered opening my first book; my chubby child's fingers struggled with the pages. I recalled taking my first pony ride, and I remembered the many times my father's soft whiskers brushed my cheek as he kissed me goodnight. Those memories I could easily summon, but the memory of my mother would forever elude me, and that filled me with a deep, gnawing sadness. Lillian Jane McIntyre, that was her name, lived to the age of eighteen and then died only six months after my birth. I felt a strange sense of guilt about her passing, although no one ever suggested that my arrival had anything to do with her death.

No. I could not remember her. But my brother Jameson claimed that he did. Although he was only two years older than I, the difference might as well have been a decade or a century. Jameson would never willingly speak about her, except to say she liked to wear black and rarely smiled. How could I believe such things? Most everything my older brother said was a horrible lie. And it saddened me to no end to see that Jacob would follow in his footsteps so well. More like his shadow. His long, cold shadow. For most of Jacob's life, I did my best to run interference between him and Jameson, to limit Jameson's influence over Jacob, but I had failed in my efforts.

Even though Jameson mocked him and treated him more like a servant than a brother, Jacob adored him.

Jacob, that dear sweet boy, was only our half-brother—as Jameson so often reminded me. And although the youngest McIntyre clearly preferred our brother to me, I felt sympathy for him. His mother died too and not long after his birth. I did not miss my father's wife as much as I probably should. Ona McIntyre had not been a loving woman, and I wondered once more why my father had ever married her; once upon a time, he had been a very affectionate man. Ona lived at Pennbrook for only four years before the cough took her. Father had not remarried after that, and I was glad for it. According to Claudette Paul, my slightly older but not necessarily wiser friend, that made me the Lady of Pennbrook now.

I earnestly attempted to correct her, "Americans don't have lords and ladies, Claudette." She paid me no mind, and as I said, I secretly did not object to being the lady of the house. Even if I had lost my father's affection somewhere along the way.

But I didn't really have to guess when that happened, for I knew the moment precisely. I recalled it repeatedly with my perfect memory, seeing again the change in his expression, the shift in his face. Even his smile changed, at least when directed at me.

What a beauty your daughter has become, Mr. McIntyre! I imagine every respectable man in the county will want to see her for themselves.

Why would you imagine that, Mr. Chapman?

Mr. Chapman had been my father's lifelong friend and business partner but never received an invitation to return to Pennbrook after his generous compliment toward me. That had been well over a year ago. That's when the change happened. My father did not kiss my cheek anymore or applaud politely at my piano recitals or do any of the things he used to do. He looked at me quite differently. Not in an evil, diseased way, but in the way a man appraises a horse.

Yes, that was it. A new awareness arose in my father that day, and with it, the sun set on my childhood.

But maybe all things were made right again? This gift came, and so lovely a gift! I wished my mother could see this dress—or Claudette! She would come today and stay the week with me as we prepared for my birthday celebration. Mrs. Tutwiler, our most respectable neighbor, was also to help me with the preparations although I liked her company much less than Claudette's. I hugged the dress as I held it up to my reflection in the long mirror. It was a sumptuous rose-colored garment with far too many ruffles and ribbons woven into the sleeves. Oh, but I couldn't wait until Claudette arrived!

I suddenly took the notion to go show my mother my gift. A silly thing to do, I supposed, but my delight overpowered my thinking. My mother's painting hung in the downstairs study; it was a small painting without much detail. Lillian Jane had dark hair, as dark as mine, and she wore a pretty blue dress and a bright sunny smile. I did not believe my brother. He was one to lie just to please himself. Or to hurt me. One day his lying tongue would cost him if he wasn't careful. I told him as much yesterday; I warned him to keep quiet about things he knew nothing about. He went on and on about Father, one thing and then another. He'd been spying on our father, reading his mail whenever he left Pennbrook, which was quite frequently as of late. Jameson claimed to know some horrible secret that I did not. He taunted me at breakfast this morning, but I refused to encourage him. After a few bites I excused myself and took to the upstairs nursery hoping that Jacob would come, but he never showed. When my father returned, I would once again insist that he hire a governess for Jacob. Someone who could tame him, someone who would love him since he'd rejected me to please Jameson.

Clutching my gown, I raced down the stairs but halted outside the study. Someone was in Father's study, and I briefly hoped that my father had returned. It was not my father but Jameson sitting at his desk with the lamp lit, the room dark because of a gathering storm. He was once again elbow-deep in papers. Papers that did not belong to him.

"Ah, there she is. The Lady of Pennbrook. Good afternoon, sister."

I shuddered to hear him call me that. The only person who called me that had been Claudette. Did that mean my friend confided in Jameson too? I felt sick suddenly. "You've been talking to Claudette," I said. It wasn't an accusation or a question. I just wanted him to know that I knew.

He didn't answer me but kept shuffling papers until he found what he was looking for. I stomped closer to him, angry now.

"What are you doing in Father's room, Jameson? I have told you before..."

He didn't appear to care about my warning. "You really should read this, dear sister. Here is your name, right here. Don't you care at all? Or are you happy to waste all your time sashaying about the house in ridiculous garments? If you are looking for ghosts, Mariana, they would not be in here."

I refused to take the bait Jameson dangled in front of me. How eager he was to always talk shamefully about our mother. He knew I would hate him for it, but he did it anyway. "I am sure if my name is on that paper, Jameson, there is a good reason for it. Now get out of the study, brother, before one of the servants finds you here and tells Father what you have been doing!" I cradled my gown tighter and suddenly felt foolish for coming in here at all.

What had I been thinking?

"And who would dare do that?" He glanced up at me, a curious expression on his plain face. Yes, he was plain, but he would certainly appear more handsome if he smiled occasionally. A real smile, not a devilish one. Not a sinister one. "What is that, sister?"

I held the garment to my flat bosom. "It is a gift for me. It came today; it is a dress, of course. A birthday gift from Father. He will want to see it when he arrives."

Suddenly he jumped up from behind the desk and came to examine the dress, like a moth to a candle. I saw that familiar gleam in his eye, the one that said, *I must take a snippet of that fabric. I must cut it*, but I snatched the gown away and tried to retreat from the study. "Where are you going, Mariana? Just let me look at the thing."

"Do not touch it!" I said. My voice sounded squeaky and frightened, just like a mouse cornered by a fat, hungry cat. My arguments would be useless. Once Jameson set his mind to a thing, he would have nothing else. I could never escape him or his strange demands. He was taller and faster, and my gown was too full and fluffy to hide away from him.

"Stop that struggling, sister. I will not hurt you. I never have, have I? Not really. Let me touch it. I just want to touch it." His voice was quiet now, but his grip was tight. I had no choice but to allow him to see my prize. Again I asked myself why I had come here.

"Please, do not destroy it, Jameson. Father will know. He bought this for me, brother. It is for my birthday. We will have a party in just a few days. Remember?"

"Oh, I won't destroy it, but you have to let me see it and allow me to take a small piece. Look at all these ribbons. You would not miss one, Mariana dear. All these touches. I do not have a ribbon this color, though your friend gives me ribbons all the time; she even allows me to cut her hair when I have need of it. I don't much care for your friend, Mariana. Her speech is not eloquent, and she smells of peppermint year-round. Oh, yes. I like this one. Just a little piece, please. I need a small sampling, I really do need it." His eyes were transfixed on the dress. He reminded me of a snake who had been charmed by the pipe of a snake charmer. I had seen such a scene myself in the pages of a book. Yes, he did look like a snake.

"You have need of nothing. Leave my gown alone. It is mine, Jameson." I slapped him as hard as I could. I had never struck him before, and he fell back on the desk clutching his face in surprise. I could see the handprint rising on his skin. I did not wait for his reply. He would surely make me pay for such an assault. Yes, he would make me pay in horrible ways.

With my dress in my hands, I ran up the stairs.

Chapter Four—Jerica

The sun beat down on me, and I wiped the sweat out of my eyes. I didn't like being up on this ladder, but if it prevented me heartache later, I'd just have to suck it up and do it. I'd made the drive to Mobile to pick up this alarm system; it wouldn't do me any good to leave it in the box. I half expected to see Jesse here and working on the interior of Summerleigh when I returned, but so far, he was a no-show.

Oh well. Probably for the best. I need a break to think about all this.

Why was I really objecting to Jesse's proposal? I mean, did I really want the whole bended-knee experience again? Look how well that worked out for me the last time. Eddie had written Will You Marry Me in the sand during our last night at the beach. To this day, I couldn't figure out how he did it because he'd never left my side the entire trip. He must have had someone scribble those words in the sand for him. I'd been so surprised when he fell on his knee and produced a ring. I never expected any of it, and I never thought twice about saying yes. I believed that I loved him and that everything was going to be okay.

Cut it out, Jer. Stop dreaming about the past.

With the power drill, I mounted the camera's brackets. I was so focused on my task and lost in my own thoughts, not to mention trying hard not to fall off the ladder, I didn't even hear Jesse pull in.

"Hey, what are you doing?" he called up to me out the window of his truck.

"Jesus!" I whispered, pretending that my knees didn't buckle in surprise. I kept my eyes on the bracket and then eased down the ladder, holding my breath the whole time. I pointed to the open box and removed the drill bit.

"So you aren't talking to me now?"

I put the camera and drill down. Wiping sweat from my face with the back of my hand, I sighed. "Of course I'm talking to you. You know I'm not good on ladders, and I'm trying to get this done before dark. Or is that a storm rolling in? Hot enough for it."

"This is a security system. Has something happened, Jerica? Did someone break into the cottage—or Summerleigh?"

"No. Nothing like that. It's just a precaution, just in case."

He laughed dryly and put the box back down. "In case what? After all the ghosts and the incident with Ben, what could you possibly be afraid of?" Then his smile disappeared. "Is this to keep me away? All you have to do is tell me, Jerica. I'm a big boy; I can handle the truth."

"I...uh. That's not what I'm doing, Jesse."

He reached for my arm as if to comfort me but thought better of it. "I know you, Jerica Jernigan. This isn't like you at all. Please, talk to me. Are you upset about my asking you to marry me? I have to admit, I wasn't expecting this response."

It didn't escape my notice that he used my maiden name and not my married one. *You can't erase my past by ignoring it, Jesse. And Eddie is my past.* "You didn't ask me, Jesse. You suggested it. Not the same thing." He leaned against the side of the house with his arms crossed over his chest now. Jesse's expression wasn't easy to read, but I recognized hurt when I saw it. He was hurt, and I was to blame. "This isn't about you. I would never install a security system to keep you away. It's Eddie. He's out of jail, and Detective Easton says he's coming here to Mississippi. I can only imagine why."

"What?" His arms bowed, and he was standing straight as a board. "Your ex is coming here? To Mississippi? Have I missed something?"

I shrugged in frustration. "That's what I said. I can't believe they are letting him out. On a technicality, no less. Once he leaves the state, they'll never find him. He's not going to be happy until..." I thought better of finishing that sentence. No need for dramatics. The situation was dramatic enough without the added histrionics.

"Have you heard from him? Has he threatened you?"

I put the drill back in the box and closed it up. "I haven't heard from Eddie and don't expect to. I have a new phone number. I won't hear from him, not until he shows up. And I expect he will do that. In his mind, we have unfinished business. He blames me for Marisol. He can't understand that it was an accident."

Jesse hugged me now, and I let him. It felt good to be close to him. Oh, God. I loved him. I did love him. "He's wrong, you know. You aren't to blame."

"Oh, I know. I was there. I remember every second of it. Every moment. It was not my fault, and Marisol knows that. She has moved on with Jeopardy. She's happy." I stepped out of his arms, refusing to cry. "Eddie has been high since she died. He just couldn't handle it."

"Let me help you with this. Then we can take a look at Summerleigh's security. Just in case. I'm not going to let him hurt you, Jerica."

"It's mostly done now. I've just got to set the software up on my tablet."

He began to walk to his truck like he wanted to roll up his window and stay a while. I would have liked nothing more, but the thought of Eddie showing up with Jesse here made me sick to my stomach. The idea of those two worlds colliding stressed me out. So like Eddie to want to contaminate everything good in my life. It was a wonder I'd kept my job at the Sunrise Retirement Home for so long.

"Jesse, go home. I've got this all buttoned up here. If you don't mind, we can finish up the crown molding tomorrow. I just need to think. I have to process all this."

"Are you sure you want to be alone?"

"I've been alone before, you know. I'm not afraid to be alone."

Jesse said in a soft voice, "Yes, but you don't *have* to be. Not this time."

I walked over to him, my wimpy ponytail sagging in the heat. I kissed him softly and whispered, "I don't need you to rescue me, Jesse. I have to do this. Me."

He kissed me back, but I knew he hoped to change my mind. He couldn't. If Eddie wanted me, I'd have to face him. I would defend myself. No more hiding and running. No more feeling like my life was spent at his mercy.

"I have to do this. This is my mess, Jesse. Not yours. I'll call you later. I promise."

"It's not like you to isolate yourself. Why are you shutting me out? What about supper? You want me to bring you something later?"

"No. I've got food. I'm not lying to you. I truly am fine. Go work on your boat and take a break from this house. And me."

"I don't need a break. Do you?"

"All I need is some time. Time to think about everything. That's all."

He paused, wavered in his boots for a minute and then climbed into the truck. With one last sad look, he shifted into reverse and drove away. His taillights glowed brightly in the growing darkness, and the smell of promised rain filled my nose. I glanced up at the sky in time to see lightning pulse through the clouds above me.

See there, Jesse Clarke. You don't know me at all.

Chapter Five—Jerica

At six o'clock on the dot, Jesse called me. I picked up the house phone happy to hear his voice. "Hey, Jesse."

"Hey. Just checking in. Did the security system work okay? You did set it for night vision, right?"

I tapped on the tablet screen and updated the settings without admitting I hadn't fine-tuned any of it. "It's working perfectly. I can see both porches." I tapped on the screen to see the other two cameras. "And the corners and even the wide-angle view. There's a good view of the back of Summerleigh too," I said as I flipped through all the angles.

"If anything goes off, any sound at all, any alarm, you call me. I mean it. I'm not happy about you being alone there. Maybe Ree-Ree should come stay with you tonight."

I smiled into the phone. "I will be just fine, Jesse Clarke. If I see anyone that remotely looks like Eddie Poole, I will call the sheriff's office first thing and then you. How does that sound?"

"Have you met our sheriff?"

I laughed at Jesse's insinuation. He had a strong distrust of any politician, big or small. And here in George County, the sheriff's office was a big point of contention for people who felt the same way. The conversation went silent between us. What should I say? Sorry? But I wasn't sorry.

"Ree-Ree needs me at the diner tonight. Something about Frank's big toe...dropped a can on it. I think he does stuff like that because he wants to get out of work. Why she keeps him around, I'll never know."

"Ouch," I said with a smile. "I've been promising to come to the diner to see her. I'll have to do that soon."

"Tonight's special is hamburger steak and gravy with a side order of mashed potatoes. My specialty," he said. I could hear the smile in his voice.

"I know what you're doing, tempting me with gravy and mashed potatoes, but I better stay here," I replied with a chuckle. And then I heard a weird beeping sound. It was the alarm system! I picked up the tablet and tapped on the screen as Jesse said his goodbyes. He asked me a question, but I wasn't paying attention.

"Okay, bye."

"Jerica? Are you listening to me at all?"

"Yeah. You said it was your specialty. I've got to go, Jesse. I've got something on the stove. Talk to you later." I hung up the phone and stared at the screen.

Nothing. I can't see anything. Wait a second. Doesn't this thing have a rewind button?

I had the cameras set to record anything that triggered the motion detector. I blindly tapped buttons, still unsure what button granted access to what feature. "Oh my God," I said as I stared at the tablet. There was a young man standing in my yard looking at my house. Looking at the camera! Then as quick as a flash of lightning, he was on my front porch. He was there one second and gone the next, but he was there for sure. I rewound the footage and watched it again.

I know that face! He looks so familiar!

And then my hair stood up. *Nobody disappears like that. Unless they aren't really there. Or aren't really alive. Oh my God! He's on my porch! Why had I hung up with Jesse?*

As I stared at the tablet in real time, my heart raced and my forehead broke out in a sweat again. I wasn't sure what to do. I'd had a ghost or two on my doorstep before. John Jeffrey Belle had even carried on a conversation with me. But I didn't get the feeling this man wanted to exchange pleasantries. He looked too angry for that.

I waited—for what, I did not know. I half expected the door handle to jiggle or doors to slam, but none of that happened. Instead, the phone rang. "Jesse Clarke, you're going to give me a heart attack," I whispered into the phone.

"I'm on the way. Don't open the door. Eddie is there, isn't he?"

I eased to the window and peeked out the curtain. There was no one there. No Eddie. No strange man with an angry face. "No. It was a false alarm. There is no one there. I think I may have set the sensitivity too high." *God, I'm horrible at lying.* "I'm adjusting the settings now."

"You aren't telling me something. What's really going on, Jerica?"

"Jesse, you're going to have to trust me. I'm fine. The alarm went off, but I've checked and there's no one there. I've got the doors locked, and I'm about to take a shower and cook some supper. Really. I'm perfectly fine." *I don't need you to rescue me, Jesse. I've been fine by myself for all these years*, I thought but didn't say.

"Alright. Well, call the diner if you need me." And he hung up, clearly unhappy with me.

I hung up the phone and retrieved my flashlight. I did need help, but not from Jesse.

I was going to have to find a way to connect with Harper. The only place I knew to find her was Summerleigh. I paused at the window and searched the yard for any evidence that the man with the angry face lingered. I didn't see him. *Well, now is as good a time as any.*

I left the safety of the cottage and walked across the yard. The air was dead still, and the sky had a strange, sepia quality to it. I felt as if I were walking in an old photograph of Summerleigh. There were white gardenias growing under the kitchen window, but there were no lights on inside.

Yes, I should go through the back door. If Harper was here, that was where I would find her.

I put the key in the lock and stepped inside.

Chapter Six—Mariana

"Mariana, of all the rooms here at Pennbrook, I think this one is my favorite, dearest. I am really surprised that you have not claimed it for yourself, as you should. Look at this view, and the new furniture is stunning. This is the new suite, correct? All the way from Bermuda? Ah, what a lovely see-dar scent." I tried not to notice Claudette's slight lisp, which tended to resurface whenever she became excited about anything. Even after all these years of regular speech lessons with marbles in her mouth, and after gargling with lemon juice and rubbing her neck with honey lotion, the lisp never truly disappeared. It was a fact that brought her much despair at times. No, it would not be kind to mention it now.

"Yes, it is lovely. Father had it delivered this week, along with a few other things. It has a peppery scent, very different from anything I have ever smelled," I said as we both rubbed our fingers across the red-tinted finish. I knew it was Bermuda cedar only because of Father's excitement about this particular line of wood furnishings. He owned the most successful lumber mill in south Mississippi but had quite recently entered the furnishings business along with his now-disfavored partner, Mr. Chapman.

"You know, as the lady of the house, you could move into this room. No one would say a word about it, not your servants or your brothers. Not even your father. If I were the Lady of Pennbrook, that is what I would do."

I shook my head in embarrassment at her reference to the title of "lady" yet again. Claudette appeared very fixated on such a silly thing, but I didn't argue with her.

"It has everything, Mariana. Shade in the afternoon, sunlight in the morning. You could sew in here, read and even paint. It is very well appointed, a picture of paradise. Much better than before, dearest." Her lisp resurfaced as her "dearest" became "dear-wist," but I smiled and nodded without flinching. I could not bear it if I caused her to break down in tears again on this particular subject.

I wondered at her assessment of the room, as I had not known her to spend much time in here previously, but I appreciated the suggestion. I most certainly agreed with Claudette's opinions, but I would never abandon my own rooms in the attic. It was home to me, and I had the entire floor to myself with plenty of space, even if it did have a tendency to get warm in the summer months. She sighed happily as she touched the blue floral wallpaper and closed her eyes to daydream about some romantic idea she had conjured in her own head. Claudette was a romantic, through and through. I sometimes felt like a character in one of her stories. She did like telling them, and I liked hearing them. Especially the one about the snake charmer and the sultan's daughter. I used to get lost in the stories she'd read to me when we were younger.

But we weren't alone in the room. Claudette's silent attendant, an older woman named Eliza, busied herself with emptying Claudette's trunk and boxes. It was as if Claudette planned to move in for a month, not spend the week with me. But then again, a lady could never have too many gowns, she would say. I watched in silence as the woman carefully removed one gorgeous dress after another, and I smothered the urge to race down the hall, retrieve my own new gown and show it to her. What a fight I had had with Jameson to keep it intact. But I had refused to open the door to him, and eventually Father called him away. No, showing off my new gown would not be polite, and I had other things on my mind. Besides, Claudette's wardrobe was far more impressive than mine and certainly more mature. I blushed at the sight of the plunging necklines and the sleeveless ball gown. I had no bosom to speak of at all. Father must have observed that, for my gown was embellished with a silk rose right where my nonexistent cleavage would have been. The stylish accent hid the noticeable lack of breasts. I could not stop staring at Claudette's wine-colored gown with the plunging neckline. She had the womanly figure that I did not.

Surely she intends to wear a wrap with that!

"Eliza, when you finish airing out the gowns, be sure to hang them up promptly so they do not wrinkle." The older woman nodded without looking in our direction, and Claudette settled in the chair next to the small round table in the corner of the room. "What time is your father joining us for dinner, Mariawana?" Her hand flew to her mouth as she tried to hide her embarrassment. I did as I always did and pretended nothing happened.

"I'm not sure. He's been very busy with his new business lately. I rarely see him anymore, dearest," I said with a polite smile.

She squeezed my hand and sighed and appeared quite pleased with her arrangements. "I do love this room." She released my hand and said, "Have you been to your father's new mill, Mariana? It is a triumph for him, you know. He truly is the captain of his industry." I wondered how she would know anything about it. Her father and mine were not friends, only neighbors, and I got the distinct impression that Mr. Anthony Paul was not one to mince words either. He was a judge on the Mississippi circuit and was gone much of the year on legal business.

"No, of course not. He has never invited me to visit the mill, nor do I expect he will do so." As usual, Claudette was two steps ahead of me when it came to gossip, even gossip about my own family. She knew something and was dying to tell me about it.

Just like Jameson.

"Claudette, I do not know anything about Father's business, but I would like to talk to you about something." I glanced in Eliza's direction as Claudette sighed and waved her away. The woman discreetly left us alone to the privacy of the blue floral guest room.

"What is it? What is on your mind, dear-wist? You know you can speak your heart to me." She patted my hand and smiled at me. She appeared so patient, even though she was less than two years older than me. Sometimes Claudette could be silly and petty and eager to share unkind secrets about her family, but she was probably my only true friend in the whole world. Once upon a time, Jameson and I had been friends, but we'd been much younger than we were now. And that was before he began to tell his lies.

"It is about Jameson, Claudette. I have questions, and I need you to be honest."

Her hazel eyes grew wide, and I could see she was curious. "Of course I would be honest with you, my true friend. You know I am your friend, dearest Mariana. I shall always be your friend and will always tell you the truth. What is on your mind? Come now, hold nothing back. You can talk to me as if I were your true sister."

"Is it true that you and my brother will marry? That you have romantic feelings for him?"

Her hand flew to her chest. She had such long, slender fingers. I could see that she was not expecting my question, and immediately I knew that I was not going to like her answer for she paled and her pale pink lips stretched into a pained smile. My friend had light olive skin, bright hazel eyes and light brown hair. I noticed that her straight hair was losing its curl; she wanted so desperately to have springy curls like my own, or at least so she said on many occasions. I had always thought that Claudette was a handsome young woman but not quite pretty. Certainly not beautiful but intelligent, humorous and even accomplished. She was in every way my equal even though my family was wealthier than hers by half. In the world that Claudette and I shared, those differences were very important. What young woman didn't want to be considered beautiful or polished in her manners?

"Surely you must know, Mariana, that I will eventually marry, as will you. We are young women of marriageable age now, and of course our families will want us to marry and have our own families. Is it so offensive to you to think of me as your true sister? Would you object if I did marry into your family? For then, we would truly be sisters."

"You know that I love you as I love my own family, but my brother is not well, dearest. He does things that are not normal." I noticed that Claudette's hand went to her ear, and I quickly discerned that a lock of her hair was missing.

So it was true, then!

Then Claudette was on her feet, her hands curled into fists. I never expected such a defensive posture from her. "I have lis...lis...tened to you discwedit your brother long enough, and I can do it no longer." Not only was her lisp on full display, but she stuttered as well. I hoped for her sake that did not mean she would have a seizure. She rarely had them, but when she did, she would sleep for days afterward and wake up with bloodshot eyes and no memory of soiling herself. I prayed for her sake that it did not happen during my birthday party.

But she would not relent. "No. I mean this, Mariana. Whatever displeasure you have held with your brother needs to end. Why must you insist on seeing the worst in him when there is good there also? Why? Is it because of Jacob? He is the one who is disturbed. Do you not understand that?"

It was my turn to spring to my feet; my gown made a strange hissing noise as the layers of fabric settled around me like an angry cloud. "It is true, then. You are positioning yourself to marry my brother behind my back!"

"That is not true, Mariana!"

"All this time I thought you were my friend. But it turns out you were more interested in becoming Jameson's *bwide*." And in that moment, I did mean to mock her. It felt good to be hateful about her speech impediment. And if it hurt her, it was her own fault. She'd done this to herself.

Claudette took a deep breath and shoved her hands in her skirt pockets. "Stop that, Mariana. You promised you would never mock me. I'm not doing anything of the sort. And as far as I know, nothing has been arranged for me; there has only been talk, and not just about me but about you too. Your father has already begun your marriage arrangements, or have you not heard? I can only hope to marry someone as wonderful as a McIntyre. Now if you don't mind, I would like to be alone to *west* before dinner. Pw...please send my servant in," she struggled to finish her sentence coherently. Claudette turned her thin back to me and stood before the open window. I wanted to talk more about this, to argue with her and explain my position, but she was having none of it and did not turn around. I was so shocked and overwhelmed by what I'd learned that I could hardly argue with her.

To think, Jameson had told me the truth!

"Very well. I shall leave you to your rest," I whispered. I walked out the door and found Eliza leaning against it. I didn't bother telling her that she should go in, for she had been eavesdropping and already knew this.

As I stumbled down the hall with tears in my eyes, I shook my head at the news. Would my father make arrangements for my hand to someone I did not know? And if it was someone I knew, who was it?

Jameson knew. I was sure of that now. I had to know! Who would I marry, and why was I the last to know? And why would Claudette want to marry my brother? She knew about his...perversions, his incessant need to cut at the things he admired.

I walked down the hallway lost in my thoughts when I heard Jacob's voice. He wasn't talking or giggling as he had a tendency to do whenever something amused him; he was reciting poetry. Sir Walter Scott, if I wasn't mistaken. That was something I had never been able to achieve with him. Perhaps Father had sent for a governess after all?

I was beginning to understand that many things happened at Pennbrook that I was unaware of. I would surely have heard about a new governess' arrival, wouldn't I? I walked toward the nursery door and was shocked to see Jacob and Jameson sitting together on the long blue settee. Jacob had an open book in his lap and was flipping the page as I paused to listen. He read a little more, not perfectly but much better than before. Obviously, he'd been practicing. And that's when Jameson saw me. He was holding a tiny pair of scissors and cutting into a stack of folded paper. Making paper dolls was an old hobby of his. I was surprised to see him working at it again.

"Continue," he said to my brother as he rose and walked toward the door. I thought about what to say to him, what to do. Should I apologize to him? Offer him some sort of peace offering? I hardly knew how to proceed. I felt lost, in a whirlwind, in a place where I had no control over anything. Jameson walked toward me, a wooden expression on his face. It was like I was invisible, like I wasn't there at all. Was I a ghost? There was no welcoming smile on his face, not a trace of triumph.

And then he closed the door.

Chapter Seven—Jerica

My exploration of Summerleigh availed me nothing. Whatever ghost or spirit showed up in my surveillance video wasn't in the house now, and there was no sign that Harper was there either.

Where are you, Harper?

I was trained in grief management. Grief counseling had been a part of my job when I worked at the Sunrise Retirement Home. Although I didn't want to admit it, I was beginning to suspect that a lot of my emotional uncertainty lately stemmed from the fact that I had not given myself time to mourn Harper. She'd been such an integral part of my life, especially during the loss of Marisol and afterward. Harper had been such a friend to me, almost a mother, that it seemed impossible to think I would never see her again.

I mean, I knew she had passed away. I understood the concepts of life and death and mourning and grief. From the day she died until recently, Harper remained a part of my life in a strange, metaphysical way. But she was gone now. Yes. That was a fact that could not be denied. She was gone, and I had to move on with my own life.

Maybe Ben Hartley had been right. Maybe it was Summerleigh itself that brought the melancholy out in me and in all who called the place home. I wasn't sure, and I didn't have all day to think about it. Trucks were pulling up in the yard. Jesse. Emanuel and Renee were converging on Summerleigh as I pondered life in my kitchen. With a frown, I finished the dregs of this morning's coffee. That's when I heard a tap on the front door.

"Coming," I called. Renee was there waiting for me with a big smile on her face and a gift in her arms. It was wrapped in tissue with a big pink bow on it.

"Brought you something, sweetie. I couldn't wait for you to come to the house; I had to give it to you now."

I smiled at her thoughtfulness. "I'm just headed that way now. Can we go over there, or should we open it here?"

"If you are ready to go, let's head to Summerleigh. That's where this belongs, anyway." Renee's long dark hair was piled on top of her head in a casual yet perfect messy bun. As usual, she sported flawless makeup and like me wore shorts and a t-shirt even though it was November. When was fall going to arrive?

"How did you get time off from the diner? I wasn't sure you were going to be able to join me with Frank's swollen toe."

She rolled her eyes. "Just lucky, I guess. And I told Frank that if he had one more injury, I was gonna fire him. He's always dropping something or cutting something or setting something on fire. I swear, the man is a danger to himself and my business."

I poked her in the side playfully. "But you are crazy about him, aren't you?"

"What can I say? I have a weakness for klutzes."

We went into the kitchen and said a quick hello to Jesse, who was busy going over the furniture placement chart with Emanuel. There were others in the house too, craftsmen polishing up various projects, but the work was largely complete. For the first time, I could see the rainbow at the edge of the storm, and my dream of restoring Summerleigh was close to coming to fruition.

Most of the furniture would arrive today, and the interior decorating was starting. This was my least favorite part, but Renee had proved repeatedly that she had an eye for those kinds of details. And Jesse knew all the historical touches that needed to be added. Not to mention I'd seen this place as it used to be many times in the dreams that Harper shared with me.

Oh, Harper. I wish you could see this place now. If you can see me, find a way to let me know.

I heard nothing but Renee chattering beside me. I followed her to the nearest guest room, which would've been Harper's old bedroom. There was a wrought iron bed with a new mattress, a curtainless window and a shabby-chic dresser against the wall.

"Go ahead. Open it." Renee was so excited, I could hardly say no.

I unwrapped the tissue and tugged on the ribbon to release the surprise. "Renee, this is the most gorgeous thing I've ever seen. I love it. What a beautiful quilt!"

"I'm so glad you like it. My neighbor Betsy works on quilts on the side, and I thought this would be perfect for Harper's room. Don't you love those cherries? That's a retro print. Feel the weight? Makes me want to snuggle up with it right now. If it wasn't so warm."

I spread the fabric out to get a good view of the complicated patchwork. "I love it, but I'm not sure I can accept this. This had to set you back a bit. I mean, look at this workmanship. Really, Renee, it's too much."

"I don't think you understand the meaning of the word 'gift,' Jerica. This is my late birthday and early Christmas gift to you. Now let's put it on the bed. I even brought sheets to go with it. I'm dying to see what it looks like in here." Renee's big smile made it impossible for me to refuse her thoughtful gift. I would never have dreamed of putting something like this on the bed, but Renee was right, those vintage cherries were perfect for Harper's room. She used to have a dresser with cherry embellishments, and I knew for a fact that she always loved that romper of Jeopardy's. We spread the quilt over the freshly sheeted bed and sat back in amazement. It looked perfect.

I wiped a tear from my eye and said, "Harper would have loved this. I love it, Renee. Thank you." It wasn't like me to dole out hugs, but I couldn't help but hug her. We were both teary-eyed as Jesse walked in the room, his eyes gleaming with excitement and not about the quilt. He had a dusty box in his hand.

"Look what I found in the attic. Can you believe this? I guess you know who this must have belonged to. After all this time, I found it."

Staring at the dusty wooden box, I knew exactly what he was talking about. This belonged to Jameson McIntyre! This was the very treasure box that Jacob and Jameson had been protecting. "Let's go into the kitchen and open it, Jesse. It's too dusty to open it in here. Did you see the gorgeous quilt Renee brought?"

Jesse complimented Renee, and together the three of us headed to the kitchen to look inside the treasure box. With shaking hands, he put it on the table and opened it. I don't know what I was expecting, maybe a box of little skeletons or bottles of poison or pieces of hair or maybe even bloody garments, but that wasn't what I saw. There were a few ribbons and, yes, a curl or two of hair, but besides that it was nothing like I expected. There were some pieces of paper, and I picked one up and began to read it. "You are cordially invited to attend..."

Jesse broke in and said, "This is for Mariana's birthday party. It's an old invitation! This must have been written around the time when she was murdered. Why would he keep this?"

I tried to read the faded writing, but it was difficult. "Look, guys. It says Pennbrook. Could that be the name of the old house before they rebuilt it? Is that the original Summerleigh? I've never heard of Pennbrook before. Have you, Jesse?"

"No, I haven't, but that doesn't mean anything. Remember, all of those old records were lost. Pennbrook doesn't ring a bell, but now I have something to research. With this name and maybe some of this other information, I can turn up something."

Renee swallowed and said, "I hope finding this box doesn't stir things up around here. I'd be really worried for you if it did. Are you sure everything is okay, Jerica? You seem a little distracted today."

"Well, I did see someone on my porch last night, a young man. But it wasn't a living person because he vanished into thin air. He was standing in the yard, and then quick as a flash, he appeared on the porch. And then he vanished. I thought it must be a glitch with the camera, but I've never heard of a glitch projecting an image that isn't actually there."

Jesse asked, "What did he look like?"

"He looked a bit like Jacob; I think it may have been Jameson, but I can't be sure. A shadow obscured his face, like he was deliberately trying to hide his identity from me. Sounds crazy, huh?"

Renee let out a sigh. "Please, from what we know of this place, that doesn't sound crazy at all. It sure doesn't surprise me. What about you, cousin?"

Jesse was staring at me accusingly but said nothing. He closed the box and said, "I'd like to take this home and check it out later if you don't mind. But in the meantime, we've got furniture trucks arriving, and I think the telephone guy is here. Can you show him where to install everything while I help Emanuel move the furniture around?"

"I'll do the bossing," Renee said sweetly in an attempt to lighten the mood. The installation man was walking in, and I quickly greeted him. For the next hour, we were all so busy that I didn't have much time to think about the contents of the box or anything that had to do with Pennbrook or the McIntyre family. The tech knew his business and quickly ran the necessary lines we would need for the house.

"You guys have it looking great in here. Must be exciting to see an old place brought back from the dead. I always wanted to see it fixed up."

I smiled at his choice of words. "Yes, we're all very happy about it." I heard the furniture trucks drive away and peeked out the window to see the dusty air stirring up behind the exiting vehicles.

Renee poked her head in and said, "I've got to get to the diner, but I think everything is where it should be. See you later."

That was disappointing. I had hoped to spend more time with my optimistic friend, but I couldn't keep her here forever. "Sounds great. Thanks for your help, Renee. And thanks again for the gift!" I called to her as the kitchen door closed. To my surprise, Jesse's truck cranked up too. Either he was still upset with me or he had that box on the brain and wanted to go home to start plundering it in earnest. Maybe I would surprise him with a visit? No. Probably not. I was the one who wanted some space.

Either way, it quickly became apparent that the phone installation man and I were the only ones left at Summerleigh. I followed him into the Great Room, and we watched the modem finally light up. He tested the connection on his tablet, and I signed the appropriate paperwork. Yes, it was all quiet in here now.

"Yeah, this is a real nice place you have here, Mrs. Poole."

I blinked at hearing that name. I might need to have that changed soon. I never wanted to think of being a Poole ever again. "Please call me Jerica."

"My older sister is getting married next summer, and she's been looking for a place for the reception. This looks like it would be large enough to have a nice wedding reception. I see you guys are going to be open soon. Would it be possible to get a business card or brochure or something?" The words had barely left his lips when we heard footsteps above us.

It was the sound of high heels clicking across the wooden floor upstairs. I could have played it off as normal, pretended that there was someone up there walking around in old-fashioned high heels, if not for the extreme coldness invading the room and the absolute feeling of wrongness that overwhelmed me. And by the look of the tech, he was feeling it too. His expression was all the assurance I needed that there was something supernatural happening right this very moment.

"I can get you a card. I have some in my purse. Be right back." Anxious to keep things normal and to pretend that there was nothing happening, I scurried off into the kitchen, opened a cabinet door and dug out a card from my purse. It took me more than a few seconds to find one, and when I returned to the Great Room the installation man was gone. And I hadn't even heard the door open or close. The paperwork was on a nearby table, but beyond that there was neither hide nor hair of him. And then I heard the truck pulling away.

I don't know why, but that really ticked me off. We were doing so much around here, so much work, we'd put in so much effort to bring life back to Summerleigh. We'd worked hard to clear the proverbial air and help those spirits that wanted to be helped. And now it looked like my work wasn't done yet.

"Great. Just great," I said to the empty house. But it wasn't empty. Who was I kidding?

Obviously, I was talking to the ghost of Mariana McIntyre.

Chapter Eight—Jerica

With my princess telephone in my hand, I dialed Hannah's number but then quickly hung up. Was I ready to get involved with the psychic again? Would she even take my call? This wasn't the time to do that. I was a big girl, as I kept telling Jesse. It was time to take things into my own hands. I washed the supper dishes and put them back in the cabinet knowing all the while exactly what I was going to do. I took the key off the latch and headed out the door toward Summerleigh. There were no phantom lights glowing in the windows, no shadowy figures and no beckoning ghosts. Just the growing sense that I wasn't alone.

And that I was expected.

But by whom? That was the question.

I half expected to see my boyfriend's beat-up old truck tooling down the driveway, but it didn't happen. Well, at least he was respecting my wishes. What more could a girl want?

I slid the key in the back door, opened it and stepped inside to enjoy the view. The renovated kitchen was inspiring. We put so much work into restoring those old details that it really felt as if one of the Belles might come in at any moment and invite me to help make a pan of biscuits. A stack of white and blue china plates waited neatly in the glass front cabinets, and there were jelly jars in a basket on the counter along with a collection of colorful red and white napkins. It was a lovely space with precious details.

We would open the Summerleigh Bed-and-Breakfast in a few weeks, just in time for the holiday season. It was exciting, tiring and nerve-racking all at once. Word had gotten out around town about the new venture, and we already had a few reservations thanks to Renee, who was really skilled at drumming up business. I was glad about the prospect of money coming in. Although Jesse and I were technically partners, I was footing the lion's share of the bills. But that's not to say he wasn't doing his share of the work. Nobody could ever say that Jesse Ray Clarke wasn't a hard worker.

I moved a few of the items around the countertops before walking into the parlor. We had not been successful in acquiring one of those old radios, but we found a nice reproduction and the space was roomy, perfect for entertaining multiple guests. Jesse and I had toyed with the idea of hosting some historical chats in this room. In my mind, I could see Ann Marie Belle perched on the couch, her knees tucked up under her, giving me a disapproving look while she absently thumbed through a magazine and looked bored.

For some reason, I felt like something was out of place in this room, not quite right. I moved a few things around but couldn't shake the feeling. *I'll think about it some more.* Then I stepped into the empty Great Room. The fireplace was beautifully restored and filled with vanilla-scented candles. The bookcases were painted white and stuffed with interesting pieces that we'd discovered in the attic. It was a nice room but not as cozy as the parlor. I walked through and headed to the hallway that led to the bedrooms. I smelled paint and carpet adhesive; strangely enough, it was a satisfying combination.

I went into Harper's room, amazed again at the beauty of Renee's quilt. Everything was in order in here, I thought as I flipped on the light and glanced around the room. In fact, besides hanging an odd picture or two, I checked the room off in my mind. Yes, this room was perfect. Besides the kitchen, Harper's room was the one that made me completely happy. I had to pinch myself—this wasn't a dream. This was my life, and it was a good one. I took a quick survey of the other rooms and then headed up the stairs. No one silently stalked me, but then again, the boy ghost was gone now. I paused in the hallway outside the nursery door and shivered, then took a deep breath and stepped into the room.

Nope. It was still uncomfortable in here, despite the fresh paint, the new door and the new light fixtures. So uncomfortable. I wasn't convinced that any amount of redecoration would help this place. It had been here that I'd offered the ghost boy Marisol's purple bear. Shaking my head and rubbing my arms against the chill, I left the room and closed the door behind me. The other bedrooms on this floor were neat and tidy with new hardwood flooring and period furniture but with modern touches like electric lamps and top-of-the-line mattresses. I especially liked the room that overlooked the backyard. It had a comfortable, peaceful feeling. I went into that room, shifted a small table, placed a book of poetry on the nightstand and left, happy with the arrangements. The other rooms were nice but not completely furnished yet. And then my eyes fell on the attic.

Jesse and I had decided to keep this room private. It had a new door with a lock, and although we had spent a great deal of time cataloging and storing many of the antiques up here, there was plenty of stuff left. No, we could never rent this room out.

This would always be Jeopardy's room. And also Mariana's, I suddenly thought. That knowledge inspired me.

"Mariana, are you here? It's me, Jerica. I'm not here to disturb you. I just want to talk to you." I sat on a nearby stack of plastic tubs and waited. Why hadn't I thought to bring a digital recorder up here? Hadn't I learned anything about paranormal investigation? I should be an old pro by now.

I watched the sun go down, and the room darkened quickly. I felt apprehensive but not fearful. I expected to see or hear Mariana; I talked a bit more and invited her to speak with me, but in the end, nothing happened. There was the groaning of the old attic floor, the occasional shifting of the air, but no ghost, no voice, nothing at all.

Leaving the attic behind, I retraced my steps to make sure I'd turned off all the lights. Everything was in order here on the top floor. I was tempted to head back home but on a whim decided to check out the bottom floor too. Turning off the light in the Great Room, I hurried down the hall that led to the bedrooms. The only light on was Harper's.

Hmm...I don't think I left that on. Maybe...

I pushed open the door and waited. Nobody was there, but something had changed.

The quilt had been turned down, just like Harper used to do right before bed. Like she used to do for all her sisters and her mother. I walked toward the bed, wide-eyed and holding my breath. With shaking fingers, I touched the cool fabric and glanced over my shoulder.

"Harper?" I asked as I sat on the edge of the bed. But I didn't really have to ask. I knew what this was.

This was an invitation.

I wasn't remotely tired, but I kicked off my shoes and slid under the quilt. After thirty minutes of waiting and watching, my eyes grew heavy and I fell asleep.

Chapter Nine—Mariana

The night before my party, Father came home, and he was in a fine mood. He was happy and kind and loving to me once again. I couldn't understand the change in his attitude. Father did not avoid me, or at least he did not avoid looking into my eyes. He even dressed for dinner and wore a new, dark blue suit, refrained from smoking at the table and drank only one glass of brandy when offered to him. To be fair, though, his cheeks were quite red during our dinner, as if he had previously imbibed. I noticed he carried a new gold watch that he repeatedly removed from his pocket to check the time. He laughed, and Claudette gave me an awkward shrug. I felt like I was missing some secret, but I could not discern it.

At least the letter sent by Mrs. Tutwiler explained why she had been absent. Her own son Donnie had pneumonia, and the prognosis was not hopeful. Donnie was a nice boy with blond hair and big blue eyes; he was as stupid as Old Edward, Father's stable hand, but it would be sad to lose him. I prayed silently for him as we waited for the first course of our dinner.

As the pumpkin soup was served, Jameson gave me a sideways smile at seeing my confusion. He and Father talked a good long time about the furniture business, and Claudette asked a few polite questions about Bermuda and the processing of the cedar from that wild place. Their chatter continued through the soup service, to the pork loin and potatoes and through the dessert, a vanilla pudding with caramel sauce. I realized that I was not as hungry as I had expected to be. I sat as quietly as a porcelain doll and listened to them talk to one another, almost as intimately as Claudette and I might from time to time.

Then my father remembered his manners and complimented me on my dark green gown. He asked if the new rose gown pleased me, and I shot a look at Jameson that said, *See there? I told you he wouldn't want the gown cut up.*

"It is a fine dress, Father. Fit for a queen."

"Or the Lady of Pennbrook, Mr. McIntyre," Claudette added.

"Please, call me Michael. Or Bull, whichever you prefer," he said, tipping his glass to her. I was shocked to see him then squeeze her hand briefly. His face flushed as he released her.

She touched her face with the hand he touched and leaned forward slightly. I heard her whisper, "I pwefer Michael."

Any sympathy I may have felt for her regarding her handicap had vanished. I suddenly hoped that she would lisp and stutter her way through the rest of dinner.

What is going on here?

I sat quietly as Father pretended to be a young man and flirt with my oldest and dearest friend. I felt sick, sick like a cat that had eaten a bad mouse. In fact, I wanted nothing more than to throw up and go to bed. Surely I had entered a nightmare.

Rising to my feet suddenly, I said, "Please excuse me, Father. I do not feel well. I think I need to rest until this passes."

"Should I call for the doctor?" my father asked, seeming genuinely concerned about me; it was the first time he had really noticed me at all tonight.

"No, Father." I pressed the white linen napkin to my lips to prevent myself from becoming ill. "Please enjoy your dinner. I am going to bed. Thank you for the gift."

"I will walk you up, dear sister."

"No thank you, Jameson. I can walk just fine."

"Let your brother help you, Mariana. Jacob, stay right where you are. You promised to read to Claudette, did you not?"

Jacob gave both Jameson and me a distrustful glance but did as he was told. Luckily for him, he had brought the book with him; he stood beside the table and began to recite. As I walked up the stairs with Jameson beside me, I heard Father and Claudette applauding politely.

"When did he learn to recite so well? Did you teach him?"

"No, the real teacher around here is Claudette, don't you agree? Is that really the question you want to ask me?"

Clutching my wobbly stomach, I whispered, "I must confess this whole night has been confusing to me, from the beginning to now." I opened the door to my bedroom, thankful that I had hidden my new dress so well that Jameson would never find it. Let him cut on one of my other gowns but not that one.

"Shall I tell you what you didn't want to hear before? Shall I tell you the truth, even though it is unpleasant, at least for you?"

"Tell me what you want to tell me, Jameson."

"Why should I? What are you going to give me?" His snake's smile returned to his face. He glanced around and could not find my dress, but I knew he wanted to see it. "Oh, never mind. Even though you treated me harshly before, I will tell you what I know, and then maybe you will give me what I want. Miss Claudette Paul has set her cap at our father, Mariana. Not me. She has no desire to marry me, nor do I have any desire for her. We talked about it once briefly when she was twelve, and we both decided it would never work. But she does like to please me sometimes and offers her hair or a ribbon as a kind of peace offering between us. And you should know, dearest Mariana, she wants nothing less than to be the Lady of Pennbrook. It's all she ever talks about, sister. She doesn't want me at all but our father; she wants to be a McIntyre. Now why that is, I don't know."

"Why would he want to marry again? He has the three of us. He does not need any other children."

"He is a man, by all accounts a young, virile man, and he needs a good wife to run his house and do the things a wife should do besides merely have children. I wonder at your intelligence at times, Mariana."

I banged my hand on the wall. "I don't believe a word you tell me, Jameson Michael. I don't believe you at all!" I said as I went to close my door. I did feel dizzy now, on top of being sick.

"Be a fool, then! You're nothing if not consistent!" Then he muttered, "Stupid girl," under his breath and stomped away still mumbling.

I slammed the door and climbed into bed. Once the room stopped spinning, I fell asleep.

Chapter Ten—Jerica

A feather rubbed across my nose. Or something. What was that? I opened my eyes and discovered it was a lock of my hair tickling my face. My eyes popped open as I recalled my surroundings.

I was sleeping in Harper's bed. But I hadn't seen my friend or any of her sisters; I dreamed of someone else last night. I dreamed of Mariana McIntyre—a young woman who had been dead for 150 years. With my eyes closed, I attempted to recall every second of the shared memory, for I had no doubt that my late friend was somehow involved in the paranormal experience. Or maybe it wasn't Harper at all. Maybe it was simply Summerleigh. Maybe it had been Summerleigh's power all this time. No. I didn't want to believe that. I hoped with all my heart to be reconnected with Harper at least one more time, just to say goodbye. But it hadn't happened. Not yet. I pushed back the quilt and sat up and stretched. As comfortable as this bed was, it was no substitute for my own. What had I been thinking?

I listened quietly and hoped to hear footsteps pattering around upstairs, maybe children's footsteps or high heels like those that had belonged to Mariana. But I heard nothing. It was as if the house had fallen asleep and slept still.

Harper, if you're trying to show me something, I don't get it. I know that Jameson murdered his sister. I don't want to witness it if I don't have to. Harper? Can you hear me?

I sighed at the lack of noise and climbed out of bed. I'd left my toothbrush and toothpaste and all of my personal items back at the caretaker's cottage, so I would have to go home if I wanted to tidy up for the day ahead of me. I made the bed quickly and fluffed the pillows. Yes, everything seemed normal.

Quiet.

Dead.

And then I saw the picture. It was a wedding picture, an old black-and-white photo in an even older picture frame. Despite the faded color and some minor damage to the photo, I could see every face plainly. This was the day that Addison married Frank! I had seen this moment in a dream. Harper had shown it to me! I remembered the moment that she looked up at the attic and saw the Lady in White staring down at her. Mariana's lips had been moving, but I couldn't make out the words at all.

This picture hadn't been here before; I was sure I would have known if it had been. I would have adored this picture; I was just in here with Renee yesterday, and we would've seen it. But it had not been here, so who put it here? That was the question. I took it off the wall and examined the back of it, then popped off the back of the frame and searched for clues, but there was nothing to see. No inscription, no faded words on the back of the picture. But I knew those faces. I loved those faces.

And then it occurred to me—Harper wanted me to see this picture. She had wanted me to spend the night here. This picture was here for my benefit, but what did it mean? As I stared harder at the scene, taking my time to identify as many of the details as I could, my phone rang and startled me.

I answered it without looking. I was too busy staring at the picture. "Hello?"

"Good morning, Jerica. This is Detective Easton. I'm calling to follow up on the status of your ex-husband, Eddie Poole."

I tore my eyes away from the picture and focused on the phone call. I really needed to listen to what she had to say. My life might depend on it. "I'm all ears, Detective. What's the latest?"

"Eddie is definitely on the move. And to make matters more complicated and ten times more dangerous, he has a gun. He robbed a convenience store and a package store just this morning, and by the way he's traveling, it is clear to me that he is on his way to you."

"Great. Just great. How many crimes does he have to commit before he gets caught?" I sat on the bed trying to catch my breath.

She agreed with me but didn't seem eager to hang up. That made it even worse because I only ever heard from Easton when something horrible was happening. Like this, for example. "Eddie is disturbed in a very real and dangerous way, Jerica. I think you need to move. Go somewhere safe."

"You aren't telling me anything I don't already know about my ex-husband. I was a fool for a long time but not anymore. I am not going anywhere. I did that once before, remember? I have a gun and a security system; I am going to stand my ground, Detective."

Her voice deepened and took on a more serious tone. "You are playing with fire, ma'am. He's made several threats online; some are quite disturbing. I think I should read a few of them to you so you understand…"

"I'm not on social media, Detective. That would mean nothing to me. So what if he's making threats? He's been threatening me for years. I'm sure this won't be the last time either." Who was I kidding? I didn't take this news nearly as lightly as I was pretending, but this detective was going to be of no help to me. None at all. Might as well get rid of her now. "I know that he wants to harm me, that he blames me for Marisol's death, but he's wrong, you know. He's wrong." I hadn't expected it, but I started crying. I cried because once upon a time, I had loved Eddie Poole; we made a beautiful and magical child together. *I am so sorry, Marisol.* Marisol's death ended all of that, not the love I had for her but my marriage. Her death ended our family, and it was a grief I felt deeply. And I knew that Eddie did too in his own way. In his own warped way.

"I have to make a few phone calls. Goodbye, Detective. Thank you for calling me, but I'm sure I will be okay."

"I am calling the local sheriff's department for you, Jerica. They have to know what they're up against. It would be wrong of me not to prepare them for the violence they may encounter if they try to apprehend this man. He is dangerous to more than just you. He is dangerous to the community at large. You should know something else too." She paused as if she wanted me to ask her what that something was. I wasn't sure I wanted to, so I waited for her to continue speaking.

"Eddie is addicted to heroin. I'm sorry to tell you that, but it's the truth. When he's desperate, he will shoot pills or whatever he can get his hands on. If we don't catch him, I don't think you'll live very long. He's got a death wish. Have you ever heard of something called suicide by cop?"

"I think so."

"Well, the doctor thinks that Eddie is a prime candidate for this type of thing. Please be careful."

I rubbed my nose with the back of my hand and promised to do just that before hanging up on her. She was still talking, but there was nothing left to say and nothing I wanted to hear.

I walked out of Summerleigh and locked the door behind me. Renee had not arrived yet. It was only around 6:30 in the morning, and she didn't usually show until about 7:30.

But I knew who would be awake. Jesse was always awake this early. I picked up the phone and dialed.

"Hey, I need your help with something. I want you to teach me how to shoot, and I might actually need to buy a gun."

"Does this mean that he's—nope. I don't really want to know, but I do believe that you should be prepared...especially if you're going to keep me away, which I don't understand at all."

"Will you just answer the question? Will you teach me how to shoot?"

"Of course I will. You want to get started now?"

"There's no time like the present," I said as I quoted my father.

"Okay, let me stop by the bank and get my gun out and grab some bullets at the hardware store. Be there in about an hour. Are you cooking breakfast?" I could hear the grin in his voice.

"I guess I could try."

"Nope. Why don't you let me bring something? I'll be there in about an hour with breakfast and anything else you might think of. Just text me. And Jerica?"

"Yeah?"

"Thank you for letting me help you."

"Yeah. I'm an idiot. Thanks for coming to my rescue." And then I added, "I love you, Jesse Clarke." I don't know why I said it, but I did, and I didn't regret it. I hung up before he could answer me.

Time to get ready to face the day. Whatever it might bring.

Chapter Eleven—Mariana

My bedroom brightened as the clouds skittered away on an invisible breeze. The half-moon above cast strange shadows in the corners of my room, and I felt I could no longer trust my eyes. I saw spirits everywhere, phantoms that looked like my mother. And other things. Darker, more frightening. But as quickly as I saw them, they vanished like smoke.

More than once, I suspected that someone was watching me, but surely that was only a feeling. Earlier, my doorknob rattled and a tapping on the wall beside my bed startled me; I assumed the noises came from my former friend. I refused to open the door or respond to her tapping or open my heart to her again if this was her. And it must be!

No. I would not make that mistake twice. My mind raced back to the moment at the dinner table. I could see Claudette rubbing her skin, obviously relishing my father's light touch on her wrist. Such an intimate and disgusting moment. How could my father play the fool with such a foolish girl? *Claudette, how could you betray me?*

My nose was runny from my earlier crying jag, and I wiped at it as I sat in the chair near the window. Occasionally, deer wandered across the grassy lawn and nibbled their way to the pond. Perhaps I would see one tonight. I did so enjoy watching them. Such peaceful animals. Goodness knows I needed something to distract me from my rumbling stomach. My sickness had vanished, and in its place I felt a raw hunger. I waited and toyed with the soft bristles of my brush as I watched the shadows move on the ground below. I saw nothing. Not a deer or a squirrel.

Nothing at all except Jacob.

My younger brother ran awkwardly across the lawn wearing nothing but his nightshirt. What was he doing? Jacob knew the pond was off-limits to him without one of us to watch him. My father had always been so adamant about that. Oh, why hadn't Father hired a governess? I could not be expected to watch over Jacob when he refused to listen to me.

I reached for my robe and threw it over my body as I raced toward the door and fumbled with the cold key. The heavy lock clunked, and the door opened to the chilly hallway. Hurrying as quickly and quietly as possible, I rushed down the stairs and out of the house. I saw no one and heard nothing except the chiming of the clock and the light scampering of a mouse. Even though our home was new, there were mice in the walls. Many mice. I could hear them scratching, chewing, moving, but no one else heard them. Just me. How strange that was.

With each step, I became more aware that I was abandoning the safety of the house. This was not something I would normally do. I did not venture outside of Pennbrook often, except for social calls. I wasn't adventurous like my brother Jameson or always out of doors like Jacob. To be honest, I only took walks in the garden when Claudette came to call. I did not like venturing out much. Yet, here I was running through the lawn in my nightgown in the middle of the night searching for my brother. The grass was wet under my feet, and my heart pounded so loudly I was certain that anyone near me would be able to hear it.

In a loud whisper, I called, "Jacob! Jacob! Where are you?"

The wind rose from the ground, and my loose hair and dress fluttered as I sailed across the lawn toward the woods. The pond was just beyond the smallish forest, and what was beyond that, I did not know.

"Jacob!" I whispered a little louder this time. The tall grasses around me spun like drunken dancers in a ballroom.

"Who is there?" I heard Jacob's frightened voice calling back to me from the line of woods just ahead.

"It's me, Mariana. Where are you?" I paused my flight as I scanned the tree line. Jacob's face rose up from the ground like a spirit rising from a grave. He waved at me and disappeared into the greenery.

With an exasperated sigh, I followed him and quickly caught up to him. Grabbing him by the shoulders, I turned him around. "What are you doing out here? You can't be out here, Jacob. It is the middle of the night. Besides, you know the pond is off-limits. Is that where you are going?"

He shook his head slowly, his bottom lip poking out to express his displeasure with my interruption of his midnight adventure. "I was not going to the pond. I followed Jameson. He is out here hiding a treasure, and I want to find it." He fumbled with the button at the top of his nightdress and avoided looking me in the eye.

"Jacob, you do know those are not real treasures, don't you? Jameson isn't hiding gold or jewels. It's something else, nothing you want to see."

"I want to find it." Obviously, he was immovable in his determination.

"I have not seen anyone out here except you and me. It is the middle of the night, and tomorrow is my birthday party. We have to go back, Jacob. I think it might rain."

He narrowed his eyes. "Why do you lie to me? Just because I am young does not mean I am stupid. It is not going to rain, and I do not want to go inside until I find Jameson's treasure."

I glanced up and down the cluttered pathway. I saw no evidence that Jameson—or anyone else, for that matter—had passed this way. "Jacob, there is no one here. If Jameson hid a treasure, it would not be in these woods. You know how much he dislikes bugs of all kinds. And he would never hide his treasure so far from the house; he is smarter than that. You know that. I never said you were stupid, nor did I think it. Why don't we do this? We will go back to Pennbrook and look for the treasure on the way. But we must be very quiet. You know Jameson never wants us to know where he hides his treasures." Jacob smiled and put his arms around my waist. This was the first hug I had received from him in so long that I could not remember the last one.

The wind increased, and again my hair slapped my face. Jacob held my hand tight, and we walked back toward the house. I did not realize how far we had ventured out. True to my word, we paused every few feet to glance around for evidence of Jameson's recent excavations. I had no desire to pry into his personal business, but if it pleased Jacob and helped bring him back to the house, then I would certainly not discourage him from looking. I thought Jameson's treasures abhorrent; I wondered why Jacob would put so much value in them. And that worried me.

After the birthday party, once things returned to normal, for surely they would, I would speak to Father again about a governess. There must be someone willing to take my younger brother under their wing.

Someone besides Jameson.

I breathed a sigh of relief once we cleared the fountain even though the return trip was taking much longer than I expected. Together, we walked ever so slowly back to Pennbrook. Jacob insisted on looking under every rock, and that's when I saw him.

Jameson!

And he was not alone. My tall, gangly brother was wrapped in a woman's embrace. But whose? As they caressed and kissed, I watched and for a moment forgot that Jacob was there. I was shocked to see that Jameson was making love to Claudette. My hand flew to my mouth. Her hands rubbed his arms, and he held her tight and kissed her so deeply I thought surely he would devour her. Like two animals they were!

I heard Jacob's breath catch in his throat. I squatted down beside him and put my finger to my lips. He nodded in agreement but continued to stare at the unseemly display. The sickness that I'd felt earlier returned, but I could not succumb to it. We could not stay here and witness this any longer.

"Let's go to the front of the house, Jacob." He nodded again and held my hand tightly. We backed down the pathway and made a loop around to the front of the house. Once we turned the corner, we both ran; we were quite breathless as we stood on the porch. I squatted down again and said to him, "Say nothing to anyone about this. I will talk to Father, Jacob. You leave it to me, brother."

"But the treasure. We never found the treasure," he whined. I kissed his forehead and hugged him.

"I do not think the treasure is out here, anyway. I have never seen Jameson hide anything out here. Tomorrow when the sun comes up, you should go to the attic and look. I know he hides things up there. But do not let him find you searching.

It will be worse for you if you do." He smiled and shook his head.

I forced myself to smile back. How was I going to tell Father about this?

Chapter Twelve—Jerica

As always, Jesse was the first one out of bed. If the sun was up, he was too; he didn't like sleeping in. I sure did, but with all the work we'd been doing, I wasn't afforded many opportunities. Still, I wasn't complaining. This was what I signed up for. At least I didn't hear the saw roaring this morning. Most of the woodworking had been completed; all that was left was the fine-tuning. Small things mostly, except for the installation of the plantation blinds. Yep, that was today. My arms weren't going to thank me. Those suckers were heavy to lift and hold.

After a few seconds of enjoying the quiet, I took a peek out the window just in time to see Jesse's truck driving down Hurlette. He'd be back soon with the shutters and window treatments. And Renee would be here too, if she wasn't already, as well as a few extra hands eager to finalize the renovations at Summerleigh and prepare for her official opening as a bed-and-breakfast.

There really wasn't much left to do, and that awareness brought a little sadness. *Why are you being so melancholy, Jerica?* It was as if the mood of Pennbrook had touched me in some strange way. Yes, I had Mariana on my mind. Why was the girl reaching out to me? I had no connection to her—not like Harper, who had been my close friend.

I heard a car horn honking in the distance. *No time for daydreaming, Jerica.* I had to get dressed so I could meet Jesse when he came back with the blinds. I looked forward to stretching my muscles and working with my hands, and I always slept better after a day of physical labor. As I headed off to my closet to retrieve today's uniform, blue jeans and a loose t-shirt, my eye caught a glint of something shiny. Was that gold? I walked over to Jesse's vacant pillow and picked up a thin necklace. *Hey, there's a pendant too!* I held the jewelry up to the light to admire it better. It was a dainty gold chain with a gold heart dangling from it. It was a choker style, and from the look of it, this was real gold. A present? From Jesse?

I smiled as I rubbed the smooth metal and turned it over in my hand. I gasped when I saw that there were initials engraved on it: MM.

Mariana McIntyre?

I looked around the room. No one had been in here, and if Jesse had mentioned anything about a necklace, I was sure I would have remembered it.

Maybe… No. Don't go there.

Jesse probably found this when he was digging around in the attic the other day. He wanted to surprise me is all. Yeah, that made sense. I put the necklace on and hovered in front of the mirror to examine how it looked on me. It was pretty, and I hoped Mariana would be happy I had it. I touched it one last time and then got dressed. Five minutes later, I tied my tennis shoes, pulled my hair up on top of my head and fired up the coffeepot. Toast would be my breakfast, that and some coffee. As I smeared cold butter on the toast, I reached for the phone.

Come on, Jerica. How impatient are you? You can wait a few minutes. He'll be back soon.

Instead of racing to the phone to ask Jesse about the necklace, I decided to be a grown-up and wait for the answers. I did a few more things around the house and then headed out with the keys in my hand. It was gorgeous out today. The sky was blue and clear with big, white puffy clouds. Not the kind of clouds that said, *Hey, I'm going to rain*, but the kind that made the sky appear as perfect as a picture. Yes, today had a dreamy kind of quality to it. A good dream, and I needed some of those after the strange hypnotic watching session I'd been having of Mariana and her family.

Jameson confused me. And Mariana's father should be ashamed of himself for being so distant, so unavailable. Did he intend to marry Claudette? I wondered how I could get more information. Surely there would be marriage records at the George County Courthouse? But maybe not. Jesse told me a couple of times that there was really no way of knowing much more about the McIntyre family since most of the historical data was missing.

I was surprised to see that Renee had beaten me to Summerleigh. She was so excited about stocking the pantry, and she chattered on and on. I listened patiently and helped her with the work. Apparently, there was a new restaurant opening in Lucedale right across the street from her diner. She was none too happy about it. Not too long after I arrived, Jesse reappeared with the promised load of blinds and some extra hands to help with them. Emanuel was there doing some work on the second floor installing canister lights in the former nursery. The wiring was giving him fits, as he put it, but he was determined to make it all work. I was glad to hear that. That room needed as many cheerful lights as we could give it. I shivered thinking of Marisol's bear hanging from the old fixture.

"Jerica, did you hear me? I said you are all booked up for November. Can you believe that, you guys? And there are three major events on the books and lots of excited locals who have already paid in advance—isn't that great?"

I nodded my head with a smile and said, "That is exciting news. I had no idea it would be so popular. I hope we can maintain the excitement."

"No second-guessing yourself, Jerica. Not having a change of heart, are you?" Renee's voice dropped, and she paused with her two cans of tomato sauce in her hands.

"Of course not. I'm not going anywhere. It's just that I've been thinking a lot about Mariana."

"The Lady in White? I haven't seen a thing, have you?"

"Not exactly, but I feel like there's something she's trying to tell me. Something about what happened to her. Everyone else has been found, and the truth is out about the Belle family secrets, but what about Mariana? Maybe she needs something too."

Renee twisted her lips and furrowed her brows thoughtfully. "I wouldn't be in too big of a hurry to solve every mystery, Jerica. Every old house needs a Lady in White, and you've got one. A real one. Look, you've done so much for Harper and those girls. You brought Jeopardy home. I mean, you've just done a lot already. Don't go putting yourself in danger again."

And for the first time today, I thought of Eddie. Shouldn't I be more afraid of the living than the dead? I'd heard that somewhere before. "I don't intend to, Ree-Ree."

"Sometimes we have all the answers we want; we can't always know everything that happened. Maybe Mariana just wants to be remembered by someone."

"Maybe." I couldn't believe Renee's attitude. What was she saying? What did she mean? That I should keep the Lady in White around like some kind of paranormal pet? I wasn't going to pay a bit of attention to that advice. I was going to find out what happened to Mariana. One way or another.

Jesse's handsome face appeared in the doorway. He pointed his power tool at me and said, "There's the girl I'm looking for. I could use your help with this. I brought Frank, but you know how handy he is. No offense, cousin."

She laughed at that. "None taken. I'll be the first to admit that Frank has two left feet and about ten thumbs. Y'all have fun. I'll catch the phone if it rings."

I followed Jesse to the front room, and we immediately began to unpack the first set of blinds. Fortunately for us, the shutter company had them all marked. "Hey, that's a nice necklace. I don't remember seeing that before," he said as the power drill whirred the screw into place.

"You left it for me. It was on your pillow." I elbowed him playfully as I toyed with the pendant.

He frowned. "No, I didn't."

My stomach felt like I was standing in an elevator that had decided to drop a few floors. "But I thought…" I dropped the pendant like it was on fire. "Okay. Then this is going to be really weird. Check this out." I held the pendant up for him to examine. He pushed his glasses up on his nose, and his eyes widened as he read the monogram.

"Does that say MM?"

"Some coincidence, huh?"

All of a sudden, Renee walked through with a basket of candles and picture frames. She got closer to see the pendant and said, "How lovely. Not to make myself look like an eavesdropper, but it sounds like The Lady in White left you a present." Jesse and I locked eyes as she walked through to the Great Room.

I dropped my voice and said, "And there's something else. I have to tell you about this photo that was in Harper's old room. It's of Addison's wedding day. I don't know how it got there because it wasn't there when I lay down. It's like both Harper and Mariana are trying to tell me something!"

Jesse had no chance to answer me because Renee popped back into the room. "Hey, I hate to interrupt, but there is a man here who wants to speak to the owner about possibly renting a room. He's in the kitchen."

I don't know why, but I stammered. Jesse said, "I'll go. Be right back."

I stopped him. "If you don't mind, let's call it a day. Round everyone up and head home, and we'll regroup tomorrow. There's some stuff going on, and I need to make sure it's safe for our guests before we open."

"Are you sure, Jerica? If you don't think it's safe, I should stay with you," Jesse said.

I put my hand on his chest and gave him a soft kiss. "I'm sure. I'll see you back at your place soon." I gave them a weak wave and headed up the stairs. I had to clear my head.

I had so much to think about. I had to figure this all out. Was this gift really from Mariana? Was she trying to tell me that she approved of what I was doing? That she wanted me to keep digging?

Nope. Nothing. I didn't have any answers.

All I knew was I had to find them.

Chapter Thirteen—Mariana

My birthday began like any other day, with the exception of the early arrivals at Pennbrook. A constant string of carriages rolled down the driveway, a precursor of tonight's festivities. I had expected to experience some anxiety at the prospect of my first official party as "the Lady of Pennbrook," but I was not prepared for this. And I'd had no idea I would spend this day without Claudette by my side.

However, I quickly realized the arrivals were here not to see me but rather to speak with my father. These men were his closest friends, or more to the truth, men of enterprise who had some business affiliation with Mr. Michael Bull McIntyre. Yes, Father obviously had some deal brewing in the pot, as he sometimes bragged, and these men were here for that purpose. They certainly wouldn't be here to see me. Would they?

The anxiety rose again, but I wasn't given much time to dwell on the meaning of it. Mrs. Tutwiler had managed to leave her son Donnie, who was faring better now after her ministrations. She'd been kind enough to come and set the house straight, oversee the arrangement of the decorations I had selected, and manage the food preparation. I had never been so happy to see the stern-faced woman. She appeared almost as excited as I was today. Her arrival lifted my mood;

despite the machinations of my turncoat friend, it was going to be a joyous day.

Mrs. Tutwiler cooed over the magnolia swags I had cut and braided. I followed her around as she relocated them one by one, and I had to admit, her ideas were far more elegant than mine. She informed me in a whisper that Father had arranged for a three-piece ensemble to play a special concert in my honor at the beginning of the ball, and she assured me that every detail had been arranged. I felt very relieved to know that the weight of this celebration, of my own birthday, was not resting upon my incapable shoulders.

Claudette obviously did not come to my room as we had initially planned and thus was not there to fix my hair or help me prepare for the ball. Mrs. Tutwiler assisted me—I wanted to wear the new rose gown from my father, but she assured me that I should wait until later in the evening to put it on. This was my first ball, so I trusted her counsel. As she finished getting me ready, she said, "Your mother would be so proud to see this day. You have grown into a beautiful young woman, Mariana. Yes, she would be perfectly pleased with the sight of you."

With some surprise, I asked, "You knew my mother, Mrs. Tutwiler? Why have you never said so?"

Before we could continue our conversation, there was a knock at my door. A recognizably confident knock, not Claudette's soft tapping or Jameson's irritating series of pecks.

Mrs. Tutwiler hurried to the door to welcome my father. Mr. McIntyre was dressed in his best suit, his newest black one, along with a crisp white shirt with a black and silver bow tie. Father looked quite the picture, almost handsome. And he had gone to the trouble of waxing his mustache, too. I twirled about one more time as he showered me with compliments. Mrs. Tutwiler left us alone to talk about whatever it was he wanted to talk about.

And to think, I've been waiting since last night for this opportunity, and now it has presented itself to me. I will tell him everything! No one makes a fool out of Bull McIntyre! Or his daughter!

The door closed behind him, and I settled into my chair by the window and invited him to sit opposite me. "Thank you for my new dress, Father. It is the most beautiful thing I have ever owned. I look forward to wearing it later on. Thank you for the party and all the gifts. I can't believe how many people have arrived already."

"The Lotts are coming too. I want you to be kind to their son, Thaddeus. He is close to your age and an intelligent young man."

I promised to do so but couldn't worry about this request right now. I had much more pressing matters to discuss with him. Father smiled and slapped his knees as if that was all he had to say and he was ready to leave. I couldn't allow that. I had to tell him what I knew now before he could be embarrassed by it. And I was afraid that if I did not speak my mind now, I wouldn't have the courage to do so later. I just blurted it out, and as soon as the words came out of my mouth, I realized this may not have been the wisest course of action.

"I have to tell you something, Father. It concerns Claudette Paul—and Jameson." He tilted in his chair and surveyed me coolly. I swallowed and continued, "Last night, Jacob and I were outside. You know how he takes to wandering at all hours sometimes. We were coming back to the house, and I...I mean, we saw Claudette and Jameson. Together." I averted my eyes, unwilling to watch his anger erupt. Like so many said, Bull McIntyre was as unpredictable as they come if you got on his bad side. I never wanted to be on his bad side. I waited quietly, expecting a burst of angry, colorful language. But to my surprise, it never came. He remained quiet, controlled. He twisted the ends of his waxy mustache with his fingers and waited. Regret washed over me.

Why had I chosen to say this now? I rarely received visits such as this from my father, and to sully the moment with what he would surely consider gossip was a horrible idea. But as they say, in for a penny, in for a pound. I stammered on, "I do not believe that their meeting was altogether a holy meeting, sir. I thought you should know about it." I tilted my chin up now and looked him square in the eye. He didn't rage or scream or berate me. A low, dry laugh rolled out of his chest.

"And what would you know about holy meetings, Mariana? Are you insinuating that your brother and Miss Paul were behaving in an intimate manner? If you are going to make the accusation, you must be more specific. For you see, the arrangements have already been made. Unless you have seen them coupling or lying naked together, I cannot break my contract. Is that what you are saying? Speak plainly."

I blinked at his question. What was he asking me? Did he want details? I would not back down because I knew that what I had seen was not my imagination. They were not spirits in the moonlight. "I am sorry to hear that, but I did see them together. Ask Jacob if you do not wish to rely on my testimony alone. He saw it too. He was there. I swear it, Father." I felt the tears rise now, and my face flushed. This was getting worse by the minute. Not only did I have to tell my father bad news, but he did not believe me. "They were kissing one another and touching and doing other things, and Jacob–"

Father raised his hand and walked to the doorway. I could hear him asking Mrs. Tutwiler to bring Jacob to him. We sat in silence and waited for my brother to appear. Music was beginning to play downstairs; the musicians were tuning their instruments. I could hear laughter and lively talking; apparently, the libations were being served. My ruffles wilted around me, my neck felt sweaty, and my face was moist with tears. Yes, I intensely regretted telling him anything. Why had I done it? This was my party, and I had allowed Jameson to take the joy from my celebration. What was even worse was I knew my father did not believe me or did not want to believe me. I could not be sure which.

Jacob entered the room, and his big dark eyes shone with curiosity. He had been playing in the dirt; it was all over his knees. I surmised he'd been digging for Jameson's treasure somewhere outdoors. *He'll dig holes in the yard and blame it on Father's dogs.*

"Son, your sister says you were wandering last night. Is that true?"

Without missing a beat, he shook his head. "No, Father. But I have been outside all day today. I am about to get a bath and get ready for sister's party."

"Jacob, do not lie. Tell Father the truth. Tell him what we saw on the way back. Go on," I said as I gripped the sides of the chair desperately.

"I did not see anything, sister. I was asleep in my bed. Maybe you were dreaming?"

I jumped to my feet and blinked back tears. "You have to tell the truth, Jacob. Why are you lying? Is it to protect Jameson? You must see how this could hurt Father. Tell him what you saw!" I stamped my foot at him, but his innocent expression never wavered. He glanced fearfully at Father.

"You may go now, Jacob. Get your bath and come downstairs for the concert." Jacob walked to the door and gave me a cryptic look before he left the room.

"He is lying," I whispered.

Father walked to the window and peered down at the lawn below. He held his gold pocket watch in his hand, apparently to check the time. I knew that he had made up his mind not to believe me. "I am sure you are confused, Mariana. Maybe Jacob is right. You were dreaming."

"I wasn't dreaming," I said as I flopped back in my chair. "I was not dreaming, Father. I saw them together."

He didn't seem to hear me. "You have heard by now that I intend to marry Claudette. I wish that whoever had told you would have done me the courtesy of allowing me to share this news with you, but I can see that the servants have been gossiping again. Or was it Mrs. Tutwiler?"

"No, Father. Mrs. Tutwiler has not been gossiping." I felt all my joy vanish in that moment, and I wiped at my tears with the back of my hand.

"Good. I know that the idea of my marrying again seems strange to you, as I have been a bachelor for so long, but it is my intent to do so. Judge Paul has agreed to the union, and as you and Claudette are friends, I believed you would be happy to have her so close by. Whatever disagreement you have with your friend, you must settle it—because she will be my wife, Mariana." He wiped my face with his handkerchief and handed it to me. "Keep it, but I want those tears gone when you come down the stairs."

"Yes, Father."

"Time to put those childish ideas away now. No petty jealousy between you and Claudette or your brother. We will be a family." He popped open his pocket watch one last time and snapped it shut. "From this day forward, you must behave like an adult. I have been patient with you, Mariana, but it is time to move on. You cannot grieve for your mother all your life; you never even knew her. There is so much you don't know." He walked to the door and stared at it, his back to me. He was struggling with the idea of telling me something but, unlike me, decided against it. "Finish getting ready for your party, and no more idle talk." He left my room without another word to me. And I could think of nothing else to say to him.

I had told him the worst, and he did not believe me. I was no fortune-teller, but I could see the future in that moment.

Horrible things were about to happen.

Chapter Fourteen—Jerica

For the first time, the nursery felt warm and peaceful. Almost welcoming. At least that's what I told myself. Tucking myself into an overstuffed seat, I rubbed my hand over the soft throw blanket. We had decided that this would become the upstairs parlor, a kind of bonus room for guests staying on the top floor. None of the ghosts of yesterday could touch the beauty of this space now. What a great idea to go with this lively blue and taupe color combination. It was the most contemporary-looking room in the house, the complete opposite of what it used to look like. And that was due in no small part to Renee, who had proved to be invaluable in the renovation and decoration process. She'd managed to completely change the room, no more dark foreboding shades of deep burgundy and hunter green covering the walls. I sighed, the warmth disappearing from the room—and my bones. This room had been such an unhappy place, and no amount of paint and throw blankets and candles would change that.

Not anymore. That can't be true. Not anymore.

Even as I thought the words, I did not believe them. Nope. As much as I pretended otherwise, the nursery still played an unhappy note, a mournful strum that hummed beneath everything else. No, this place did not want to be happy.

"Well, it's going to be," I said to no one in particular. And that's when I heard the notes, soft and sweet at first and then more frantic. *Oh yes, this was a familiar sound. Was that a piano? Yes, it was a piano!*

I sat up on the settee and moved the pillows to the side. I heard nothing, but then the music returned, only louder, more present. Yes! There it was again. The sound of the piano! But we had no piano. I had to investigate this noise immediately. Jesse and I had talked about installing a stereo system but had not taken steps to do so. Not yet. Was this a CD player? It couldn't be; the sound was too close, too full, like there was a recital taking place downstairs. I walked to the open door and poked my head into the hallway. I suspected that as soon as I stepped into the hallway the sound would disappear, but it didn't. Now, I heard the piano playing even more loudly. I swallowed and checked the other rooms. All the doors were closed. I checked every room, but there wasn't a soul in the place, no CD player and certainly not a grand piano.

"Renee? Jesse? Are you still here? Anyone?"

No one answered, and I swore silently under my breath. I wasn't one to swear much and didn't do it well, but this was definitely a swear-word moment. Why had I sent everyone home? I was beyond goose bumps, and my hands and arms felt icy cold. Instinctively, I rubbed them to try to warm myself back up. Out of the blue, a stabbing pain in my stomach struck me so hard that it made me bow forward slightly. I clutched my gut in surprise and felt a wave of nausea hit me.

"Oh God," I whimpered as I gripped the nearby doorframe. I waited for the pain to pass and then flicked off the light and closed the door behind me as I headed to the stairs. The piano notes became softer, the music calmer; it was a familiar tune. Was that Chopin? It was certainly not Mozart. I racked my brain trying to remember, trying to recall those long-ago days in my Music Appreciation class. Back then I would've known who I was listening to. Then it dawned on me. Beethoven! That was it! Beethoven's Moonlight Sonata.

As I put my foot on the top of the stairs, the music stopped and I heard the moving of furniture, as if someone had hurriedly pushed back the piano bench. But again I had to remind myself that there was no piano here and no piano bench. I hurried to the bottom landing and stood there, steeling my nerves to make the final few steps into the Great Room. Once more, the pain twisted in my stomach. I leaned against the wall gasping for breath between spasms.

When I could finally breathe normally, I called, "Jesse?" I hoped he would answer me, that someone would answer me, but I knew I was alone. My hand went to my stomach, and I half expected to pull it away and see blood there, so deep and painful was this sensation. I closed my eyes as they watered and waited for the pain to pass. As the pain loosened its hold on me, I waited. A board creaked below.

Probably the house settling. That's all. Just the house settling. Please be that.

A familiar voice echoed from the Great Room. "Hello, Jerica. I have been waiting for you. Impatiently waiting." With heavy legs and even heavier footsteps, I walked down the last few stairs and stepped into the Great Room. The custom-made furniture had arrived earlier, and the place was beautifully accommodated, ready for guests. But this visitor was certainly unwanted and unwelcome.

How did he get in here? Had I left the door unlocked? I couldn't have. I never do!

Eddie Poole sat in one of the chairs near the large picture window. His bony arms were crossed as if he were some sort of demented physician waiting to diagnose his patient.

"Please, Jerica. Dear wife, come and join us."

I stepped closer. "Us? Who are you talking about, Eddie?"

I had another visitor, who manifested like an inky portrait image being developed right before my eyes. She sat like an old-fashioned wooden doll in the chair beside Eddie. I watched her touch my ex-husband's hand as if they were the greatest of friends. The closest. The most intimate. I couldn't believe what I was seeing.

I was looking at the ghost of Claudette Paul.

Chapter Fifteen—Jerica

The deep, stabbing pain returned, and my knees buckled. *No, please. Don't do this now. What is happening to me?* My nurse's brain worked on a diagnosis, but the agonizing ache was like nothing I could describe. I had to be hallucinating. That couldn't really be Claudette Paul.

"What are you doing here?"

"I think you know why I am here. I was invited, dear wife. I am here to collect on a debt that I am owed."

I put my hand up to fend him off as he walked toward me slowly. Eddie behaved like a man impaired, under the influence of some sort of narcotic. But he was clearing the distance between us rather quickly, and panic rose within me.

"What debt? You have to get out of here. Get out of my house, Eddie!" I yelled as the pain increased. "Leave before the police arrive. I have this place wired. They'll know you are here."

Eddie walked up beside me and stared down at me, and he seemed to enjoy my pain because I heard him laughing. "By the time they arrive, I will have collected my debt and then it won't matter. Will it?" He chuckled, and it was a low, horrible sound. How was Claudette involved in all this? Was it she who had summoned Eddie here? Or was it just his pure hatred for me, his absolute disgust for me, that led him to Summerleigh?

Whatever the answer, I knew I was in trouble. Why had I told Jesse to go home? He had wanted to stay, but I had to push myself. I had to be here at Summerleigh by myself. I had to visit the nursery just one more time. Check it out, just to make sure everything was safe. But it wasn't safe. Not at all. And now I'd made a horrible mistake.

I had my cell phone in my pocket, and that gave me hope. If I could get to it, I could call for help. But right now, I had to focus on getting to my feet.

Harper! If you can hear me—I'm in trouble!

Finally, the pain lifted, but Eddie had me by the back of my hair. He dragged me to my feet as I screamed, more in anger than in pain. "Stop, you bastard!"

"Oh, nice. So classy, Nurse Jerica. Is that any way to talk to your husband?"

With a twist of my upper body, I lifted my foot and kicked backward, hitting him in the leg. It wasn't enough to take him down, but it freed me from his grasp. *No way! I wasn't going to die alone at the hands of Eddie Poole!* I backed away from Eddie but didn't dare make a fast move, and I sure didn't risk pulling out my phone. Not yet. I had to make a run for it first, but I needed more time.

You know how to do this, Jerica. You were a counselor and a nurse, for Pete's sake. You can do this. Focus on the patient.

"Okay, Eddie. I know that you are hurting, but you have to explain to me why you are here. Tell me, what do you want? What can I help you with?"

And then I had the opportunity to look him fully in the face. This man was a shadow of the man I once loved; I had loved him so deeply that I had been willing to do anything for him. His long, narrow nose looked so out of place in his face. Had he broken it recently? Yes, it was crooked. There was no trace left of the man I had loved. He'd shaved off his hair, and I could see scars on his hands, face and arms. For an instant, I felt sympathy for him until I saw what was in his right hand.

Eddie was holding a pair of silver shears.

"Eddie, put those scissors down. You don't need those to talk to me. I think we can work this out if you..."

And then to my complete surprise, Eddie swung the shears in front of him like a child swinging at a piñata. But this was nothing as pleasant as that. He wanted to cut me, to kill me, to make me bleed. And now, a few feet behind him, Claudette was moving closer. She appeared washed out like a black-and-white picture, and she wore a raggedy ball gown. Claudette looked like an awful creature. Her dead eyes were ringed with black shadows, her white lips moved, and she wore a hungry expression as if she would love nothing more than to devour me. She was speaking but not to me—she was whispering to Eddie.

I screamed as I tumbled backwards, tripping over my own two feet, but I quickly regained my footing. I sprinted around the couch to escape them, but I didn't make the mistake of trying to run any further. Claudette's image flickered out and reappeared near the front door, as if she knew I was going to try to escape. Eddie growled like an animal next to me, and he began to sob as he waved the shears again. He waved them wildly like some sort of macabre puppet under the control of an invisible, devilish puppeteer.

"You killed my daughter! I knew you hated me; I knew you were going to leave me. You planned the whole thing, didn't you? I thought you might try to take Marisol from me, but you murdered her instead. Why, Jerica? Why? You merciless bitch! You took everything from me."

I sobbed at the accusation. He believed it—he really believed it! "Eddie, I wasn't leaving you. I never even considered that. I loved you, and that is not what happened. How dare you believe that I would harm Marisol? I loved her! I loved you! I am sorry. If I could take it back, I would. Don't you think I wished it was me that died and not her?"

As if to answer my question, he plunged the shears into the couch nearest me, his hateful glare focused on me. With all his rage, he stabbed the couch again and again. I should have run, but I was stunned by his savagery and could do nothing but watch.

"You are a liar, Jerica. A murdering liar!"

Remember, stay focused. Talk to him. All you need is ten seconds to get to that door.

"I don't know what's going on with you, Eddie, but it's not too late. If you are sick, and you must be, I can help you. You are delusional if you believe that I would hurt our daughter!" I replied to him as calmly as possible. Yes, I had to be calm. Being calm would help him. The police should arrive soon. The alarm system had been active, or so I hoped. Surely they would arrive any minute now.

"Eddie you shouldn't have come here. There are spirits here that influence people who are sick. You are sick, Eddie. You need a doctor, and I can help you find one. You know I can. Remember that time your appendix burst? I was there. And that time you wrecked out on your motorcycle? I was there every minute. I loved you, Eddie."

I continued to move to my left around the back of the chaise, and I couldn't stop the tears from coming. I didn't want to cry, but I also didn't want to die. It didn't appear that I would be able to get to the front door, but there was an alternate exit in Ann's bedroom. If I could just get there.

That's what I would do. I would make my move and run down that hallway. The kitchen would be too far, but this way...I could make this run.

And then the lamp crashed to the floor. Eddie struck it down with his hand, and I jumped at the sound of the breaking pottery.

"Don't talk to me, Jerica, and don't speak her name. You are not worthy of her! And you were never worthy of her, you crazy—" Before he could finish his slur, footsteps banged across the ceiling above us. *Someone else was here.* "Is your friend hanging around? Isn't he man enough to come face me? Hey! Come down here, you punk! I've got something for you too!" He was distracted, or so I thought, so I tossed a glance at the door that led to the hallway. The footsteps continued, louder now, as if someone in heavy boots were stomping around. Those weren't high heels clicking on the wood but the boots of a soldier. Then the floor shook and the chandelier began to swing.

Immediately, I saw Claudette's image change. Her face morphed into one of terror, and she wavered as if she were an image on an old television screen that flickered in and out. And just like that, she vanished. Eddie's eyes widened; I saw confusion and terror there. Was it possible that the spirit's hold on him, the evil influence of

Claudette Paul, had been broken or at least weakened?

"Eddie, we have to leave this place. You have to stop this. This is madness!"

He was crying now but still had the scissors in his hand. "My daughter! You killed her, Jerica. You took her from me." He continued to cry and swear, and now he was waving the shears in great arcs as he came toward me. I could run to the front door now if I wanted to, and I might be able to make it. But maybe not. Even as I glanced in that direction, his eyes followed me. His pale lips were cracked and covered with sores. As he snarled at me, I could clearly see his broken teeth. Oh, how could I have loved this man? This couldn't be my ex-husband. This creature was nothing but a disgusting doppelgänger of Eddie Poole.

"You aren't going anywhere, Jeri girl. You are gonna pay for what you did to my daughter. She was the only good thing left for me. The last of my soul, Jerica. She was the last of my soul."

"No, Eddie. You are still in there. You can still have a life. Marisol would want you to live, and you know I would never harm her. I loved her as much as I loved you."

"I told you not to say her name! You'll pay for that!" The gaunt skeleton of a man launched himself toward me. *I have to make my move now! No more stalling!*

I pushed the armchair over as hard as I could. It wouldn't stop him for long, but maybe it would slow him down. I raced toward the hallway that would lead me to the bedroom hallway. I slammed the door with a scream of anger, wishing it had a lock. I ran as fast as I could, but the pain in my stomach returned and seized me again. I flung myself against the wall opposite Harper's bedroom. I couldn't speak or breathe; all I could do was lean against the wall and wait for the pain to subside.

What is going on? What's wrong with me?

Eddie slung the door open, and I crept away as far as I could until the pain was so great that I collapsed on the floor. He laughed as he walked toward me. And here I would die. Here in the hallway at Summerleigh, so close to Harper. So many had died here—why not one more?

Although my stomach pain intensified, I dragged myself away with both my hands. Surely this pain would only last a few more seconds, just like before. If I could wait it out, I could get away. I still had a chance.

I crawled a few inches, but then Eddie was next to me. I could see the scissors in his hand. They were old scissors, antiques, really. They were severely rusted, or was that dried blood? I could hardly tell.

"Eddie... Don't do this."

I expected him to say something cruel, to taunt me as he did his horrible deed, but that didn't happen. I heard a door squeaking and shoes walking toward us. Then I could see the shoes. Whoever she was, she wore old-fashioned saddle shoes, the black-and-white ones. I couldn't look up as pain held me in its grip, but I knew by the bobby socks and shoes who it was that approached. Was this Harper come at last to collect me since I was about to die?

"Harper," I whispered. And then I heard Eddie scream. I realized that I could move again and that the pain had lifted.

"Harper?" I screamed as I ran down the hall. I wanted to look back, to see her one last time, but I wanted to live even more. I propelled myself down the hall on wobbly legs until I reached Ann's bedroom. I opened the door and practically slung myself over the bed. I raced to the side door, but it was locked. I could hear Eddie screaming and running after me. He called me foul names again and again, but I wasn't listening to him. I could hear a second pair of shoes slapping on the floor.

Finally, the door opened for me and I tumbled out onto the porch. *Oh God, this hurts! Had I twisted my ankle on top of everything else?* The door slammed behind me, and I heard Eddie swearing again. A great crashing sound echoed in the bedroom behind the closed door, as if someone had knocked the dresser over and moved the bed around. I heard Eddie's frightened cry once more. I crawled off the stairs into the yard and finally dug into my pocket for my cell phone. Eddie's screams continued, and my hands shook with fear. How long could Harper keep him there? I wasn't sure. I don't know why I didn't call the police, but I couldn't think straight. I dialed Jesse's number.

"Jesse? I need you to come to the house. Eddie is here. Please!" And then the stabbing sensation hit me again, and this time the pain was so great that I felt a great tide of blackness wash over me.

When my eyes fluttered open, I could see the face of a young woman in front of me. I knew this face. This was Mariana McIntyre.

Mariana, I see you. Am I dead?

A peaceful smile stretched across her face, and I felt her cool hand touch my cheek. And then she was gone. She was no longer there; I was looking into the face of someone I had never seen before.

"Ma'am? Can you hear me?"

"Yes. I can hear you. Am I dead?"

The woman in the nurse's uniform shook her head. "No, but you are one lucky woman. You had an ulcer, but you're on the mend. I think you have a visitor if you're up to seeing him."

"What? I'm in the hospital?"

"Yes, ma'am. You've been here a few days. You are going to be alright now, Mrs. Poole."

"It's Jerica. I'm Jerica Jernigan," I said with all the strength I could muster.

I heard another voice beside me, a familiar voice and one that I wanted to hear with all my heart.

"Look who is awake. I thought…I'm glad to see you, Jerica."

"Me too, Jesse. I'm glad to see you too." And then I felt so tired, so very tired. I had to close my eyes for a few minutes. Just a few. "Don't leave, okay?"

"Never. I'm never leaving again."

I started to say, "Thank you," or "I love you," but the words didn't come.

I fell into a place beyond sleep.

Chapter Sixteen—Mariana

The striking pianist's fingers moved over the ivory keys so effortlessly that it seemed like a bit of magic to watch him play. Thaddeus Lott, as he was introduced to us by my father, leaned into Beethoven's Moonlight Sonata as he closed his eyes. This selection always made me weep, but tonight no tears came for I could not take my eyes off the young man's face. It was certainly a handsome face; many other young women in the room obviously agreed. It was angular, elegant and illuminated by candlelight. His pink lips moved slightly as he allowed the music to carry him to faraway places. I traveled with him. Dark-fringed eyes stared into the darkness beyond the conservatory windows, and then they were watching me, but only for a second. He did not leer at me. However, I could not take my eyes off of him.

Oh! He caught me staring, and I believed I saw the hint of a smile tug at the corners of his mouth. But then it disappeared, like the music that vanished into the night air. Suddenly, my gown felt as if it tightened around me; I was short of breath and reminded myself to breathe evenly.

Keep your composure, Mariana.

Someone was watching me; the hair began to prickle on the back of my neck. Angry to be torn away from Mr. Lott's musical performance, I glanced sternly in Claudette's direction. She smiled at me politely, but I gave her no hope of being forgiven. *She may fool my father, but she will not make a fool of me. Never again.* And then suddenly Thaddeus Lott's music recaptured my attention as it intensified, the notes precise and persistent. I felt the audience's collective breath catch as he picked at the notes like a madman. A handsome, wonderfully talented madman. The lady beside me, whose name escaped me, began to frantically fan herself as if the speed of the music had raised her temperature. I smiled at the idea but kept my eyes on Mr. Lott.

Father had asked me to befriend him; I suddenly became very open to the idea of a friendship with this talented musician. *In this I shall be obedient, but I will certainly wait for Father to make my introductions.* It would hardly be proper to extend my hand to him without first being formally introduced. Would this piece never end? I wanted to meet this young man, talk with him and maybe even dance with him. The ballroom would be ready now; I could not wait to see it. Suddenly, Claudette sat beside me. Her posture was perfect, her face the picture of grace and beauty, but I could sense her worry. She knew that I knew. She'd figured it out. I wondered if Father mentioned it to her. I moved my skirt a few inches to avoid touching hers as if she would contaminate me.

"Sister," she whispered without leaning too far in my direction, "I must talk to you."

"Must you?" I whispered back and shifted in my chair. It would be the height of rudeness to walk out on my guest's performance, so I would not, but I did not believe I had to endure chitchat with my former friend.

"Mariana," she began in a low whisper.

"Please, be quiet," I hissed as I turned my full attention back to Thaddeus Lott, and as quick as that, the sonata ended and the applause began. I eagerly applauded too as he stood to graciously accept our praise for his beautiful performance.

Father stepped into the aisle and offered his hand to me. Claudette rose too and smiled in an overly friendly manner. Without frowning at her—and that was a tremendous feat—I accepted his hand and we began to greet those who had gathered to celebrate my birthday. I knew many of the faces although some names escaped me. Even after introductions, I was unable to remember all their names. But Thaddeus Lott and his father, George Lott, I would always remember. Two more handsome faces I had never seen.

"Please allow me to introduce my daughter, Mariana, and her friend, Claudette Paul. Ladies, this young man is Thaddeus Lott. And this is his father, George Lott."

"Ladies, we are honored to meet you both." Thaddeus bowed slightly to the two of us but barely glanced in Claudette's direction. I liked him even more. Jameson passed by behind Thaddeus but did not dare intrude.

"Thank you for playing, Mr. Lott. I wish I could play the piano with such precision, but alas, I have two hands with ten thumbs."

"Do not pretend that you are not talented, Mariana. You have the voice of an angel," Claudette purred with faux sincerity.

"Whatever my other skills might be, I could never play the piano so beautifully as my mother did. They say musical talent skips a generation. Many people say my mother was such a moving pianist that people wept when they heard her play. But alas, as I said, I have no such talent." My father's dark eyes pierced mine as I realized he was very unhappy with me. Yes, I had pushed him too far. Claudette frowned too, but both our guests were oblivious to the tension.

The younger Lott's lips curled and revealed two dimples, one in each cheek. "I hear there is a cure for that," he said in a warm, friendly voice.

"What would that be?" I asked curiously, happy to be in conversation with this beautiful young man.

"Practice," he said. My heart sank at his reply, but he obviously did not mean to insult for he followed up his comment quickly with a surprising offer. "Perhaps you need a better teacher. I would of course be happy to offer my services. Music is my passion, Miss McIntyre."

"Oh, yes. I would like that."

The five of us stood awkwardly for a few seconds until Thaddeus said, "If I may be so bold, Miss McIntyre, I wonder if you would dance with me. Your father has mentioned that you enjoy the waltz. I do as well, but I fear I am not a skilled dancer."

I smiled and answered, "I hear there is a cure for that, Mr. Lott." Everyone laughed except my father, who merely watched the exchange. Was I being too flirtatious? I had no time to wonder, for the ballroom doors slid open and the violins began to soar. I could not hide my delight. Mrs. Tutwiler had exceeded my expectations—the place looked like a scene from heaven. Gold-toned candlesticks held white candles, and green and white ribbons hung from the curtains that were elegantly pulled back from the massive windows. I felt that I was indeed the Lady of Pennbrook tonight.

As if she read my mind, Claudette came to my side, but I turned away only to walk into Jameson. He would not budge but stared down at me rudely. I nudged him in the chest with my elbow and swirled around him as he tugged at one of my ribbons. I could see a gleam of devilish delight in his eye. My brother would love nothing more than to cut off all my hair and strip every ribbon from my gown, but my rescuer, Thaddeus

Lott, remained close and said smoothly, "Miss McIntyre, how about this dance? It is a waltz, and I am anxious to make your further acquaintance."

"Thank you, Mr. Lott. I would be delighted," I replied, trying not to smile too broadly or speak too hurriedly.

"Please call me Thaddeus," he said as he offered his hand. I put my gloved hand on top of his and ignored the whispers.

"Very well, Thaddeus. You may call me Mariana."

"Mariana. What a musical name."

For the next hour, I sailed around the ballroom with various guests, but none pleased me as much as Thaddeus Lott. As we laughed and enjoyed one another's company, I decided then and there that I would behave. I would not tempt Father's anger again as he had arranged this new friendship and clearly, he and Mr. Lott hoped a deeper friendship would bloom between Thaddeus and me.

Soon, the ensemble rose and received their prize, our applause and admiration. The ballroom had grown warm, the faces of the cheerful attendees were pink, and many folks headed for the porches and the gardens beyond. Confused, I asked Mrs. Tutwiler what was happening.

"Oh, my dear, I forget how young you are sometimes. This is the intermission. It will last for an hour, and then there will be another hour of dancing. During the intermission, the men will take cigars and bourbon in Mr. McIntyre's study."

"What will the ladies do, Mrs. Tutwiler?" I felt ashamed that I did not know, but I was grateful to have her insight.

"Why, they will tidy themselves, tend to their hair, their gowns, whatever they like. But you can be sure many will be talking about you and that young Mr. Lott." She patted my hand and led me up the stairs. "In my time, the ladies took naps, but that was for afternoon balls. As you are the hostess of the party, you have the upper hand. You could change your gown if you like and then return to the ball looking fresh and beautiful while your guests will look a bit wilted. It is after all your birthday."

My eyes lit up as realization dawned. "Oh! Is that why you told me not to wear my new gown yet?"

"You are a very bright young woman," Mrs. Tutwiler said with a smile. She rarely smiled, and I hugged her to thank her. She patted my back and kissed my cheek. Another first for me. "Your father has thought of everything, Mariana. And Thaddeus Lott—you approve of him, obviously."

"How generous Father is to me! I cannot believe he would be so kind. I should go apologize; I have hurt him, Mrs. Tutwiler. I really should." I pulled my gloves off and chewed my nail until Mrs. Tutwiler fussed at me.

"He is busy at the moment making arrangements for his own happiness. You can talk to him later, Mariana. Now come on, let's go get you changed."

What could that mean?

Just then, a housemaid interrupted, "Excuse me, Mrs. Tutwiler? Jacob needs you. He's very sick and has thrown up all over himself. I don't know what to do, ma'am." The girl appeared sick herself and certainly not capable of taking care of Jacob. Yes, we needed a governess. Then I had an idea, what if Mrs. Tutwiler became Jacob's governess? She knew how to take care of the house. She had one of her own. But why would she do such a thing when she had Oak Lawn to run? Her husband died five years ago, but the house was her family home.

"Go ahead, Mrs. Tutwiler. I can get one of the house servants to help me. I will come down soon."

She left me alone in the hallway. There were people everywhere, including Claudette who stared at me with fierce determination. I immediately spun on my heel and went into my room and closed the door.

I sat on the bed, but Claudette did not knock. I waited another few minutes and heard nothing at all except for the voices of other excited young women in the hallway. I imagined I heard my name on their lips.

Yes, Thaddeus and I would be the talk of the town by now, or at least the talk of Pennbrook. With furious fingers, I began to tug at the ribbons that had me bound. No. It was no good. Mrs. Tutwiler had knotted one or two of them. I would need an extra pair of hands. As I walked to the door to call for a servant, a voice behind me surprised me.

"Please, sister. Allow me to help you with that."

I spun around to see Jameson, and as quick as lightning, his hand wrapped around my throat.

Chapter Seventeen—Mariana

"What do you think you know, sister? I know so much more than you do. I always have. I know about our mother. Fever didn't take her. Sickness didn't claim her. It was Father who did her in."

My throat hurt so badly, I could barely breathe, and I was so frightened I believed I might die. "Jame-son, st-op," I gurgled as he continued to apply pressure to my throat.

"Say, 'You know more, Jameson'. Say it!" Jameson's voice was flat, and his face was the picture of hatred. And it was me that he hated—his own sister. Partially releasing my neck, he said in a near growl, "Say it!"

"Jame-son...please stop." He squeezed me again, and I gasped for breath and my eyes watered. *Would he kill me on my birthday?*

"Say that I know more than you or I will put you to sleep, Mariana. You could go to sleep and never wake up. Just like Mother." He leaned over me, his face just an inch from mine. The weight of his body forced me down into the mattress, and I began to cry silently. *I will die! I will die tonight! Any second!*

But the bedroom door opened and to my surprise, Claudette walked inside. She closed the door behind her and immediately I knew I was doomed. She did not come to my aid or try to stop Jameson from performing his evil task.

They were going to kill me to keep their secret. *But it wasn't a secret anymore. I told Father, only he didn't believe me!* I saw spots form before my eyes. I saw bright lights, and then everything went black. I was dying. I had to be dying. One would die if one could not breathe. My lungs burned, my eyes ached, and I passed out.

Or maybe I died.

No. That's not right. I'm awake now.

I was in my bed, finally wearing my new gown. But I could barely move. Jameson had left us, but my former companion Claudette remained. I noticed that she held a pair of silver shears. I wanted to speak, but I could not, not yet. My throat hurt, and my heart beat rather slowly. I wasn't sure I was still alive. Maybe I was dead...*yes, please let me be dead*.

"I know you cannot talk to me, Mariana. You cannot speak because Jameson crushed your windpipe. That is unfortunate, because I would like to hear your apology. Why did you have to ruin everything? Why? You should not have spied on me, Mariana. You should have left well enough alone. For you see, I am going to be the Lady of Pennbrook now. You should have accepted me, accept that I do not love your father, that I love Jameson. Your father is a killer. Would you rather he kill me too?"

I tried to speak but only hissed. She smiled as she clipped at my hair. She held up a lock of it to me and then tossed it on the floor beside the bed. "Jameson and I love one another, Mariana. And we understand one another. You cannot spoil it, although this pains me, you just cannot. But now, I am going to claim a souvenir first. Just a few to remember you by when you have gone. Yes, I am afraid you must die, sweet Mariana, but do not worry your pretty head about it. I will make sure you are buried with all the respect due you, and as your father's wife, I will mourn you immensely."

Suddenly, I began to scream, but nothing came out of my mouth. Not a sound, just an empty scream. I called for Father, Mrs. Tutwiler and Jacob, but no one heard me. Not even the people in the hallway outside could hear me. But I could hear them. Life was so close! Thaddeus was so close!

"What a lovely new dress, Mariana, dear. So lovely. The perfect dress to die in."

I squirmed away from her, but she was on me like a hungry cat on a fat mouse that had been foolish enough to give away his position.

And I was murdered as quickly as that.

Horrible, gut-wrenching pain pierced me, accompanied by hot warmth on my skin and then coldness in my body. The cold was so fierce and chilled my soul. I did not feel anything after the first stab. She stabbed me a second time and then rose from the bed to watch me bleed. I stared at the horrible smile on her face. That's when I saw him. My little brother was hiding beneath the table and no one had seen him. He'd seen the whole thing. I wanted to tell him to run, to go tell Father, but I felt dizzy, like I was falling down the staircase. Or like my soul was falling out of my body.

I died so quickly. I died too soon.

I never kissed Thaddeus as I had hoped to.

I hovered near my body...waiting for what, I didn't know. And another door opened; it had been a part of the wall. I never knew that was there! Jameson stepped back into the room, and although I could not hear them, I could see that he was angry. Angry with Claudette! She pleaded with him about something, but what? I could not hear, and the room was growing dark now.

And then I heard Father's voice. Father's voice calling me, his fist banging on the door.

Finally, the door was open and I saw him, his face broken in tears as he witnessed my bloody end.

And then everything changed.

I could no longer see my father. I was in another place. No, wait. This place was so like home but not quite. The color had faded from my new dress, my face and everything about me. I walked up and down the halls looking for Jacob. Poor, frightened Jacob. I did not hate him. He could never have saved me. I worried for him, hoped he would love. I had to show him that I was alive.

And then I found another child. A little girl with golden hair; she wore it in two braids. We talked often. Her name was Loxley. She lived here now, but this was no longer Pennbrook.

This was her house. This was Summerleigh.

And I was the Lady in White.

Epilogue—Jerica

With only thirty minutes to kill before my drive to Mobile, I felt antsy this morning. This was a recent development but not an entirely unwelcome one. In the past, this kind of anxiety often preceded a supernatural encounter.

No, I didn't feel afraid. I was excited by the prospect of seeing someone I loved. Would I see Harper? Maybe Jeopardy? I couldn't guess what was about to take place, but I felt compelled to go for a walk. And even as my feet stepped onto the familiar pathway, I knew my destination.

The potting shed.

I zipped up my jacket and waved goodbye to Renee, who was busy preparing for a new infusion of weekend guests. How could I manage all this without her? I hoped I never had to know. One day soon, very soon, she would be my cousin-in-law, if that was a real thing. Closing the door behind me, I shoved my hands in my plaid jacket pockets.

Only thirty minutes to kill, Jerica. You can't miss a minute of Jesse's big day.

And I wouldn't dream of it. Jesse's latest book, *The Ghosts of Pennbrook*, was a regional hit, and his publisher was very excited about his future. I remembered the night he typed THE END. We celebrated with a kiss, a little champagne and a completely wonderful marriage proposal.

And this time I said, "Yes!" without hesitation.

"But I want to do it quickly," I told him.

"Afraid you'll change your mind?" he asked while he posed in his signature power move, leaning back against the couch with his arms crossed.

"I'm not changing my mind, Jesse. My only concern is my dress." I slid my arms around his narrow waist and smiled coyly.

He gave a low and sexy laugh and kissed me, his relief obvious. As if I wouldn't want to marry him. "Jerica, I am sure any dress you choose will be perfect. Just like you."

"Thank you for the compliment, but we both know I'm not perfect." I kissed him back. "It's not my style selection I'm worried about. It's the fit." A dark strand of hair fell into my eyes, and Jesse tucked it behind my ear as he always did. I blushed thinking about his voice purring in my ear earlier during an intimate session.

I always want to see your beautiful eyes, Jerica.

I tried not to chuckle at his confusion now. "You lost me, honey."

Still smiling up at him, I rubbed my stomach and held it protectively. "I don't want to waddle down the aisle, Jesse. So sooner rather than later, please."

"What?" His puzzled expression made me laugh out loud. Then realization dawned on his handsome face. "You mean...we..."

"You are going to be a daddy, Jesse Clarke." And to my surprise, he cried. He held me and cried. And I couldn't have loved him any more than I did at that moment.

"When?"

"Let's see. It's December now, and I'm three months...so June, I think. At least that's what the doctor says, but it's subject to change by a week or two."

"What do we do now? I mean, is there anything I can do?"

I laughed again. "I think your contribution to this process is over for now. But thanks for the support." We hugged and laughed and cried some more. Yes, it was a wonderful moment.

A little more than a year had passed since we'd solved the mystery of Mariana McIntyre. And to think, Hannah had even gotten it wrong. Jameson had not murdered his sister—Claudette committed that heinous crime. But now the world knew the truth, thanks to Jesse's hard work. He gave me credit in his book for my part, but I didn't really care about that. The ghosts had been put to rest, and all was well here at Summerleigh. If a little lonely.

I was glad everyone was at peace. Except with the way I was feeling, that may not be true. Someone was waiting for me! *Just a quick walk, Jerica. Get moving. If you miss your fiancé's book signing, you'll never hear the end of it.* The gravel crunched underneath my boots, and I flipped the jacket collar up to shield my bare neck from the growing cold. Why had I worn a ponytail today? A few brown leaves fluttered to the ground, the last remnants of fall. Suddenly, I paused as I heard a sound. A familiar sound, like a shovel digging in the dirt. I hadn't hired a gardener yet, so who could be out here digging on our property? I heard the sound again—clearly someone was here. I cleared the potting shed, the direction I assumed the noise was coming from, but there was no one there. Just a shovel on the ground. An old rusty shovel and the beginnings of a hole.

"Who's out here? Come out now!" I yelled, ignoring my own goose bumps. Then I heard movement in the shed beside me. Yes, someone was hiding in there. I moved as quietly as possible toward the door and turned the knob slowly, hoping to get the drop on whoever might be inside. I was wasting my time—there was no one in here, no one at all, and no sign that there had been anyone in here recently.

Not at first, but then I saw them. Pink rose petals scattered around an empty bed of soil. Where had those come from? We hadn't had roses in at least two months. I realized the petals weren't just scattered...they spelled something. I studied them and after a few seconds could clearly read two words: *Thank you*. I reached into my pocket and retrieved my cell phone to take a picture. Jesse had to see this. Before I could hit send, I saw a figure walk past the shed window. Instantly, I knew who it was.

That was John Jeffrey Belle! I raced to the door and yelled, "JB!" But he wasn't there, and the space where I was standing was icy cold. I spun around and called again, "JB! John Jeffrey Belle, I'm here!" But nothing happened. I didn't see him again, but I knew he had been there and had come back for one reason—to thank me. To thank us. And something else. The hole that I saw just a few moments ago was deeper now, and I spotted a rusty can peeking out from the soil. Quick as I could, I got on my knees and pried the can out of the clay.

"What is this, JB?" I whispered to the air around me but received no answer. And try as I might, I couldn't remove the lid. It was rusted on there. Feeling desperate, I whacked it against the rusty shovel, and the can released its long-hidden treasures.

I couldn't believe my eyes. Inside was a tangled assortment of oddities, including dry rotted ribbons, pieces of fabric and jewelry. Old jewelry. With shaking fingers, I plucked out a wad of silver and gasped at the diamonds that twinkled back at me. After a few seconds, I had the ribbons unwound and spread the elegant web of diamonds on my knee. "What in the world?" I kept pulling items out: an ivory brooch, a pair of ruby earrings, a thin gold cuff bracelet with a dangling pendant. I held the pendant up to the sunlight and could clearly see the initials MM. "Mariana? These were Mariana's?" And the rest of the contents were similar and familiar. Yes, I'd seen these before! These belonged to the McIntyre family. JB must have found them, and now he wanted us to have them.

I quickly put the lid back on and told myself, "I have to show Jesse." I packed everything back in the can and headed back to the house. I whispered, "Thank you, John Jeffrey Belle. Thank you all. Go be with your girls and Dot. She's waiting for you too. Kiss Marisol for me." As I left the potting shed behind, there were tears in my eyes. But I wasn't hurt or broken.

I was whole now.

And unlike Eddie, becoming whole wasn't about money or making someone hurt because I hurt. It was about family, loving family, staying together and keeping your promises. In some strange way, the Belles had been my family. Harper, Jeopardy, Addison and Loxley were all my sisters. I did for them what I couldn't do for myself, and that was bring everyone home.

But that wasn't true. Harper had brought me to Summerleigh. She'd entrusted it to me, and I had done what she could not, and I was glad that I could do it. Summerleigh, with all her shadows and mournful ghosts—all her secrets were revealed now. The Belles and McIntyres could rest knowing that there were no more secrets. That everyone was home and not forgotten.

Yes, it was time to let them rest. I got back to the house and climbed into my car with the can of treasures. With one last whispered, "Thank you," I turned off Hurlette and onto Highway 98. Time to look to the future. Of course, I wouldn't be gone long. Jesse said the book signing would only last a few hours. And then we'd come back home to Summerleigh.

And it would be just the two of us...until our little one joined us. We would fill Summerleigh with what it had been missing all these years. Laughter and love.

Connect with M.L. Bullock on Facebook. To receive updates on her latest releases, visit her website at M.L. Bullock and subscribe to her mailing list. You can also contact her at authormlbullock@gmail.com.

About the Author

Author of the best-selling *Seven Sisters* series and the *Desert Queen* series, M.L. Bullock has been storytelling since she was a child. A student of archaeology, she loves weaving stories that feature her favorite historical characters—including Nefertiti. She currently lives on the Gulf Coast with her family but travels frequently to explore the southern states she loves so much.

Read more from M.L. Bullock

The Nike Chronicles

Blue Water
Blue Wake
Blue Tide

The Seven Sisters Series

Seven Sisters
Moonlight Falls on Seven Sisters
Shadows Stir at Seven Sisters
The Stars that Fell
The Stars We Walked Upon
The Sun Rises Over Seven Sisters

The Idlewood Series

The Ghosts of Idlewood
Dreams of Idlewood
The Whispering Saint
The Haunted Child

*Return to Seven Sisters
(A Seven Sisters Sequel Series)*

The Roses of Mobile
All the Summer Roses
Blooms Torn Asunder

The Gulf Coast Paranormal Series

The Ghosts of Kali Oka Road
The Ghosts of the Crescent Theater
A Haunting on Bloodgood Row
The Legend of the Ghost Queen
A Haunting at Dixie House
The Ghost Lights of Forrest Field
The Ghost of Gabrielle Bonet
The Ghost of Harrington Farm
The Creature on Crenshaw Road

*Shabby Hearts
Paranormal Cozy Mystery Series*

A Touch of Shabby
Shabbier by the Minute
Shabby by Night

Lost Camelot Series

Guinevere Forever
Guinevere Unconquered

The Sugar Hill Series

Wife of the Left Hand
Fire on the Ramparts
Blood by Candlelight
The Starlight Ball
His Lovely Garden

The Desert Queen Series

The Tale of Nefret
The Falcon Rises
The Kingdom of Nefertiti
The Song of the Bee-Eater

Made in the USA
Las Vegas, NV
22 June 2021